THE AWAKENERS

SHERI S. TEPPER

NORTHSHORE

✦

SOUTHSHORE

ORB

A Tom Doherty Associates Book

New York

For my children,
Alden, Cheryl, Mark, and Regan
a password

THE AWAKENERS

This is an omnibus edition, consisting of the novels: *Northshore: The Awakeners, Volume 1*, copyright © 1987 by Sheri S. Tepper, first Tor edition March 1987; and *Southshore: The Awakeners, Volume 2*, copyright © 1987 by Sheri S. Tepper, first Tor edition June 1987.

Cover art by Thomas Canty

An Orb Edition
Published by Tom Doherty Associates, Inc.
175 Fifth Avenue
New York, N.Y. 10010

Library of Congress Cataloging-in-Publication Data

Tepper, Sheri S.
    The Awakeners / Sheri S. Tepper.
        p.   cm.
    Originally published in two separate vols. under titles: Northshore ; Southshore. New York : T. Doherty Associates, c1987.
    "A Tom Doherty Associates book."
    ISBN 0-312-89022-2
    I. Title.
[PS3570.E673A95   1994]
813'.54—dc20   94-2978
                                                                              CIP

First Orb edition: August 1994

Printed in the United States of America

P1

• 1 •

There was no need for watchmen on the boats that plied the World River. Since everything moved at the same speed, pulled by the same invincible tides, there was little chance of collision; this no less on the barge *Gift of Potipur* than on any other boat. Thrasne, third assistant owner's-man, had appointed himself watchman nonetheless, borrowing the title from those who manned the gates between townships on Northshore.

Northshore.

Northshore with its Awakeners and frag powder merchants, its oracular Jarb Mendicants and blue-faced priests of Potipur, glittering with sacred mirrors. Northshore, with its processions of black Melancholics, flailing away at the citizens with their fishskin whips and given good metal coin to do it. Northshore, with its puncon orchards and frag groves and wide fields of white-podded pamet and blue-tasseled grain.

And Northshore's River edge, where lean forms of stalking Laughers, tight-helmed in black, announce their approach with cries of scornful laughter, ha-ha, ha-ha, making the heretics run for cover. Echoing the Laughers, stilt-lizards hoot through their horny lips, scattering the song-fish from around their reedlike legs only to snatch them up one by one to gulp them down headfirst. Ha-ha ha-ha.

Once in a while Thrasne would see the up-pointed finger of a Tower scratching at the sky, fliers gathered around it like flies around dead fish. Once in a greater while he would see the lonely knuckle of a Jarb House. And the River itself, some places smooth as a rain pond, other places full of rocks as a worker pit, everywhere dotted with blight-buoys and striped with jetties, as wide as half the world.

Township after township, town after town, with fences between to keep people from moving east and gates between to let people move west, the World River tugging the ships along on the endless tides, and all the panoply of life laid out for Thrasne's watching.

He knew watchmen were necessary on land to keep foolhardy youths from sneaking between townships in the forbidden direction or greedy caravaners from rushing too quickly westward, clogging the orderly flow of commerce. He knew that on a boat a watchman could only watch, but that was what Thrasne did best. He wasn't bad at handling sails or sculling oars. He could make the fragwood deck gleam as well as any boatman. He could give orders and see they were carried out, which is what gained him the third assistant's post. And he could stow a cargo so that what was wanted next was always on top. These were necessary and useful talents, but he felt his talent for watching was better than these. Certainly it was more developed.

He had created a little cubby in the forewall of the owner-house, up top deck, where the ventilation shaft opened from the forward hold. Across this shaft he rigged a high grating of poles with a sack of loose pamet on top. When his round was done for the day he could sly up to top deck, wait until no one was looking, then hang himself by his fingertips from the owner-house roof with his toes on a handwide railing and shinny around into the cubby. No windows there; no owner's wife looking for anyone not occupied so she could find something unnecessary for them to do; only the sun-warmed boards of the owner-house wall vibrating to the ceaseless flow of the tides. Sometimes he'd stay until dark, and sometimes past that if there were things to see.

It was from the cubby he had first seen a flame-bird set fire to its nest, from the cubby he'd first seen a strangey, rising from the depths like some great green balloon, looking at him out of huge, wondering eyes from its fringes as it spit its bones at him.

It was from the cubby he had first seen a whole ship and its crew caught by blight, drifting ever farther into the unknown southern currents with wooden men standing at the rail as though they'd been carved there.

It was from the cubby he had watched the golden ship of the Progression gliding by on its seven-year journey, the doll-like figure of the Protector of Man held high on the arms of the personal guards.

It was from the cubby he had watched the crowds on shore, thousands of shouting townspeople and file on file of mirror-staffed Awakeners and gem-decked priests all shouting the Protector's name, "Obol, Obol, Obol."

It was from the cubby he had seen all there was to see for the four years he had been Blint's man, and it was from the cubby he now noticed the hard lines of jetties wavering over the River surface not far ahead, where no jetty was supposed to be.

According to the section chart-of-towns, there were no piers closer than Darkel-don, a good ten-day's tide yet, and just yesterday owner Blint had told them they could fish as they liked till then with no worries at all. Now, having seen what he'd seen, there was nothing to do but slither below and tell Blint of this, though it might put him to wondering how Thrasne had seen the piers. They wouldn't be visible from deck level for some time yet, and it wasn't Thrasne's shift to work the rudder deck at the high stern of the boat.

He reported the sighting in a quiet voice, hoping his very mildness and lack of excitement would throw Blint off the scent. Which it might well have done had not Blint-wife been standing near, overhearing him, going at once to peer over the rail.

"Jetties? There aren't any jetties! I can't see any jetties!"

"Well, boy?" demanded Blint.

"Yessir. Piers."

Blint's eyes crinkled at the corners. "He saw them from

above, wife. I told him to be sure to check the owner-house roof was tight.''

"Tight? Of course it's tight, Blint. It was rebuilt only a Conjunction ago. What do you mean, tight?''

Blint, who answered few of her questions, did not answer this one. "How close?'' he murmured.

"Close enough, sir. We'd better get our nets out of the water or the fisherman caste of the place—assuming there is one, for why else have piers—they'll be heaving stones at us.''

"We could move into deeper water.''

"There was that bunch in Zebulee with the catapult.''

"Ah. So there was. Well then, go tell the boys. Haul in and hide the evidence, tell them. No fishskins drying on the deck. No strangey bones lying about. I'll leave it in your good hands.''

"Any chance of trade, you think?''

"Well, we'll have to see, won't we.'' Owner Blint strolled away, no whit disturbed, leaving it in Thrasne's good hands. If Thrasne hadn't been available, he'd have left it in firstman Birk's good hands, or secondman Thon's. Thrasne scrambled into action. At least the boatmen wouldn't argue with him. The memory of that catapult was too recent.

When they were hard at work getting the nets in—they'd have to be stowed wet, which would stink up the net locker—Thrasne went to the chart room to take another look at the Northshore section chart. They were passing Wilforn now. Nothing of interest listed on the section chart for Wilforn. Next place was Baris, and the section chart didn't say a word about Baris having jetties. Baris had pamet, art work, confections, puncon fruit—when the weather was right—and toys. The Baris Tower was listed as middling active, not fanatical, which meant the Awakeners weren't likely to search the *Gift* for any kind of contraband, books or such. And that's all Blint had written down six, seven years ago when he'd been by last. Thrasne made a mental note to hide his own books—if there were changes in one thing, there might be changes in others—and to add a description of the piers as soon as he'd

had a good look at them. Probably some fisherman moving
west had come to Baris and decided piers would be a good
idea. Probably sold the local Tower on the idea and got a
worker crew to build them. In which case, Thrasne snorted,
spitting in habitual disgust, it was sheer luck they were still
standing.

He returned to the deck in time to help empty the nets. Not
much in the way of fish and two or three hard, clattering
things bumping on the deck with an unmistakable wooden
sound.

"Blight-fish!" one of the boatmen cursed. "I swear by the
carrion birds of Abricor, it's too much. All we get lately's
the blight."

"Come on, Swin, it's not that bad. We haven't really seen
any of it since Vouye. Be careful!" Thrasne pulled him back.
"You almost touched that one."

"It's hard. Probably blight's gone out of it. Almost."

" 'Almost' gave the boatman a wooden leg."

The men snorted. An old jest, but a true one. What the
blight touched, it turned to wood, slowly or quickly, and if it
touched the boatman's hand he would have the choice of
cutting the hand off—if he moved without hesitation—or
becoming a life-size carving of himself.

Some said once the blight hardened completely it lost its
power of contagion, but Thrasne had seen a man lose a foot
kicking something that seemed very hard indeed. "Just push
it over the side, Swin. Don't stand there looking at it, or
you'll forget what you're looking at and pick it up."

Swin grunted and pushed the fish overboard with a boathook.
The few remaining fish were free of blight, thrashing around
on the deck making high-pitched squeals from their air blad-
ders. The men began clubbing and cleaning them, tossing the
gutted fish down where other crewmen waited with the salt
kegs. Thrasne turned to stowing the nets. Blight meant extra
care there, too. They would have to be lowered into the net
locker without touching them and sprayed with a mixture of
sulphur and powdered frag leaf. Only when they had steeped
in this mixture for a day or two could the men safely handle

them again. Now they were plying the long hooks in gingerly
fashion, pushing the nets below, and Obers-rom was already
mixing frag powder. A good man, Obers-rom. Never needed
to be told anything twice.

Thrasne leaned over the rail to watch the blighted fish
moving alongside, sinking very slowly as they went, still
visible after long minutes had gone by. They floated right
side up; they looked almost alive, only the lack of movement
betraying that they were fish no more. Or perhaps fish of a
different kind. Thrasne had seen a man touched by blight
once. In fact, Thrasne had been the one to use the axe, and
he still woke in the night sometimes sweating from the
memory of it. The boatman had kept his chopped-off leg in a
netting sack, sprayed down with blight powder. He carried it
about with him to taverns, where he sold topers a look at it in
exchange for drinks, daring the foolhardy to touch it and see
whether the blight had left it or not.

"Dangers in every caste and trade," said owner Blint from
time to time. "None free of peril."

Thrasne supposed that was true. He went below to change
his shirt and hide his books. Not that he had many, but those
he had he wanted to keep. His book of fables about the
Southshore. His *History of Northshore* in three volumes,
nine-tenths of it nonsense, Blint said, and all of it forbidden.
Thrasne didn't care. It made a nice thing to do some evenings
when the winds were warm, sit on the deck in the light of the
owner-house windows and read about how humans first
landed on Northshore, down from the stars, and about their
great wars with the Thraish, whoever they may have been.
Winged creatures, by the sound of it in the stories, who could
talk just like men. And all the men using metal tools and
weapons, which was enough right there to show you why it
was all false and unapproved. But who wanted to read approved books? Lives of the Great Awakeners. The biography
of Thoulia. Poof. One might as well read the chart-of-towns;
it was more interesting.

They'd be in Baris by noon, and owner Blint would likely
seek trade. Most of the towns along this stretch were short of

spices and salt. They'd want to give pamet in exchange, and the *Gift* couldn't take it. No room left in the holds. It would have to be something less bulky. Dried fruit, jam, jelly. Candies, maybe. The confectioners were supposed to be something special along here. Something about candies in one of their Festival myths. And toys. Little things for children. Mechanical ones that could be wound up. The toymakers on this stretch were notable. Not that Thrasne had been along this stretch before; he'd been only four years on the *Gift of Potipur*, starting when he was twelve as go-get-boy.

As he struggled with the buttons of his shirt, he examined the row of carvings set on his storage chest. There was a long, slender piece of clear fragwood he'd been saving, and he thought he'd make a fish of it. A surprised fish, with blight halfway up its tail. The carvings stared back at him from the chest top: merchants, children, the tall robed figure of an Awakener, even a worker, shapeless and hopeless in its canvas wrappings. The little figures seemed almost to breathe. One at the near end of the row looked at him in eternal supplication, and Thrasne took it into his hands with a little groan, warmth pouring into his belly.

"Suspirra," he whispered. It was his name for her, the otherwise nameless ideal, loveliest of all women, created out of his head and his aching loins. She lay on his pillow when he sought his solitary comforts. She watched him when he dressed and washed himself, always with the same expression of supplication and entreaty. "Love me," she begged silently. "Love me." And he did love her, in a lonely fever, almost forgetting sometimes that she was no longer than his forearm. He had carved her in one daylong frenzy of creation, the wood curling away from his blade as though it sought to reveal what lay within it, the pale soft grain of the face, the darker grain of the long, smooth hair, the gown, clinging to her as though wet so he could see every line of her sweet breasts and belly, the curve of her thighs and the soft mound where they joined. Even her feet had sprung out of the wood magically, every toe perfect, the lines of the nails as clean as the line of her lips.

"Suspirra," and he set her down, turning her slightly away from him.

"You should be artist caste," Blint had said when he first saw Thrasne's carvings. "Some of these towns give high status to artists."

Thrasne had shaken his head. "I'd rather see everything. Not just stick in one town. Maybe, someday, when I'm tired of the River."

Though he could not imagine being tired of the River. There was always something to see on the River. As there was right now—the new piers fringing the edge of Baristown.

When he reached the deck he gave it a careful look over. No signs of nets or hooks. The net poles were put away. He could still smell the sulphur and frag, but the River breeze would carry it outriver this time of day. He checked the hatch over the net locker to see it was tight. Funny the way shorebound fishermen resented any fishing done by the Riverboats. Even though the Riverboats caught different kinds of fish, to say nothing of the deep River strangeys, which probably weren't fish at all. Glizzee spice, now. Everyone wanted that, even fishermen. And Glizzee spice was nothing but ground strangey bone, though the boatmen didn't tell everyone that.

When he'd completed the round, he went back and climbed up to the rudderman. "What did Blint say?"

"Told me to pick the longest pier and see could I come around it."

"No side wharfs, hmm?"

"None we can see from here." Some of the towns had at the end of their piers sideways extensions that ran along the River flow rather than across it. A Riverboat could steer close, toss a line to be made fast, then let the tide turn the boat on the line to lay alongside. Coming around a long pier was harder work than that.

"Is Blint getting the sweeps set?"

"He got Birk out of his hammock. Said for you to stand by here where you could see everything." The man sniggered, not maliciously, and Thrasne grinned at him. Taken all in all, the boatmen rather liked having a carver aboard. There wasn't one of them he hadn't carved something for, as a pretty for themselves or a gift for someone they treasured. When a man only came to his home place every six to eight years, he wanted to have something special for his children, at least. Though it wasn't uncommon to find more children than reason suggested was appropriate. Many a man gone six years came back to find two- and three-year-olds, but such was the life of a boatman and accepted as such. The women couldn't be blamed, not with the procreation laws the way they were. And after all, if things like that mattered to a man, he wouldn't be River.

The pier was coming up on the right, a long one, not completed yet. The oarsmen had the sweeps set in the rope locks to turn the ship as soon as the pier was past. The tide wasn't strong just now, not with the moons all strung out like this, not like Conjunction, when no one in his right mind would try to tie up except at the Riverside itself.

"Hold fast," breathed Thrasne, locking the sculling oars out of the way of the rudder. "Hold fast."

"I see it," grumbled the steersman. "Been doing this for twenty years."

Thrasne ignored him. If Blint wanted him on the steerhouse, it was to take charge of things.

"Hold fast," he muttered again. "Now! Hard over!" He bent his back to the rudder as the bite of the oars took hold, taking up the slack on the tackle until it was tied hard over and they could watch the sweating men at the sweeps. Blint himself was at the line cannon. In a moment it went off with a dull *thwump* of its huge wooden springs, and the line arched out over the pier, where half a dozen standabouts made it fast.

"Sweeps up," cried Blint. "Stand by the winch!" The ship shuddered as it began to draw toward the pier, moving against the surging tide. Thrasne shook his head, remembering the time they had taken on a boatman from a place called Thou-ne. "Born in Potipur," he said he was. Sanctimonious half-wit. Insisted that no ship had the right to oppose the tide, and the only way to moor was at the end of a line along the bank. Fool had said winching was evil, antilife, and against the will of Potipur. He lasted until the time he took an axe to the rope during a winching operation. Assuming he had been a good swimmer and hadn't encountered the blight, he might still be alive. Since Blint had dropped him over the side in the far mid-River after dark, however, his survival was only conjectural.

There were no other boats at the Baristown piers. Despite this, there was a considerable gathering at the end of the jetty, engaged in some noisy set-to.

"What're they doing?" Thrasne asked.

"Couldn't say," offered Blint. "Have a look if you like. I'll need the walkway down anyhow for those fatbellies coming." He nodded toward the town. Several members of the merchant caste were bustling toward them, each trying to be first without being ostentatious about it. None of them quite broke into a run. Thrasne set the walkway, then strolled over it, hands in pockets, down to the end of the pier.

Most of the crowd were simple standabouts, though there were a few fishermen and merchant apprentices who should have been elsewhere. There was one Laugher in his polished black helm, fiddling with the flasks at his belt, staring at each member of the crowd in turn, as though he would see through to the bones. Those at the end of the jetty, however, were Awakeners directing a worker crew in dragging the River.

Thrasne got a whiff of the workers and moved back a few steps. Using workers to labor in Potipur's behalf was a religious requirement in every town they traveled by, but Thrasne thought it a stinking one, literally and philosophically. The shambling figures were so damned inefficient. Everything had to be done six times over. It took a crew of Awakened workers four times over a field to plow it, and Thrasne had never seen a ditch dug by workers fit to run water through until some competent irrigation manager cleaned it out and trued the sides. Now they were heaving hooks at the ends of long lines, tossing them about a fourth of the distance Thrasne could have thrown them, dragging them back with slow tugs against the tide.

"What're they looking for?" he asked one of the stand-abouts.

"Some woman went in the River. Drowned herself."

"So? Why the dragging?"

"She did it to get out of bein' Sorted. So they say. I don't know. All I know is the Awakener's mad as a fisherman with a blight-fish on a new line."

The Awakener was indeed very angry. He could hear her clearly as she spat at a long-faced, miserable-looking man before her. "Fulder Don! It was your duty to come to us if you thought she would do this!"

"I didn't think she would," the long-faced man said plaintively, his voice flat, almost without expression. "I thought it was just her talk. She talked about a lot of things she never did. I didn't think she'd ever leave the baby. She cared so for the baby." The little girl in his arms was crying. About three or four years old, Thrasne thought. Old enough to remember what was going on, without being old enough to understand it.

An old woman with a tight, lipless mouth stood beside the depressed-looking man. "Fulder Don," she said, "I've known since you married that silly fool she'd do something like this. I wouldn't have thought heresy, but who could put it past her? She hadn't an ounce of loyalty in her."

"Mama," begged the man placatingly. "Now, Mama . . ."

"Don't 'Mama' me. You married beneath you and beneath artist's caste, and that's all there is to it. Take that idiot child and give her to Delia, will you. I can't stand the sight of her. It wasn't enough her mother had to do this dreadful thing, now you're saddled with the child for her whole life."

"Well, Mama, she's my child, too."

"I'm not even certain sure of that." The old woman stomped off down the pier, the cane in her hand slamming down in a furious *whap, whap, whap*, which sent angry echoes booming under the pier over the lick and slap of the water.

The Awakener threw up her hands, twirled her staff, and began a slow, mind-curling chant. Thrasne shut it out, humming to himself. He couldn't stand Awakener chants. If it was to escape this, this chant-driven pretense of life, this shambling excuse for existence, he did not blame the nameless woman who had drowned herself. The band of workers turned from the River to shamble back up the pier, following the glittering staff, eyeless, faceless, only their feet and hands indicating what lay beneath the loosely woven canvas sacks and hoods they wore.

"Papa," the little girl was pleading. "Papa."

The man paid her no attention, merely stood staring at the River as though he wanted nothing more than to be deep inside it himself. The passivity of that face moved Thrasne. His hands twitched, wanting to capture that face. This was a man who had given up. He would not do anything, not ever again. He would only float, pushed by the tide of others' lives, waiting his end under the canvas hood, deserving it. The child turned, caught by the watchfulness in Thrasne's face, stared at him, eyes wide and accepting with something of that same passivity. "Papa," she said again, hopelessly.

A woman came out of the crowd to take the child, a nothing much of a woman, small and plump, older than middle-aged. "There, there, my Pammy," she said. "There, there." The child sobbed once and laid her head on the woman's shoulder. That, too, Thrasne coveted, that line of child against the woman's body, limp and exhausted, giving up everything in the acceptance of this comfort.

Thrasne moved toward the man. What had the old woman called him? Fulder Don. "Fulder Don," he asked casually, as though he were only another standabout, "why did your wife go in the River? How do you know that she did?"

The man looked at his feet, mumbling. "A fisherman saw her. She was sick. She was afraid to die. Afraid to risk Sorting Out. My mother . . . was always at her. Telling her how bad she was. How incapable. I guess she thought . . ." His voice trailed away into nothing as he stared into the water, his long, mournful face intent upon another time.

"She was so beautiful," he whispered at last. "So very beautiful."

Something in the intonation made Thrasne look at him again. Yes. Under the shabby cloak the man wore the smock of the artist caste. An artist. Not a successful one, from the looks of it. For which Fulder Don's mama probably blamed the dead woman. Thrasne turned quickly to return to the *Gift of Potipur*, his hands itching for his carving knife. The man, the woman and child; if he was lucky, he could get both the carvings started before Blint found something else for him to do.

They spent three days in Baris. The merchants wanted spice, but they insisted on trading bulk pamet for it. Blint would take no more pamet. "Silly blight-heads," he complained as still another delegation left the boat unsatisfied. "Can't seem to understand every town in this section has more pamet than they can use. We'll have to go all the way to Vobil-dil-go before anyone will want pamet. I told them we'd take toys, or those dried puncon candies, or woven pamet cloth, provided it was something out of the ordinary. They'll come to it eventually. Just takes them two or three days to make up their minds."

On the third day they did make up their minds, and Blint did a brisk business. By dusk all the trading was done, and the crew of the *Gift* went into Baristown for some jollifications. Thrasne offered to guard the ship. He wanted to finish the carvings and brought them on deck to do so, working in the lantern light from the owner-house windows. He had caught Fulder Don to his own satisfaction, the sorrow, the loss. Now he was finishing the carving of the woman, Delia, and the child.

There were no sounds except the soft push of the water along the sides, an occasional burst of laughter or song from the taverns. The soft bumping had gone on for some time before he even heard it.

Once alerted to the sound, it still took him a while to find it. It seemed to come from everywhere and nowhere. At last he leaned over the side and heard it clearly. Something in the River, knocking against the side of the boat.

He lowered a lantern on a line to see only the oily shifting of the water. Then she came from under the wavelets to look up at him for an instant, turning in the ripples to glance sideways at him from half-closed eyes.

"Suspirra!" He set the lantern down, shaking, rubbing his eyes with his hands. The face was Suspirra's face. The bumping went on. He lowered the light again, and again she shifted to look upward at him, the water flowing across her face, the line in which she was tangled making a silver streak across her breast.

Sick cold in his belly, he could no more have left her there than he could have burned his own Suspirra for firewood. It took long moments to realize the bumping made a wooden clattering rather than the soft sound of flesh. He thought of a carving, first, and only then of the blight. This was the woman they had been dragging for. The woman who had been so beautiful, who was so beautiful. Blighted now. Wooden. And deadly. Still, he could not leave her there.

He brought up one of the small nets, safe enough after its frag powder soak. He rigged a line to the boom. Working silently, cursing the amount of time it took, he pushed the net under her with poles, then heaved the boom all alone against her weight, heavier than he'd thought, to lift her dripping body to the deck.

She turned in the lantern light, toward him and away in a silent dance, eyes half-open in invitation, lips curved as though about to speak. "So beautiful," he murmured, wanting to touch her, holding himself from doing so only with difficulty. "So beautiful."

A burst of laughter as some Riverfront tavern opened a door and spat revelers into the street. Blint would be bringing the crew back shortly. If Blint saw her, he would sell her to the family, or to the Awakeners, though what good she would be to either, Thrasne could not imagine. No. He wouldn't do that. She had fled from them, family and Awakeners both. The woman who had fled was gone. This was his own Suspirra now. He plotted furiously, discarding one notion after another.

Then he thought of the ventilation shaft beneath his own watching post. Up went the net once more as he guided it from the owner-house roof, down into the shaft, suspended there in its netting bag from the pole grating upon which he so often sat, where none could see it, wonder at it, touch it—save Thrasne himself.

When Blint and the crew returned, he was crouched beneath the owner-house window, finishing the carving of Delia and the child. That night, for the first time since he had made her, he did not even look at the small carving of Suspirra.

• 2 •

Night on the River in the township of Thou-ne. Lanterns gleaming along the River walk, on the quays and jetties, where the oily water throws back slippery reflections, fishbelly lights, momentary glimmers. Rain misting the cobbles into fishscale paths, River sucking at the piers with fishmouth kisses, all watery and dim, silver and gray, evasive as dark bodies turning beneath dark water. Lantern man strolling along beside his wagon, wagon boy tugging, head down, sliding a little on the slick stones. Fish-oil cans in the wagon; fill the lanterns; trim the wicks; light the lanterns; then move on. Behind these two the lantern light lies in liquid puddles on the stones, pools of light, wetter than water as the crier follows after, "Dusk falls, night comes, let all abroad take themselves to home and hearth." The call so well known over lifetimes it comes out in drawn vowels, "Uhhhs aaaahs, aiiit uhmmms, aaaad ohhhhm arrrrrh."

Peasimy Flot trots along the River path, behind the crier, stepping carefully into each puddle of light to splash it onto the path. Slap, slap, slap with the soft soles of his boots, slap, slap. Light has to be distributed. Nobody sees to it but Peasimy. What good are these puddles with all the dark in between? Have to splash the light around. He does not look behind him to see the pools of light still separate and rimmed with black. He has splashed them; now the walk is lighted.

Never mind what the eyes see. Never mind. It is what the soul sees that's important.

"Uhhhs aaaahs," the crier calls. "Aiiit uhmmms."

Night is already here. Potipur glares in the eastern sky, full and ominous, his face half-veiled in River mist. Viranel is half herself at the zenith, skittish behind clouds, as she becomes at these slender times; Abricor has whetted his scythe on the western horizon and goes now to harvest the crops of night. Peasimy stops in midsplash to contemplate the scythe-moon. "Harvest," he calls in a whispery fishvoice, full of bubbles and liquid gurgling. "Cut down the lies, Moon of Abricor. Foul weeds of untruth. Cut them down, down, down." Then back to the splashing once more. Pitty-pat, pitty-pat, slap slap slap.

Twelve years old, Peasimy is a neat one in his high-collared coat with the shiny buttons, his tight dark trousers fitting down into the soft boots, his perky little hat perched high on his tight, shiny hair. Daytimes he sleeps, like a strangey, lost in the depths of his sleep as in a cavern. Nighttimes he comes up for air and to look at the moon and splash lantern light. Peasimy knows Thou-ne would wither away if he didn't splash the light around. It doesn't matter no one else knows it. All night long he will continue this perambulation, spreading the light. Dawn will mean a bite of breakfast, then pulling the shades down, hiding in the dark. No one knows why, but he's been that way since childhood. No trouble to anyone. Just see him decent dressed and let him go. So says Peasimy's mama, the widow Flot. So says her kin and kith. Let him alone. He doesn't hurt anything. Poor little fellow. Lucky when he can remember his name.

Peasimy . . . well, Peasimy remembers a lot of things. Peasimy remembers catching his mama putting Candy Seeds on his bed when it was supposed to be the Candy Tree growing there that did it. Peasimy remembers things Haranjus Pandel said in Temple. Peasimy remembers every lie ever told and some he only suspects. Peasimy can recognize true things when he sees them.

Lanterns, now, they are true things. Water is true, and the

widow Flot. The lantern man is true, and the crier. Daylight
is so true he needn't even stay awake to watch it. All light is
true. Dark is a false thing, full of lies, making you think a
thing is one way when it's actually another. That's why
Peasimy splashes the light. Have to fight the dark. Can't just
let it overcome.

There's an image Peasimy sees sometimes in the dusk,
maybe in the dusk, maybe only in his head, he's not sure
always where things are. But the image is there, somewhere,
shining. A glowing thing. Looking at him. Looking at him
and shining with its own light. Truth. Shining. He doesn't
know what it is, but he expects to find it. Somewhere. Along
this alley, perhaps, between splashes of his boots. Along that
street.

And until then, he goes along.

"Aiiiih uhmmmms," calls the crier.

"Night comes," whispers Peasimy. "Light comes."

• 3 •

It was six days before Thrasne was left alone and could look at the drowned woman again. Under a grove of enormous frag trees, tied up at the Riverside past Shabber, he was able to lift the net once more. He stood on the owner-house roof, staring at her in lantern light where she swayed in the net. She was dry now. Her hair had fluffed out like fine pamet fiber, a warm, lovely brown. Though he had thought her eyes open when he brought her aboard, they were closed now, the lashes lying softly upon her cheeks as she seemed to sleep. His eyes marked her, measured her, trembled over every part of her, fascinated and aroused. He had to hold his hands behind him to keep from touching her. At last he could stand it no longer. He went below and took a live fish from the cook's cage where it hung over the side. Carrying this squirming burden, he went back to her to thrust the wriggling thing against her, careful not to touch the part of it that touched her. He laid it on the roof, watching closely, and within moments the front part of it stopped thrashing and began to bump against the roof, moved by the tail, which was still alive. The blight lived in her still. He brought the sprayer up and covered her with a powdery, golden shower before lowering her into the shaft once more. The fish was still bumping, and he shoved it overside with a pole.

"Suspirra," he whispered down to her. "It's all right, Suspirra. A few more days' drying, the good powder will do

its work, then you can come out of there. . . ." Except, he
told himself, she could not. Where would he put her? How
would he explain?

"Blint, sir, would you mind making me a small payment
on my wages?"

"How small, Thrasne? And what do you suddenly find
yourself so needy of? Isn't wife Blint seeing well enough to
your food and clothing?"

"It isn't that, sir. I have a mind to make a large carving,
and I'd like to purchase a block of wood from a frag
merchant. . . ."

Which block of wood was not easily come by. Some were
too crooked and others too straight. Some had harsh graining
that would spoil the features, others were too dark. Thrasne
found one eventually, at the bottom of the pile, and paid for
it with good coin. He put it in one corner of his little room
aboard the *Gift*, knives and chisels ostentatiously by. When
he began to carve it, the wood opened up to reveal the
Suspirra within. Still, it was a largish thing, life size, and it
was longer than he liked before it resembled her, longer yet
before it was her, line for line. Then was a long time between
towns, during which he was never left alone, so that when he
finally came to take the drowned woman from the net, replacing her with the carving—in case he might ever need to
hide the real woman again—it seemed a season had gone by.

The drowned woman came gladly to his place, standing in
one corner of it as though invited there for dalliance. She
looked at him through barely opened eyes, lips not quite
curved, as though she were thinking of smiling but had not
yet accomplished it.

"Well," said Blint when he saw her first. "I still say you
should be artist caste, Thrasne. Not that I'd like doing without you. Still, that's a beauty, that is. Pure fragwood, is it?
Surely not the hair? That doesn't look carved?"

"Well, no sir," he lied without a change of expression.
"That's a wig I bought in Tsillis. Somehow the carved hair
didn't look . . . well, it didn't look soft." Her hair had not

looked soft, either, when he had raised her that last time, matted and filthy as it was from the frag leaf and sulphur. He had rinsed her time and again with buckets of clean water, brushed her hair, and run soap through it. Now it lay gleaming on her shoulders, not unlike the color of frag, yet more silken. The rest of her gleamed in nut-brown colors, also, with a hint of rose at nipples and lips.

"What do you call her?" asked Blint.

"Her name is Suspirra. It was the name of a girl I knew once back in Xoxxy-Do, where you found me."

"And where you'll be again in a year or so. What will she think of this, your having a life-size doll of her to keep you company?" Blint was roguish, twinkling.

"She wouldn't mind." Since Thrasne had invented such a girl on the spot, he was not concerned about what she might think. What Blint would think had concerned him, but evidently Blint thought nothing untoward. If a boatman wished to have a life-size carving of a beautiful woman in his cabin, well, so be it. It took all kinds, as Blint would say, to do all the things needing doing.

At first Thrasne merely looked at her in the lantern light before he slept or in the early morning before he rose. He touched her face sometimes, almost reverently. He did not presume to touch her breasts, though once he laid his cheek against them, almost sobbing as the promise of softness was betrayed. After a time he stopped touching her at all and began talking to her instead. At a short distance he could forget the blight, forget her petrification, believe that she was living flesh. He still called her Suspirra. He told her all the things he had never been able to tell anyone, not even Blint.

"Blint saved my life," Thrasne told her.

"I lived in Xoxxy-Do. Halfway round Northshore from anywhere. A mountainous place, where the falls come over the cliffs into World River, and the ships have to tie up behind great shattered rocks along the sheer walls and the boatmen climb steep, twisty stairs to reach the towns above. My father was a builder there, a builder in stone. My mother was an artist—though there was not so much of the caste system there in Xoxxy-Do as I have seen elsewhere. It was she who taught me to carve—or let me learn it, I suppose. She gave me a knife when I was only five. She was a wonderful carver. When Father finished a place, it was she who ornamented it. They had a great success together. They were very happy. So was I.''

He was silent then, waiting for Suspirra to say something, to comment. He heard her saying, ''I was not happy. I envy your happy family, Thrasne. My own was not like that.''

''I saw your husband's mother,'' he replied. ''My father's sister was like that. All pinch-lipped and hating. She could not bear it that they were happy. Could not bear it that they were in love. She had predicted doom on them, and the doom did not come. Not the kind she threatened.'' He fell silent again, this time out of pain. The memory still had this power to undo him, to turn his muscles to water, his bowels to aching void.

''Ah,'' said Suspirra. ''Then we have much in common.''

''They died. They had gone to the quarry together, and there was a great storm. The worker-built road was inadequate even in calm weather. In the storm it dissolved like sugar. They were found at the bottom of the gorge, crushed beneath the stone. My father's sister took me in.''

''I know that kind of taking-in,'' said Suspirra.

''The first thing she said to me was that my father and mother were in the worker pits of Ghasttown to the east, being raised up by the Awakeners. I could not stop crying, but she went on saying it. She took my knife away, saying I might hurt myself. It was the knife Mother had given me. I stayed with her for almost a season, but then I lay awake one night planning to kill her.''

''You had to get away,'' prompted Suspirra.

''I had to get away. Blint found me along the Riverside, half-starved, talking to a little carving of Mother I had made.'' It had been his first attempt at carving Suspirra, but he did not remember that.

''A kindly man, Blint.''

"Blint is kindness itself." He stopped talking, appalled. She could not have spoken, and yet he had heard her speak. He left the little room to go out on deck and stride about, back and forth, hour on hour.

"What's troubling you, boy?"

"Do you ever find yourself talking to yourself, Blint?"

"All us boatpeople do, Thrasne. Never known one that didn't. Married Blint-wife just to have someone to talk to and found out it didn't work. Have to talk to yourself. How would you find out what you think about things otherwise?"

"Did you ever—did you ever pretend it was someone else answering you?"

"Always. Makes it more interesting that way."

So he came to accept it. Boatpeople came to the River because on that everflowing current they could talk to themselves about Northshore without that world forcing its own opinions on them. On the River one could repudiate the Awakeners, hate the workers—both for their hideous existence and for the shoddiness of the work they did—cogitate upon Potipur and Abricor and Viranel, question their very existence, perhaps, without being accused of heresy.

"Do you think Potipur is loving?" whispered Suspirra.

"I don't think Potipur is anything," he answered. "Except a moon which pulls the tide around. And a moon-faced god in the Temples with the priests all bowing and waving incense and sparking their staffs at the congregation every tenth day and twice at the end of the month." Ten days make a week, and when five weeks are gone, then you've a month with a holy day tacked on. Or so Thrasne's mother had always said.

"Then why?" Suspirra murmured. "Why, why, why? . . ."

They had been on the River some forty days from Shabber when Blint complained that the pamet stacked in the forward hold smelled of mildew. "Must be something blocking the ventilation duct," he said with a sigh. "We'll see to it next mooring."

Thrasne was annoyed with himself. The wooden likeness

of Suspirra was undoubtedly blocking the duct, and he should
have seen to it long since. "Let me do it, Blint. I've a cubby
up top where I sit and watch things. Perhaps I've let something fall into the duct."

"Have you now? Well then, you see to it. I'll leave it in
your good hands."

He did it at night, with all the crew ashore, the fitful light
of torches from the pier throwing orange stripes across the
netted burden as it came out of the shaft. Once lowered on
the roof, he stripped the net away to have a long look at it
before giving it to the tide.

There was something wrong.

He had carved it to be like the blighted woman. Like her
line for line, eye for eye, lip for lip. And this was not like.
These eyes were half-shut, these lips not quite curved, as
though about to smile, but the Suspirra in his cabin had
wide-open eyes, her lips were compressed. Leaving the statue
where it was, he went below to make sure. Her eyes met his
as he entered the room, her lips set tight as though humming,
as though admonishing, as though about to say something.

"I'm going mad," he whispered to himself, knowing he
was not. "Suspirra, am I going mad?"

"The world is mad," she said. "You see what you see."

He put the carving into the tide, watching it until it vanished on the wavelets, casting a glance at the moons. Slack
water would not come until early morning. It would travel far
by then. He would never catch up with it again. Perhaps
someone would fish it out along a pier and wonder at it.

Below in his room he began a small carving like the one
just thrown away, line for line. When it was done, he did
another of Suspirra as she was now. If the drowned woman
was changing, he would make a record of those changes.

Over the next five years he carved forty little Suspirras.
They were stowed under his bunk, numbered on their bases,
and once in a very great while he would take them out and
stand them in a long file before him, from first to last, the

position of each slightly changed, the eyes and lips slightly opened or closed. Something about this silent throng oppressed him and bothered him at once, as though he should infer some meaning that evaded him. He still spoke to the drowned woman, and she still answered him, but this throng of small Suspirras seemed to shout at him in silence, a mute demand: "Pay attention." He looked and looked, not understanding.

"Are you alive?" he asked her.

"What is alive? Perhaps you stopped the blight before it was finished with me."

"Do you want me to put you back in the River?"

"It is cold in the River, and lonely. Perhaps you will let me stay a while."

So for five years he let her stay, carving each new expression as it showed itself, recording this strange slow life, if it was life, in every minuscule manifestation. Day succeeded day, river, pier, town, boatmen leaving and new ones coming aboard. Blint grew grayer and Blint-wife more loquacious. They had made almost a round since the drowned woman had come aboard. They had come to Xoxxy-Do to find Thrasne's aunt long dead, had passed it by, and were almost at Baristown once more.

"I wish you'd carve a baby for that woman," said Blint-wife in an unaccustomed tone. There was worry in it, and sorrow, and a kind of aching that Thrasne had never heard her use before. He was surprised.

"What woman?" he asked. "What do you mean?"

"That woman, those women, the little ones. All in a row, saying, 'My baby.'"

He went below to look, she behind him, peering over his shoulder at the array. "I came down to change your bed. I hadn't seen them all standing that way before. You see, look from the front to the back, that's what she's saying."

He was only puzzled. His artist's eye had missed it. Blint-wife left him, returning after a time with a box of children's toys from the hold.

"See here," she said, handing him one of the little books they had traded all along the River. On each page a festival clown was drawn, each drawing slightly different. When one flipped it rapidly between thumb and fingers, the picture of the clown seemed to cavort and jump. Seeing his puzzlement, she went away.

That night he drew Suspirra's faces and arms on small squares of paper, binding them into a similar book. When he flipped the pages the hands and eyes moved, the mouth said, "My baby."

Blint-wife, of course, had talked to Blint of the matter.

"Murga—that is, Blint-wife—she lost the only baby we ever had," said Blint. "She used to sit before the mirror down there crying, saying it over and over, 'My baby, my baby.' It's no wonder she thought your carvings were saying the same."

The carvings weren't, but the drowned woman was. "My baby." The little girl at the end of the pier, the one saying so hopelessly over and over, "Papa. Papa."

"I'd like some time ashore in Baristown, sir," he said. "There's some private business I'd like to attend to."

He had no real idea how to find her. He had left Xoxxy-Do when he was twelve years old, not old enough to have perceived or understood the intricacies of town life. He had had no substantial contact with a town or village since. Still, intuition told him that there would be someone who made it his business to know things, all kinds of things. It did not take long to find him.

"Fulder Don?" the barber asked, waving his scissors in a vague gesture toward the center of town. "Oh, surely, I know Fulder Don. Him and the old lady, and isn't she a termagant. Makes his life a misery, she does. Oldest girl got married young just to get out of the house, and the story is that Prender—that's the middle one—can hardly wait for the same chance."

"There's a baby, isn't there?"

"Baby? There's been no wife there for six, seven years now. No. There was a baby when the wife killed herself, little girl, about four. But she's tennish, now. Half-grown. Lives with old Saint Delia the gardener on Outskirt Row.''

"Saint Delia?''

The barber laughed, amused at himself. "Well, that's what they call her. Anybody needs something, anybody hungry or sick, they can go to old Delia and get taken care of. More of a saint than I ever thought Thoulia was, that's for sure.'' He laughed, somewhat uncomfortably, making the ware-eyes gesture to keep Laughers away.

Thrasne went to Outskirt Row to find Delia's house. It was the one with the greatest profusion of flowers, the most sweetly scented with herbs. He stood in a redolence of fragrance and color, peering over the low wall. The little girl was there, crouched over a book as though to protect it from thieves, twiddling one long lock of hair with her fingers, winding and unwinding. The book was licit from the looks of it. It had the Tower seal on the cover.

"Pamra,'' came a voice from inside. "Come have your supper.''

The girl rose, half sighing, closing the book unwillingly. As she turned, she caught sight of Thrasne standing there and hesitated for a moment, puzzled, almost as though she might have remembered seeing him before. Then she shook her head and went into the house, leaving him as shaken as he had been by the first sight of the drowned woman. For it was she again, line for line, in a smaller frame and compass, a younger face. There was the same passion, the same willful disbelief, the same stubborn intensity turned within. He knew, having seen her face, that she lived inside herself, seeing her own visions, making her own world, not seeing half of what went on around her.

Seriously shaken, he made his way back to the *Gift*. What message could he give the drowned woman? How could he pierce the isolation of her blight to tell her her child was well? The child who was like her, line for line.

At last he printed a message large and put it upon the wall before the drowned woman's eyes. "PAMRA IS WELL. DELIA CARES FOR HER." He could think of nothing briefer, nothing more reassuring. He did not really know whether she would see it or not. Perhaps time was slower for her. Perhaps it would take her a year to see it. He was careful not to move her so that her view of it would be undisturbed.

They still talked.

"Blint is getting older," he confided to her. "He talks to me all the time about not being as young as he once was and needing someone to be a son to him."

"If he says that, he hopes you will be such a son."

"That's what I thought. Almost as though he needs reassuring about something. When he talks so, Blint-wife makes a kind of face, as though she had tasted something bitter."

"It is bitter for women not to have the fruit of their bodies when they are denied the world's fruits. Bitter to have her man seek for a son in his old age. Men, who harvest the world's fruits, care less for their own."

"It's true she gets little of the world's fruit," Thrasne agreed. "The River is a man's world."

The thought stayed with him as he moved among the boatmen in the following years, proving its truth to himself again and again. Those who had little enough of the world's fruits were most needy of their own. He thought often of the old woman, Fulder Don's mother. What had she had, after all, but Fulder Don himself? Had him, and had been disinclined to share him. Had she driven his first wife to her death, too? As she had his Suspirra? If she were dead, which he was not at all certain of.

Blint came to him one day with a bulky document, wrapped about with tape and sealed with wax. "My boy, I want you to keep this. I want you to swear oath to me you'll see I go into the River when my time comes and not into any town workers' pit." He looked deep into Thrasne's face, gray lines around his eyes, loose jowls betraying a loss of flesh. His hands trembled, too, and Thrasne was moved to such a

sympathy of feeling, it was a time before he could bring
himself to speak.

"You know I would do that without any oath, Blint. You
have been a father to me. You may rely on me."

"Tie ballast to my bones, boy. Don't let the Awakeners
get me into those damn pits." Put me deep as the strangeys
swim."

"I'll do it, owner Blint. And where no blight is, either."

The man looked at him oddly then, and for a bit Thrasne
thought he had given something away, but nothing more was
said. Time went on. Blint seemed to recover some of his
jovial ways. He put on a little weight. Thrasne sighed in
relief. He was to open the document if anything happened,
and he knew Blint-wife would be furious that Blint had not
given it to her. Still, he owed much to Blint.

"Why didn't he give it to her?" he asked Suspirra.

"Because he knew he could rely on you to do what he
wanted. He knew she might not. Often she does the opposite
of what he says, you know, only to remind herself she is still
a person. Otherwise, she forgets."

Thrasne knew it. He made a carving of it. A man, climbing, carrying a woman on his back, not looking at her. She,
gazing at him, tripping him as he went. The faces were not
anyone's faces. Still, Blint blinked when he saw it and
looked at Thrasne with widened eyes.

Suspirra went on changing. Now that Thrasne had the hang
of it, he simply drew a picture of her every twenty days or
so, binding them together as he had previously. He thought
she was beginning to say the same thing again. More than
that, however, her body was changing shape. She who had
been slender as a frag sapling, yielding as a reed, seemed
thicker, more stolid, as though she fattened upon the air of
the little room, gained substance from their conversation.

They came one warm second summer to the Straits of
Shfor. All the boatmen were on deck with the fending poles.
They had lashed great bundles of rope and sacks of pamet to
the side of the boat to protect it against the fanglike stones of

Shfor. One could not go through at slack water on the oars, for the way was too narrow. One wanted a low, easy tide and a slight wind to get through the straits, or one wanted a long voyage out into World River to go around. As they moved into the canyon, Thrasne looked up to see great birds gathered in hundreds along the rimstones.

"Owner Blint," he called, pointing up.

"Ah? Oh, this is a Talon, boy, full of fliers as a strangey is of bones. There's many of 'em up there, isn't there. Servants of Abricor. Takes a clear day to see 'em. Last time we were through was wrapped up in fog like a blanket, remember? Those peaks up there are all full of holes and caverns, so I've heard. And you never see any young ones at the Talons, so they say. Certain the big ones gather up there, though. Other things, too, from what I hear tell."

"What other things?" Thrasne drew nearer, drawn by something mysterious in his tone.

"There's Talkers and Writers up there."

"Now, owner Blint! Are you joshing me?"

"Well now . . ." The old man squinted against the sun, moving along the side to assist a boatman who was thrusting against a toothy rock. When he came back panting, holding his chest, he sighed. "I'm trying to remember what it was I heard about that. My old owner told me. He was a flier watcher, he was, and he said there was two kinds of fliers."

"Sure." Thrasne laughed. "Big ones and little ones."

"No, no. Two kinds of big ones. He said the kind that nested up there on the Talons could talk. And write."

Thrasne could not help himself. He sniggered. "Like in the stories about when men came to Northshore, owner Blint? Talking fliers?"

Blint shook his head reproachfully. "I didn't say I believed it, Thrasne. I just said that's what he told me. According to him, there's some people up there, too. They live there, to talk to the fliers."

"Where did he hear that?"

"I don't know. He didn't say." Blint seemed vague,

clutching his arm as though it hurt him, disinclined to discuss it further.

They came through the straits without incident and tied up at Shfortown. Blint started to move a bale of pamet, gave a startled exclamation, and fell down. He breathed hard for a moment, cast a frightened look at Thrasne, and lost consciousness.

"Plank aboard," called Thrasne in a calm voice.

"We just got here," grumbled a boatman.

Thrasne whispered to him imperatively, nodding at the pier where several Awakeners walked, and the man moved to pull the plank aboard. Two other boatmen carried Blint below as Blint-wife lamented. They moved quickly out onto the tide.

"Sorry, Thrasne," mumbled the boatman. "Wasn't thinking. You think he's took bad?"

"I don't know," Thrasne murmured. "Just I've been watching him. He keeps clutching his heart as though it hurts him. . . ."

Blint regained consciousness only for a few moments, learned they were well out in the River, gripped Thrasne's hand gratefully, and died. They put him into a small net with ballast stones and dropped him in the deepest part of the current while Blint-wife sobbed.

When she had had time to steady down, Thrasne went to the owner-house with Blint's document.

"Blint asked me to look after you," he said, seeing the fear leave her face a little as he said this. He and Suspirra had thought it out, this approach, after Suspirra told him Blint-wife was afraid.

"I agreed to do it, Blint-wife. He wanted me to take over as owner."

"You!" she screamed. "You, boy! You nothing boy we picked up from the rocks! Why not me, who was his wife these thirty years? Hah? Tell me that?"

He let her rage, saying nothing, until his silence weighted her down and she quieted, lips trembling.

"Because the men won't obey you, Blint-wife, and you'll

not be able to find others who will. If you take the *Gift*, soon
she'll be against a rock in quick-River with none to fend her
off. And if you sell her, you'll not get enough to keep you
for your life. But if I'm owner, I promised Blint I'd set you
safe ashore and bring payment to you each time the *Gift*
comes round. Enough to live on and be well cared for. So,
that's what Blint planned, and I promised. Unless you have
some better plan.''

Which she didn't. The only thing she cried about then was
the possibility of falling into the hands of the Awakeners, but
Blint had thought even of that.

He had written: ''There's secret groups in most towns call
themselves Rivermen—not boatmen, they've had nothing to
do with the boats—who see that their people end in the River
and not with the Awakeners. See Blint-wife is set near some
such group, and give them what gifts they require to see to
her.'' So Blint had written. Boatmen wrote a good deal more
than other folk, it being the kind of business it was. Thrasne
wasn't the only one aboard with hidden books, either. Blint
had some secreted in the owner-house, Awakeners or no
Awakeners.

Thrasne, when he went looking, was surprised to find
many groups such as Blint had described. They were secretive and careful, but open enough once they knew who he
was and what his life had been. Boatmen in general were
known to be rebels against the laws of the Awakeners,
Thrasne no less than others. He set Blint-wife down in a
pretty town called Zephyr, about midway between Shfortown
and Baris, full of ponds where lily flowers grew, in a stout
little house all her own near a quiet cluster of Rivermen and
-women.

''You'll need to hold your tongue, Blint-wife,'' he said to
her, carrying the last of her goods into the new place to the
accompaniment of her incessant clacking. ''Else you'll betray
those who would want to help you.''

She quieted, turning a weeping face on him at the last. ''I
know, Thrasne. Believe me, I hear myself and I know. It's

only I was so lonely there on the River among all those men and not a woman, not a child to talk to. So lonely. I'd have come ashore long since had I not loved him so. Blint. Don't judge so harsh, Thrasne. There's more pain in us clacking old women than you'll ever know, most likely.''

He went shamefaced to Suspirra with this.

"She talked just to hear a voice. A woman's voice," confirmed Suspirra.

Which didn't make Thrasne feel any better about it. Blint-wife had given him all Blint's books, and he was feeling he'd been ungrateful for all her care over the years. He wrote her a letter, saying so, which he had no means to deliver. It was not to his liking, so he wrote another. And as the days passed, he wrote still others, to Blint-wife, to Blint, to himself. In time, he began to keep them in a book, which he called, to himself and very secretly, "Thrasne's book." He was sure the things he wrote there would mean nothing to anyone but him.

From Shfor to Baris was only a few days' float, if one did it without stopping. Suspirra had asked once more, "My baby?" and it had been seven years since Thrasne had seen Pamra. So they came to Baris, and owner Thrasne went ashore, leaving the boat in the good hands of firstman Birk. In the same shop he found a new barber, who might well have been the old barber for all the difference between them.

"Fulder Don's youngest daughter? Why, boatman, she surprised all her kin and became an Awakener. Been at the Tower four or five years now. Seems someone told me just the other day they'd seen her with an older one herding a bunch of workers out on the piers.''

Sick at heart, Thrasne took himself off to the house he remembered from before.

"Pamra?" Delia asked, surprised. "Why, boatman, why would you come looking for Pamra?''

Thrasne mumbled something about having known her mother.

"Oh, sad, sad. Pamra's mama was the loveliest thing I've

ever seen. Like a flower. Like a flame-bird, bright and
graceful, and like a flame-bird gone too soon. Ah. Well,
Pamra's an Awakener now. Did it out of rebellion, I think.
To get even with her grandma and her half sisters. They were
always at her. It was because she looked like her mother,
don't you know?'' She wiped the nose of the infant she was
juggling and called a quick set of instructions to two toddlers
who were picking herbs, explaining, "Their mama died, too,
and they needed a place for a few days until their papa could
make arrangements. Well. You didn't come to talk about my
kiddies.''

Which he hadn't. He left her with words of thanks, taking
himself off to the vicinity of the Tower, far enough away not
to be questioned by the Awakeners but close enough to see
her if she came. When she did, he knew her at once.

"Pamra," he called, not certain it was allowed to speak to
her, but needing to do something more than merely look and
go away.

She turned to him, that expression he so well remembered
intensified, if anything, into a stubborn, blind naiveté, a face
that said, "I will do what I will do!"

"Do I know you?" she asked, a little haughtily, as all the
Awakeners were.

"I knew your mother," he said.

"She went in the River." Her voice was forbidding. Cold.
"She was a coward, a heretic."

"That's very harsh," he said, shocked at her tone.

"No more than she deserves. Did you have something to
say to me?"

"Nothing," he said. What could he say to her? "Nothing." He turned away, confused,·not liking her and yet not
wanting to leave. "You look like her," he called over his
shoulder. "Exactly like her. And she loved you." There, he
thought. Let her make what she will of that.

He went back to the boat downcast and miserable to write
a new sign for Suspirra. "PAMRA IS WELL." She was
well. So beautiful it put his heart into his throat, half longing
and half anger at her, at what she'd done. About sixteen or

seventeen now, and the perfect copy of the drowned woman except that Pamra was slim where this woman had a rounded figure, gently swelling.

"How could she?" he whispered.

"She believes," Suspirra said. "Truly believes. Not in my love, for I abandoned her. Not in her father's love, for he left her, too, in his way. But in the love of Potipur, for she *must* believe in love—of some kind."

Sickened, Thrasne could not believe in the love of Potipur. It was with a kind of guilty relief he put Baristown behind him.

Haranjus Pandel, Superior of the Tower of Thou-ne, saw fit to visit the home of the widow Flot.

"There's this law, Widow Flot. You know it, and I know it." He said this in his usual manner, as one might who is dreadfully bored with the necessity but feels it wise to go through the motions.

Widow Flot, unawed, shook her head at him. "If you're talking of Peasimy, have a little sense, Superior."

"He's thirty years old."

"He's thirty in years. He's four or five in his head, and as far as his wee private parts go, he's not got enough to bring a blush to a maiden's cheek. I'll swear that part of him hasn't grown since he was born." She flushed a little saying it, but it had to be said. Gods, hadn't she said it to her friends, many a time, and hadn't they breathed it around? Sure Haranjus knew it, just as he knew every other blessed thing that went on in Thou-ne.

"Still, there's the law." It didn't come out with the force Pandel would have wished. He had suddenly remembered several other things about Peasimy that he had known at one time but had conveniently forgotten until that moment.

The widow Flot was no more awed by the law than she was by his presence. "The law says no celibacy, no boy-boying, that's what the law say, Haranjus Pandel. The law says there must be wedding and bedding and enough children born to keep our numbers strong. That's what the law says.

And Superior or no, don't come all over haughty with me, Haranjus. I knew your ma, and I've known about you since you were no bigger than Peasimy's cock. Peasimy's not celibate, no more than any infant is. And Peasimy's no boy lover, neither. Peasimy's a ninfant, a neuter, no more sex to him than to a blade of grass. So what's this about the law? You got some ugly, godforsaken maiden you've got to get matched up, is that it?''

Haranjus had the grace to blush. He had, as a matter of fact, the daughter of the Merchants' Guild Hetman to get mated, somehow. She with the face like a song-fish and the body like a tub. No matter, face nor figure, so long as she was able to produce. With the constant drain on their numbers, producing was important. And rumor was that human numbers needed to be slightly increased for a . . . well, for a reason. No way it could be done unless the birth rate went up.

Seeing him redden, she went on relentlessly, ''You'd be laughed out of Thou-ne. And if word got back to the Chancery you was wasting your time on such silliness—and I'd see it got there, one way or another—they'd put an end to any hopes you might have. Give it up, Haranjus. Find your ugly girl some other housemate, but give it up so far as Peasimy's concerned.''

He argued some, but it was only halfhearted, a kind of face saving before he went away with scant courtesies. It had been a silly idea. Everyone in Thou-ne knew Peasimy, and the idea of Peasimy with a wife would strike them all as a mighty funny thing. Compromising to the dignity of the Tower. Meeting the letter of the law, but contrary to its spirit. Besides, it wouldn't gain the favor of the Merchants' Hetman, either, if he got no grandkids as part of the deal. Widow Flot was right. Leave it alone.

Behind him in the little house, Widow Flot wiped one or two tears away. Hadn't she suffered enough? No hope for grandbabes. No hope for someone to care for her in her old age. Just Peasimy, sweet as any toddler, and with no more sense. "There, there," she told herself, cheering a little. "Still, he's good as a pet anyday."

In the bedroom, Peasimy sprawled in moist, infant sleep as he always did daytimes, unaware of the catastrophe that had narrowly missed him, dreaming of a time when all the darkness should be driven away and the light made whole. There were no words in these dreams, only visions in which winged figures moved through radiant space. Dreams, not unlike those dreamed by many, except that Peasimy remembered them when he woke. When he rose, walked, prowled through the dark, splashing light where he could, he always remembered them and longed to be deep in that dream again.

Days and nights go by. Moons swing up from the east in round, ripe glory and fade to mere slivers of rind on the western sky as time passes. Conjunctions come and go.

Comes a night. Dusk in Thou-ne, a misty dusk in which all is veiled, mystery made manifest, ghost faces in the wisps of fog that waft in from the River, ghost voices, too, which become, on long listening, the sounds of song-fish, wooden bells, the tinkle of glass chimes, the crier's call. Only the Tower has a brazen bell, metal being too scarce to waste on anything except coin and holy purposes, but it is silent tonight, its voice withheld. Tower bell only rings when something is wrong. There is seldom anything wrong in Thou-ne, edged as it is on the east with the scarps and valleys of the Talons. No workers come to Thou-ne from the east. Potipur knows what the Awakeners beyond the Talons do with their dead, though Peasimy supposes a workers' pit somewhere. Peasimy has it all figured out. Lies, all lies what they say. It was lies what they said about his father being Sorted Out. It was lies what the body fixer said about his arm, that time it broke. There hadn't been any Sorters, and the arm had hurt, terribly. Peasimy no longer listens to what they say. Only what they do is true, so he watches but does not hear. He has turned his ears off, long and long ago, to most words. Sounds, now, those he will condescend to hear, and tonight

he listens from his post beside the warehouse wall. Chimes
and woodbells and the crier's call.

Night along the River in Thou-ne. Mist, tonight, blowing
in from the slupping surface, softly suffused globes of it
gathered around each of the lanterns, holding the light in
glowing spheres that hang along the jetties like a string of
ghostly balloons. Song-fish making a chorus under the shore
reeds, harummm, rumm, lummm, rumm. Three of them.
One soprano-fish and two deep-voiced droners. Harumm,
sloo, harumm.

Light cannot get far enough from the lanterns to make
puddles on the cobbles. Lanterns are scarcely bright enough
to see by. Jetties lying in shadow. He stands, Peasimy, head
cocked, listening to the song-fish. Something there, disturbing them. Most nights they've finished up by now, danced on
their tails, done all their calling and telling, but tonight
there's something keeping them awake. So Peasimy listens,
almost understanding what it is the song-fish sing, as much in
tune with them as with the dark and the fog.

"Oh," he whispers to himself, "don't I hear you, don't I?
Somethin' comin'. Somethin' wonderful comin'. Don't I
know that? Haven't I been told? No need to keep sayin' it,
over and over. No matter was it tomorrow or forever, I'd still
be here, waitin' for it." He rocks to and fro on his heels,
thinking they may stop now, now that he's told them, but the
song-fish go on, harummm, harummm. No, whatever they're
telling him, it's something different from the ordinary.

Peasimy tiptoes along to the Riverbank, out onto the jetty,
down to the place the reed bed thins out and the fish sing,
flings himself down with his head snaking out over the slosh
and slurp of the black water.

Harumm, lumm, sloon, rumm. Fish playing with something, pushing it back and forth. They do that. Push an old
barrel back and forth. Push a log, a stump. Chunk, chunk on
the jetty, far down. Chunk, chunk, coming closer. And he
can see it! Even in the dark, down there under the water,
glowing, shining, a greeny glow, like new leaves in the sun,
like moon on grass, light!

He stares and stares as the fish bring her up, up to the surface, she glowing ever more brightly, until at last he looks directly into her face. All around her the fishes, singing, the glowing fishes spread either side of her like wings. Bump, bumping her against the stones, looking up at Peasimy as though to say, "Here she is!" He knows her at once, one of the creatures from his dreams, one of those who bring the light.

Oh, but she has changed since Thrasne carved her and put her into the River. All the features are the same, and the hard fragwood has not softened, but the little creatures of the depths have been at her, smoothing her all over with their phosphorescent slime so she gleams, shines, beams up from the waves like a beacon of greeny light, smiling, one hand held out as though for Peasimy to take it and welcome her ashore.

And Peasimy reaches down, stronger than he could possibly be, tugging and lifting, pulling like a boatman at the capstan, hauling with an excess of power he has never had and will never have again, until she stands there, dripping on the jetty, peering at the town of Thou-ne. Only then does he go screaming off after the crier and the watch, hallooing for the lantern man, for the people to come see, and such is his fervor and volume of voice it is not long before there is a crowd gathered, full of muttering as the reed beds, staring at the woman from the River, who smiles back at them, shining, shining, shining in the dark.

"There," Peasimy cries, over and over, in a voice totally unlike his own. "There in the River. The Truth Bearer. The Light Bearer. She shines, oh, she shines!"

"What's he saying?"

"Says she's the Truth Bearer."

"What's that?"

"Somebody who brings the truth, I guess. Look at her. Ain't she lovely."

"What'd they say?"

"Said the lovely Truth Carrier was come, I think. That's her. Up there."

"What's a Truth Carrier?"

"Oh, that's religion, that is. Foretold to happen." This
from one of the standabouts, a know-it-all who makes up half
of what he says and switches the other half around to suit
himself. No one believes a thing he says in daylight, but the
dark and mist make him an anonymous voice, speaking with
the authority of conviction. "Foretold to happen," he says
again, pleased with the way this is received.

And the circumstances of it all, the mist, the dark, the
voice saying things that seem authoritative, Peasimy's trans-
figured face, the beauty of the carved woman, all that reaches
them so they go away from the place nodding their heads,
believing she is whatever Peasimy calls her. Believing they
had heard of the Truth Bearer all their lives, pleased and
delighted, though mystified, that she has come.

The day after goes on with saying and saying until what is
said by one is said by everyone and believed by everyone.
Someone—years later the distinction is claimed by half the
families in Thou-ne—someone says the glowing image belongs in the Temple. By evening she is there, in the Temple
of the Moons, there at the top of the sanctuary steps in front
of the carved visages of the gods, looking down at the people
in kindness and wonder. By evening the ritual surrounding
her has begun. From the balcony high above, a novice ladles
water from buckets, an endless line of buckets carried from
the River itself, and in this dank sprinkle the image of
Suspirra stands, shining wetly and smiling, as though forever. Peasimy kneels at the altar rail, his face glowing like
the moon.

Behind him in the sanctuary, Widow Flot stares at his
back, not knowing whether she is thankful for this or not.
Peasimy hasn't been up in the daytime for a dozen years or
more, and this could mean he will start sleeping at night, like
most people. Which means he'll be underfoot, during the
day, most likely.

"Flot-wife," says a voice behind her in gloomy tones, and
she turns to confront Haranjus Pandel.

"Superior," she says formally in her most discouraging

tone. What is he going to make of this, now? Some new thing to bother honest people with?

Instead he asks in gloomy tones, "What is all this? You can tell me, Widow Flot. Haven't I the right to know? All the responsibility, and no one tells me? Did he carve the thing? Did he?"

She stares, laughs, stares again. He doesn't expect an answer. He doesn't even believe it himself. He sits there on the hard, uncomfortable bench, head propped on one hand, his long, lugubrious face attentive to the glowing woman behind the rail. Is he thinking, too, that it may really be a miracle? Behind the shining woman are the faces of Potipur, Abricor, and Viranel, so familiar the worshipers do not even see them. Now, for the first time, Widow Flot sees these carved faces of the gods contrasted with a human face, the shining woman's face, and knows them for what they are.

"Haranjus," she breathes in the grip of discovery. "Potipur's face! That's a flier's face!"

And he, casting his eyes upward, sees the faces of the gods for the first time. Really seeing. Peering down at him with a hooded-eyed cynicism, beaks gaped a little as though hungry. Fliers' faces. He has never questioned them before, never before even noticed the expressions they wear. How long, he wondered in sudden panic, how long had he been worshiping the fliers without even knowing it?

• 5 •

In the Awakeners' Tower in Baris, Pamra Don lay sleeping. The Candy Tree filled all the space above her, glitter and shimmer of leaf behind leaf, blossoms squirming open in a sensuous dance of hue and scent, explosions of amber and gold, bursts of gemmy reds, all rustling, flushing, burgeoning into every empty space, thrusting its light and color upon her, drawing her up into itself, weightlessly . . . toward glory. . . .

Something rasped, scraped. A hard sound. Nothing alive in it. Metal on stone. The Candy Tree shivered. Pamra ignored the sound, hating it, clinging to the tree. . . .

"The new drainage ditches along the Tower wall," a voice in her mind said clearly. "A worker crew digging drainage ditches."

With that recognition the Candy Tree dream slipped away like smoke, and she woke thinking of Delia.

Tangled warmth of bedcovers; a ghostly reflection staring back at her from the glass across the cubicle. Last evening, the bleeding. This morning, heavy sleep and slow waking. A longing for comforting arms. That was why she was thinking of Delia today, when she had not thought of her for a season.

Groaning, Pamra rolled herself half upright, huddled at the edge of the bed, hugging herself as the weak tears runneled her face. Oh, it was hard enough to waken oneself after bleeding without thinking of Awakening the workers. She should have known better than to have angered Betchery with her comment about the woman's appetite. Betchery was well known as a glutton, but she hated being reminded of it. Bleeders had ways to retaliate; unconscionable, but predictable.

She mouthed the furred, foggy taste of sick depression; only the result of weakness, true, but enough to make one doubt one's strength. For a moment, predictably, she regretted being an Awakener. Why keep on when it meant submitting to Betchery and all the other necessary unpleasantness?

She responded to both regret and question as she always had. "Because of what my mother did." Muttering, the words coming out in a single connected string, as though they were all one word, an incantation uttered from habit.

It was years since she had actually heard herself saying those words. At one time they had stirred her anger, renewed her resolution. Now they were only part of the morning litany, the childhood humiliation buried beneath ten years of ritual and acceptance. She slumped away from the bed, aching, sagging, knowing her face must be pale as ice. What a lot to go through. And yet she was so close to senior grade.

Senior grade. Senior retreat first, learning the mysteries that juniors were not privy to. Danger there, carefully avoided in thought. Not all those who went on senior retreat returned afterward. Skip over that. Senior retreat, then senior vows, then a luxurious room of her own on the upper floors. Meals cooked to order, not ladled out of the common pot. Respected by everyone, without exception. Even Papa wouldn't be able to think of her as a failure when she was senior grade.

She leaned against the window, letting the glass cool her skin, remembering Grandma Don's sarcastic voice: "Pamra's mother was a coward and a heretic. Pamra herself shows no sign of expiating that sin. She will never make an artist."

And her own words in response, unplanned, unintended, raggedly defiant in the subdued gathering. "I can be an Awakener. That's better than artist anytime."

Silence had opened to receive that statement, an embarrassed silence that grew into coolness, into distaste, into

disaffection. There had been no way to back down, no way
to change her mind. They had rejected her when the words
were said; she could only go on after that.

Once in the Tower, she had not seen Prender or Musley or
Papa or Grandma again. Someday she would see her half
sisters and Papa, perhaps. After she was senior, not before.
And not Grandma Don, of course. Grandma would have been
taken to the Holy Sorters long ago, though Pamra doubted she
had been Sorted Out.

Disgusted at the memory, she pushed herself away from
the window. Nothing was real this morning. Propelling her
weakness through the day would be like swimming through
mirage. Stripping off her gown, she began the morning ritual
which got her dressed, her hair braided in the distinctive
Awakeners pattern. Robed and sandaled at last, she left the
cubicle to pause at the top of the women's stairs for the
Utterance.

*"Rejoice! I go to Awaken those whose labors sustain us.
Thanks be to the Tears of Viranel, to the Servants of Abricor,
to the Promise of Potipur, and amen."* Though her shaking
hand upon the banister belied her voice, the statement was
made firmly aloud, requiring response.

"Rejoice and amen!" chanted a voice from down the
corridor, echoing and anonymous.

So released, she stumbled down to the women's refectory
and a deserted table. The smell of the morning grain ration
sickened her, but she held her breath and forced the porridge
down. Her body would not make new blood if she didn't eat,
and no amount of religious posturing would get her through
the day unless she felt stronger.

Ilze's voice came from behind her, formally cool, yet with
a slight tone of anger. "Pamra, you're white as pamet. Have
you just been bled? Who did it?"

Pamra kept her face forward. While talking at morning
meal was not forbidden, it was considered indicative of a
lack of seriousness. Still, he was a senior and her mentor. He
had a perfect right to come into women's quarters, a perfect
right to question her. She whispered, "It was Betchery."

"Betchery indeed. I should have known without asking."
He was lean and brown with a bony, handsome face and
hungry eyes. Despite his evident concern, Pamra felt a sense
of danger whenever he was near, as though she might burn if
he focused on her more closely. She shifted uncomfortably
beneath his unsmiling regard, keeping her eyes down where
they belonged, uneasy under his stare.

"You're in no condition to be on labor roster. Take it easy
today, and I'll see what I can do." He touched her, almost a
caress, lingering longer than necessary. Beneath his hand,
her skin quivered, not welcoming the touch, not daring to
reject it. He turned, saying, "Well, enough of this rejoicing.
I have yesterday's plowed fields to inspect."

"*Rejoice!*" Pamra responded formally. "*The Awakening is
at hand.*"

He left her with an amused smile, shaking his head very
slightly. Ilze frequently seemed to find her amusing, and this
slight, half-concealed mockery often puzzled her. This morning, however, she was too weary to be puzzled by anything.

In the open corridor between men's and women's quarters,
she waited at the bleeders' hatch for someone to bring whatever supplements the Superior had ordered. Betchery brought
them out, fat Betchery, sneering and popping candies into her
mouth as Pamra tried to choke the pills down dry. It was
Betchery's habit of gluttony that Pamra had commented on to
Jelane. Unfortunately, Betchery had overheard the conversation.

"Rejoice, Awakener," said Betchery, handing over the
two daily flasks of blood and Tears. "Lookin' a trifle pale,
there."

"Rejoice and amen." Pamra would not give her the satisfaction of anything but ritual. Rejoice and amen, and amen to
you, Betchery, bitch. If you come dead under my hands,
you'll not be Sorted. She went out into the morning, no
longer trembling, merely angry-sad as bleeding usually made
her. It brought a brooding melancholy that made the world
seem colorless—a painting done in shades of brown and tan
with none of the usual life and vitality.

The water in the trough on the high steps riffled in the light wind of the year's second summer, warmer and less rainy than the autumn that had just passed. Thin, early-morning clouds streamed north in the onshore winds; later they would puff like pamet pods to hang their heavy veils over the fields. A flight of young flame-birds fled across the sky, their orangey feathers spark bright in the sun. Down in the Baristown plaza, a line of swaying Melancholics moved across the pave, chanting to awaken the people. Only they or the Awakeners would be up this early. The parkland that separated the Tower from Outskirt Road at the edge of Baristown lay green in this early light, quiet, silvered with dew.

Beyond the park and the plaza, the avenue stretched south to the bank of the World River. There the tidal bulge pulsed westward as it followed the god-moons Viranel and Abricor, hanging like pale, round lanterns in the western sky. Potipur brooded beneath the horizon. Conjunction would come at midwinter this year, more than a season from now. Conjunction, when all the Servants of Abricor disappeared for a time and the workers were allowed to lie quiet.

Along the pulsing waters of the Riverside a worker crew was dumping loads of rock to extend one of the fishing jetties, the workers crawling like gray maggots on the clumsy structure. Beyond them on the brown-dun flow a boat passed, pushed onward by the tide, and the striding form of a Laugher moved on the River path at the same speed, as though boat and man were tied together. Pamra made the sign of Aversion, turning her eyes from the Laugher. Always better not to see them. Against a hillside to the west another worker crew was plowing, the shapeless forms oozing among the occasional copses of broad-leafed puncon trees left standing both for their shade and their fruit. Beside each crew an Awakener leaned on a tall mirrored staff, blood flasks hanging from the shoulder. Pamra was usually first to the day's labors. Seeing these others before her reaffirmed her weakness, her tardiness. She must move, get the day's work under way.

But first she could receive her own Payment, that moment of her day blessed by Potipur. No matter what else happened, the early-morning rapture made it all worthwhile.

She took a deep breath and raised both arms in the ritual gesture toward the west, the direction of the World River, of the moons, of the sun, toward which all things moved. Her breathing slowed, her skin began to tingle. Eastward then, holding her hands before her face in the gesture of negation, the unworld direction, the way no one could go, from which all things came but into which nothing could return. She bowed north, to the forests that carpeted all the lands to the edge of the Great Steppes and beyond the steppes to the Chancery, where the Protector lived, mighty and omniscient, behind the Teeth of the North; bowed south to the River, World-Girdler.

Then she held her breath, waiting for it.

A welling joy that had no focus in this world, a transcendent glory in her flesh, a dizzying beat of her blood, a rush of pure pleasure throughout her body, a bath of ecstatic fire.

"It's the pills they give you," Jelane had said to her. "It's the pills that give you that feeling." Jelane was a junior who had come into the Tower shortly after Pamra.

"No," Pamra had told her. "It couldn't be just pills. That wouldn't be fair."

"Well, it is, Pamra. By all the three gods, but you're dumb. Why do you think you get that rush every day right after they give you your supplements! It's kind of a little Payment, for being a good girl when they bleed you."

"No," Pamra had said, choking down her resentment and anger. Why should anyone listen to Jelane—Jelane, who spent every third day being restricted or getting two lashes for infractions? Jelane was a selfish, heretical little fool. If it was the pills, then how explain that the rapture came at other times, too? She said this, definitely, not expecting Jelane to believe it and not caring whether she did or not.

"Well, maybe you get it other times," Jelane had sniffed. "None of the rest of us do."

How could one live in the Tower without the rapture? How could one do recruitment without the rapture? How could one get through the day? The rapture came from Potipur as Payment to His servants; nothing else made sense.

When the glory faded, she went to Awaken the workers.

Of the twenty or so fresh bodies brought every week from
Wilforn, the next town to the east, several still lay in the
Baristown pit, their canvas wraps virtually unstained, the
masking hoods whole and untattered. Only the swollen blue
feet emerging from the wrap showed the first signs of corrup-
tion. These were the Wilforn dead who had not been Sorted
Out, who had instead been left in the workers' pit to fulfill
their obligation.

Pamra bowed her head and gave the invocation in a calm,
beckoning voice, then raised the first hood just above the
purple-lipped mouth to pour the mixed Tears and blood from
her flask between the dead lips.

"Drink and rise," she intoned. "For work awaits you."

One never raised the hood high enough to see the faces—
though every Awakener had probably done it once. Having
done it once, no one would do it again. A few years before,
she might have waited to verify that each worker did indeed
rise up. Now she merely dropped the hood and moved on.
Other Awakeners would arrive soon, and she wanted as many
of these fresh workers in her own crew as she could get. Too
many times lately she had had to take shambling forms
directly from the worker pits to the bone pits because some
other Awakener hadn't bothered to put them where they
belonged the night before. Of course it was unpleasant to get
something barely able to hold itself together to walk the extra
few hundred yards, and of course they had to be moved in a
barrow sometimes, but that was part of the job. Though,
thank Potipur, not a part she would need to do today.

"Thanks be to Viranel," she intoned, meditating upon the
Tears that were mixed with the blood.

Long ago, said Scripture, Viranel had revealed the power of
Her Tears, shed for the sins of mankind, to the Holy Sorter
Thoulia, and in furtherance of that revelation all the Towers
and Awakeners had come to be. In class, Pamra had been
told that the fungus, brought into a spate of growth by fresh
blood and sunlight, grew rapidly throughout the dead bodies,

duplicating nerve and muscle cells with tissues of its own, copying and revivifying the structures that were there. Pamra thought there were other things the Tears did as well, but it was better not to ask questions. Undoubtedly she would be told whatever was important for her to know, in time.

"Anything you do badly reflects on me," Ilze had said to her that first day.

Pamra, half-terrified, had trembled. "Yes, Mentor," she had murmured.

"Anything you do badly, I have to answer to the Superior. You understand?"

She had bowed, hands folded, eyes down, only to start at the lash of something around her ankles, a stinging on her bare feet. She was staring down at a whip, coiled serpentlike around her feet, and the shock brought her eyes up to confront the snakelike stare in Ilze's eyes, covetous and cold.

"And if I have to answer," he had whispered, "so will you."

Pamra had never forgotten. Ilze had never had to answer for anything she had done. She had kept the rules, not asked questions, done what she was told. As she was doing now.

"Drink and rise," she said again and again until she had the full hand of workers on their feet. Five was about all one could manage while plowing, though up to ten could be used in carrying stone. She twirled her staff as she led them northwest to the pamet fields, the mirrored facets throwing sparks of light before them. The harnesses and plow lay where the last crew had left them. Driven by the mirrored lights and her murmured chants of command, the workers shambled into the harness and began to plow, slowly, soundlessly, the blind hoods faced in the direction Pamra faced, seeing, if at all, through her eyes.

When evening came, she led them back, judging the distance carefully so that the power of the last blood she gave them would last just until the workers reached the pits. None of them were ready to be dropped into the bone pits, thank Potipur. A good fresh crew. She would rise early the next few days and attempt to keep them for herself. The thought frayed away, lost in weariness at the thought of any next few days, fatigue wrapping her with an aching sigh. She could not consider tomorrow. She could not even consider the night. Though she felt stronger than in the morning, the mindless evening hours in the Tower seemed more than she could bear.

She'd been neglecting Delia lately. It was a good time to visit her.

The gardens of Outskirt Row spilled over their walls, shedding perfume into the evening, fragrant with herbs and warm from the day's sun, as welcoming a place as it had always been. Delia's house was at the end of the row.

Despite the welcoming appearance of the place, Pamra delayed as she went down through the parklands, heavy with nostalgia, last night's dream and the morning's resentments all mixed together. Skittering sparks of light fled from her mirrored staff to scramble across the path and the stones. The lights attracted Delia's attention, and she came to the gate of her garden, waving her cane as though it were a wand held by some good witch to make a welcoming enchantment.

"Pamra! Something told me you would come, so I baked spice cakes. . . ." No reproach for all the days she had been forgotten. Reproach was not Delia's way, and Pamra warmed to Delia's way, as she always had.

"I haven't had a spice cake in . . . oh, a thousand years." She could not help smiling. This was good Saint Delia, who always remembered things, all of them warm and happy, even when there were few enough of those to choose among. "Not since I was a child. A long time ago, Delia."

"Not all that long. No. Scarcely yesterday. Only a conjunction of the moons or two, nothing to mention." Delia laughed, but the cough turned into a hacking convulsion that left her weak, wiping her eyes and shaking her head. "Oh, me, me. My days are surely few before I am carried to the west and put into the Sorters' hands. Tsk."

Pamra made a gesture, her revulsion scarcely concealed. "You mustn't say things like that."

"Oh, Pamra, child! All us ordinary people talk like that.

You know it. Only you Awakeners never talk of going into the west. Do you worry so that we have no faith? That we will not be taken into Potipur's arms?''

"It isn't . . . it isn't that, Delia. I have no doubt about your being Sorted Out and received by Potipur. Among us it's just accounted bad manners to talk of it with . . . people close to us.''

"But child, we're not among you Awakeners. There's just you and me, and haven't we always said honest things to one another?''

"Of course we have." Pamra took the old woman's hand in her own, feeling the fragile flesh give way between the slender bones. Delia's wrists were like a flame-bird's legs, like a reed stem. "And when all the family turned away from me because I decided to be an Awakener, only Delia stayed my friend.''

She smiled into the old face, reaching out to touch the tiny, leaf-shaped blue birthmark on Delia's chin as she had when she was a little one. "Wiggle the leaf, Deely. Make it move!" She had been only two or three, but she could remember saying that.

"Well, I hope more than any friend, child. You were more like my own child, and you stayed my child, stubborn though you were. And *angry,* sometimes. I remember how excited you were about the Candy Tree. And how furious you got when Prender told you it didn't really exist. You were seven. Lots older than the others were when they found out. Ah, you flew at her with your little fists, hitting and screaming at her that she lied, she lied. You cried for hours.''

Pamra protested, "But it was *you* told me about the Candy Tree, Delia. Of course I believed you. You made such a story of it. And sure enough, in the morning the seeds were always there. So good. I can taste them yet. And how hard it was to save even one as 'seed' for the next year's tree! I tried so hard to stay awake and see the tree grow, even though you said it wouldn't grow at all if I did. And then Prender . . . well, I didn't like her much anyhow, and she was calling you a liar.''

"Oh, child. Now, you know that isn't true. It wasn't a lie. It was just a kind of story. A pious myth. To make children behave well. And they get such fun out of it."

"Well, I got more fun out of the myth than I ever did eating the candy after I knew you had put it there. Especially since it was Prender who told me."

"Prender wasn't supposed to tell you. She was supposed to let you believe as long as you could. We always let the little ones believe as long as they can; they get such pleasure out of it. She probably wouldn't have told you if it hadn't been for jealousy in the family. You two didn't get along then and most likely never will. I've told Prender a hundred times, 'We eat the crops the workers grow! Why should we turn our backs on the Awakeners?' Ah, well, but you know your oldest sister."

"I know her well enough." Pamra was grimly certain about this. "The whole family. Rejecting me because of what I chose to do."

"Oh, child. They just doubt sometimes, that's all. Don't you ever doubt? Are you always sure Awakening is for the best?"

"Della! What do you expect me to say? That's the kind of question Mother would have asked! And you know how everyone felt about that! Of course Awakening is for the best."

"I know you believe so, child. But lots of people don't, truly. It doesn't make them bad. Perhaps you know something they don't. It's better when all the people know, Pamra. It's better not to be alone." She sighed. "I wish you'd forgive your mama, Pammy. What she did wasn't so bad."

"It was bad enough! Deserting me and Papa that way!"

"She had her reasons, Pammy. She was pregnant, sick, frightened."

"That's no excuse! How could she give up an eternity of blessedness in Potipur's arms for no more reason than that!"

"Perhaps . . . perhaps because she doubted she'd be Sorted Out, child. We all have our little sins."

"And Potipur is merciful," Pamra grated, teeth tight together. "Delia, stop this. I didn't come here to argue with you!" Remembering, suddenly, why it was she had not come more often. Delia always pressed her for forgiveness. And it always evoked this old guilt. This old pain.

"All right, all right, child. We won't fight over it. I wish you'd forgive her because you'd be happier so. But you won't. And that's that. It doesn't change I-love-you."

"No," she said, softening enough to put her arm around the old woman. "No, Delia. It doesn't change I-love-you."

They sat beneath the flowering puncon tree, the sky beginning to flush with sunset. "I'm glad you've come, Pamra. I prayed you would, because your old Delia wants your help to break a rule. Just a little bit."

Pamra's mouth twitched. Because she could not imagine Delia breaking any rule at all, it took a moment for the enormity of the woman's request to sink in. "You want to *what?*"

"I want to go back east, to the village I was born in, to see my sister. She's old. I want to see her."

For a moment she did not believe she had heard. Then she believed and was appalled at the fury of anger that took her. Anger. At Delia. She choked on it. "By the three, Delia! You want to get us both whipped? Or used? That's no small rule breaking. That's a major infraction—*the* major infraction. No one crosses town lines eastward. No one!"

"Oh, well, child, sometimes people do, you know. They just lie about it a lot. I heard that someone on the other side of Baristown went to Wilforn and stayed for the Conjunction festival and then came back, all in one piece and in his right mind."

"Don't tell me!" she demanded, feeling her face grow white and stiff. "Honestly, Delia. Of all the things I'm sworn to uphold, the direction of life is one of—is *the* most important."

"Why?"

"What do you mean, why? Because it's Potipur's commandment, that's why. The World River moves west, the moons move west, the sun moves west, we move—all west,

in the direction of life. To go east is antilife, against the
Three. It's evil, in and of itself! Blasphemous! It's like those
foul same-sex lovers who refuse to propagate in accordance
with Potipur's will, like those rotten celibates the Laughers
keep rooting out. If you want to visit your sister, you'll have
to go west to Shabber, and keep on going until you come to
it.''

"But it's only to Wilforn," Delia whispered forlornly.
"Not more than a day or so walk east from here, even for an
old woman like me. If I go west, love, I won't live to get
there. How long do they figure it takes to come all the way
around? Twelve years if you walk, isn't it? Six or seven
years on a Riverboat. Something like that? I don't have
twelve years, Pammy. Not even six.''

Pamra shook her head angrily. This wasn't fair. Not when
she was so tired. Oh, Delia. What could she do? Travelers
did go all the way around the world, traveling west, some on
boats on the River tide. Some afoot. Pilgrims did it afoot,
making Potipur's Round. They carried messages and told kin
of kin, and walking it did take about twelve years, more or
less, and Delia was right. She couldn't survive such a trip.
She fought to be calm, forced herself into quiet.

"Now, let's talk it over. If it's so important you go back,
how come you ever left there? You never told me you had a
sister there.''

"I came from there when I was about your age, following
my curiosity. Oh, Pamra, truth to tell I was following a man.
He wanted to see somewhere else. So we came here, and he
wanted just to go on and on, but I didn't. I'd had enough of
him by then, and your grandma gave me a job doing the
garden in this place, and time went by. Your papa was only a
child then, and he needed me.

"When he was grown, I could have gone on around west
until I had come home again, but I delayed and dillied, and
by the time I thought of it again, there was you. You, with
your mama gone and that family of yours gnawing at you
because you looked like her. . . .'' She fell silent, stroking
the little blue birthmark at her jawline. Then she shook

herself and went on. "It's just that lately I've been thinking
of my sister. Wanting to see her. Wanting to say, 'Well,
Miri, how has it been with you?' " She stood up, clapped
her hands as she tried to smile.

"It's not important. Not at all. Not important enough to
worry my girl. Now, have another cake. After all, I baked
them for my own Pammy."

She did not speak of it again while Pamra sat in the garden
in the glow of evening, smelling the kindly smells of the
growing things, hearing the cries of the fishermen on their
way home from the long jetties, sitting quiet as the sun fell
lower to touch the horizon in blazes of crimson and orange
and streaks of crushed berry color, bright and bruised at
once. It should have been a time of contentment, of quiet,
but too many memories had been jostled awake in Pamra.
She kept the calm smile on her face, kept her voice low and
peaceful not to distress old Delia, but it was a quiet surface
over a turmoil of remembering.

Mama. Lovely as a dream and as fragile. Pretty as a soap
bubble, and as useless. What did one remember about her?
Softness and singing, sadness and tears, and at last—at last
the unforgivable thing.

And Papa. Winning that second mention when he was
young, very young, enough to set Grandma talking of his
great future as though it were real. But there was no future.
No other awards. No other mentions at all for Fulder Don.
Not a second, not a fifth. And even that fact was blamed on
Mama, somehow made out to be Mama's fault—in turn to
become Pamra's fault, who so resembled lovely Mama.

And saintly Delia had been there through it all, the substitute mother, the kindly one, the only one who did not turn
away when Pamra made her choice and went to the Awakeners' Tower. She squeezed Delia's hand now in remembrance
of that. If it hadn't been for Delia . . . Well, there must be a
way to repay her now, a way to solve this problem.

"Delia, I'm not promising anything, but I'll ask around.
Honestly I will. I'll have to sound out a few people, find out
who to ask, but maybe there'll be a way we can send a

message or something." She surprised in the old woman's face an expression of longing—no, more passionate than mere longing, a fanatic desire, an impassioned pleading with fear in it. "Delia, why does it matter so?"

The old woman sighed. "I wronged her, Pamra. My own sister. I wronged her with him, the one I followed away. He was hers, my sister's man, and he turned from her to me. He told me if he couldn't have me, he would not have her, he'd go to the west without either. And oh, I followed him, foolish as it was, and then did not care enough to follow him farther when he went on. I must ask her to forgive me. *It must be done, Pamra child. It must be done.* Otherwise . . . I may die unforgiven, and it may be Potipur will not take me up. I'm so old, child. There isn't time to do anything but just go to her and ask. . . ."

The old woman sat there, head bowed, grieving over a wrong done forty or fifty years ago. Pamra shook her head. Even though it was dangerous for ordinary mortals to die unforgiven, it was silly for Delia to be upset like this.

"If you did a little wrong when you were young, you've made up for it a hundred times since. If there is any person within twelve days' travel who will be Sorted Out to receive Potipur's kiss, it will be you, Delia, so stop this grieving. I'll figure something out for you."

She felt better for having said it. It was all true. Delia was one of Potipur's own. If reaching Delia's sister was important to the old woman, Pamra would do what she could, and she told Delia so again, and yet again as she left after taking a last breath of the clean garden air.

The water in the ritual cleaning trough was chilled by evening, holding little of the day's warmth as she dipped her hands, sprinkled her face and feet. She leapt away from the trough as black wings swept by, buffeting onto the step where a great flier fixed her with a calculating eye, clacking its huge serrated beak softly together. She leaned against the wall to let her heart stop pounding. It was only one of the Servants of Abricor. They seldom landed on the Tower steps, though they clustered thickly around their aerie on the Tower

top and in the bone pits, always silent, never making a
sound. She dried her hands on the towel by the door, aware
suddenly that door was open.

"Pamra." It was Ilze in the doorway. She realized he had
been there, watching her. "Pamra? Come on, you'll miss
your meal. Where've you been?"

"I'm sorry, Senior. I've been down in town. Visiting my
old Delia. She's half-stuffed me on spice cakes. I'm not
really hungry."

"Spice cakes don't build blood." He sounded irritated.
"Come on. I've arranged something for you."

The hall was busy, echoing with feet and the clatter of
plates. From the men's refectory there was a bass rumble of
voices, a harsh shout of laughter, quickly repressed. The
women's tables were half-empty, only a few tardy diners
plying their spoons, breaking their bread. Ilze waited with
her at the service hatch, then drew her away to an empty
table. "I've got you on recruitment tomorrow."

"Senior! That's kind of you. I thought my turn on the
roster wouldn't come up again for ages."

"It wouldn't have. But I told the Superior that no one was
better at recruiting than you are, that you have a sincerity
which is very effective." There was a moment's odd hesitation in his voice, but then he went on, "And I told her you'd
been bled dry."

"You told the Superior!" Pamra was momentarily aghast.
While some said the lady Kesseret was only human, and a
kindly human at that, Pamra could only think of her as a
moving presence beneath the shining crown and floating
veils, a mystery and a glory. Despite her reputed more than
hundred years, her unlined face and clear eyes implied she
had already received the Payment. "Mentor, I heard someone
say once that she's a Holy Sorter. I'm still petrified to go near
her."

Ilze looked at her in that coldly amused way of his, head
tilted to one side. "One needn't go that far," he said. "It's
enough that she's Superior of this Tower. I told her, also,
that if someone didn't do something about Betchery, she'd

end up killing someone. The Superior agrees you need light duty, so you do your usual sincere job of recruitment for the next two days, and by then you'll be feeling better.'' Actually, it had been the Superior who'd suggested this, but Ilze did not say so. He preferred to let Pamra think he was responsible for the favor.

Pamra chewed thoughtfully, lulled by his informality into an almost social feeling. ''I sort of like recruiting. It's a pain dealing with all the crazy stories they have about us, of course, but I guess I heard the same ones when I was that age.''

''Better you than me, young one. I hate mixing with the damn other-castes. You'd think they'd been touched by Potipur not five minutes before, the way they look and act.'' His face was hostile, nostrils pinched.

Pamra shrugged. ''Nobody could be any worse than my father's family was. I just ignore them.''

''Well, you can't ignore them on recruitment duty. You're expected to be reasonably diplomatic, and that's what pisses me off most about it.'' He flushed, abruptly aware of his manner, not the appropriate one for a mentor to a junior, certainly. ''Why were you so late?'' Now he was her mentor once more, demanding an accounting.

''I shouldn't have been. Except Delia was after me—Senior Ilze. May I not be judged harshly if I ask a question which may be . . . not in accord with doctrine?''

He gave her a dramatically astonished look, lifting one eyebrow. ''A question, Pamra? From you? Are the final days upon us?''

She flushed. ''I know I don't ask many. I wouldn't ask this one, either, except for old Delia. She came from the next town east, Wilforn, many years ago. She has a sister there, or thinks she does. She'd be a very old woman. . . .''

''And Delia wants to go east to see her sister?''

Pamra nodded, relieved not to have had to say it. ''She says some do.''

Ilze nodded. ''It's quite true. If you asked an occasional question, you'd have known it. It's common talk.''

"Where? How? There are guards! There's a fence!"

"Through the workers' pit at night. They go in there and sneak up the other side of the pit where there's no fence."

Pamra's face wrinkled in concentration. At the other side of the pit, marked by a burning lantern, was the Sorting place. Surely . . . "But they might encounter the Sorters on the Sorting ground! That's sacrilege!"

He paused, eyebrows drawn together almost as though she had angered him. He seemed about to say something, then changed his mind. "I've answered your question, Pamra."

"That's the only way?" She was disappointed. "Isn't there some way to send a message?"

"That's much easier. You go to the east gate and pay one of the gate guards on the Wilforn side of the fence to take the message into his town, and you tell him you'll pay him that much again to bring you an answer. That's not really licit, but it's not heretical, either. It's quite common. Even if it's reported, it would only count a day's duty against you. The gate guards might abuse an old woman, but they will not trouble an Awakener. You can tell your old nursemaid that after recruitment tomorrow."

But she could not wait until then. She went early in the morning, moved by an urgency she did not try to identify, to explain how a message could be sent.

To which Delia nodded, frowning a little vacant frown, as though this was not what she had wanted at all, as though this new suggestion had come between her and the comfort of some long decided action with which she had reassured herself in time of pain.

"Just get the message written, Delia. Exactly what you want to say, just as you'd like to say it to your sister—Miri, wasn't it?—and I'll take it to the border either tonight or tomorrow. Tonight, if I can. Much better to do that than go sneaking off through the worker pits in the dead of night. That's not something I want you to do. I'll be back as soon as I can, and you have it ready." And she went off, late already, looking over her shoulder to catch that same expression of stubborn puzzlement, which she saw with a catch in her throat, wondering if she could not somehow have been more convincing and more hopeful.

But then it was, all driven from her mind by the day's work, so different a day from the one before. As she went toward the plaza she passed the merchants' hall and the gardeners' mart and the guildhalls and artists' council houses, and from each of them representatives were coming out in the customary garb of their professions and guilds, all wandering in the same direction. They took no notice of her, or she of them, but each one of them had to give way when she came by, and she knew it ate into them like acid. "Scoff and sneer," she murmured to herself, "but stand aside when I come by, other-caste."

At the plaza each representative went off to his own booth, there to spend the day in earnest conversation with the caste-less youths who were not yet fastened into any way of life. For her there would be the usual curiosity seekers and those who came on a dare. And among them might be the one or two she would recruit, though they had often not intended it when they came. It was true that Pamra could recruit better than any of the senior grade. Perhaps because she was not much older than the young people she talked to. Perhaps because she cared more about it. Though Ilze was a stickler for duty, sometimes he seemed almost to mock the Tower and the law. Almost as though it were no better than law mongering, or body fixing, or garbage shifting, some low-caste activity that no one would bother with if they could do something better. Occasionally Pamra wondered if any of the high-grade Awakeners took it seriously, though of course they must! The religious glory, the ecstasy, would only come if one were serious. How could they remain in the work otherwise?

And it was the ecstasy she talked about with the recruits. By midmorning she had collected a small group—two gig-glers and one swaggering boy with a perpetual sneer. There was also a narrow-chested, fire-eyed youth who glared at her as though she guarded the gate to a treasure he sought. She could almost feel the spear of his glance skewering her, as though he feared she might oppose him rather than help him!

"Do you remember when you were children," she began, "at the time of Conjunction, at festival time, when the Candy Tree grew in your bedrooms at night?" She smiled at them, and they back, unable not to smile, even the gigglers and the swaggering one, though he covered the smile with a sneer pretending mockery. "When you awakened in the morning, the evidence of the tree was there, on your bedcovers, sweet and marvelous.

"Later, of course, you learned that it was your kin who put the candy there, and you believed the story of the Candy Tree must be false, a simple myth for little children. You did not realize that there was a greater truth—that the Candy Tree did indeed grow on the night of festival, not in your bedroom alone, but over all the land of Baris, to drop its festival spirit into the hearts of everyone. If you looked into their faces, your mothers and fathers, you would have seen that festival spirit blooming." Her voice began to sing, she herself began to sway. Her exhilaration in what she said began to catch them, and herself. She felt the blood rising into her face and knew she was beautiful to them.

"There is indeed a Candy Tree, though it is a more complicated concept than children know. And just as the sweetness spread upon your bedcovers is the physical evidence of the spiritual tree, so the existence of the Awakeners is the Northshorely evidence of a greater mystery, the love of Potipur. It is true that we Awakeners raise up those who come to us from the east to provide a service they failed to provide in life. It is equally true that we carry the dead of Baristown to the place of Sorting, west of here. There the good and righteous, their faces shining with the radiance of a life well spent, are Sorted Out by the Holy Sorters to be dressed in silk and placed in the arms of Potipur. We know this. We can testify to it. We are the evidence of it, the evidence of the love of Potipur, and Abricor, and Viranel.

"Because we know this wonderful thing of our own experience, we believe we are more likely to live in accordance

with Potipur's will, more likely to be Sorted Out at the end."
Pamra swept over this point quickly. She was sure. She
wouldn't lie, not to recruits. It wouldn't be fair. But she
didn't really know whether all Awakeners had the radiance in
their faces. All Baris's dead were collected at the Tower for
transport to the place of Sorting, and though Pamra had been
on duty in the death room several times, there had never been
the body of an Awakener there.

She took a deep breath and went on, "Other castes deni-
grate us, it is true, calling us names and making jokes about
our caste. When I was a child I thought this was because of
something atrocious or dirty about Awakeners. I came to
know that it is simple fear. The other castes know they will
come into our hands, and they are afraid. That is all." She
looked firmly into the eyes of the gigglers, of the sneerer,
and found there the fear she sought. "Just as you are fearful
now. Perhaps you worry that the Awakeners somehow can
decide whether one is Sorted Out or not. I tell you we cannot
control it, but without us it would not happen. Your fear,
however, is a key which may open the door of our Tower. If
you fear us, join us and conquer your fear. Learn the truth of
what we say." The rapture was seething within her now, as it
did on the steps of the Tower at morning dedication, or
sometimes during prayer, or when she had gone long without
food, or during these sessions of preaching to the youth of
Baris.

She felt herself smiling, felt the radiance of it, knew that
her face was glowing as she did it. This was her heritage
from pretty Mama, this smile, and her gift from Potipur. The
gigglers had stopped their fidgeting, the sneerer his facial
contortions. She might not have them as applicants, but they
would not mock for a time. The other one, the pale-faced
youth who had fastened himself upon her words as a baby
upon the breast—him she had.

"Will you show me?" he begged. "Show me the Tower?"

She took his hand, letting the others go with an expression
of tender regret. They would remember what she had said.
"Remember the Tower with your gifts," she whispered to

them as she turned away. They would make gifts in the future, certainly they would when they were old. None of her effort was wasted. She sighed, feeling the rapture fade. Until next time.

She took the youth to the Tower, as she had taken others. So precious they were. Young, full of idealism and wonder. She could not resist them, nor they her. From a great distance, the lookout had seen her coming, and when the door opened the Superior stood there in all her robes with the entourage around her. "Come," said Pamra, giving the youth her hand once more. "Come into the Tower." Then he was welcomed with wine and praise and flattery and a very late night, as she had been in her time.

She hadn't known what it really meant then, no more than he did now: the bloodletting, the endless hours in chapel without sleep during those first years, the constant repetition of litany. She had only seen the robes and the glittering staffs, the solemn figures at the forefront of any procession, only heard the whispers concerning the Payment of Life. The rest—the rest hadn't been mentioned. She had been only twelve when she'd said, "I can be an Awakener. . . ." Said it out of bravado and hurt and in ignorance, only to have the rapture become her reason for living.

She woke late. An officious senior caught her lingering at her ceremony upon the steps and sent her with two or three others onto the wastelands north of the Tower to gather Tears of Viranel. So, she had lost the second day's recruiting by her own inattention to duty. "My own sin," she'd told the Three in a whisper. "My own sin. Forgive."

The Tears were so small as to be almost invisible against the stones, transparent, drop-shaped, attached to the soil from which they grew by a glassy, hairlike root. They grew thickly but in widely scattered patches, each patch marked by a tall, skull-topped pole. Impossible to transplant, fruiting only during second summer, Tears grew throughout the lands of Northshore, when and where they would, and the skull poles warned away the unwary. Of late, the patches of fungus had been even more scattered, more difficult to find, almost as though something had been rooting them out. This was an unholy thought, and Pamra made a religious gesture, ashamed of herself.

Gathering was hard, back-bending work that made bones and muscles ache. The Tears had to be scooped into baskets without touching them. The sun was hot, the dust sticky, provoking an unending damp itch that distracted and annoyed. Attention could not be allowed to waver. There were many cautionary stories about those who had touched the Tears accidentally, only to feel the tiny fungi passing through the skin in an instant of fatal error for which there was no cure. Those who touched the Tears were possessed at once by Viranel. Those possessed by Viranel were living workers. Unlike the dead, they were able to speak, for a time. Like the newly dead, they knew what they were and felt the agony of possession.

It was only as she returned to the Tower, her basket full, that she remembered what she had promised Delia. The sun bulged upon the horizon like a single oozing drop before she came to the garden and the little house to find both empty.

The note was there on the table, half-written, scratched and erased, tried again and again. The words fumbled, crawled like crippled fliers on the page. "Miri, forgive . . ." "I did not know . . ." "Only now, in my age, Miri . . ."

Pamra heard her own words in the silent room as though someone had spoken. "Much better than to go sneaking off through the worker pits in the dead of night," she had said. "Sneaking off through the worker pits . . ." Cursing herself that she had not kept her word, that she had not even guarded her tongue.

So. Delia had gone. There was not even a chance to say good-bye. The house did not feel of parting. It welcomed, even now, even empty. In the kitchen the pots shone in the level rays of the sun. Pamra ran her hand over them, smooth and cool, as she had used to do when drying them for the old woman. Spice cakes filled a covered jar. Dried fruit rested upon the sill. High in the rafters bunches of herbs hung like autumn brought home, smelling of the fields. In a cupboard

her own child's apron was folded away where she had left it
the day they took her to the Tower. She felt it now, shaking
out the sweet-smelling buds that lay in its folds. "Delia, ah,
Delia. Why didn't you wait?" knowing as she whined into
the silence that it was her own fault, her own. And at the
end, as the sun darkened in startled ambers and bruised
purple and the kitchen room settled into a quiet she remembered from childhood, all she could say was what Delia had
said to her then, time after time: *"Rejoice. May the Sorters
protect you and bring you to Potipur's arms."*

She skulked out late that night, a shadow in her robe,
striding to the hill overlooking the pit where the little light
burned to guide the Sorters, where all were forbidden to be
after nightfall. She sat there, invisible. It was no good. Delia,
if she had gone this way, had gone long since. It was too late
to do anything about it. Against the stars she could see the
wings of the great fliers, moving in and out of the bone pits,
seeming to peer down into the worker pits. What was the
sound she heard? A croaking murmur? As though someone
had spoken? A chill went through her. If she sat here until
the Holy Sorters came to bring those who had not been
Sorted Out, they would turn her to stone for her presumption,
and it would still be too late to do anything for Delia.
Suddenly fearful for herself, she turned back, sneaking into
the Tower as silently as she had left it.

Each evening thereafter she took herself to the Tower by
way of Delia's house, hoping the old woman had returned.
On the third day she found her half sister, Prender, sitting in
the silent room, dusty now and beginning to smell of disuse
and damp, weeping over the scribbled note. Pamra had not
seen her for years. The face raised to her was familiar and
strange at once, familiar in its outline, in the well-known
quirk of the lips, the expression she had so often interpreted
as a sneer, but strange in its softness, in the lines above the
eyes, around the mouth, lines of pain. "Gone," her sister
said. "Pammy. She's gone."

"I know. She went east. Crossed the line. I was going to
help her, but I was late. . . ." The words came out without

planning, naturally, even kindly. They might have been children again, before any terrible things had been said or done to be forever remembered.

"Delia. Oh." Prender's weeping went on. "She was always there. When Grandma was having those rages of hers, when Papa shut himself up and wouldn't talk to anyone—I'd come here to Delia. It was Grandma's house, you know. She didn't like it, here so near the edge of town. She put Delia in it, just to keep it. It was all bare then. No garden. But Delia . . . Delia . . ."

Without knowing how she had come there, Pamra found herself at her sister's side, stroking her hand as she had not done since they were children. "I know."

"Delia said we treated you badly. We did, you know. It was Grandma. You looked too much like your mother, and she said we were Papa's girls, but you—you were your mama's girl. And then when your mama . . . when she did it, Grandma was just hateful about it. I know you became an Awakener just to make it up. Just to prove you had faith, even if your mama . . . I used to hate you, Pammy, for that. I don't anymore. You need to know that. Papa's gone. They're all gone but me. I don't want to be like Delia, unforgiven by my own kin. Forgive me, please. Please."

Musley gone? Papa gone? Not to see her reach senior grade? Not to know what she had become. She choked with surprised tears. "I forgive you. Really. I do." Saying it, astonished to find that it was true.

And was even more astonished afterward to find that nothing had changed. There had been an hour or so when they had been friends, a transient solidarity of grief that gave way almost at once to old habits. For a few days Pamra went to the house in the evenings to hear if there were any news of Delia, but other people began to frequent the place now that Prender was there, and the stiff discomfort of these encounters drove Pamra away. Even Prender could not keep herself from suggesting that Pamra leave the Tower, give up her life, return to them in some more acceptable form and manner.

"There's no reason anymore, Pammy! You could come live with me!"

As though Pamra's oath were nothing!

Pamra could preach the rapture to strangers, but she could not bring herself to discuss it with Prender, to defile it by letting Prender mock at it as she would, setting it to nothing. She nodded, said nothing, went away as soon as she could, and did not return.

Nothing had changed except that for a time the rapture failed her. It seemed to fail others, also, and there was much use of the whipping post in the courtyard. More than once she looked down to see Ilze plying the long whip on some crouched, tortured junior and gave thanks through dry lips that she found compliance easy. He had never whipped her, though she had never doubted he would if she did not keep her oath. If it were not for that, perhaps she could have heard Prender's words, but it was too late for such words now.

The weather grew windy and harsh. Summer robes were laid away and the winter ones taken from the chests. The moons were moving toward a winter Conjunction—there had not been a winter Conjunction for twenty-two years, not since the year she was born—and the festival season began to fizz on the horizon of her time like something boiling in an adjacent room, a small excitement, a new possibility, the end of another holy year.

"You've been selected," Jelane announced at evening meal, grinning as the bearer of bad news. "Tomorrow you get to get the first load of wood for winter!"

"Oh, Jelane! No. Why me? I hate that trip. The forest is all dim and murky. It takes forever to get there with the wagon. The workers are no good with axes, half the time they cut themselves to pieces and the wagon comes back full of worker parts instead of wood. . . ."

Jelane made a moue. "Politics, junior Awakener. Some of us play and get out of things. Some of you don't play and so you get to go for wood."

It wasn't fair. Pamra conducted herself strictly by the

rules, and the favors went to those who broke them. She shut her mouth in a grim line and said nothing. When Pamra became senior, she told herself, Jelane could expect an accounting.

The forest trip required an early start. It was scarce dawn yet, half-dark still, and the first worker lay under her hand, blood trickling between its lax lips before she saw the blue, leaf-shaped mark upon its jaw.

Her hand moved to raise the hood before she could stop herself.

In the instant she had known what would be there. Delia's eyes, full of knowledge and terrible awareness, staring into her own.

She dropped the hood to stand frozen in position, one hand still holding the dripping flask. A voice that she could not hear, could only feel, screamed inside her, "*Strangers*. You're supposed to be a stranger! Always strangers. No one we know. Not our family, our friends, our people. Others. Sinners. People from the east. People who are being punished for the sins and omissions of their lives. . . . Oh, shame! Shame Potipur that he did not take you. Shame Sorters that . . . that . . . that . . ." But as her voice screamed mindlessly, her eyes saw the little lantern at the eastern lip of the pit and knew it for what it was, knew it for what it had always been—the light to guide the Awakeners from the town to the east to the place they might leave their dead.

There was no Holy Ground.

There were no Holy Sorters.

If either of those things had existed, then Delia would not be here. Delia was here, therefore they did not exist.

"Delia!" Her throat bled at the rasping agony of her own cry. A great cloud of black wings rose from the bone pits to circle above her, looking down, aware of her.

"Delia," sobbing, knowing finally why it was the people scorned the Awakeners, lived by them and hated them. Before her the canvas-covered shape rose up to confront her. Despite the heavy veil, she knew that it saw her still. "A lie," she whispered, wanting that shape to know that she,

Pamra, had been lied to no less than any; used and betrayed no less than they; knowing as she whispered that all the truth had been there for her to read, all the lies open, all her life long, as they had been open and easy to read for children when they woke to find candy on the bed. "A lie," she said once more, hopelessly, disbelieving it. Not even a pious myth. Merely a blasphemy.

She could not bear the blank canvas of the hood. She could not bear what lay behind it. She turned to flee, only to turn again. If she left, another Awakener would come to begin the long punishment, the seasons of unending labor while the flesh reawakened by the Tears of Viranel diminished slowly through an eternity of time and the rotting brain within the corrupted flesh counted each hour, each day, until time could be laid down forever in the bone pits to be eaten by the fliers.

And then a calm came, a calm more terrible in its cold quiet than the frantic horror that had gone before. She went down into the pit and raised up all the workers who were there, a small pitful. Thirty-five or forty, perhaps. She led them away, chanting them along the road, her mirrored staff casting a glittering warning before her in the rays of cold sun. "Rejoice," she gargled. "Work awaits you." Her voice was a mockery. "Work awaits you."

It was very early. No one saw her go. She led the workers away from the city, away from the Tower, north into the forested lands where they could not be seen, then farther still, farther than she had ever gone before among the endless trees of the roadless wilderness, using the blood and Tears for distance only, not for labor. She went in wild ways, guided only by the pale sun, leading a tangled, shambling line that stumbled in its witless wandering through the day, into the evening, into violet dusk. She found a chasm at last, a rocky place, deep and solidly ranked about with high-piled edges of balanced stone. The workers had begun to stumble, but she had driven them on with the last few drops in her flask and then by her voice alone, a harsh cawing, like one of the carrion fliers. She led them onto the sparse brush and hard

stone of the chasm, and there she let them drop. There she let
Delia fall as well.

When she raised the hood, Delia's eyelids lifted to give her
one look of terrible intelligence before they closed once
more. Pamra told herself it had been the final look, the last
awareness.

"It's over," she whispered. "Over. Done. Soon the dark.
Soon the silence. The forgiving silence. Soon the true peace,
Delia. Delia. Forgive me."

Then dark surrounded them, the sound of night fliers, the
rustle of small living things, the dim ghostlight of Abricor,
the silver radiance of Viranel, the red looming power of
Potipur, gathered together to stare down at her as she stared
up, daring them to strike at her. In their light she raised the
hoods, leaving them up to see whether any still looked at her
or whether they were only dead. She could not tell, for the
moonlight shifted and threw strange shadows on the faces.
From the top of the chasm wall she levered the loose rimrock
until it tumbled in a thundering avalanche across them, a
growl of stone that piled above the pathetic bodies and shook
the silent fabric of the wilderness.

It ended in a shivering cascade of gravel, a roil of dust that
hung for long moments in the still evening, moving as though
it were sentient. She dropped onto the rimrock, choking on
the dirty air.

Where had the stubborn naiveté come from that had kept
her enthralled with myth long after those around her knew the
truth? Where had her blindness come from? Had it been
willful? A way of getting even with them all?

Slowly, so slowly that she did not know if she truly saw it
or only imagined it, a line of fliers moved across the face of
Potipur toward her, bent and moved as though a lip had
moved upon that face, mouthing a word. Was it "Go"? Or
perhaps "Good"? Or "God"? Fliers. Investigating the sound
of the falling stone.

"A lie," she said defiantly. It made no difference what the
Servants of Abricor said. It was all a lie.

She broke her mirrored staff and threw the shattered pieces

into the pit. Her hands went to her hair to remove the
identifying braids. When it hung loose as any marketwoman's
locks, she remembered she had never seen an Awakener die.
Had never seen one dead. Perhaps there had been many come
beneath her hands, their hair unbraided, hidden behind the
canvas hoods.

After a time she climbed down from the high rimwall and
began to walk through the dark trees into the west. She
would pass through the workers' pit on the westward bound-
ary and come to Shabber.

What would she do then? Tend garden, as Delia had done?
Go westward farther still?

Or stay in one careful place, close to the River, so that in
good time she could seek her own end in deep water as
gentle, fearful Mother had done. Seek the long pier's end
deep in the lonely night as Mother had done. As Mother had
done, so that no amount of fishing could bring her forth
again. No amount of dragging bring her to answer to Potipur
for her sin in not trusting to the Holy Sorters to Sort it all out.

Wise in her weakness; better able to face the truth than
Pamra herself.

Behind her the dust settled. Hands moved feebly beneath
the rocks. Through chinks in the stones, eyes stared upward
at the red light of Potipur.

Out of the night the black wings settled upon the stones.
Great fliers walked here and there, thrusting the rocks aside
with monstrous beaks and talons.

"Rejoice," a croaking voice chuckled softly, almost inau-
dibly. "The Sorters are here."

• 6 •

Ilze had spent the day inspecting the plowing of pamet fields northwest of Baristown, a vast stretch of fertile soil that lay between two slightly raised banks, as though at some time a side channel of the World River had run there, depositing its sediment over centuries. The inspection was perfunctory, more a matter of ritual than actuality. Pamet did very well when scattered on unplowed ground. The uneven scoring of the soil by a crew of stumbling workers neither helped nor hindered the crop. Nonetheless, the workers had to be kept moving if the Tears were to permeate all the flesh, growing throughout it, reducing it in volume by at least half and making it suitable for the Servants of Abricor to eat. Worker flesh was all that they ate. Presumably Abricor had destined the fliers for the purpose of eating workers, or workers for the purpose of feeding fliers—though Ilze regarded this idea cynically. In his opinion, fliers were outrageously ugly, and they stank.

Also, junior Awakeners had to be kept busy. All juniors—like the populace at large—were supposed to believe that the labor provided by worker crews was necessary. They were supposed to believe it until officially told otherwise during senior retreat. Most of them did believe it, or pretended to. Therefore he stalked across the field, a solemn junior trailing behind as he commented aloud on rows that were uneven or corners that were scamped, twitching his whip suggestively from time to time to enjoy her shudder.

He lunched in Baris in a small cafe where he went from time to time and was a familiar-enough figure that the tables did not automatically empty as soon as he entered. Townsmen had a way of sniffing the air when Awakeners entered a shop or tavern, sniffing ostentatiously, then moving away, perhaps leaving the place. Ilze had known since childhood that Awakeners didn't smell. Still, the rudeness rankled, and he went to the town tavern from time to time to exercise his fury. They did not dare press too far, and Ilze was readier than most to make them pay for each jot of license. The Superior of the Tower occasionally ordered a conscription of townspeople. One or two, usually, for some mysterious purpose of her own. Next time Ilze was sent on that errand, he had certain individuals in mind.

A singer enlivened the hour at the cafe. Perched in a shadowy corner, the boy's voice crept over the conversation, into the pauses, into the hesitations.

> "Devious as fire,
> Ubiquitous as care,
> Cruel as the flame-bird's byre
> And the waiting air,
> Your love encompassed me
> And left me dying there."

Ilze smiled. It was a kind of love he recognized, his own particular kind. He knew the singer's voice very well but had no intention of recognizing him. That was over. Superficially enjoyable, slightly dangerous, and over.

> "High as the flier soars,
> To Abricor's breast,
> From such height I fell
> Onto my nest,
> To burn, to burn, to die,
> Like all the rest."

Ilze snorted. Why was it they all thought reproaches gained

anything? He fingered in his purse for the smallest coin possible, summoning a servitor. "Give this to the singer." He smiled. "Tell him his song is pretty, but boring."

He stayed to see the message delivered, delighting in the bonelike pallor that suffused the boy's face and the tears swimming in his eyes. Stupid. He would end as a living worker, a felonious boy-lover brought to justice. Ilze considered turning him in. No. Not yet. Perhaps later, when he needed amusement.

The boy picked at his instrument, sang again, sadly:

> "When we are sunk so deep
> in madness' sleep
> Who, who shall be our Awakeners? . . ."

After lunch there was pretty little Seesa, the fish merchant's wife. The fish merchant had been one of those who moved away in a tavern while making some ostentatious statement about the odor in the place. He and his wife had since learned how dangerous such an impudence could be. Now they took no license with Ilze whatsoever, though the lesson had taken them some time to learn—an interesting time for Ilze. Seesa's submissiveness bored him now. Soon he would find another woman or another boy. What he needed he could not find among colleagues in the Tower— that is, not yet. When Pamra came to senior status, perhaps then. With her naiveté she would not know she was allowed to refuse him. Until she learned that, perhaps he could enjoy her. In anticipation of that day, he had never whipped her, though the thought of her body tied to the stake made him grunt explosively at odd times, his penis twitching in spasms almost like orgasm.

He returned to the Tower very late. There were no juniors at the trough, none who had been with the workers enough to need the cold ritual bath, and it was not required of seniors. He passed it by, humming, not dissatisfied with the day, a little puzzled at the unusual buzz of conversation in the junior dining hall, the air of mystery. The puzzlement gave way to

amazement and then to baffled anger as he learned that
Pamra seemed to be involved in some strange occurrence.
Pamra! Obedient as any dog from the first day, with only that
dazzling beauty to make him hold his hand! Never even
whipped, and now this?

No one seemed to know what had happened. She had not
returned from the forest, and the worker pit was empty. No
one had known about the workers until late in the day. Each
Awakener had assumed that other juniors, rising earlier, had
taken what workers there were. There were shortages from
time to time when the people of Wilform obstinately refused
to die. Or, as Pamra would have said, "when most of those
who died were good ones who were Sorted Out." Ilze snorted,
remembering, a slow, hot anger beginning to build in him. It
was very late, unexplainably late, and she had not returned.
No one had seen her.

By morning it was assumed Pamra and the missing workers were connected. There were only half a dozen new
workers in the pit, scarcely enough to keep one Awakener
busy. The work of the Tower would be disrupted for weeks.
There was a feeling of unease in the place, a whispered buzz
of conjecture and secretive hissing of words like heresy and
conspiracy. The day wore slowly on, and the Superior did
not put in an appearance.

Ilze received the message at the evening meal. It was
delivered by the Superior's own servant, veiled, silent Threnot,
she who spoke no word except what she was told to say by
the Superior. "Now?" asked Ilze. Threnot gestured toward
the stairs. He laid his napkin down and followed her, feeling
a twitch of fear, an uncustomary emotion, one he did not
like.

They stood outside the heavy door at the head of the stairs,
waiting for a response to Threnot's tapping. Though he had
spoken often with the Superior in her office on the ground
floor of the Tower, Ilze had been summoned to the Superi-
or's personal rooms only three times before. Once to receive
senior status from her hands. Once to be commended for zeal
in recruitment. Once to be assigned the supervision of a

clutch of juniors, Pamra among them. He knew this summoning had to do with Pamra. It had to be. He wet dry lips and entered behind Threnot, eyes downcast in appropriate humility before the throne. The Superior wasn't alone, but he would not risk looking up to see who else was there.

"Ilze."

He bowed deeply, waiting.

"One of your juniors has disappeared."

"So I heard this evening, Your Patience."

"The one in which you found such amusement."

"Amusement, Superior? I'm sorry, I—"

"At her naiveté. So I am told. You were most amused at Pamra, a true believer. Such is the gossip among the seniors. Never mind, I have been amused at naiveté in my time. I am told the old woman who reared her went east."

"I was not told so, Superior." The other figure in the room shifted impatiently from foot to foot. Ilze wished he could look up. There was a strong musty smell in the room, like a wet pillow. And something in the Superior's voice that rubbed upon his ears, knifelike.

"I was told so. Pamra had been unlike herself recently. She was seen making frequent trips to the house where the old woman had lived. I sent Threnot to find out why. Threnot found a sister living there. Prender, her name was. She told my servant the old woman had gone east. Pamra, it seems, was deeply grieved."

"I didn't know." Ilze was puzzled. It would not have been his job to follow Pamra or inquire about her, unless the girl's work had suffered. Why this note of accusation in the Superior's voice?

"Since Pamra was naive enough to cause you amusement, Ilze, would it not have been prudent to watch her? Just in the event the old woman showed up in the pits?" There was a tone in the Superior's voice he did not recognize, one he had never heard in her before.

"It would have been, certainly, Superior. Had I known the old woman was gone . . ."

"Perhaps if you had paid less attention to Pamra's body

and more to her emotions, you would have known?'' The
Superior sighed, and Ilze dared look up, just for a moment.
The other figure was a flier. A Servant of Abricor. He
dropped his eyes, gulping. Here. In the Superior's own rooms.
A Servant. Nausea roiled in him. He had not known this was
possible.

"Have you heard of Rivermen, Ilze?''

For a moment he could not hear her voice, could not
understand her words. Rivermen. What was she talking about?
"Yes, of course, Superior. Those who bring cargoes on the
boats. . . .'' Suddenly he knew what it was in her voice that
so cut at him. Fear. Nothing but fear.

"No. Rivermen have nothing to do with boats. Rivermen
are members of an heretical sect who place their dead in the
River. They do not trust in the Holy Sorters. A cult of
apostates, Ilze. Had you heard that Pamra's mother was a
Riverman?''

"I knew she was a madwoman, Your Patience. A sick
woman. A heretic, if you like. I had never heard she was a
member of any cult.'' He gulped, heard only the silence,
went on. "The initiation master told me Pamra was deeply
shamed by her mother's behavior. It was probably her mother's heresy which brought Pamra to the Tower in the first
place. Her dedication had some redemptive quality to it. So
he said.''

"So I thought. So you thought . . . perhaps. But now she
is gone, with a pitful of workers. And the . . . Talkers have
sent for you, Ilze. And me. They have questions about our
orthodoxy.''

Talkers? In this context the word didn't make sense. He
opened his mouth to ask—to ask anything that would help
him out of this confusion. . . .

"I think you had best let me speak with him for a moment
alone,'' she said to the Servant of Abricor, her voice whee-
dling and groveling. "He is totally ignorant of your existence. As naive, in his way, as Pamra was in hers.''

"And did you find this amusing?'' croaked a strange

voice, not a human voice, though using human words. "Was he amusing to you?"

"No. He knew as much as any senior. Seniors are not privy to the decisions of the Chancery, Uplifted One. May I appeal in the name of the Protector?"

"The Talons do not recognize the Protector."

"Surely you jest, Winged One." There was a note of desperation in her voice. "Your treaty is with the Protector, and through him with the Chancery and with the Towers. How can you have a treaty with an office you do not recognize?"

Ilze had heard the Superior's voice for years, leading the observances, reciting the litany, directing, assigning. He had never heard it as it sounded now, tight as a harp string, aching with strain, almost with panic.

"We do not recognize the Protector in this instance, human. Still, we do not desire further disruption of your duties. I will give you not long," the inhuman voice croaked again. "Other Talkers await you on the aerie. You will not attempt escape." There were sounds, wings, clacking of beak, a harsh scrape of talons upon the floor.

"Ilze?"

He breathed deeply, trying not to vomit. "Superior."

"You must help me in this, Ilze. I am depending upon your strong sense of self-preservation."

"What was it?" he grated, furious at himself for this loss of control.

"A Talker. A leader among the Servants of Abricor. One of their Superiors, I suppose you could say. Though this one seems rather higher in rank among its people than I consider myself among mine."

"Talking?"

"They talk, yes. Though not to us. Never to us. This is the first time I have heard one talk. I have been told that only a few of the Servants can talk. The ordinary fliers do not. Only these, these others. Or perhaps only these are allowed to talk. That also is possible."

"What does it want?"

"It expects to take us to one of the Talons. The closest one is east of here in a tall mountain range near the Straits of Shfor. The Talons are where their leaders live, as the Chancery is where our leaders live. They want to take us for questioning." Where I cannot go, she thought. Where I must not be taken. For they will certainly learn what I know, in time, and I know too much. "They want to take you, Ilze. And me, me as well. This is not the way it should happen, Ilze. Listen now. In the northlands, the Protector of Man dwells with his people, his retinue, the officers of the Chancery. You know of the Protector. You have seen him."

"During the Progressions. Of course. I saw the golden ship. Everyone does. The last Progression was years ago."

"So long ago that the next Progression is almost due. Once each eighteen years the Protector makes the trip, taking six or seven years to visit Northshore, allowing himself to be seen at every township. You have seen him!"

"I've seen him." He was sharply attentive. Why was she telling him this? "All citizens are required to observe the Progression."

"I remind you of that so you will remember it. The Protector exists. He lives in the northland. He heads the Chancery. He is my Superior, as I am yours. I work at his command." She reached for the man before her, reached into him. By all the gods, this unworthy tool must bend to her purpose—for all their sakes.

"I understand." He did not understand, though his hard, clever mind was beginning to chill, beginning to listen attentively. He had accepted that his life might depend upon that. She smiled at him approvingly.

"There is a treaty between the Protector and the Servants of Abricor. It is the treaty which prohibits the Servants from . . . from troubling us. It prohibits our troubling them as well. If the Servants are troubled by men, the treaty requires them to report it to the Chancery. This Rivermen business, this heresy . . . if there is something like that going on, *if they think we have something to do with it, we should*

*be summoned by the Chancery, not by the Servants them-
selves. Do you understand that?''* She was begging him, and
for the first time he came out of his own bewilderment to
hear her. He thought she was frightened for herself, and this
focused his attention.

"I . . . yes. Yes. If this Servant is disturbed by something
we've done, something it thinks we've done, it should have
gone to the Chancery about it. And they would have questioned us."

"Yes. Exactly. And our one chance of coming out of this
alive is to get to the Chancery. Not go with this one to the
Talons. We go to the Talons and we're dead."

He did not ask her how she knew. It did not seem to
matter. His heart was drumming, and he felt the blood rush
to his fingers, making them tingle. "Can we escape from the
Tower?"

"They will see us. They see well at night, and there are
dozens of them."

There were dozens, of course. All around the Tower top,
the bone pits, here and there in the forests. Ilze himself had
counted up to twenty of them in the air over Baris at one
time, as many over the neighboring towns. "Stay inside
where they can't get at us? Send a messenger? Ask for
help?"

"We could not live locked inside the Tower that long. The
Chancery is half a year away, through the Teeth of the North
by way of the Split River Pass. It is how the Protector comes
down to make the Progression. By the Split River. We could
walk there in a year or two if we stopped for nothing."

"And the Talons?"

"Not so far. East instead of north."

"How do they plan to get us there?"

"In a basket, the leader said. In a basket, carried by two or
three of them. Through the air. For four or five days. He
spoke of flying without stopping. He spoke of a 'tailwind.' I
can guess what that is."

He had looked at the Talker only briefly, but it had not
looked unlike the usual Servants. The long, almost human-

looking legs with their feathered, two-taloned feet. The folded
wings, tips almost dragging the floor, three-fingered hands at
the wrist joint. The face, not long-beaked like the small fliers
but flat-beaked, so that in profile it did not look unlike his
own except for the absence of a nose. Ear tufts. Wide-set,
round-orbed eyes surrounded by plumed circles. The chest,
protruding at the center like the keel of a boat. And the neck.
Not really long, but it would be stretched out in flight. He
thought on that, anger moving him now, a well-known kind
of anger. So, they would misuse and mock him, would they.
They would break the rules of respect. Well then.

"When you were senior, lady, did you use the whip?" he
asked, whispering. "And have you whips here still?"

When she nodded, he whispered again, and she sped to
find the things he suggested. She knew then she had guessed
aright in choosing the tool to save her life and in saving that
to save more than that. She took a moment to speak to
Threnot, dictating a message to be sent to Tharius Don,
Propagator of the Faith, at the Chancery, in case they did not
arrive there themselves.

"Enough," croaked a voice from behind her. "Enough
time spent enlightening your lackeys. We will go now."

"Of course," said Lady Kesseret of the Tower of Baris, as
though she were going for an afternoon walk into the parklands.
"We will go now."

In a monstrous fanged circle halfway between the River and the pole, the Teeth of the North gaped at the swollen sun, their peaks thrust eight miles or more into the glittering sky. Here, driven deep into the frozen stone, were the only mines on this metal-poor planet, icy tunnels plunging into the heart of the towering range, warmed only by the feeble lamps of the slaves who dug the ore, the mines incessant in their demand for new flesh, for few men lived long in these frigid, airless holes.

The wall of the Teeth was riven in only one place. High against the southern light the jagged jaw of Split River Pass gaped at either side of the sky-filled notch, bared now and briefly, before the snows came again. There black rock tumbled from black rock down an ogre's stair to the loess of the slopes and taiga of the plain, with the river lunging over it in frantic starts and sorties, like a drunken man-at-arms waked suddenly from dreams of battle.

Within the lofty circle of the mountains stretched an enormous basin, taiga and grassy plains, dotted here and there with a few tens of migratory weehar and thrassil. When the Teeth leaned toward the sun, the lands of the northern basin bloomed and burgeoned toward a hasty harvest. While the people along the River shivered in the chill rains that separated their first and second summers, above the Teeth the sun rolled up from the north around the circle of the sky like a swollen fruit upon the sides of a bowl, never setting, and the

Chancery folk walked out of doors in their shirt-sleeves to
smell the flowers while the woodsmen piled thick fortresses
of firewood along the walls. Axes, axes on the height! Oh,
yes, the summer sound in Chancery lands was the crack of
the axe and the creak of wagon wheels behind the plodding
feet of weehar oxen.

In the winter, when the Teeth turned from the sun after
months of lengthening autumn dusk, the long night came
down to drown Highstone Lees under a cold cataract of stars.
Then the weehar and thrassil dug deep into ice caverns to
sleep the three-month night away, and the residents of the
Chancery retired to their tunnels and rooms burrowed into the
rock below while they made other tunnels into the mighty
walls-stacks of wood, carrying it inside load by load, leaving
snow-covered, canvas-roofed tunnels behind, widening as the
winter went on until the outside walls could be taken in to be
burned in the half sun of early summer.

And it was summer yet, though there were few flowers left
and evenings brought chill winds to curl at the corners of
buildings and rattle the fastenings of windows. The broad
leaves of the mime trees in the ceremonial plaza were beginning to roll into tight cylinders, fronds of papery green sheets
becoming brushes of fine needles, black as jet. The fountain
in the plaza still played, but plaintively, and North Split
· River rattled a shallow complaint upon its black stones beneath a hundred high-backed bridges. There would be little
more melt from the heights to feed it and then no more at all
until spring came again.

It was the time some people of the Chancery liked best,
after summer's labor and before the cozy hibernation of the
snow time. The High Lodge of the Jarb Mendicants preferred
the season, the fading sun of autumn, the needling of leaves,
the plaint of water. The Mendicants moved abroad to draw
into their pores each scant ray of the slowing sun, drug pipes
hanging cold in their lax hands, for a time unpossessed by
oracular visions. And the Mendicants were not alone in their
enjoyment.

To the palace garden, tippy-toe with tiny mandarin steps, sweet as a leaping lamb upon the grass, came the Protector of Man, Lees Obol, in his padded robes, one Jondarite at either arm, half carried, half escorted in his gentle perambulation of the cloisters. Such an old, old man, Lees Obol, beneficiary of the fliers' Payment for almost five hundred years, all the youthful passion spilled away over the centuries to leave this vague contentment in its stead. Not that all that youthful urgency leaked away unremembered and unremarked. At the center of him was an ache sometimes, a feeling of vacancy, as though an essential vessel had been drained, an important room left untenanted. This hollowness echoed occasionally, a dim seashell sound, the susurrus of his blood, perhaps; or a thudding like the boots of armed men come to rob a temple of all its valuables, only to find it empty and the worshipers gone.

So he quivered once in a while, shaking with a memory of passion, knowing he had cared once and unable to think of any reason he should not care now, but too frail to hold the notion for long. So he moved on the strong arms of his guards in the pale sun of polar summer, stopping to sniff at the brilliant northern blooms in the carefully tended gardens, easing through the muslin veils that clouded the doors, flung open now to the sweet airs and the sound of water, when it could be heard over the sound of chopping.

Still, at this noon hour the axes had fallen silent and the fountains could be enjoyed by the Protector of Man, held aloft and protected from harm, like a little doll, by the strong arms of his keepers. So he was held up during the last Progression; so he would be held during the next one if the Payment proved efficacious and he lived still longer. Though, said those who performed the functions of the Chancery, there was little enough left now to work with. An occasional spark was all, like the last glow of a fire banked against the morning and left too long without fuel. A fugitive gleam, without heat, consuming itself in the instant.

He stood on the gently curved span that crossed Split River, his old eyes seeking a gleam of golden fishes in the

complaining flow. There was no peace in Split River. From
the cold white heights it ran north into the Chancery lands,
and from those same heights it ran south across the steppes of
the Noor, and from there through Ovil-po township to the
World River. Once each eighteen years a caravan carried the
Protector through the pass and down the other side as far as
Ovil-po, where the Progression ship was docked, its gold and
gems wrapped against the harsh winds of early first summer.
Six or seven years later, the Progression done, he returned to
be met by the caravan and taken home to the Chancery, home
to the warm familiarity of near five hundred years.

"Looky," said the Protector, staring up at the distant
mountains in senescent surprise. "The pass is all melted
black."

The uniformed Jondarites shared a conspiratorial glance
and suggested it was time for his tea. His acquiescence was
no less charming and inconsequential than his participation in
the walk. One item of ritual more or less gracefully done. Let
us move on, he seemed to say, to the next and then the next.

The next being tea before the soft warmth of a porcelain
stove. Cuddled deep in his curtained bed, Lees Obol nodded
over his cup. His alcove was just off the main audience hall,
its thick, squat walls dwarfed by the lofty barrel vaults above,
its rock floor warmed and softened by carpets. Though it was
too early for fires, the Protector of Man had a fire. The
Jondarites were careful for his comfort, solicitous for his
welfare. They would die for him without a moment's question, just as they cared for him day by day, hands busy in his
service, knives ready at their belts, eyes watchful. Two of
them stood guard outside the alcove now. Two more stoked
the tiny stove and closed the curtains. The stove burned only
a few pieces of charcoal at a time, but with the alcove
curtains closed, it developed a cozy warmth. Stretching in the
heat like an old, pained cat, Lees Obol puffed a little sigh
and sipped, remembering a sense of sharp discomfort without
being able to identify the memory at all. Outside the alcove
the Jondarites heard the sigh and remembered it. General

Jondrigar would demand an accounting of them. Each sigh, each word, each breath, had to be remembered.

High on a parapet of the household wing, Maintainer of the Household Shavian Bossit peered through a glass into the southern sky. Sun glow filled the wedge of sky that marked Split River Pass, and a flying speck showed black against this fruity shine; a Servant, maybe even a Talker, here inside the Teeth, where no flier of any kind had any business being. Shavian frowned, his mouth making a point-up triangle of concentration. Not merely *a* flier. More than one of them, he told himself as the speck wobbled toward the Chancery lands. Several. Two or three at least. Trouble of some kind coming, and Lees Obol vacant as ever while his people plotted, some against one another, some against the Protector himself. Bossit did not pretend to himself that he was not one of them, even while breathing a quick prayer that Gendra Mitiar and Tharius Don could set their growing enmity aside for a few hours or days, if real danger portended.

"Do you think it's Servants?" he asked the guard, one with younger eyes than his own.

"It looks like it through the glasses, Your Grace. Carrying something. It's a new one on me. I've never seen those fliers carry anything."

"If you're in attendance when they land, Captain Velt— that is, assuming it does land—remember not to say 'flier.' The correct title, if there's a Talker, is 'Uplifted One.' If there's no Talker with them, order the bowmen to kill them as soon as they land."

"I'll remember, sir." The captain flushed.

"In the meantime, perhaps you'll be good enough to find the Deputy Enforcer and suggest he join me here. . . ." He took the glasses back from the guardsman and peered into the wedge of sky once more. At least two Servants of Abricor, flying north of the Teeth in defiance of the treaty, carrying something. "Hurry, Captain," he suggested through clenched teeth.

Shavin Bossit was not the only one to have spotted the

flier. From a window of his suite high in the library wing, Propagator of the Faith Tharius Don stared through a glass both newer and more powerful than the one used by the Maintainer. After much searching and many trials, he had had it secretly procured from the lens makers in Zebulee, an acquisition not to be displayed but to be kept wrapped in an old sheet in the bottom of his clothes chest. He had had his own watchers posted here and there throughout the Chancery. More than one rooftop at Highstone Lees carried his men, one of whom had called his attention to the approaching blot on the sky. When he identified the winged speck as probable Servants of Abricor, he buried the glass beneath his clothes once more and stood gnawing his lip, cold beads of sweat starting out on his forehead and in the edges of his beard. Servants. Possibly one or more Talkers. If a Talker, then certainly one concerned about heresy. It had been all the fliers had wanted to talk about at the recent convocation. Heresy. By the waters of surcease, he was not yet ready for this. Not ready at all. It was too soon. But if he avoided being part of whatever confrontation was about to take place, the others would interpret his absence not to his credit, though they might assign him varying motives depending on who was doing the assigning.

"So long as they do not know my true motives, it should not matter," he told himself. It was a kind of litany. There had been a time when Tharius Don had cared much for the opinions of others—even of others here in the Chancery. That time was long gone. Now he played the moralist, sometimes the fool, and told himself it did not matter. Wiping the sweat from his forehead, he slipped out onto the stairs. Like it or not, he would have to be obtrusively present—a need with which the Maintainer of the Household might not be entirely sympathetic.

Gendra Mitiar was told about the approaching Talker by a servant sent by Shavian. "His Grace says to come to the small council room as soon as you can." The servant bowed.

Thin and dried, a woman of great age, her face long since

settled into a vertical assemblage like eroded gully walls, her skin the same dun color as the winter fields, Gendra Mitiar stared at the messenger. When she spoke, it was to reveal vast yellow teeth jutting like monuments from her pale gums; flat, inexorable teeth that ground together from time to time, making the sound of millstones. Her voice was like herself, colorless and strong, betraying an unostentatious but terrible will.

"Tell His Grace I will be with him shortly," she said.

"And may Potipur help us," she added to herself, grinning in vicious humor. "For it is certain old Obol won't."

Shavian Bossit was irritated beyond measure. "I can understand your annoyance at being . . . ah . . . flown here against your will, Uplifted One. I can appreciate the discomfort of having a whip lashed about your throat in midair and being threatened with strangulation. However, I can also understand the panic felt by our Superior of Baris. Your action was in defiance of the treaty. You admit as much." He tapped his fingers impatiently, glaring at the Talker standing against the wall. The damn flicr would not take tea, would not act like a rational creature, would not sit, though they could and often did. Shavian hated looking up at people, much less fliers, though his diminutive size let him do little else. He ran his fingers through jet-black hair, dyed each ten-day by his mute body servant, and frowned in exasperation. Where in the hell was Gendra!

"I have explained already," the Talker croaked from a throat not only unaccustomed to human talk but largely unfitted for it by the recent and lengthy half choking he had experienced at Ilze's hands. The flight had taken some days, and the whip had been around his throat for most of that time. "The treaty does not apply in this instance."

"You have said so." Shavian kept his voice carefully without emotion. "You have not said why."

"I am not required to do so. I demand you accept my word that such is the case."

Shavian pondered the possibility of simply sending this

creature away. He would never have thought of insulting a Talker, any Talker, when he was younger and the promise of life offered by the Payment had seemed irresistible. Now he toyed with the idea. It was sad to think the wisdom and resolution of age might be only weariness and pain. Effort avoided became pain avoided, and ennui masqueraded as good sense. So he told himself, not speaking any of it aloud. When he spoke again, with every appearance of courtesy, it was to remark in an uninterested voice, "The treaty does not permit you to demand anything of the kind. I will listen to reasonable talk, flier. I will not listen to bombast, which is what you have given me thus far." To call a Talker "flier" was no less an insult than to turn one's back, which Shavian also contemplated doing.

The Talker's beak flushed red, a deep, winey color betokening fury. Shavian regarded this without apology or change of expression. The damn thing had very nearly forced his way into the Protector's bedroom. Potipur knows what old Obol would have made of that! Or what the Jondarites would have done! Killed the Talker, probably. Then they would have had to kill the others to keep the word from getting back to the Talons. Which might not have worked, for other Talkers or mere fliers might have seen these during their long flight toward the Chancery.

Well, it had been a disaster narrowly averted. Shavian had called on a hand of Jondarites to bring the Talker here, to the small council room. So far as the Lord Maintainer was concerned, Talker of the Sixth Degree Sliffisunda of the Talons had received as much courtesy as was due him.

This thought, or some similar sentiment, must have occurred to the angry Talker as well, for in a few moments the furious color faded. When the flier spoke again it was with grudging courtesy.

"We believe these two may be implicated in the Riverman heresy."

"Indeed? I find that hard to credit. In any case, this suspicion should have been reported at once to the Propagator of the Faith, and he would have sent for them to accuse and ascertain the truth.''

"We did not wish you to send for them. We wanted to question them at the Talons." The words were clear enough, though it was hard to tell what the intonation was meant to convey.

"So you have said. Still, you have not said why."

"I will not say." Sliffisunda's beak flushed again, only slightly this time.

Oh, these Talkers didn't like subordination. High mucky-mucks, all of them, and proud! By Potipur, they're proud. A servant came forward with tea. Shavian took a cup, offering none to the flier. It had refused before; let the refusal stand. When the silence was broken by a rap on the door, he called, "Enter," knowing already who was there. The woman and the man who came in wore faces as carefully blank as his own; their bows toward Sliffisunda were sketchy, a bare politeness. The Talker stood against the wall, unmoving, looking them over with unblinking eyes.

"Uplifted One, these are staff members of the Chancery. At the most recent convocation you met the Dame Marshal of the Towers, Gendra Mitiar. The gentleman with the large knife is Bormas Tyle, Deputy Enforcer to Lord Don. Put the knife away, Bormas. The Talker is not threatening us. Yet.''

He beckoned them to the table, offering cups only to them, interrupted in this calculated insult by another tap at the door and the entry of someone he had not sent for.

"Lord Maintainer," said Tharius Don with an ironic bow. "I saw my Deputy Enforcer waiting upon you and came to inquire if I might be of assistance."

Shavian Bossit poured another cup, seething inside. He had not wanted Tharius Don this morning. Lately he had not wanted Tharius Don at all. The man had a chilling way with him. Like the knife cut of cold conscience. "The Lord Propagator of the Faith, Tharius Don," he said, making introductions. "The Uplifted One, Talker of Sixth Degree Sliffisunda of the Talons. I have apologized to the Uplifted One for the absence of other members of the council." Of

the seven, four were present. A quorum, he thought. Though
he would have traded Tharius Don's presence in a moment
for that of the Ambassador to the Thraish, Ezasper Jorn.

He turned back to the table, making a wry mouth at the
Dame Marshal and commenting, sotto voce, "Ezasper Jorn
should be conducting this little exercise as Ambassador to the
Thraish, but both he and Koma Nepor are off somewhere.
The Protector, of course, would be of no help." He shrugged,
taking more tea for himself. "I know I am discourteous. This
Uplifted One has set my teeth on edge."

"I assume you have reason for discourtesy?" She turned
toward the Talker, millstone jaws loud in the quiet room.
Only the Talker heard it. The others were too long accustomed to the sound to be aware of it.

"Indeed," he murmured, loud enough for the other humans to hear. "This Talker and two of his subordinates, also
Talkers, went to the Tower at Baris and abducted the Superior and one of her senior Awakeners. They went with him
under threat of great harm to all those within the Tower. His
reason for doing so is that he believes them to be part of the
Riverman heresy."

"He need not have troubled," said Tharius Don, his gray
brows pulling together over black, suddenly angry eyes, in a
face become as suddenly and unnaturally pale. The pallor had
struck him at the mention of the Superior of Baris, and it did
not leave him now. The bones of his striking face stood out
in relief as he sucked in his cheeks, biting back a set of too
revealing words to replace them with, "We would have
fetched them here had he but sent word."

"Ah, but it was not his intention to fetch them here at all.
He sought to take them to the Talons."

"The Talons! Human prisoners?" Bormas Tyle slid the
knife in and out of its sheath, cutting his words as he cut his
hair, short and soft as velvet. The hair grew upon his forehead and down his neck onto the bulging muscles of shoulder
and back, joining the velvet beard that half hid his mouth,
making his head appear upholstered except for his cold serpent's
eyes. "By what right? The treaty forbids this."

"Indeed." Shavian smiled his three-cornered smile at them all and then at the Talker once more. "So I have said. To which the Talker replies that the treaty does not apply in this case, though he will not say why."

There was a silence that began as mere hesitation, becoming tumescent with something more ominous than that, a brooding expectancy broken only by the hiss of the Deputy Enforcer's knife and the grinding of the Dame Marshal's teeth. These hostile sounds pervaded the room, sliding in it like serpents.

The silence was broken by Tharius Don. Such tension could breed nothing good, and in the absence of the Ambassador to the Thraish, someone had to take the responsibility of ending it. He moved with practiced ease, crossing the room and bowing the Talker to precede him into the corridor. "I am sure the Uplifted One would like to sit down. Perhaps he would honor us by joining his subordinates and having a cup of tea. I will prepare for him below, and we will beg his return when we have finished our discussion."

The Lord Maintainer sighed. For a moment there, he had felt something almost wonderful within, like lust, or youth, or rage. The possibility of hot conflict, maybe some blood spilled? His hands trembled. Whose blood? Most likely his own. "By all means, Tharius." He sighed. "By all means. Uplifted One? Will you go with the Lord Propagator? We will meet again a little later, when we have considered this matter."

It was quiet in the room after Tharius left. Gendra Mitiar cast questioning glances at Shavian Bossit from time to time, which he affected not to see. Gendra Mitiar had been uncollegial latterly. No, not only latterly, but for some time. Irascible. Given to ineffectual quarrels about trifles. She would not be content until her enmity for Tharius was out in the open, where she could gnaw on it publicly, something Bossit wasn't sure he wanted to see. At least, not yet. He sighed, and then sighed again, drifting toward the window, his inconspicuous form gliding like a shadow.

Suppose Lees Obol dies. Shavian considered this, not for the first time. Suppose Lees Obol dies of ostentatiously natural causes, and suppose, therefore, that General Jondrigar does not turn Highstone Lees into an abattoir seeking the cause of Obol's death. Suppose this not totally unlikely state of affairs. Who would be the next Protector?

Gendra is in line, but she is not popular among the members of the Chancery council who will elect the next Protector. There are factions there. The Mendicants have a faction for themselves. Meaning what? Potipur knows. Shavian has his own supporters, of course. And Ezasper Jorn would be supported by the Thraish, who have their own way of bringing influence to bear. Research Chief Koma Nepor has been in Jorn's pocket since Jorn got him his first dose of elixir, so those two council members could be said to make up a faction. And there is a faction for Tharius Don among the lower ranks of the Towers. Perhaps a stronger one than is generally known. Which would explain Gendra's antagonism toward him, if an explanation were needed.

Shavian ticked the connection into memory. He did not doubt Bormas Tyle had also a claque, ready to come forward. Bormas Tyle, however, could be managed, though he sometimes needed simple reasons to do what more complex motivations required, able to accept the former but being only confused by the latter.

So, of the six surviving council members, there would be at least four contenders. Only Jondrigar and Nepor would not seek the office of Protector for themselves. Four would, including Shavian himself. Enough, he thought, to make rampant confusion.

The door opened, closing behind Tharius Don with a final snick, like a scissors.

"Guarded?" Bormas Tyle asked, his knife sliding with creepy persistence in the sheath. "You have them well guarded?"

"Relax, Deputy. I've put them in the reception room at the end of the corridor over the garden, the one with barred windows. You'll recall there's a grilled gate at the end of the corridor, and I've stationed six Jondarites there, all growling at the insult almost offered to Lees Obol. Sufficient?"

"The damn things fly, is all," snarled Bormas. "You have to remember they fly."

"As we do remember," Shavian commented. "Well, you've all heard everything I've heard. If you'd care to offer advice." *As when haven't you?* he asked himself. *All of you. Endlessly.*

"How did the captives end up here?" Gendra, shaking her head and running one fingertip up and down a long wrinkle on her cheek. She did this sometimes for hours at a time, engraving her fingertip into her face as though to deepen the crevasses already there. Up, down, up, down.

"The senior Awakener—Ilze, his name is—brought a couple of whips with him, wrapped around his body under his clothes. Once in the air, he snapped them around two of the fliers' necks—evidently he has had considerable practice with the whips—and Lady Kesseret told the Talkers they had the choice of flying to the Chancery or of being strangled to death. Luckily, she knew the way up the Split River Pass, or they'd have died on the heights. Damn fliers can't get high enough to come over the Teeth. We may regret they came through." *Bossit already regretted it, but it was not time to talk of that.*

"And where is the lady Kesseret now?" asked Tharius in a carefully neutral voice. "And the Awakener?"

"I've got them both in the Accusers' House. It seemed prudent."

"Prudent!" *He covered his terror with a pretended scorn. Kessie! In the Accusers' House!*

"Until we know a bit more."

"Such as why they are suspected?"

"Among other things, yes," sighed the Maintainer. "I was much tempted to send this Talker packing. Something told me it would be a mistake to do it or not do it, either way." *Shavian pondered this. Prudence had come with age and was as tasteless in his mouth as food had become. Lacking the spice of feeling.*

"And the Talker won't say why the treaty does not apply."

"I think we can figure it out," Shavian murmured, mov-

ing across the room to the tea service, taking a cup with him
to a comfortable chair, where he sat, face wreathed in fragrant steam, making owl eyes at them through the mists. "At
the recent convocation with the Talkers, we learned they are
barely reasonable upon the subject of the Riverman heresy."

"That's true," said Tharius Don carefully. "It was all
they wanted to talk about. We traveled a great, uncomfortable distance to cross the pass to the place of meeting. There
were matters of true import to discuss. This demand of theirs
for a higher food quota in order to increase their numbers, for
example. Gods, but that needed talking of. But no! All they
wanted to do was huddle in dusty groups, ruffling their
feathers—full of dander as they are to make me sneeze
endlessly—and fulminate about the heresy." He fished a
hankerchief out of his sleeve and erupted into it with a great
play of gloomy recollection. Let them think him a fool. It
was safer than the truth. Besides, the kerchief helped to hide
his face.

"True." Gendra considered this. "It was the same with all
of them. They spoke of nothing else, always watching out of
the corners of their eyes, as though to catch us in some
cover-up. The Riverman heresy, and was it connected to the
homosexuals or the celibates? As though they had anything in
common!"

"And we?" Shavian smiled a tiny, three-cornered smile, a
mouse smile, wicked on that small face. "What did we do?"

"I told them it was all nonsense," said Tharius. "No more
to it than the usual few Awakeners who can't get past their
junior vows and a coven or two of recalcitrants who put their
dead in the River out of misplaced sentimentalism. I told
them in my opinion it was not a widespread heresy, and not a
conspiracy of any magnitude. Probably not more than a
dozen or two Rivermen per town, mostly individual families.
I doubt there's a Riverman anywhere in the towns who even
knows that Talkers exist, so it would be hard to imagine a
conspiracy against them. And I told them the boy-lovers were
only aberrants! Genetic, if anything. Not a matter of politics
or belief at all. And the same with the celibates. They want

to believe all humans think of nothing but endless breeding, and it's hard to disabuse them of the notion. Though the gods know, Talkers ought to understand that if any creature can. They don't breed. They can't.''

"And I told them the same thing," sneered Gendra, as though having agreed with him for any reason was of questionable taste.

Bossit bowed. "Your Graces were no doubt right to do so. However, if I were one given to paranoia, deeply suspicious that some human group was plotting my downfall, and if the Propagator of the Faith told me it was all nonsense and then the Dame Marshal of the Towers told me it was all nonsense—both of them telling me this as a mere aside, mind you, not with any appearance of grave consideration—might I not feel even more suspicious? Why would the leader of the humans be so offhand unless he wished to mislead me?"

"You mean the Talkers thought we were lying? That there is indeed some vast Riverman plot which we know about?" Tharius kept his voice calm, unmoved, feeling the sweat crawling on his forehead but trusting the shadows of the corner where he sat to hide him.

Trust Shavian, thought Bormas Tyle, drawing no attention to himself whatsoever. If there is one conspiratorial breath inhaled within ten thousand paces, trust Shavian to hear it and smell upon it what rotten fish the speaker ate for dinner. He sat quiet, watching the others think about this.

"It would fit," Gendra continued. "It would explain this particular action. They wanted to do some independent questioning." She raked both sides of her face simultaneously, fingers up and down the gullies, up and down. "And, of course, they could claim the treaty wouldn't apply if they really thought we were breaking it."

"There's something more here. . . ." Bormas Tyle turned to stare out the window. "Something going on."

"It may be wise to give them the Awakeners," Gendra said. "A quick way to show them we aren't lying."

Tharius turned pale, miming another sneeze to hide his pallor and his tight lips. Behind the linen veil he composed himself. "It would show them nothing of the kind. They will find whatever they believe is true. The Talkers are experts at torture. What do you think the lady Kesseret of the Tower at Baris will tell them under torture? That she knows nothing? Perhaps, for a time. At last, however, she will say whatever they most want to hear. 'Yes, there is a conspiracy. Yes, they are heretical. Yes, all the homosexuals and the celibates and the Mendicants are part of it. Yes, I was in on it, and so was my senior Awakener; in fact, so was the whole Tower and all the Chancery, including the Dame Marshal of the Towers and the Protector himself!' "

Gendra blanched, compressing her lips. Obviously she had not thought deeply enough, but she resented Tharius Don's immediate apprehension in the matter. He was too often right. She longed for his pride to be riven, longed for his downfall.

He, seemingly unaware, went on. "No, Dame Marshal. Allowing our people to be questioned at the Talons is the last thing we should allow, if for nothing but humanitarian concerns, much less for the sake of our own skins."

Gendra hated admitting he was right, but she was forced to agree. "Still, if we keep them here, the Talkers will believe their suspicions about us were true."

"It would be better not to upset them. . . ." Bormas frowned. The mutual benefits conveyed by the Treaty of Thoulia included provision of elixir for all high-ranking Chancery officials. His next scheduled Payment was to occur very soon. Not a good time to have the Talkers upset, angry, or suspicious.

"Then we must do something to make them believe their suspicions about us are false." Gendra moved to the table, stroking the polished wood as though it were some cowering animal she sought to tame. "Let us give them the Awakeners, but don't let them be taken away. Let the Talkers question them here. Under the eyes of my own Accusers."

Shavian agreed, turning his wicked three-cornered smile upon them. "Yes. Let the Dame Marshal supervise the questioning. The lady Kesseret will no doubt be willing to bear some discomfort for her faith.'' His glance at Tharius might have been only casual, though there were needles in it.

"Allow her to be questioned by Talkers? When we know she is innocent of any wrongdoing?'' Tharius Don turned on them, hands knotted, lips tight. They moved away, annoyed at his challenge of conscience. Expedience often dictated, but Tharius Don would seldom let it dictate in comfort. "Let her be questioned under 'discomfort,' as you put it, Bossit, when we all know she is a faithful Superior, guilty of absolutely nothing? Shameful!''

"Come, come, Tharius. She may not be entirely innocent," Gendra challenged him, grinding her teeth like stones in an avalanche. "We are all guilty of something. Some minor thing. Sufficient to warrant some suffering, no doubt. It will not compromise her receiving further Payment, as she has been promised. In fact, we might make that day come sooner, as a reward.'' The younger one was when the elixir was first provided, the more powerful its effect, and to provide it earlier than promised could be a powerful inducement to many things. Enduring torture included.

There was another brooding silence. Tharius Don seemed about to object once more, but he contented himself with an internal monologue and an angry glare before subsiding into his chair, one foot tapping at the carpet, a muffled heartbeat of annoyance. At last Bossit asked, "Are we agreed? The Accusers and Ascertainers are your people, Dame Marshal. I trust you will not allow more harm than necessary to come to these Awakeners. They are, after all, *our* people.'' He used the royal possessive with heavy irony.

Tharius gave him a hard, intent look, as though to see whether this was to be interpreted as a sensible instruction or as something with double meaning.

Gendra, who wanted no interference from Tharius Don, returned her agreement in like form. "No. Our people shall receive no more harm than is necessary, Lord Propagator. No more than is necessary.''

Later that day, Tharius Don leaned in a window of his

rooms. The Library Tower overlooked the Accusers' House. Somewhere behind one of those windows in that cold pile was the Superior of Baris Tower.

Tharius Don put his head in his hands, for the moment unconscious of those on distant Towers or roofs who might be watching.

"Kessie," he moaned in an agony of empathetic pain. "Oh, by the gods, Kessie. Kessie."

• 8 •

Thrasne had not wanted to think of Pamra again. He had put her out of his mind; he had refused to speak of her to Suspirra; he believed he could forget her in the years that followed his last departure from Baristown.

But during those six years, the drowned woman had moved her lips once more to say, "My baby!" This time Thrasne had not needed to draw the sequence of facial expressions. He knew them as well as he knew his own. What should he have done? he asked himself in irritation. Should he have abducted Pamra there on the steps of the Tower? Should he have dragged her away like some impetuous lover? What could he have done? After a time he stopped thinking about what he might have done and began thinking what he would have to do next time.

When he came to Baris for the fourth time, Thrasne was thirty-six, a stocky, thatch-haired man with a boatman's crinkles around his eyes from looking into the sun half of every day. He had stopped to give Blint-wife her first promised moneys, surprised to find her stout and healthy, happier looking than she had ever been aboard the *Gift*, eager to come aboard and hear all the news, bearing gifts of cakes and a keg of ale. She asked Thrasne, somewhat shyly, and with careful attention to who might be by to overhear what she said, if he had time to carve some gifts for her. "I'm being married again," she said. "To an old Riverman [this in a whisper] who lost his wife long ago. He has grandchildren.

His daughter has gone to the River [whisper], and the children spend much time with me."

So he carved a jump-up-jakes and a dancing doll and a set of fancy building blocks, knowing as he did so that Blint would be glad of this marriage. Blint had loved her once, likely more as she was now than as she had become aboard the *Gift*.

And he left her to come to Baris at the beginning of the cold season, well before festival, with the tides pulsing ever higher. By this time there were many cross piers to tie to in Baris. There was a procession of Melancholics, dark faces fierce and demanding, waving their fishskin lashes in invitation to the watchers. Thrasne saw more than a few citizens taking a lash or ten in return for Sorter coin. When he found the barber's place he remembered from before, Thrasne sat in the chair, commenting on the scene.

"I don't know why they do it, barber. Let themselves be whipped in return for a worthless bit of glass!"

"Ah, well," the barber remarked, snipping around Thrasne's ear with close attention, the obsidian shears making a repeated *snick*, like the teeth of a stilt lizard, unpleasantly voracious. "It's harmless, I suppose. Who knows, maybe the Holy Sorters would Sort you Out if there were enough Sorter coins in your purse."

"Superstition," muttered Thrasne. "Even the Awakeners don't allow as how that's true." Then, seeing argument about to fall from the barber's lips, he changed the subject. "I wanted to ask you about the family of Fulder Don. Would you remember them?"

"All that family's gone, boatman. Fulder Don died a year or so after his mama. One of the older daughters died, too. The youngest girl, she that became an Awakener, she up and vanished not long ago. Quite a scandal!"

Thrasne was silent, shocked. Vanished? Pamra? "The old woman who cared for them? Oh, sure now, I heard something about that. Went east, I think. Bad business, that was."

"Wasn't there another daughter?"

"Oh. Sure there was. Prender. She's staying at the house the old woman had. Now how did I forget Prender?"

Prender was stiff and cold, angry at being questioned. "She's gone, that's all I know. A servant came from the Tower. I couldn't see her face for the veils, but her voice was hard. Then a Laugher to question me about it, sent from somewhere else. He was stone in his face, and mean. His words were like threats. He said they'd find her no matter where she's gone. They don't know where she went, except she went early one morning. She was supposed to take workers to the forest for wood. Very early. All the workers were gone."

She started to shut the door against him, her face creased deep with all the bitterness of the years, opening it just far enough to spit a few more words at him through the crack. "He wanted to know what she had said to me about Delia. About Delia going east. As though she would have said anything to me. This is all her fault, Pamra's. She and her mother both. Neither of them could ever be sensible about anything."

"When did she disappear?"

"I said. Early in the morning."

"No. I mean *when*? How long ago?"

"Not long. Twenty, thirty days, perhaps."

As he turned to leave, she called after him, "She only did it to get even with us, you know. That's what I told him, that Laugher. She only did it to hurt us."

Thrasne didn't turn. He was too busy feeling ashamed of himself. He had blamed Pamra, blamed her, when all she had really done was flee from voices like the one behind him.

What would he tell Suspirra now?

He told her nothing. When he entered the owner-house, she was turned toward him. He saw her lips, her teeth, the lower teeth touching her upper lip. He copied it with his own, breathing out. "Ffff." He did not need to wait to know what she would say.

"Find her!"

"How can I find her, Suspirra? No one knows where she went."

"Find her!"

"She will have gone west, probably. Why? Why did she go at all?" And even as he asked the question, he knew the answer. He could see it as clearly as the pictures he had drawn of Suspirra. The barber had said Delia went east. He saw Delia leaving. She was old, too old. She died there, east of Baristown. He visualized her returning in the pit, Pamra's arrival there, early in the morning. He assumed the Awakeners looked at faces. So, she would have seen the face, seen, known, all at once known everything she had not wanted to know. That stubborn rebellion, that rigid naiveté, breached, overcome. Suspirra had said, "She had to believe in love—of some kind."

And having seen, having known, where would she go? Not to the River, not at once. No. West. For a time.

He took the *Gift* west, stopping at every town, no matter how small. He searched everywhere, talking to Rivermen, patronizing barbers.

And he found her, as much because she had not had time to go far nor strength to go fast as for any other reason. She was serving drinks in a tavern, hair loose as any market-woman's, silent as a wraith with haunted eyes, and yet more beautiful in her fear than she had been in her complacency at the Tower. There were men drinking in the place only to look at her, but she was blind to all their looks.

"Do you want drink?" she asked, her haughtiness gone and only a haunted, terrible conviction of danger remaining.

"Pamra, I've been looking for you."

She started with fear, thinking he might be someone the Awakeners had sent after her, but he put a hand upon her arm as she trembled.

"It's all right. Your mother wants to see you."

"My mother is dead," she said, eyes wide with horror. "She's dead."

"Yes. But no. Will you come with me?"

"She went in the River. You're mad!"

"Say I am mad. But I will not harm you in my madness. I swear by all that is good and holy. . . ."

"Then you swear by nothing!" Her face was wild. She would have run from him if she had had anywhere to go. She would have screamed, except to do so was to attract attention, and only in being quiet and unnoticed did she have any chance of life at all.

"I swear by the River, then, the River you have planned to go into, the River where your mother went. Come with me."

He coaxed her as he might have coaxed a frightened animal, until at last, terrified of him but more afraid of the looks being cast their way by those in the place, she consented to come with him to the place the *Gift* was moored. He led her along to the owner-house, letting her stand there in the door while he fumbled with the lantern, she ready to run, but too weary and beaten to do it.

The light shone down on Suspirra, facing the door, lips slightly open, though they had been closed when he'd left. And it was Suspirra's twin who stood in the doorway, eyes wide and lips open in surprise. They were alike, line for line. From the drowned woman came a sound, the only sound ever heard from her, almost a sigh, or perhaps a sigh of dissolution.

"Mother?" Pamra cried. "Mother!" She went to touch the still face, drawing back her hand in horror. "You lied. A carving."

"No," said Thrasne, heartbroken. "She is as I brought her from the River."

Pamra sobbed, laying her hand on the hard breast. Above that head the lips curved upward, moving visibly. The lips moved, seemed to utter a word. "Remember?" A question, perhaps. In that instant the smile vanished, smoothing like windswept sand, becoming a hinted curve, coherent only for the moment, cloud-edged, shining with light, as Pamra reached out to hold it.

"Mother?" she said.

The word released the last ties that held the figure whole. Suspirra went, all at once, the golden cloud falling in the instant into a hillock of powdery dust, leaving behind a transparent golden pillar in the beam of light as though something incredibly tenuous maintained its structure still, after all that was dross had fallen away. Something solid fell as well, resting upon the dust like a little moon, softly glowing. Pamra knelt to pick it up; Thrasne was too late to stop her as he muttered, "Blight!"

Undeterred, she knelt there, stroking the thing, round and heavy as a melon. "Was that what made her like that, the blight?"

He nodded, watching her hands. The globe seemed to breathe between them. "Out of her womb," Pamra whispered. "She was pregnant when she died. I was too young to know at the time, but Grandma saw that I heard the story often as I grew up. Mother almost died when she had me, and the midwives told her she would die next time. She was afraid. Afraid of the Awakeners. Of us. . . ."

"You are not an Awakener now."

She turned her haunted eyes upon him. "Once past the junior vows, an Awakener is an Awakener forever. They will remind me of that when they send a Laugher with the flask of Tears for me. I have been lucky to escape them this far."

"What would they do to you?"

"They will feed me Tears of Viranel. I will remember who I am, but I will have no will of my own. I will exist for long years until I truly die and can be eaten by the Servants of Abricor. Perhaps, since I will not be dead and stinking, the senior Awakeners may use me for a while. Jelane says they do that. I saw a woman like that in the Tower once. They have almost caught me twice already. I cannot sleep, cannot live, for fear of them. They will find me. I have nowhere to go."

"You have somewhere to go." He took the strange roundness from her hands, turning it in his own. It shifted as though something within it moved, turning in slow sleep. "What shall we do with this?"

"It lives," she breathed. "See, that place on the side seems to swell, like a pamet pod opening."

A thin, light-colored line upon the roundness widened, stretching as they watched. He set it upon his bed, and they leaned over it, not daring to breathe too loudly. The line strained, shifted, strained, opening wider over a lighter lining, which began to tear with a thin ripping sound like rotted canvas.

From inside came the sound of shallow breathing, slow as the tide.

Pamra reached out to tear the shell open gently with her hands.

A child lay within. Tiny. Perfect. Brown as Suspirra had been, yet moving. Breathing. Opening its night-black eyes to look up at them as though it saw them entirely and comprehended them utterly, moving its lips as though to speak.

They said nothing. It was a wonder too great for speech. They could have made exclamations of disbelief, but in the quiet of the room it would have seemed blasphemy to speak at all. When those eyes closed at last and the baby half turned as though into sleep, they took the shell away. It was connected to the child by an umbilicus, a dried, brittle cord that shivered to fragments when they moved her. A girl child. Pamra reached a tentative, fearful finger to touch that flesh, warm and soft as her own. Silently, she wrapped the child in one of Thrasne's towels and laid her in the basket he used for his mending while Thrasne stared and stared, lost in the wonder of it.

"Now you must come with me," he said. "To care for her."

"Who . . . what is she? How can I care for something like that? Surely this is no human child."

Thrasne took her by the shoulders, shook her gently. Though the child was a wonder and a miracle, had not Suspirra been both a wonder and a miracle? "A strange child, yes, but I believe she is your sister. Born of the same parents." He did not say what other strange parents might have been involved in that birth. The strangeys of the depths? The blight?

"Where will we go?"

"For a time, we will simply go on," he said firmly. "They will not look for you on the River." He would make this so if it were not so already. Perhaps it would not be safe enough forever; perhaps some other provision would have to be made. For the time being, it was enough that Suspirra— who had been in turn a dream, a small carving, a drowned woman, an almost carving once more—was with him now, alive.

· 9 ·

The Accusatory of the Chancery at Highstone Lees was a cold stone building, built high along one side of the ceremonial courtyard, where dark-needled trees made a solemn shade around a jetting fountain. The room in which Ilze found himself confined was no less chill. He could walk around and around in it to warm himself. He could stare out the high, shuttered windows at the mountains along the horizon, which seemed to nibble at the sun as it moved along them. After a very long time of alternate walking and staring, Ilze realized that the sun would get no higher than the low northern sky where it swung in a long arc from east to west barely above the peaks. When darkness came, he huddled on the narrow bed, beneath the two blankets.

There was nothing else to do: walk, stare, or huddle on the bed, staying as warm as possible. There was food in the room and two buckets, one of water, one for his waste. The sun went once around the mountains before anyone came near him. Then it was only a silent guard with more food and a lackey to deliver two clean buckets, one full and one empty, and take away two dirty buckets, one full and one empty. Ilze had a vision of himself spending years in this cold room, moving water from one bucket to the other by way of his guts, moving solids from the plate to the bucket, consuming, being consumed. Somewhere nearby was another such room, he imagined, with the lady Kesseret in it. He had been separated from her almost immediately, but he thought he would be released as soon as she had had time to tell their story.

He slept for a time, woke again, looked out the window to see the sun rolling upon the mountains, the day not quite half-gone. He stared, walked, huddled, began inventing pictures from the crevices and holes in the walls. There were a line of rounded depressions that looked like fish. He half slept, the fish emerging from the wall to swim about him, slowly, like blight-fish. He woke. The shadows had moved. Now the same depressions were eyes, watching him.

Another day passed before the door opened again to admit two tall Servants of Abricor. Talkers. They had come, they said, to accuse him. They were accompanied by a silent human in a dark robe and half veil. Ilze was angered by this, horrified by them.

"What am I accused of?" he demanded. "Tell me! What do you think I've done? I knew nothing about Pamra's disappearance until after it happened. I know nothing about it now."

"Tell us about Rivermen," they demanded. They were taller than other Servants he had seen, cleaner, their feathers gleaming with blue highlights. One of them might have been the one who had been in the Superior's room. Perhaps not. He could not tell. The fingers at the last joint of their wings were hard and clever. When he didn't answer quickly, they pinched him. Their beaks were soft, almost like lips, and though the words they spoke were more croaked than enunciated, he learned to understand them very quickly. "Tell of Rivermen," they repeated.

"I know what the Superior told me. They are a heretical cult who put their dead in the River."

"Tell us something more."

"I don't know anything more."

"Do you think they infiltrate the Towers? Put their own people in as Awakeners?"

"I have no idea. It seems unlikely."

"Do you think Pamra was a spy? For the Rivermen?"

"She was only twelve when she came to us. Would a spy be that young?"

"For a person, she was very pretty, wasn't she? Did you like her a great deal? Did you lust for her?"

"Seniors are not allowed that sort of contact with juniors. Yes, she was remarkable looking. Everyone thought so."

"Did you lust for her?"

"Not really, no. There are always plenty of women in the town."

"Did she confide in you?"

"No. She did ask me about sending a message east for her old nursemaid."

"Did you tell her to do that?"

"I told her it wasn't particularly in accord with doctrine, but it wasn't actually heretical. I told her how to do it."

"When did she tell you her old nursemaid had gone east?"

"She never did," he said in a fury.

They went on asking these same questions for hours. From behind the veil a grinding sound emanated from time to time, as though the veiled person were chewing stones. That person said nothing. Tomorrow they returned to ask the same questions again. These returned, or others who looked exactly like these. Until his anger got the better of him.

"Where is my Superior? Ask the lady Kesseret!" It was obvious, even to him, that they had already asked the lady much. Where else would they have gotten the information they needed to question him? "She knows I'm telling the truth. What do you want from me?"

When they left him alone at the end of the day, he was too tired to move, too angry to care. He lay on the bed, the blankets drawn carelessly over him, letting the night come. There were bruises all over his body where they had mishandled him. He had stopped eating. The food tasted foul. The water tasted foul, too, but he was always thirsty.

"Why did you choose Pamra to be your junior?"

"It doesn't work that way. I didn't choose her. She was assigned to me."

"Who assigned her?"

"My Superior. But even she didn't pick Pamra. Pamra was just one of the handful who came in about the same time. As soon as the initiation master was through with them, I was in line to get that clutch. And the next senior got the next clutch. A clutch is five. It didn't mean anything. Whichever of us was next senior got the next bunch that came in."

"Did she confide in you?"

"No. She didn't confide in me."

"Did you lust after her?"

He hadn't, really, not in any way that was culpable. "No," he said. "I didn't lust after her."

"Tell us about discipline. It is said you never whipped Pamra."

"I never whipped any of them unless they deserved it. Of the five of them assigned to me, I only whipped three."

"Why did you whip them?"

"Because they were lazy."

"Was Pamra never lazy?"

"No. Pamra was a zealot. She was never lazy. She believed. She believed everything."

"Didn't such excess of belief seem at all suspicious to you?"

"Why would it? That's how I believed when I was seven or eight years old. It seemed childlike. Endearing. I thought it was funny."

They went away again. He pushed a shutter aside and leaned in a window, exhausted. His room was on a corner, with two windows. On this side the flat, bleak moorlands stretched to the foot of the jagged mountains, the sun rolling like a red ball on their tips. He could not see the moons.

For a moment the world whirled, shook, and there was a great darkness behind his eyes. He could not see the moons. After a time he figured it out. The moons circled this globe at its center line, above the World River. He could have seen them, low on the horizon, except for the mountains. The Teeth had bitten off the moons. Not seeing them was like an accusation. But an accusation of what? "I really haven't done anything," he snarled furiously into the dark. A dark anger welled up from within him, and he tried to wrap himself in it. Sleep would not come. He rose to run around and around the small room until he was panting, gasping, his heart thundering away inside him as though it would burst. His hands knotted, unknotted. He would kill the fliers. Strangle them. If he ever got out of this place, he would kill them. One at a time, lingeringly. Wherever he found them. At last, worn out, he fell once again into that sleep from which they always woke him.

"Where did Pamra take the workers?"

"I don't know that she took them anywhere. If she took them anywhere, some of you must have seen her. How could she take a whole pitful anywhere without the Servants seeing it? I didn't see her. I don't know."

One of the Talkers looked at the other, almost disconcerted, he thought. Had he told them something they didn't know? Suggested something? They gave him no time to think about it. "Did you ever discuss the workers with her?"

"Discuss? No. Except in class. I had her for a class in hermeneutics. Scripture. The Scripture talks about workers."

"Did she doubt the Scripture?"

"Pamra? I told you Pamra never doubted anything."

"Did you lust after her?"

Perhaps he had. Perhaps he had. "Yes," he said. "Sometimes. But I didn't do anything about it."

They went away, leaving him, returned again, went away. After an endless time they seemed to tire of it.

"Tomorrow," they said to him. "Tomorrow you will go to the Ascertainers."

He didn't know what that meant; he didn't care. It would be different from this, something to look forward to. Perhaps they would give him an opportunity to kill some of them. He went to sleep, dreaming of them tied to the stake and he with the whip in his hand.

• 10 •

Pamra, at first fearful and hostile in equal measure, became gradually accustomed to being aboard the *Gift*. Thrasne had given her a room in the owner-house with a comfortable bunk, a basket for the child, Lila, and a chest full of simple clothing such as the boatmen wore. He taught her to braid her hair in River fashion, high in the back, with bead-decorated locks around the face. He named her Suspirra, as he had named her mother before her and his lady of dreams before that. Relieved of the constant bleeding of the Tower, which kept the juniors both slender as saplings and free of any trace of sexual feeling, she put on a little flesh. Though she looked unlike the woman he had found in the tavern and much unlike the Awakener he had seen outside the Tower, she looked more like his Suspirra than ever, and with this Thrasne was content.

Had to be content. Though he wooed her with his eyes and his gifts and his constant, calm solicitude, she showed no sign of perceiving what was in his mind. He kissed her cheek, and she accepted it as a child might a kiss from an uncle, not unwillingly, but as though it did not matter. Nothing moved her. Nothing stirred her. At certain times, when she was drowsy, perhaps, she would answer his questions about life in the Tower, though never at length or in any great detail. From these infrequent comments he formed a picture of her existence there and on the basis of that trouble-some image forgave her much. She could not feel attraction toward him, he told himself. She did not know what it was. She was like a child, innocent of sexual feeling. She was sometimes angry, but it seemed an anger unformed and unfocused, and if she had any feelings toward Thrasne at all, she did not recognize what they were.

Still, she began to keep house for him, at first absentmindedly, and then with a small show of concern for his comfort. She learned to cook in the same way, at first from hunger, and then with a kind of dim pleasure, remembering the aromas of comfort found in Delia's house without having to remember Delia herself. She could not remember Delia. Would not. The fall of rock in the lonely place was shut away inside her. The faceless regard of the canvas hood was shut away. Herself as Awakener with the flasks at her belt was shut away. There, inside, where love might have lived, was a stone house into which all such things were put. There was no room for love. The house was so large it took up most of the room there was. It had to hold too much.

Thrasne, looking deep into her eyes, knew it was there, for he could see the shape and shadow of it and the feral glow of eyes that peered out of its windows now and again. A ghost house. Tenanted by her mother and by Delia and who knew how many more. He hoped the hard prison space inside her might grow smaller in time. He had time.

She never went ashore. He showed her his watching place in the high cubby by the owner-house, and she sat there for hours watching the Riverbanks flow by. Long months went by. He brought the shore to her, little gifts, bits of foliage and flower, fruit and confections. And toys. And carvings he made for her, which said all the things his mouth left unsaid. And she did not much notice.

Meantime the child of the drowned woman grew like a little tree, slowly yet observably, and moved like a reed blown gently by the wind. They had tried feeding her everything, softly stewed grain, vegetables, bits of fish. She took only the brackish River water and sunlight. On days of cloud, she lay quiet in her basket, scarcely moving. On sunny days

she learned gradually to crawl about the deck with the deliberation of a tortoise and the curiosity of any infant confronted
with a new world to experience.

She seemed to love best to be held on Suspirra's—Pamra's—
lap facing the sun, being shown things—a fish, a bit of rope,
a frond of flowers from a tree they floated under when early
first summer came. The boatmen stopped to talk with her,
never touching her, regarding her half with affection, half
with superstitious awe. So far as they knew, Suspirra had
brought the child with her when she came, her arrival as
mysterious as anything else about the matter. The carved
woman in the owner-house was gone. A live woman who
looked like the carved woman was there, except that the live
woman had a child that could have been carved. Except that
it lived, of course. A wonder. A living wonder.

Thrasne and Suspirra had agreed to name the child Lila. It
had been Thrasne's mother's name. He liked the sound of it.
The crewmen accepted this as well but did not use the name.
Instead, they were inclined to hint to Thrasne that they
suspected a story that might be told, at which he shrugged
and smiled, unresentful. Suspirra made the matter no less
complicated when she referred to Lila as her sister.

"They'll talk ashore, you know, Thrasne," said Obers-rom.
"Seems to me you aren't sayin' much about this and would
rather the matter was kept quiet. But they will talk, Thrasne.
You know that. Best you give them something to say, or
they'll say something you won't like."

Thrasne thought on this. It was true. The men would talk
ashore, and the more mystery they made, the more likelihood
of curiosity seekers trying to sneak aboard to catch a glimpse.

Something close to the truth would be best. "Tell them the
baby's mother was pregnant. She drowned in the River and
was blighted. So the baby was born different from you and
me. She has a different sense of time, that's all. Perhaps all
creatures which are blighted have that sense of time. Maybe
blighted fishes live their whole lives out but do it a lot slower
than we do. Now, my old friend Suspirra—her I had the
statue of until she herself came aboard—Suspirra calls the

baby her sister because the drowned woman was her . . . her friend, and she cares for her friend's child as she would for a baby sister. It wouldn't be fitting for her to call Lila her own child, her being an unmarried woman. And Suspirra came to stay with us because the Awakeners wouldn't leave the child alone, not if they knew. You know that. She had to come to the River to be safe. That's all there is to it."

This won their sympathy and went a way to shutting their mouths. Boatmen were accustomed to avoiding Awakener attention and keeping shut about River business. It began to seem to all of them that Lila and Suspirra were River business right enough.

Obers-rom gave it considerable thought. Next time he stopped to speak to Lila he stroked her face, at which she made an indeterminate sound of pleasure, almost a word. "She's not so different, really," he said to Pamra. "She just moves real slow, that's all. Real slow. I'll call her slow-baby." He turned away, smiling, the smile vanishing as he thought of the watchful, perceptive expression in the child's eyes. "Not so different," he repeated to himself, "except for that." He still determined to call her slow-baby.

Which, thereafter, Lila heard more often than she heard her name.

• 11 •

Where the great log came from, Thrasne could not say. It had the look of something prehistoric about it, like some ancient monster heaving up from the depths to wreak havoc upon the works of man. As it did. The *Gift of Potipur* ran upon the log—or the log came up beneath her—with such force as to stave a man-sized hole in her bow planks, through which the water alternately poured and gurgled as the *Gift* rocked from the shock. There were several hours of panicky struggle, after which the *Gift* gurgled rather less, though still dangerously, and the most threatening part of the damage had been controlled for the moment.

"What will you do now?" asked Pamra. She had stayed out of the way during the worst of it, trying not to show how frightened she was, clinging to Lila as though to some raft on which she might have expected to float to safety. Later, when they had patched the hole, she had gone below to see the black water oozing around the patch and had realized it could be only temporary. "You'll have to fix it ashore, won't you?"

Thrasne nodded, still numb. It was the first real injury the *Gift* had received, and he felt it himself, looking at his ribs from time to time as though expecting to see great bruises and rents there, surprised to find himself whole. "It'll take a while. That third rib back is sprung all out of line. All the planks are loose along there. They're not leaking now, but they will be. Next town's hopeless, no piers, no shipwrights. Next one on down's some better, but I'll have to do most of it myself, most likely.''

''How long?''

''A long time. Thirty, forty days, at least. Probably more. They won't have the planking we need. It's almost impossible they'd have seasoned wood available. Chances are if they have any, it'll be green. Or, more likely, still standing. Over a month.'' A month was fifty-one days. ''Sixty days, maybe. Seventy.'' Still in shock, he wasn't thinking of her at all. Then he turned to see her look of fear and apprehension, understanding it in the instant. ''That'd be too long for you to be in one place, wouldn't it? Dangerous for you. Those hunting you would likely find you. I should have thought of that right off.''

''I can stay here in the owner-house.'' She tried to smile. ''If the men won't talk about it.''

They would talk, of course. No way he could prevent it. ''You can't stay cooped up that long. You'd turn all pale, like a mushroom.'' He tried a not-very-successful smile. ''No. We'll think of something else.''

When he came back to the owner-house some hours later, he brought the local chart-of-towns with him, laying it on the table under the lantern where she could see it. ''I've found something,'' a tired smile telling her it was the only thing he'd been able to find. ''I'd forgotten all about it. Strinder's Isle.''

He pointed to the chart, the ragged edge of the River at one side, with its endless list of places, products, local idiosyncrasies, religious taboos. There to the south, a good day's sail out into the World River, lay a long, wide, inky interruption among the careful notes and the River flow. The eastern end of it was behind them, two towns back. The western end was three towns yet ahead. ''The only people there are the Strinders,'' he said. ''And only a few of them left. No guards. No gates. They have a pier here, a little east of Chantry. Chantry's where we'll have to get the boat fixed.''

"An island? I never heard of an island in the River."

"There's many of them. Most of the ones close to shore are so small they're only rocks on the charts, dots, places to steer clear of. But Strinder's Isle, well, it's a good way out. Out of sight of the shore. Blint used to call there every time he came around. Used to bring in flour and cloth and sweetening. Take out dye shells. The thing is, we can run down along the island, drop you off, then pick you up again at the western end after the ship is fixed. All we'll need is some kind of signal so you can come down to the west end of the island when it's time. That way we'll be with the current, taking you in and getting you off."

He misinterpreted her doubtful look. "It's safe enough, Pamra. We've got time to drop you off. The *Gift* isn't going to sink under us."

"No, no, no," she said, hating herself for seeming to question his provision for her when that very provision might delay and endanger him. "It just seemed—is it an empty island? I mean, *are* there still any people there?"

Now he was doubtful himself. "There used to be. Right along here. A bunch of little houses, some of them scattered back in the trees. Of course, the island mostly belongs to the Treeci. They're a little like the fliers."

"Servants of Abricor!"

"Not carrion eaters. No. Not the Servants of Abricor. A different kind of creature. I've never seen them anywhere but there, on the island. Bigger legs than the Servants. They have beautiful plumage, but they don't fly. Flat kind of beaks on them, almost like lips only harder, not those hard, hooked beaks the Servants have. From a distance, they look almost human. I've only seen them at a distance, of course, but the Strinders got on well with them." He ran a hand across his face, as though trying to wipe away the tiredness. "If there's any way to let you stay there, Pam, it's best. Truly. Even if you had to stay alone in one of the old houses. The people looking for you won't find you there, I can guarantee. And we can make it safe and reasonably comfortable for you, even if you have to stay alone."

It sounded like abandonment, and he knew it. She could not help but know it, and it made a slow, burning anger in her that there could not be some other way. There was no other way. The alternatives were worse. The Awakeners would send Laughers after her, they weren't going to stop looking for her, and even death alone on an island would be far preferable to their finding her. She shook herself, made herself sound cheerful about it.

"I'll go there, Thrasne. Even if there's no one there. I'll take Lila, she'll be company for me. However long it takes, I'll wait for your signal."

When they came to the island, however, she was less sure.

There were little houses along the shore, most tumbled into piles of gray fragments, log and plank silvered by the sun and the River wind. At last they saw a vague line of smoke ascending, and this led them to a rickety pier and a ramshackle dwelling showing light among the trees.

The woman who answered their calls had aged like the house. She was rust and dust held together by a net of wrinkles with gray hair wisping around her like smoke. "Strinder? Me? Well, of course I'm Strinder, and damn near the last. Did you say you were old Blint's boy? I seem to remember he had a boy. Think of that, and come in."

There were two others on the island, as old as she; an old curmudgeon named Stodder and her own cousin, Bethne. "Joy," she said to Pamra with a keen glance from under bushy brows. "That's my name. You wouldn't think it, would you? Not exactly a joyful object, am I? Often wished I'd had a name that aged better. Sophronia. Eugenia. Something with some dignity to it."

She looked them over, Pamra and the slow baby. She did not remark then or ever upon the baby's strangeness, and Pamra came to believe for a time it was because human babies were so far in her past she had forgotten what the usual ones were like. Lila might have fitted her memories of babyness as well as any other.

When Thrasne left her, it was with a goodly supply of food and with a large supply of wood cut for the old woman's fires. Though it was warmer on the island than on the shore, the evenings would still be cold for the next three months. Thirty days was the minimum time the repairs would take, but it could be three times that. After thirty days she was to watch the northern shore each evening, a little before dusk, to see three pillars of smoke. When she saw them, she was to make the two- or three-day hike along the flat shore to the western end of the island and camp there until he came for her. "If it takes us longer than that, we may be delayed by the Conjunction tides," he told her. "So don't be impatient. You can get down to the west end all right?"

"Oh, yes, yes," said the old woman. "She can get there easy enough. There's no more wilderness on Strinder's Island. No more wildness at all. Except for . . . well, except for what there is, of course." If this had been meant to convey something, it failed. Pamra was too agitated at being left behind to pay much attention.

The *Gift* pulled away from the isle, Thrasne turning from the high rudder deck to wave to her. When sight of him had faded into the River haze, down and cross stream toward the distant shore, she turned back to the house, the old woman meeting her halfway there.

"Oh, girl, I saw he left you puncon jam. Couldn't help but see it. I haven't had puncon jam since my youngest daughter was born, she that's gone now and left only the memory. Would it be ugly of me to beg puncon jam on our fry cakes tonight? I do have a light hand with fry cakes." For a time it was as though Joy had returned, so young she sounded, and Pamra was ashamed not to greet this enthusiasm with more spirit of her own. Though she kept counseling herself to be calm, not to consider herself injured, still she felt bereft, grieved, and abandoned, senseless though that was. She found herself blaming Thrasne, senseless though that was as well, ashamed of it and yet unable to stop. Still, faced with the old woman's delight in having company, she assented to the scheme of puncon jam, assented to having Stodder and Bethne as guests.

These three were the entire remnant of the Strinders. There

had been some younger who had gone away on the River, there had been many younger and older who had died. And now these three remained, not one among them who had ever seen the northern shore or an Awakener or a Servant of Abricor. They knew only the island and the waters around it and the Treeci, who shared both with them.

It was some time before she met the Treeci. First there were days of walking here and there, weeding a bit of garden, checking the nets to see if anything worth eating had been caught, raking shellfish from the River to dry upon the shore, carrying the dried shells to the pier, where great, wobbly baskets bulged with this reeking harvest awaiting the next Riverboat.

"Not many stop here," creaked old Stodder. "Let's see, there's *River Queen*, and *Moormap's Fish* (Moormap died, but his daughter's husband kept the *Fish*), and the *Gift*, o' course, and the *Startled Wind* . . ." He went on with his enumeration, Riverboats afloat, Riverboats long gone.

After their supper they sat on the rickety porch beneath the trees to watch the moons assemble before the old man and the other old woman stumped off to their own falling-down houses in the woods. Pamra stood looking after them, wondering why they did not live together. It would mean only one house to heat, less wood to cut. Far off in the trees came a plangent, bell-tolling sound, and she remembered the creatures Thrasne had mentioned.

"Treeci?" she asked old Joy.

"Treeci," whispered Joy, face in the lamplight alive with old memories, eyes gentle as doves. "Treeci. Honoring the moons."

They went next day to rake shells, Pamra, Lila, and Joy. Three Treeci came through the trees, calling in bell-like voices, then in human sounds. "Joy! We greet!"

The old woman waved. "Binna! Werf! Come meet a visitor from over the River. Her name is Pamra. And the baby, Lila." The Treeci bowed, acknowledging the introduction, while Pamra stared.

They were as tall as she, standing upright on legs not

unlike her own, with feathered buttocks that curved as hers did into a narrow waist. The long, two-toed feet might have been human feet stuffed into feathery socks except for the knifelike talons. Above the waist the likeness to humans was less. The arms, ending in three-fingered hands, were fully feathered with long, winglike primaries; their breasts were keeled; their large-eyed faces were full of candid intelligence. "Pamra," they said, bowing again.

She bowed in return to Binna, to Werf, then turned to bow to the third member of the group, feeling Joy's hand tugging at her as she did so. She looked down to see the old woman shaking her head, embarrassed, whispering, "No, don't bow. That's a male. You don't bow to them."

"Why?" It was startled out of her, not really a question.

"Shhh. Later."

"Are you having a pleasant visit?" Binna asked her, taking no notice of this gaffe. The words were clearly articulated, slightly accented but in a pleasant way. Though the lower part of each Treeci face was visored by their shallow beaks, those beaks were soft and flexible, protruding little, moving almost as lips did.

"Yes, thank you." They talked of the weather for a few moments, of the tides. The third, unnamed Treeci wandered to the shore and stood there, watching the water.

"I came to tell you, Joy," said Werf, "there's a new bed of inedible shellies just below the big rocks, beyond the frag grove. Good dye shells! They're small now, but by Conjunction after this one, they should be good size for your gathering."

"That's kind of you," she responded warmly. "Will you return with us and take tea?"

They demurred, demurred again, then accepted. It had the pace and quiet predetermination of a ritual. At the house they were joined on the porch by Bethne to drink tea out of fragile old cups as they recited memories of former times, so many memories it was obvious they were more than acquaintances. Joy had brought six cups. Without saying anything to anyone, Werf filled the extra cup and carried it to the rock, where the third Treeci perched in lonely silence. The two conversed in low tones. Werf returned. No one seemed to notice. Before leaving, Werf retrieved the cup and set it upon the table with the others.

"We rejoice in your friendship," they called as they were leaving. "May your lives extend."

Joy gathered up the cups. "If you could get me a pail of water, child, I'd get these washed."

"In a minute. First, tell me about the—the male. Why don't we talk to him? . . ."

"It isn't done." The old woman laid a trembling hand on Pamra's own. "Werf is Neff's mother. She talks to him, you see. And his own sisters do, of course. But no one else. It just isn't done."

"Cruel," Pamra said, remembering herself as a child. "It's cruel to treat people like that."

"Ah, but child, they aren't people, don't you see."

"They're people, Joy. You wouldn't sit here drinking tea with them unless they were." She said this as she would have done to Delia, mistaking Joy for Delia, perhaps, without realizing it.

"In that sense, yes, they're people and my dearest friends, but you know what I meant." She turned away toward her wash basin, holding out the empty pail. "They aren't human people."

Pamra forced her feelings off her face. She was living in the old woman's house, a good old woman, not unlike—not unlike another good old woman whom she had failed in a time of trouble. Let her not trouble this one more. As a guest, she had no right.

But she felt a sympathetic rebellion for the lonely Treeci, even as she admitted to herself the loneliness might be more in her than in Neff. The rebellion in her was the same it had been when she was eleven or twelve, the same that had led her to say, "I can be an Awakener." She did not think of this, but only of the sad Treeci. His separation spoke to her.

Among the Treeci, it seemed, hospitality must be returned. Two days later Joy dressed herself with unaccustomed atten-

tion, digging through dusty boxes in search of old finery. She
found a glittery scarf for Pamra, a shiny bit of ribbon for
Lila's blanket, and they set out along the shore.

"I suppose eventually you'll tell me where we're going?"

"Well, Werf and Binna will expect us. Among the Treeci
it's considered nice to drop by in a couple days so's they can
show hospitality. They call it returning the opportunity. Very
set on it, they are."

"Why all this sparkle?"

"Do them honor. You wouldn't have noticed, not being
island reared, but they were got up fine for us t'other day.
Talons painted; feathers around the eyes dyed. They were
making an opportunity to honor us—so they call it. Curious,
I expect. About you and the baby. Not been a human baby on
Strinder's for thirty years."

Pamra found herself lost in wonder at this, not so much at
the fact of it—another race of creatures upon the world with
its own habits and customs, speaking not only its own language but a human language as well, curious about human
babies—no, not so much at the fact as at her ignorance of it.
How could she have grown to be adult without having heard
of them? Why had no one spoken of them? And if no one had
spoken of the Treeci, how may other wonders in the world
might there be, unspoken of?

Joy had something to say upon that subject. "My brother
used to say all the Northshore people were so stuffed full of
Awakener shit they hadn't room for anything else. Is it true
they forbid books there?"

It was true. Or true enough. There had been books in the
Tower. Homiletics. Hermeneutics. Scripture. Difficult books
breathing an atmosphere of dusty mystery, unenlightening.
There had been no others. Without books, without travel,
Pamra could explain her own ignorance. She could not really
forgive it.

The Treeci lived in houses, better kept and better made
than those of the human occupants of the island, and there
was a teahouse set in a grove where water burbled tranquil
music into a stone basin. Young Treeci, half the size of the

adults, gathered on the meadow in murmuring groups. Tea was served in ceremonial fashion. Pamra watched the others to see what was proper, getting through the formal bits with some degree of grace. When everyone had a cup, when every cup had been tasted and approved, when the nuts and cakes had been passed around and those had been complimented, then the group could sit back and indulge themselves in conversation. Joy had been right. It was curiosity. All the questions they had been too polite to ask on Strinder territory they felt empowered to ask on their own.

"Is the child yours?"

"Is it a customary child?"

"We thought it was not a customary child. We believe she is *t'lick tlassca.*" After some discussion, this term was translated as "wonder."

"Yes," Pamra agreed with a rare smile. "She is a wonder."

"Would Pamra stay long?"

By this time Lila lay on Werf's lap, patting her feathery bosom with long, stretched gestures, murmuring her own legato music. Werf dripped tea into her mouth, and the baby smiled, an endless smile, like dawn.

"Why had she come?"

Without thinking to censor what she said, Pamra told them why she had come. Not all, merely some. Awakeners were part of the reason, and the Servants of Abricor. There was a sad murmuring, a shaking of feathered heads.

"They were kin to us one time, those fliers of the Northshore. Those you call Servants of Abricor. We remember that time in our histories. There was a time when honor could have been retained. Our tribe, the Treeci, chose the way of honor. They, those who remained, chose otherwise. There are certain words in our language which go back to that time which those on the Northshore no longer know. Words like 'decency.' And 'dignity.' It makes us sad what they have become." Werf shook her feathered head in sadness, widening the plumy circles around her eyes.

Binna changed the subject, and Pamra kept quiet, abashed at the sadness she had caused.

"We thought you might like to see some of our dancing," said Binna, nodding at a young Treeci, who went racing away with this message. In moments there were sounds of a drum and a rhythmic tinkling.

From the teahouse the Treeci watched indulgently, even proudly. On the lawn the young Treeci sat, whispering, a few going so far as to point with wingtips, as though accidentally. Looking at these youths, Pamra could not tell whether they were male or female; they had no distinguishing colors, they were merely young. Perhaps there was a stage in development in which it did not matter, for all the young ones murmured together, moved about in giggling groups, walked with entwined fingers and heads tilted toward one another.

The dancers, however, were all male. Pamra could feel it. They twirled and postured, stamped, wings wide with each feather displayed, chest feathers fluffed, those around the eyes widened into flashing circles. Their flat beaks had been rouged, their talons painted. Beside her Werf sat smiling, wing fingers tapping in time to the drums, eyes moist. Pamra followed the direction of her eyes. Werf's son, Neff, among the dancers, magnificent in his grace and strength, the dance itself stimulating, breathtaking. Without thinking, Pamra started to say something about this, some small, complimentary remark, only to feel Joy's fingers biting into her arm. Confused, she confronted the old woman's forbidding eyes with wide, excited eyes of her own. This, too, was not to be spoken of. Pamra pulled her arm away. She wanted to say something, do something. Her face was flushed, red; she could feel the heat in it, in her arms trembling with the music.

Binna had been watching her. Now she said something loudly, a cutting metal sound, and the dance ended in a ragged cacophony of drum and bell. There was conversation then, apologies, a rapid murmur of polite talk covering the sudden end of the entertainment. Pamra did not understand it.

Then they were on their way home. "Binna apologized," said Joy. There was sorrow in her voice, as though she had been given news of a grave illness or death.

"For what? I don't understand."

"For the dancing. They had not realized you would be—moved by it."

"It was exciting! That's wrong?" Pamra wanted to laugh. "Isn't that the object of it all?"

"No. Never. That would be unseemly." This, too, was forbidden ground. Joy would not talk of it further.

Her reticence broke the fragile confidence that had been building between them. Now Pamra could not feel comfortable. Each remark had to be weighed for acceptability. There were too many areas of taboo. She began to take long walks, carrying the slow baby in her shawl, far down the shore toward the west, far into the forest toward the south, roaming the rolling island woods to pass the time and leave the old woman alone. Joy did not object. She seemed to have withdrawn from Pamra as though Pamra had been culpable of some social error that only time would dilute. Her feelings did not seem to convey disapproval so much as sorrow. It was easier for them both when they were apart.

Once or twice she encountered Binna or Werf on her solitary walks. She transgressed politeness to ask them a few things about old times and the Servants of Abricor. They were not reluctant to talk, merely distressed by it, their pain so palpable that she gave it up. What she had learned from them was already a lumpish knot in her throat, confirming her knowledge that in the Tower she had been used and lied to.

Pamra found a favorite place along the shore, high among a cluster of lichened stones. It was almost a little room, sheltered from the sky, with a tiny moss yard and minuscule pool of rainwater. Here Lila could lie for long hours on the moss, singing her drawn-out notes of gladness. Pamra merely sat, hypnotized by the sound and the River flow.

It was there that Neff came.

She arrived at her sitting place one afternoon to find a spray of flowers laid upon the moss, a delicate crimson bouquet tied with a knot of violet grass, the whole displayed as in a picture. Someone.

From the top of the rock she searched the area. He was sitting on the Rivershore, face turned from her as though to make it easy for her not to see him. She did see him, and the frustration that had simmered in her for days brought a flush to her cheeks. She would not take part in this silly custom of silence when he had been so thoughtful. She waved, beckoned, called, "Come up!"

He came leaping up the rocks in one flowing motion of power, posed upon the ridge in a posture so unconsciously graceful that she drew breath, belly clenching and loosing like a knot untied. "Artist's blood," they might have called such a feeling on the Northshore. "Artist's eyes," Thrasne would have said. She was not thinking of Thrasne; she was breathing deeply, almost unaware of her own body.

She motioned to the rock across from her, a flat place with a convenient arm and back for leaning, her own favorite seat. He sat there, looking at her from enormous eyes. "You're Neff," she said. "Aren't you." He would not speak, she thought, unless she spoke to him first.

"Yes," he said in his bell voice. "Neff!"

"Your mother has been very kind to me. Won't you tell me something about that dance you did the other day? It was very beautiful."

"Just the dance." He turned away in shyness, looking at her from one eye only. "The dance we do."

"I see." She was at a loss. "We have no dances like that on the Northshore. At least none I have seen."

"Tell me of the Northshore," he begged, the words tumbling over one another in their eagerness. "Tell me of the Northshore. There! Over there!"

Poor thing, she thought with immediate sympathy. He's an explorer at heart. She told him about the Northshore. Wary of those subjects that caused discomfort, she did not speak of the Awakeners or the Servants of Abricor, but of more usual things. Festivals. The Candy Tree. Planting pamet and gathering the ripe pods. Fruit harvest in the puncon groves. As she spoke, she realized how little she actually knew of the life of the people. All her memories were of childhood, before entering the Tower. She could not share with him any memories after that.

"The one who brought you, will he come back for you?"

"Yes. He'll be back. When the boat is fixed."

"Would you—would he let me see the boat?"

"Haven't you seen boats before? Haven't you seen them when they come to pick up the dye shells?"

"I mean, would he let me go on it? See it? See the inside of it?"

"I'm sure he would." If those biddies will let you, she thought. "Would that be all right with the . . . others?"

He shook his head, the edges of his beak flushing as though rouged. "Mother wouldn't let me."

"We'll have to arrange it without her knowing, then." There it was, out in the open. Rebellion.

He seemed frightened by this; frightened and stimulated at the same time. He stood, posing, stamped, extended his wings, looked at her flirtatiously out of one eye. Then she blushed, and he turned away, as suddenly shy. "That would be wonderful. Please. Do that." He jittered from foot to foot, finally murmuring, "I have to go now." He sped away down the rocks.

"Neff," she called, unable to let him go. "Thank you for the flowers."

"We give them like that," he called. "We Treeci. To our sisters."

So then, she thought, half in amusement. I'm one of his family. So much for the old woman's distinctions. If he thought of Pamra as a sister, then it would be all right to talk to him. They did talk to their sisters.

That night she got out the puncon jam. Jam seemed to loosen Joy's old tongue. Forbidden subject or not, Pamra wanted to learn about the Treeci.

"The young ones," she said casually, "all appear to be about the same age. I didn't see any babies."

"No, there won't be any babies for almost a year. They only breed one year in ten. My brother used to say it had something to do with keeping the population in balance.

They don't have any more than the island can keep. Sensible of them, he used to say."

"I didn't see any males among the children."

"You probably did. Far as the Treeci are concerned, children are just children. Can't tell male from female till they get to be about fifteen."

"So the one that came here, with his mother, he was over fifteen?"

"Nineteen," said Joy, burrowing into the jam pot. "Nineteen last Conjunction."

"You know that? So exactly?"

"Well, of course. I know all Werf's children, have for years. She used to bring Neff and his sisters here from the time they were just hatchlings. I used to feed them nut cookies and play hide and go find with them in the woods."

"But now you don't talk to Neff? After being his friend when he was a child?" She could not keep the outrage from her voice.

The old woman pushed her chair back from the table, stood to confront her accusing look. "Girl, you're my guest and I'll give you guest rights, but don't lay your voice on me for things you don't understand. I never said I couldn't talk to Neff, being almost his mother and him as dear to me as my own ever were, I said *you* couldn't. I said to you before, they're not people. Not human people. You've got to give them their own way!"

There were tears in the old woman's eyes, and it was that which softened Pamra. If she was already grieved over whatever it was, there was no point in adding to her grief. So. Pamra bowed her head in submission, making her apologies, promising not to bring up the matter again. It did not change her mind. Cruelty was cruelty. If Neff got pleasure out of making her an honorary sister, why, then she would be his honorary sister.

At the end of thirty days, she began to make regular trips at dusk each day, looking for Thrasne's signal fires. More and more often during these excursions, Neff appeared, though he never did when one of the old people accompanied her. At

other times during the day she would find flowers strewn in
her path, a necklace of bright petals strung on grass, bou-
quets of herbs smelling of damp woods or sunny meadows.
She began to look forward to the evening walks, began to
slip away early without inviting Joy or Bethne or Stodder to
come along.

"Your man, he'll be back for you," said Joy.

"I know he will. He said it might take a long time."

"Thought you might be worried. You're spending so much
time alone." This with a sidelong, questioning look.

For several nights thereafter she invited the oldsters to
come with her, paying particular attention to being chatty
with them. Thereafter she included one or more of them
every few days, merely to allay their concern, she told
herself. No point in distressing them.

"Tell me about the baby," said Neff. He would hold Lila
for hours, fascinated by her leisurely, graceful movements.
Pamra saw him trying to mimic them in dance, long, stretched
extensions of wing and leg as though he would reach himself
through into Lila's timeless world and make himself a place
there. Often he danced for Pamra, without music, humming
to himself in a strangely moving, unmelodic way.

"What is that music?" she asked at last.

"Just . . . just music. The music," he said, flushing. He
had done that more in recent days, the red moving in from
the edges of his beak toward the center. The feathers on his
chest were turning crimson as well, and the wide, plumy
ones around his eyes. When he looked at her like that, she
wanted to hold him, tell him everything was fine. It made her
ache for him.

"Tell me of this man who hunts you!" he asked.

"How did you know about that?"

"I heard Mother talking. They think the Awakeners are
very cruel to raise up the dead, who should lie asleep. Also
our kin, the Servants. They think them stupid, vicious, and
cruel, also."

Not more cruel than they, she thought, stroking the line of

his jaw, the feathers of his chest. She could tell he liked having her do that, liked having her near him.

"I suppose every group of people has its own cruelties," she said, wondering if he would say anything about his own treatment at the hands of his people. Remembering her own rebellion as a child, she could not accept his passivity. Perhaps it lay in the fact that all males were treated much alike; perhaps that made it seem less cruel. "Don't your friends miss you when you're off here with me?"

"They are mostly alone. Besides"—he flushed—"I am a Talker. They aren't Talkers. Males aren't much. Only one in each thousand males is a Talker, they say."

"You mean other males don't talk? Never did?"

"They talk like everyone when they are children. When they grow up, though, talking goes. Except once in a while, one like me. It makes it harder."

She could not bear the thought. The safest one to ask seemed to be old Stodder.

"Is it true the male Treeci can't talk?"

"Oh, they can talk. They just don't much."

"What do you mean, they don't much?"

"They just lose interest, that's all. I suppose they figure why talk if you don't have to?" This seemed to her to be Stodder's own philosophy. She seldom heard him speak unless asked a direct question.

Upon examination, his comment made some sense. During visits to the Treeci village, Pamra noticed how cosseted the males really were. Why would they talk when every need was met before they had a chance to utter it? Each one had a circle of children seeing to his grooming, his food, his drink. Every male had a mother, sisters.

Though she went to the watching place each evening, there were still no signal fires. Stodder counted the days until Conjunction and remarked that the *Gift of Potipur* would likely not come until after the flood tides. "Thrasne's a good boatman. He won't risk the *Gift.*"

"Do you really think he won't come until after the flood tides, Stodder?"

"Ah, girl, he could still get here. Don't leave off looking for the fires. Just don't be disappointed."

Was she disappointed? Did she care if Thrasne came soon or late? What were they to one another, after all? She frowned at this new consideration. It was an uncomfortable thought because she should have been able to answer it and could not. She didn't know. "Does he love me?" She whispered the question, looking for the answer in Lila's eyes, which lightened almost imperceptibly into a smile. "Does Thrasne love me?" Suddenly she thought of things he had done, gifts he had given. Was that why?

What did the question mean? If he did or not, what difference did it make?

She wrapped herself warmly in a heavy shawl and went to the rocks with Bethne, seeing nothing on the Northshore, hearing nothing but the usual *shush* of wind and River sounds. They turned to walk back along the ridge in the dusk, the light of Potipur casting a ruddy glow along the slopes, making black pits of shadow. In a clearing at the foot of the hill, there were two Treeci dancing, male and female. "Beautiful," whispered Pamra. "Look, Bethne. Look how beautiful."

The male Treeci called plaintively into the dusk; the female responded, the two voices like a duet, sweeter than one could bear.

"What are they saying?" Pamra stopped, straining to hear, until Bethne tugged her along.

"Come along. It isn't polite to listen in. What he's singing is 'Tell me of my children . . .' It's a song the young males sing. So she sings to him of his children, how strong and graceful they will be."

"Tell me of my children," Pamra mused. Sentimental, that. Unlike Neff. He was all "tell me," but about a hundred other things.

"Tell me about the Southshore."

"Neff, no one knows anything about the Southshore. Maybe people went there once, but no one does now. Thrasne says the World River is twenty-four hundred miles wide, and no one goes farther out than Strinder's Isle. All the measurements are in the old chart-of-towns. That amazes me, but it's true.''

"Are there Treeci there?"

"For all I know there could be."

"I could get there, in a boat. With a sail."

"Why would you want to do that?"

"I just thought of it, that's all." He rose, jittering, unable to keep still, pulled her up to dance with him. This was new, their dancing together. When they were exhausted by it, they lay curled in the moss bed side-by-side, she stroking his feathered chest, dreamy and quiet.

"You are my sister," he said. "Aren't you. It's all right for me to be here. You really are my sister."

"Of course," she choked. "Of course I am."

The next evening Pamra and Joy found the approach to her lookout place ankle deep in water. "Conjunction," said Joy, measuring the water with her eyes. "Moons are pulling that water right up here, aren't they. Well, if Thrasne doesn't get back for you in the next few days, he won't come until low-water-after-the-moons. There's no place to tie up for long at the west end. He'll have better sense than to try."

Pamra tried to feel disappointment. The feeling would not come. She was not concerned. Not upset. All it meant was she would have more time with Neff. More time to dance, to sing, to lie together in the dusk watching the moons move among the stars. He had become so beautiful in recent days. Because of their friendship, she told herself. Because he had someone to talk to.

"Only ten days or so to Conjunction," said Joy, saddened by some recollection, some nostalgic connection that Pamra could not follow. "Think I'll go over to the village tomorrow to visit . . . Werf. Few days she'll be too busy."

"I'll go with you."

"No. No, just a friendly visit between Werf and me, I think. Two old friends. You can visit later. After Conjunction. There'll be plenty of time. Thrasne's not going to get here before."

The drums began to sound nightly, throbbing like hearts, like bruises, like the pulse in wounds, painfully immediate. Joy stood at the window, listening, tears standing in her eyes. "Memories," she said abashedly, wiping the tears away. "So many memories."

Of her childhood, Pamra thought. Of her young womanhood, of her children. Sad to be old and almost alone with only these other-people for company; sad to think of their children as one's own because one has none of one's own.

Still the drums. Pamra put Lila in a shawl and started to go visiting.

"No," said Joy. "You wouldn't be welcome."

"I thought I'd just watch the dancing."

Joy didn't speak.

"It's their religious time," said Bethne. "Their farewell time."

"The old year?" Pamra asked, unwillingly taking off her shawl, remembering the celebrations of her childhood when they said farewell to the old year and welcome to the new.

"Something like that," said Bethne.

Neff came earlier each day. He was thinner, fined down to pure muscle and bone, light as reeds in the wind. "All the dancing," he explained. "I haven't been hungry."

She tested this, bringing cakes, bringing tea in a bottle. He drank the tea thirstily but gagged at the cakes. "Too much dancing."

She worried about him as he lay in her arms, eyes shut in sleep. And yet he didn't look at all unhealthy but vital and alive, his beak bright red along the edges, the feathers on his neck and chest turning a brilliant crimson. He had never asked so many questions, had so many things he wanted her to tell him. He seemed to want to be with her so much it was an agony to leave him and return to the house.

"We must have festival," exclaimed Joy. "We must have a celebration of our own! I haven't made a festival dinner for twenty years. With Pamra and Lila here, we must! With wine! We'll open up the big front room we used to use!"

Pamra found herself drawn in, involved, sent scurrying

here and there for everything imaginable, pulled in to help
with long, detailed recipes. There was something a little
frantic in the way Joy set herself to this task, as though she
wanted terribly to remember, or to forget. Or perhaps it was
only to make a festival for Lila. Festivals were for children,
after all. The Candy Tree. That was for children.

On conjugation evening, Pamra went to the lookout rocks,
watching for Neff, seeing no sign of him. Well, she told
herself, he couldn't come. Not until after Conjunction. With
the water this high, it was sure that Thrasne wasn't going to
be signaling, either. Still, she climbed the rocks one more
time.

There were flowers on the stone. She went on to the mossy
place, holding her breath, to find him there, already there,
moving like a windblown cloud in a tiny circle. "Pam-ra,"
he sang to her in a voice unlike his own. His eyes were so
bright she thought he might be drugged. "Pamra, tell me
about the River."

He wouldn't wait for her to tell him anything, wouldn't let
her sit down. "Tell me about the Towers. Tell me about
fishing." He wanted to know everything, couldn't sit still to
listen to anything. "I have to go back."

"Come again tomorrow, Neff. I'll wait for you tomorrow."

"Come again tomorrow," he cried. "Oh, Pamra, tell me
of my children. . . ."

Her mouth fell open in surprise, but he did not wait to be
told. He fled, leaving the smell of himself behind, a rich
fragrance that made her breathe as though she had been
running. When she returned to the house, her trousers were
wet between her legs. She washed herself at the spring,
hanging the clothes out to dry, drying herself in the wind.
Her nipples were hard, like little stones. She had never felt
them like that, so painful. She put her hands over them,
trying to soften them, but it only made them worse. She
should have been cold in the wintery wind, but she was
warm, fiery, alive with the dance. It was the drums, she
knew, the hectic batter of the drums, like her own heartbeat
gone mad.

The oldsters made their festival dinner, scattered the seeds of the Candy Tree upon Lila's cot, sang festival songs in quavering old voices, unsure of the words. There was wine, more of it than was good for any of them, Pamra felt, repeatedly emptying her own glass out the window, only to have it refilled solicitously by Joy. Then it was over. They had exhausted themselves as if purposely, worn themselves fine and dry so they could only fall into their beds.

"You'll sleep, won't you?" asked Joy, nodding with weariness, half-drunk. "You will sleep."

Pamra yawned. Of course. Even without the wine, she would sleep.

In the deep dark she woke, sitting straight up in the bed, hearing Lila stir beside her, where she, too, had heard the sound. Pamra had not heard it before but knew in the instant what it was. Neff's voice calling in the night, bell-like, insistent, reverberating with an inexpressible vitality. "Come. Come. I'm waiting for you." Farther off were other such sounds, other such calls. Come, come. She heard only Neff, disregarding the others as so much noise.

She threw a cape over her nightdress, sandals on her feet, went out into the night, three moons from the top of the sky casting diffused shadows under every tree. "Come," he called. "Come." The voice came from the woods, from the meadows deep in the woods. She began to run, wondering what wonderful thing he had found to be calling so, her breath eager in her throat and her skin burning. She had never run so before, never so long and tirelessly, never run before without pain or effort.

Trunks of trees going by, dark and light, masses of moon and shade, splashing of stream shallows, silver fountains beneath her feet, meadow grass dotted with pale faces of winter-blooming flowers. "Come." A hillside of moss velvet. "Come."

Far to her left another voice called, and across the valley before her a figure ran toward that voice, wings extended as though to fly, feet seeming scarcely to move as they skimmed

the grass. Two met; two danced. There were angels alive in
the night. Treeci.

"Come!" He danced upon the hilltop, posed in glory,
silver and black in the light of the moons, head back, carol-
ing, bell sound on the hill, voice of joy. "Come!"

She ran toward him, panting now a little, wondering what
marvelous festival this was, what occasion called the Treeci
out into the night, remembering only then that it was Conjunction. Of course. A second celebration.

He turned, seeing her, eyes wide in their circles of feathers, wider yet as he realized who it was ascending the hill.
"No," he cried, a wounded sound. "No. No."

What did he mean? She paused, puzzled at this denial,
stopping short when he threatened her with widespread wings.
She could see him clearly now, feathers on his abdomen
spread wide to disclose a pulsing, swollen organ on the bare
skin, black in the night, oozing silver. "No," he begged.

She went toward him, her thighs sliding slickly, wetly on
one another. "Neff? It's Pamra. Neff?"

An agonized cry from him as he clasped her, his body
beating against her, one thrust, two and three, breaking away
only to close again, then away, this time really away to flee
down the hillside faster than she could pursue him, no longer
calling, now only crying, more like a child than an adult. She
stared after him stupidly, brushing at the front of her cape,
where the copious jet of sticky fluid clung, slowly, very
slowly flushing as she realized what had happened, what she
had been too preoccupied with her own feelings to see.

"Mating," she whispered to herself, aghast. "It's their
mating time. Oh, by Potipur, but I've shamed him and
myself." Sudden tears burned hotter than her skin, and all at
once she felt the cold.

She trudged homeward, a longer way than she could have
imagined, trying various apologies in her head, how she
would say it, how she would rectify the situation. Her cape
stank of his juices, a smell as wild as the woods themselves.
She would have to wash it. When she returned to the house,

however, she could only fall into bed, leaving the cape where she dropped it beside the door.

She was wakened by Joy shaking her, shaking her, screaming at her. "What have you done, damn you, Pamra, what have you done?"

She sat up stupidly, drawing the blanket over her breasts as though against attack. "What . . . what do you mean?"

"Did you go out? Last night? You didn't go out. Not with all the wine I gave you. You couldn't have. No. You couldn't have done that to him. He was my son, like my own son."

"I woke up." Pamra cowered, trying to explain, still half-asleep. "I intruded. But I didn't hurt him. I'm sorry. How in hell did you find out, anyhow?"

"I smelled it. Smelled it. On your cape. That smell. Oh, stupid, stupid, selfish, unhearing, unheeding stupid girl." She was weeping too hard to talk, weeping herself away, out of the room, leaving Pamra to stare foolishly at the door. In the cot beside the bed, Lila made a sound of pain, a creaking agony. Pamra pressed her hands over her ears, willing not to hear it.

It was Bethne who came to her about noon. "Joy asked me to have you pack up your things. Food in the cart. Stodder'll help you take it downshore to the west end. Joy'd rather you weren't here. Makes it too hard for her."

"Bethne, I told her I was sorry. I didn't mean to intrude. Where is Joy? Why doesn't she tell me herself?"

"Look, girl, I'd have just thrown you out. I might have killed you. Didn't she tell you not to talk to that Neff? I know she did. I heard her say so."

"He thought of me as his sister. He said so. They can talk to their sisters."

"Sure they talk to their sisters. That's so their sisters recognize their voices and have the common decency to stay away from them on the night. You didn't have the decency to listen to Joy, and you didn't have the decency to stay away from him, either. Now he's gone, wasted, all for nothing."

"Gone? Away?" .

"Gone. Dead. Lying on the funeral woodpile down there

in the village, all dressed in his pretty feathers, all spent. All the pretty males. Dancing, dancing, all danced out, mated out. I've thought about it sometimes, how it would be. Knowing it would all go so fast, all in a few years, a few days. Losing friends, losing words, becoming what they are at the end. No wonder they comfort themselves by asking their sisters to tell them of their children. Remember! I told you about that. 'Tell me of my children!' Did Neff ever say that to you? Probably not. He was a Talker, poor little tyke. Talkers shouldn't have to go through it. They want to know so bad. He wanted to know so much. . . .

"No one to tell him of his children, now no children. Him gone. His seed gone. His line gone."

The old woman was crying. "He was like a son to Joy. Like her own son."

"I'll go there. I'll explain."

"Oh, stupid girl, stay away from them. They're singing now. They'll sing each name, and some young Treeci girl will stand up and sing that she carries the children of that one. They'll sing Neff's name, and there'll be no one, no one at all, but that's better than having it be you, you stupid human, trying to explain!"

Bethne cried herself away. Pamra crouched on the floor, unable to move, to think. Dead. Unable to move. Dead. The smell of him was still in her nostrils, the sight of him dancing.

Tell him of his children.

· 12 ·

Apprentice Melancholic Medoor Babji accepted a fat copper coin from her weeping victim, gave the paunchy shop-keeper a dozen halfhearted strokes of her fishskin whip, then put a glass Sorter coin into the sweating merchant's palm.

"May the Sorters accept the pain you have already borne as payment for your sins," she singsonged in formula, slipping the merchant's warm metal into her own jingling purse. Medoor's purse was almost as stout as the merchant, full of the coin paid for whipping Northshoremen across a hundred towns this season before ending here in Chantry.

"Amen," said the merchant, wiping his eyes. Though why he should weep, Medoor could not say. Medoor had not struck him hard enough to get through the lard to anything essential, a fact brought forcibly to Medoor's attention by her Leader, Taj Noteen, who came up behind her and cuffed her across the back of her head.

"The man paid you, Babji! Put some muscle into it! What's all this patty-pat, as if you were playing with a babby."

"He was such an *old* fart," Medoor responded, knowing it was the wrong thing to say.

"So much more in need of Sorter compassion!" The leader leered at her, daring her to say anything more, an invitation Medoor sensibly refused. She knew as well as Noteen did that Sorters, Sorter compassion, and Sorter coin were all equally mythological, but it was Melancholic policy to appear to believe in the myth, at least when moving among the shore-fish—so-called because the townees schooled at the edge of the River, waiting to be caught, just as song-fish did in the waters along the shore.

"The shore-fish believe, they pay because they believe," Noteen was fond of saying. "Who are you to 'question their belief?"

Which was another way of telling Medoor not to bite the hand that offered her hard metal coin. Coin that would buy food, wine, woven pamet cloth. Coin to send to the Noor kindred on the steppes—some for the near-kin of each Melancholic; some for the coffers of the Queen. Thinking of Queen Fibji, Medoor made a reverent gesture and saw the leader's glance change to one of understanding approval. He thought he understood how she felt, but he did not, not at all. Medoor Babji had more reason than most to care about Queen Fibji. It was Queen Fibji's need for coin that made any of them willing to serve a term as Melancholics, despite the precarious life of the Noor steppe dwellers and the relative luxury the Melancholics knew. But Medoor's feelings for the Queen were of a different kind and intensity. And private, she reminded herself. Very private.

"I don't know why the Queen needs all that coin," Riv Lymeen had said once during a fireside argument with Medoor. "I've been at Queen Fibji's encampment, and even her big audience tent isn't that wonderful. My uncle Jiraz has one almost that big."

The leader had intervened in that argument, too, saving Lymeen from a pounding. "None of your business why she needs it, Lymeen. It's for some great plan of her own, for all us Noor; for us here on Northshore getting coin out of shore-fish pockets and for them on the steppes, fighting off the Jondarites. She's planning for all of us, woman, so we don't question what she needs it for. She needs it, and that's enough."

These reflections fled as the leader raised his signal bells and struck them with a flexible hammer, blindingly fast, the shrill tunes cutting through all the babble of the marketplace. "Assembly," succeeded rapidly by "Stores," "Wagoneers," and then "Return to camp."

Medoor had been on stores detail for one Viranel, with some days of the duty yet to run. She coiled her fishskin whip into its case, slinging it over her shoulder as she looked around for the others. Riv Lymeen, very white teeth in an almost black face and a voice like a whip stroke; Fez Dooraz, plump and wobbly with sad brown eyes; and old white-headed Zyneem Porabji, who could add up in his head faster than the merchants could on their beads. The three of them were already together at the head of Market Street, waiting for her.

"Come on, Babji," Lymeen called, her fuzzy head wagging disapproval and her lips curled to show her fangs. "Step it up, Medoor. All the camp will go hungry waiting on you."

Which was unfair, for Lymeen often scamped her whips late in the afternoon. "Match coin!" Medoor growled at her, pleased to see the other turn away without accepting the challenge. Whatever Riv might say about Medoor being distractible and absentminded, she couldn't say Medoor was lazy—something Riv Lymeen had often heard said of herself. The amount of coin each Melancholic gained was an accurate measure of the amount of effort each Melancholic expended. "Match coin" was a way of ending argument on the matter.

"Leader says to see can we get song-fish," remarked old Porabji. "Fillets or whole. Some to eat tonight and some to dry and smoke for the trip. I'll see to that. You, Babji, go along to the wine merchants. Lymeen, you to Grain Alley, and Dooraz will see to the greens. If there's fresh puncon fruit, call me. They'll want the price of a copper bracelet for it, but maybe I can talk them down. Remember, we're buying for tonight plus two days. We're westering tomorrow. Three or four more towns, Taj Noteen says, and then back to the steppes.

Three or four more towns. Then the long walk northward, through the dry, white-podded pamet fields on the arid heights and the wet grainfields along the little streams, blue with

tasseled bloom. Many days with no markets, no one allowed
to sell them food, and fliers hanging high, black dots on the
pale sky, to see they ate nothing from the fields. Many days
living on what they pulled in the carts. Then the line of
watchtowers, marking the edge of Northshore, and beyond
that the steppes. There would be roasted jarb root. Medoor
would never understand why anyone would dry jarb root
skins and smoke them as the Mendicants did—visions or no
visions—when one could bury them in the coals in their skins
and eat them, sweet and satisfying as nothing else edible
could ever be. And there would be stewed grains from the
traveler fields, small grain patches that were harvested, weeded,
fertilized, and replanted by any Noor who traveled by. Every
Noor carried seed grain in a pouch, and every Noor learned
to control his or her bladder, too, so as not to waste fertilizer
on empty sand.

Medoor longed for the steppes, that great sea of grass
dotted with the gray-green rosettes of jarb plants and interrupted by occasional thorn trees with their tart, crimson fruit.
The rivers of the steppes were full of silvery cheevle—tiny
toothsome fish, perfectly safe to eat—and equally full of
shiggles—plump, ground-running birds that could not be eaten
at all unless one cooked them with grain but when cooked
with grain tasted of heaven. Medoor told herself she would
trade all the wines and sweetmeats of Northshore for the food
of the steppes.

She hurried toward the wine merchants' stalls, as though
by speeding this part of their necessary preparation she could
speed their departure. She was heartily sick of Northshore;
tired of the babble and bellow of its people, the muddy taste
of its food, and the stink of its workers, glad as she had never
been glad before of her dark skin, which prevented the Tears
of Viranel from invading her body, dead or alive. Tears
wouldn't work on black folk. Something about the light not
getting through. It didn't matter why they wouldn't work.
The fact was enough to be thankful for.

"Thanks be to the Jabr dur Noor," she murmured to
herself in the ritual prayer of the Noors. "Thanks be that I

am black." Thus assured of the attention of the All-Seeing, she lifted a merchant's purse as he pressed through the market throng, slipping it into her trouser leg. At the wine merchant's she bargained well. Between what she bought out of the merchant's purse and what she slipped into her wide pockets without paying for, the price would be acceptable, even to Porabji. There was fresh puncon for sale, but Medoor did not bother running to the old man with word of it. When they returned to camp, she simply emptied her capacious trouser legs, placing russet fruit after russet fruit onto the meal wagon tailgate, grinning as she did so until Porabji, who had begun by scowling at her, had to grin in return.

"You'll be caught one of these days, girl," he said, shaking his head. "You'll be caught and brought up before the Tower charged with theft."

"What'll they do, let the fliers eat me?" She grinned. Criminals were dosed with Tears and given to the fliers for food, at least white ones were, or so it was rumored.

Porabji shook his head. "They'll burn you, girl. That's what they do to us Noors. If the fliers can't eat someone, they'll burn him and scatter his ashes on the River."

Medoor sobered somewhat, if only for a time. She had witnessed a burning once. It was not an end that appealed to her. She promised herself for the hundredth time to be more careful. Still, stealing was the one thing she did really well, and it was hard to give up one's only talent. She went toward the campfire in a mood of mixed self-congratulation and caution. One more night among the stinking heathen of this town, then three towns more, then home, to the tents of . . . well. Home. That was enough.

When the Noor had been fed, Medoor was free to amuse herself until roll call. There was never any question where she would go or what she would do with her free time. She had had only one passion since she had first seen the River. Boats. Boats spoke to Medoor. Their planks oozed with mysterious travel, far destinations. Their crews had been all-the-way-around. They had seen everything, been every-where. Sometimes the owners would let her come aboard.

More than once she'd gone aboard at some lecher's invitation and had to show her knife and whip to get off again, but no owner was going to bring the curse of the Melancholics down on himself. He might hint a little, or make an outright proposition, but he wouldn't try rape. At least, Medoor thought with some satisfaction, none had yet. It had been the danger her mother had most feared for a Noor daughter, here among the heathen. Medoor had had to promise utmost prudence before she had obtained permission to join the Melancholics.   ᶜ

For some days now, there had been one particular boat at the Chantry docks that interested Medoor, and it was certain the troubled man who was owner of the *Gift of Potipur* wouldn't bother her. Though he seemed to like to talk to her, he hadn't once looked at her with that particular expression men sometimes got. It was almost as though he didn't know she was a woman at all, and this was part of the fascination. Most boatmen were garrulous sorts, full of tales and exaggerations, but the crew of the *Gift* was of a different kind. Quiet. Almost secretive. Not fearful, she thought, but with a kind of separation about them, as though they knew something the rest of the world didn't. Thrasne himself had a habit of standing on the deck, staring southward over the River at one particular spot, as though there should be something there he could see.

"Thrasne owner," she called, making her way up the plank.

"Medoor Babji," came the call in return. He was below, where she often found him, supervising the repair of the ship's planks stove in by some great floating tree on the wide River. She poked her head down, attracted by the strange smell from below. Most of the crew was there, caulking the new planks with frag sap. The hot pungency of the caulk took her breath away, and she wondered how they could bear to work in the close heat of the hold. She went back to the deck, pausing for a time to admire the great winged figure that poised at the bow of the vessel, a giant flame-bird, perhaps, or a winged angel. Tired of this, she leaned against the rail, watching the water. There, after a time, Thrasne joined her.

"Another day or two," he said, wiping his hands on a scrap of waste. "We'll be done with it."

"How can you breathe down there?"

"Oh, after an hour or two, you get drunk with it. When everyone starts giggling and stumbling, then's time to call a halt for the day. They'll be coming up soon." He nodded at her, a friendly expression. "Medoor Babji," he mused. "What does your name mean? It must mean something."

"It does mean something," she retorted. "As much as yours does."

"Thrasne?" He thought about this for a moment. "It was my grandfather's name. It was the name of the place he came from, inland, where they had a farm. So, what does your name mean?"

"The Noor have a secret language of naming. We usually don't share our secret names with Northshoremen."

"Oh."

He said it flatly, accepting rejection, and she immediately sought to make amends.

"I just meant it wasn't customary. All our names are two words, and the two words put together have another meaning. Like in our home tribe, there's a man named Jikool Pesit. Jikool means 'stones,' and Pesit means 'nighttime,' 'dark.' Stones in the dark are something you fall over, so that name would mean 'Stumbler' in Northshore language."

He turned an interested face, so she went on. "I have a good friend whose name is Temin Suteed. Temin means 'a key,' and Suteed is 'golden'—ah, like sunlight. If you lock up gold with a key, that means 'treasure,' so that's her name. Treasure. . . .

"My grandfather's name was M'noor Jeroomly. M'noor is from the same word as our tribal name. Noor. Noor means 'a speaking people.' And m'noor means 'spoken.' Jeroomly means 'promising,' so the two together mean 'oath,' and that was his name."

"How about Taj Noteen?" asked Thrasne, who had met the troupe leader.

She laughed. "In Northshore he would be called Strutter."
Thrasne shook his head, not understanding.

"It comes from the words for cock and feather, that is,
plume, and the plumed birds always strut, you know."

"But you won't tell me what your name means?"

She flushed. "Perhaps someday." Actually, Medoor Babji
still had her baby name, and it meant something like "dearest
little one." She did not want Thrasne to know that. Yet.

He let it go, staring out across the River, upon his face that
expression of concern and yearning that had so interested
Medoor.

"What's out there?" she asked, taking the plunge. "You're
always looking out there."

"There!" He was startled, stuttered a reply. "Oh, someone—someone from the crew, is all. Someone we had to
leave on an island when we came in for repairs. We're to
pick . . . her up when we're solid again, and it's been longer
than we planned. We thought it would be before festival."

"Oh." She didn't comment further. With some men she
might have teased, but not with Thrasne. Whatever bothered
him, it was no light thing. And whoever he had left behind, it
had been no common crew member. "Well, we may see you
down River, then. Our leader says we'll visit three more
towns before turning north."

"Possibly." He wasn't interested. She could tell. His lack
of interest was irritating enough to gamble on. "Thrasne?"

"Hmm?"

"Who is she, really?"

His silence made her think she had overstepped, but after a
time he turned toward her, not looking at her, heaving one
hip onto the rail so he could sit half facing her.

"Did you ever dream of anyone, Medoor Babji?"

She had climbed onto the rail and teetered there now,
trying to make sense of his question. "Of anyone? I guess
so. Mostly people I know, I suppose."

"Did you ever dream of someone you didn't know? Over
and over again?"

She shook her head. This conversation was not going as

she had thought it might. Nonetheless, it was interesting.
"No, Thrasne owner. I never have."

"I used to. When I was only a boy. A woman. Always the
same woman. I called her Suspirra. A dream woman. The
most beautiful woman in the world. I made a little carving of
her. I still have it." He was silent again, then, and she
thought he had talked all he would. Just as she was about to
get down from the rail and bid him a polite farewell, he
began again.

"When I was near grown, I found a woman's body in the
River. It had been blighted. You know what that is?"

She nodded. She had never seen it, but she had a general
idea.

"It was the woman I'd dreamed of. Line for line. Every
feature. Face. Eyes. Feet. Everything. I brought her out of
the River and kept her, Medoor Babji. Kept her for many
years. And then one day I met the daughter of that woman.
Found her, I guess you'd say. Truly, her daughter. The
daughter she had borne long ago, before she had drowned.
And the daughter was alive and the same, line for line. And
she came onto the *Gift of Potipur*. It was before Conjunction,
winter, when I found her. And that was more than a year,
now."

"And it was that woman you had to leave on the island?"

"That woman, yes."

"Why? Is someone after her?"

He looked her in the eyes for the first time. "Can I trust
you not to go talking about this business, Babji? It could be
my life. And hers."

"Laughers?" She held her breath. This was the stuff of
nightmare and romance. Laughers and dream women.

Seeing his discomfort, she changed the subject. "It's nice
you found your dream woman, Thrasne. Things like that
don't often happen."

"I don't know what's happened," he said in a kind of
quiet sadness. "Her body lives on the *Gift*. But her spirit—it
isn't here yet, Babji. So, I'm patient about it."

He went on then, for some time, talking. He told her

everything he knew of Pamra Don, everything he had ever thought, even some of the things he had hoped, though he did not realize that. Far off along the shore she heard the sound of "Noor count" shrilling over the water.

"I must go, Thrasne owner," she whispered, interrupting him. "My leader will whip me with my own whip if I am not in place very soon." Though he would not if he knew who she was, she thought. Still, it was important he not know.

"Ah," he said, his unfocused gaze coming to rest on her and gradually clearing to reveal the girl perched there before him, dark smooth skin gleaming like the surface of the River. Her hair fell in a heavy fringe all the way to her knees, twisty strands of fifty or so hairs, each of which hung together, never tangling, like lengths of shiny black twine beneath a beaded headband, all gold and blue in the evening light. The scales of her fishskin vest gleamed also, laced tight over the long, full-sleeved shirt she wore tucked into pamet trousers died blue with mulluk shell. Her dark hand rested upon the rail, inches from his own, and he took it, turned it over to examine the pink brown of her palm, scarred and calloused from the whip. Her eyes were dark, and her pink lips parted in complaint.

"Come now, owner. I must go."

"Go, Babji. I didn't mean to keep you. It's just—I had not really seen you until now."

She ran down the plank and along the shore, wondering at the expression on his face. A kindly, surprised alertness, like a child finding something interesting and unexpected. Well. What to make of that. Nothing. Nothing at all.

Still, she was not sorry to hear him calling after her.

"Return again, Babji. Talk has done me good. Perhaps your people would like a ride to the next towns west?"

• 13 •

When the *Gift of Potipur* left the Chantry docks, Babji's troop of Melancholics was aboard, paying nothing for the transport and living on their own provisions. Thrasne had come to trust them, and, wisely, had seen their presence as a kind of camouflage. The *Gift* put on sail and headed out into the River, cutting across the tidal current toward the west end of Strinder's Isle, hidden in the southern mists.

Two days later, decks crowded with the curious Noor, Thrasne lowered a boat with two men to row ashore at the west end of the island, shot them a line, and tied fast to a great tree that leaned above the flood. It was twenty-two days after Conjunction.

Pamra had been camped on the tiny beach for most of that time. She came aboard with Lila, hardly noticing the dark faces of the crowded passengers, not seeing at all the concern on Thrasne's face. Her eyes were deep set in a haggard face, and her hair was tangled as though she had not combed it in days. She was no less beautiful than ever, but it was a terrible, anguished beauty.

"Are you all right?" he begged, appalled. "You look as though you'd been ill."

"I should have seen there were no older males," she told him earnestly. "I should have seen how worn away he was."

"Pamra?"

"I was so sure it was cruel. So sure. Sometimes things are cruel and can be changed. Sometimes we only make them worse. Sentimentalizing. Pretending. So tied up in my own ideas, I couldn't see what was in front of me.''

"Pamra! Who are you talking about?''

She shook her head, handed Lila to him, made her way on board to her old refuge in the owner-house, glancing over her shoulder as she went, scarcely noticing the curious group of Melancholics at the rail, the young girl who was pressing close to her with open curiosity on her face. Passengers. Well, sometimes the Riverboats did carry deck passengers.

She did not really need to look behind her to know that Neff still followed her, as he had since the night after the fires. The smoke had risen in the village, and he had come. Stodder hadn't seen him. Pamra had. He had been with her since, face alight with curiosity and wonder, flowers in his hand, a recusant ghost.

And he was not alone. The pillar of golden dust beside him was her mother. And the accusative formless shadow was Delia. Three.

"Pamra, love. Are you all right?'' Thrasne asked, following her into the house.

She let him hold her, even held him in return, aware at some subconscious level of the need in him, perceiving feeling in him she had never recognized, not even in herself until it was over, depending upon his kindness not to bother her with whatever it was.

"I'll be all right, Thrasne. I'll be all right.'' She stepped away from him, shutting him out. She had to be all right. There was something Neff wanted her to do, something she owed him. Him and her mother, and Delia.

When she was very quiet, she could hear their voices.

• 14 •

The Ascertainers maintained a domiciliary compound with dining hall, exercise yard, and dormitory, some above the ground, some below for winter occupancy. All was gray, splintery, very old. They kept it neat but could not keep it clean. The dust was too ancient, too deep in the cracks. When Ilze was given a broom to sweep it away, he knew he swept only the top layer of something that had been there for longer than he could imagine. Lifetimes. Some of the boards in the walls were newer than others. Some of the beams a lighter color. He saw it being replaced, piece by piece, over the centuries, never changing, always renewed. Why had they needed a place like this that long ago? Why did they need it now?

His Superior was in the compound, as well as some dozens of others, all with the same dazed look of incomprehension that Ilze knew he wore. There was no prohibition against talking together, but they seemed reluctant to do it, as though someone might be listening. As though anything said by anyone might lead to more questions. Even conjecture seemed dangerous. Only with his own Superior did he whisper his questions, await her answers.

"I don't understand," he said, gritting his teeth, trying to reach her with his voice as he had been unable to reach the fliers. "I thought if we got to the Chancery, we were safe! I haven't seen any humans at all except the guards and someone in a veil and some half-wit carrying buckets. Why were

those foul poultry allowed to misuse me so? I don't understand any of this. Help me understand it."

"Shh, shh. Ilze. Be thankful you are alive. I am thankful I
am alive. You were not the only one mistreated, so hush.
Think. You will need to think."

"Think of what? I've done nothing but think since I've
been here, and I've been here forever. I need some answers."

"I meant for you to think strategically. Listen to me. We
came here, to the Chancery. We demanded to see the Protector. Instead, we were sent to the Accusatory and sometime
later were there questioned by the Servants of Abricor. But
there were human Accusers watching, Ilze. Behind the veil
you may be sure was a human Accuser." Her mouth twisted
bitterly at these words, as though she needed to spit. "And
the Servants of Abricor didn't take us away. We stayed
here."

Her hand on his arm stopped his quick, angry words.

"We stayed here, Ilze. And we're alive."

He was forced to consider the implications of this. "You
think . . . you think it was some kind of agreement?"

"I listen in my mind, Ilze, for hints of conspiracy or
ignorance or trouble. What words were said here? I can
imagine what the Talker said, the one who came for us, the
one you forced to bring us here. He demanded that you and I
be bound securely and given to them. And then Lees Obol,
the Protector of Man, would have said, 'No, no, my friends,
my treaty mates, but these are humans. Humans are not sent
to the Talons. Humans must be examined here. By us.' And
then the Talkers would have blustered and demanded. What
would they have said?"

Ilze thought about this, frowning, realizing he knew quite
well what the Talkers would have said. "They would have
said they did not trust the humans. They must question us,
they would have said, because they did not trust the humans.
Perhaps that is not what they said, but that is what they
meant."

"Such was my own thought. A certain lack of trust. So,

the Protector, for some reason—which I will learn if Potipur grants me time—allows us to be questioned by the Talkers. But not taken away. And not seriously injured. I will not even have scars.'' Think about that, she urged him silently, wanting him to realize that both of them had been equally mistreated. Both of us, Ilze. When you leave here, you must remember they tortured both of us.

Ilze, who believed he carried scars he would never lose, did not reply to this. ''And now?''

''And now something else. Some further part of the game. These fliers . . . oh, but they are concerned with Rivermen. Endlessly they asked me about the Rivermen. They asked you as well, I suppose. Always about the Rivermen.'' About which we know nothing, she urged him silently. Nothing at all. Either of us.

''They did. But I know nothing about the Rivermen! I'm not one!''

''But they must find out, Ilze. If they cannot find one who knows, then they must ask those who do not. They must find out.''

He ignored the illogic of this, still trying to comprehend. ''I didn't know the Servants could talk. I didn't know they had . . . had a society of their own.''

She became very dignified, almost prim. ''Just as there are secrets seniors do not share with juniors or novices, so there are secrets Superiors do not share with seniors. You would have learned all about the Talkers in time, if you had earned advancement. As you would have done.'' Oh, yes, she told herself. He would have done. And pity the Tower he would have headed in his time.

''These others, the Talkers . . . ?''

''There are not many of them. They come from the flier caste, from the Servants of Abricor. They do not seem to run in particular lines of descent, so I am told. They are hatched infrequently, once in a thousand hatchings. It is what our scholars call a sex-linked characteristic. All Talkers are males. When the ordinary flier males breed, they die. The Talkers are identified while still young; they are fed a special diet to prevent both breeding and death.''

"A special diet?'' He thought about this before answering. "When we're through with the workers, we drop them in the bone pits and the Servants of Abricor eat them. We all know that. No one cares. What do the Talkers eat?''

"Our flesh is poisonous to the flier people, Ilze. In time you would have studied our history, how we came to this world to find the Servants already here; how they grew monstrously in number until the world could not feed them, until the herds of thrassil and weehar were gone; how they hunted us, only to find us poisonous. You would have read of Thoulia, one of their Talkers. Thoulia the Marvelous. It was Thoulia who showed them how to soften our flesh with the Tears of Viranel, and it was then the wars began in earnest between our two races. We killed them by the hundreds, Ilze, and they killed us, until there were few of them left and not many more of us. Until the treaty was made at last which allowed them to take our dead. . . .

"Our dead are what they eat. Do you see why they fear the Rivermen so?''

He did not see. He could not see because of his anger. He did not realize she had not answered his question.

She went on, voice calm, willing him to listen and understand. "If the cult of the Rivermen were to prevail, the fliers would die. All the Talkers. All the Servants. They would starve. There would be nothing for them to eat.''

Gradually he perceived the implications of this, implications so enormous he could not face them. All the philosophy, the theology, all his studies—oh, one knew there were evasions, one knew there were euphemisms employed, but still. Basically, one believed. Every senior Awakener knew that all the dead go into the worker pits except the Awakeners themselves. Even knowing this, still, still one believed. One understood the need for a pious mythology to keep the ordinary people quiet, but that did not nullify the essential truth. Senior Awakeners knew that truth. They had been accepted as the elect of Potipur. Common people—common people had to be led, instructed, used, then purified through that final agony. It was not Holy Sorters who put the sainted dead in Potipur's arms, it was the Servants of Abricor who carried their souls to Potipur. The common folk could not expect a fleshy resurrection, but that did not affect the spiritual one. But for Awakeners—for Awakeners it was a real immortality. In the body. It was the Servants of Abricor who carried the bodies of dead Awakeners directly to . . .

The thought stopped, blocked, destroyed by what she had been saying. Obviously this was not true. Obviously.

"What happens to us, to the Awakeners?" he snarled at her, his fingers digging deeply into her arm. "If the Servants don't carry our bodies directly to Potipur, what really happens to us?" He hated himself for asking the question, sure she was laughing at him as he had always laughed at Pamra.

"If we are not clever and if our colleagues detest us sufficiently to take vengeance, we go into the pits with common folk," she said haughtily, ignoring his grasp. "With our hair rebraided to make us look like merchants or carpenters. In this way the myth is kept alive that no dead Awakener is ever seen in a worker pit.

"If we are more clever, or less disliked, we are burned to ashes at one of the crematories of the order. There is one here, at Highstone Lees. And if we are very clever, if we do our jobs well and cause no trouble to the Chancery or the Talkers, we are given the Sacred Payment. We are given what the treaty requires we be given, the elixir. If we receive that gift, we live a long, long time. Hundreds and hundreds of years. So be clever, Ilze. Let go of me."

He let go of her, let go of her entirely, left her, did not try to speak with her after that. He had seen angry laughter in her face, bitter amusement. It was not unlike the amusement he had hidden so often from Pamra. The lady Kesseret thought him funny. Because he had believed. He burned with savage, humiliated shame at this. Because he had believed!

*   *   *

When the day came, he went before the Ascertainers, a kind of court with several humans sitting on high chairs to hear what was said. These, he was told, were members of the Court of Appeals of the Towers. Judges, he thought. His Superior, the lady Kesseret, was there. She appeared little worse for her experience, though Ilze knew he looked like shit. Bruised, uncombed. They had not let him put his hair in braids, and it hung about his face like tangled rope. The Talkers were there, both the ones who questioned him and others he had not seen before. Old ones. With silvered feathers.

It was one of these who asked for the Accusation.

"Ilze, senior of the Tower of Baristown, is accused of heresy; of conspiracy to aid and comfort the Rivermen; of sheltering a Riverman spy in the Tower. He is accused of erroneous beliefs. He was led astray by lust. It may be he is essentially orthodox." The humans on the bench accused him. He did not believe it.

He was given no chance to answer these charges. The silver-feathered ones merely nodded as they turned to the human people on the high chairs, and one of these said clearly, not looking at either Ilze or the lady Kesseret as he spoke, "We will allow the Uplifted Ones to be present as Ilze is examined by the Ascertainers."

The Talkers left. Ilze stood in the room alone with Lady Kesseret, he in the cage they had put him in, she behind the railing that separated him from the others.

"Poor Ilze," she said. "If you can withstand it, they will let you atone." There was a strangeness in her voice that he could not identify. Only her words were sympathetic.

She went away then, saying nothing more. In the days of pain that followed, he remembered her words.

They threatened him repeatedly with the Tears of Viranel. He defied them. "Give them to me. I don't care anymore. I might as well be dead." They did things to him, things he had in the past done to others to shame and humiliate them. Ilze, however, felt no shame, only a slow, burning fury. He knew too well their purposes, but he learned his resolution and understanding could be weakened by pain. When they hurt his body, it insisted upon healing itself so they could hurt it again. When he tried to starve himself out of fury at them and to deprive them of their obvious pleasure in his pain, they fed him by force. They would not let him kill himself. And through it all the veiled watcher stood, listening, peering, silent except for the sound of millstones.

And yet, even throughout it all, he knew they were not hurting him as much as they could. It was as though they did not really want to break him. As though they were playing with him. Waiting.

Finally he demanded they give him the Tears of Viranel in order to prove he was telling the truth.

The Talker was amused.

"Accused, if these Ascertainers gave you the Tears, all you would tell them would be the truth. Then we would eat you. A temporary pleasure which would not advance our cause."

"Oh, by the lost love of Potipur, isn't the truth what you want! Isn't that what you've been putting me through this pain for, to get the truth!"

"Oh, no, accused. If we wanted only the truth, we would have given you the Tears long since."

The winter wore on. He was moved to a cell below. Gradually, through the pain and his own anger, he realized what they wanted. Something to confirm their suspicion. Something to save them embarrassment before the Chancery officials. Something to justify their opinions. Not merely whatever it was Ilze did or did not know, but something more. Not the truth that he had, but some future verity, something they could build upon to make themselves secure. It came to him slowly, through the agony of their knives and pinchers. It came to him slowly, and clever as he was in the ways of submission, he did not realize they had led him there.

"If you will let me find Pamra," he said at last, believing

he had thought of it himself, "I will find what it is you need to know. Just let me find her."

"Well," mused the Ascertainer who twisted the iron, "it would serve her right. To have repaid your concern in this fashion was an abomination. To have treated you so when you had been so kind to her. This accusation came about through her, Ilze. Your pain is due to her, Ilze. If it weren't for Pamra . . ." Against the wall the veiled watcher made the sound of grinding.

"Let me find her," he begged.

After that there was a long quiet time when the pain passed and was more or less forgotten. "Your heresy came about through her," they told him, both the human Ascertainers and the Talkers who watched. "We're sorry for your suffering, but it was all her doing." It was a revelation that he knew to be absolutely true. He had almost compromised his own future. Because of her. Because of Pamra. If they had not been so understanding, he would have been condemned, because of Pamra.

"Are you feeling well, Ilze?" It was the lady Kesseret once more, rather gaunt and wan looking, as though she had been many nights without sleep. She wore a robe he had never seen before, one that covered her hands and feet. When she moved, she winced. "Are you recovered?"

"Quite recovered, thank you." It was early spring. He had recovered. Obviously, the lady Kesseret had not.

"The Ascertainers met this morning. I was in attendance. They have ascertained that you were not entirely guiltless, but misled. Tricked. You have been offered an opportunity to atone through special duty. As a Laugher, I understand, for Gendra Mitiar, Dame Marshal of the Towers."

"I know," he said, his anger hot at her tone. It would be more than atonement.

"I am told they plan a reward for you when your mission is done. A Tower of your own. An initial offer of the Payment." Her voice was without emotion or encouragement, uninvolved in this, as though it had happened quite separate from her life and without any connection to it.

He bowed, silent. Hatred moved him, not ambition. When he felt his wounds, hatred moved him.

"The Payment comes from the Talkers, and they must approve its recipients. That they have done so speaks well of your future expectations, Ilze."

Hot curiosity still burned in him. "Tell me again about the Talkers. Who are they?"

"They are the leaders of those who lived here before we came."

"What was it they ate before we came?"

"Beasts, so they say. I've told you."

"Tell me again."

"They ate hoovar and thrassil and weehar, animals with hot juicy bodies. They ate them all. All but a very few who survived here behind the Teeth of the North. The Protector has small herds of thrassil and weehar here in the Chancery lands. A few hundred animals. The hoovar are extinct." She rose, moved about the room, stiffly, uncomfortably. Again, Ilze wondered what they had done to her. "When all the beasts were gone, they had no choice but to eat us—us or fish."

"Why not fish, then?"

"Because, so they say, fish eaters lose the power of flight and thereby blaspheme the will of Potipur, who made them fliers. Some essential ingredient is missing in fish. Eating fish changes them in other ways, too—makes their females more intelligent, for example. The female fliers are as you have seen them. Dirty, quarrelsome. I am told they, too, can talk but do so very little. Eating fish makes them less aggressive, as well. There is a tribe of fish eaters somewhere, so they say, a tribe called the Treeci. In their language, 'treeci' means 'offal.' Talkers speak of fish eaters as we do of heretics." She winced, sat down, cradled her hands as though they pained her.

"No, given a choice of eating fish or dying, they might

well eat fish. However, they prefer to eat us. And the Talkers eat us alive, Ilze. Not dead. There are not many Talkers. Two or three living humans taken from each town each month are enough to feed them. You will learn how to do it when you are Superior of a Tower. It will be your task to *recruit* citizens for this purpose. The Talkers do not eat the dead. The fliers would not eat the dead if they had anything else to eat.''

"So they might feast on me, or on you!"

"The Servants have nothing else to eat," she said simply, as though his statement were irrelevant. "They are the Servants of Abricor. We worship Abricor. We worship Potipur, and Potipur promised them plenty." These are truths, her voice said. Truths beyond question. "Do you think you will be able to find her? Pamra?"

Was this another test? He stared through her, not seeing her. Who was she, really? Another like himself or one of them? A betrayer? Or a betrayed? Had she, too, really been tortured? If she had, he knew with sudden certainty, they would have told her the suffering was Ilze's fault, and she would have had no choice but to use him as he would use Pamra in turn. What was she up to now? "I will find her," he said.

"Find her. That's good. Bring her back to the Tower."

"I will give her Tears."

"No, Ilze. You will not. That is an order. Not at first. She can only tell us the truth if you give her Tears. We must have more than truth. The Talkers need more than that."

He knew that already. The Talkers needed far more than truth. He had learned there were occasions the truth did not serve, when only the presumptive lie would serve at all. He had not yet learned what they needed to know, but he would. He was resolved upon that.

They set him down in the glowing springtime upon the Rivershore far west of Baris. His scalp had been shaved clean and covered with a curious dark helmet, close as a second skull. None of the scars they had put upon him showed. He turned his face to the west and began the hunt. Pamra. Rivermen. Along the river in both directions others like him moved; others with similar scars. Everyone called them Laughers because of their scornful cries, ha-ha, ha-ha. Even the Rivermen they sought called them that. And they never really laughed.

• 15 •

On an evening not long after the *Gift* had been repaired, Pamra stood on the quiet deck watching Thrasne lay out the boom lines while the ship rocked gently along a pier at Sabin-bar. The Melancholics had gone ashore, even Medoor Babji, who these days seemed reluctant to leave the *Gift*. The sun lay low along the River, making a dazzle that beat against their eyes. Neff stood in the dazzle, and her mother stood there as well, bathing in that effulgence as though to draw nourishment from it. Delia was lost in it, a black shadow obscured by brilliance, so that she, Pamra, could not distinguish one from the other but merely stood at the edge of a glowingly inhabited cloud. All was very still. Sometimes at this hour an expectant hush would fall upon the Riverside, upon the waters themselves, calming and stilling them, making the song-fish hum in voices one could scarcely hear, so soft they were. So it was tonight.

And so it was that Ilze appeared at the edge of her vision like a striding monster, all in black, the black soaking up the glow as though to empty it, to absorb it all, and it flowing toward him as water flows toward a drain, whirling down into blackness.

"Ilze!" she breathed, quiet, her stomach telling her the truth of this more than her eyes. There was a striding figure there on the River path, but she did not truly perceive it. Her belly saw it before her brain knew who it was. Then it shivered her, all at once, like a tree cut but not yet fallen, and she collapsed across the rail. "Ilze," she breathed in a tone of mixed relief and horror. "He is a Laugher. Come for me." It was relief he had not seen her yet, horror to know he was seeking her, a verification of everything she had known all along. He bore a flask at his waist, and she knew what it contained. Tears, and a little water to keep them fresh. They would last like that for years, remaining potent to the end, her destiny there swinging at his hip, a threat more monstrous in that she had almost escaped it.

"Lie down," Thrasne whispered to her, pushing her below the line of the rail. She seemed hypnotized by that distant figure, leaning out across the rail as though asking to be noticed. He thrust her down into the piled nets with one hand, then set his foot upon her, holding her there as he tied off the lines to the boom, his stance betraying nothing except attention to the task at hand.

Across the stretch of water the striding figure stopped as though it had heard its name. Sound carried over the River. Perhaps her voice had been loud enough for the Laugher to hear, for he stared out over the long pier to the place the *Gift* rocked slowly on the tide, holding his right hand to shield his eyes from the brilliant glow in which the *Gift* was bathed. Thrasne watched him covertly, memorizing the face, the form, the strange helmet he wore. Thrasne had seen such helmets before. This hunter was not a new thing but an old one, at least as old as Blint's youth, for Blint had told him of these men—always men, the Laughers. Beneath the contorted helmet the face was narrow, full of an unconscious ferocity, a violence barely withheld. It was a cruel face in repose, one that could lighten into sudden, dangerous charm when it was expedient to do so. Thrasne looked at his own hands, square upon the ropes, thinking of men he had known with faces like that. Often they died of violence. One time his own hands had pushed the knife home. Sometimes the knives were held by women. Such men were always feared. And hated. Had they not been Laughers, still they would have been hated.

When he looked up again, the Laugher was gone, perhaps into the town.

"You can get up now," he told her. "The hunter has gone."

"It was Ilze. Come after me."

Thrasne decided upon calm acceptance of this. There would be no point in lies between them. "Pamra, you knew that someone would come after you. It is time to talk of that now. Make plans. Decide how we will avoid them."

The moment stretched between them. For a moment he thought she would answer him, for she was looking at him as though she actually saw him. Ilze had made her aware of her surroundings, of him no less than of all other things. He waited, breathless, hoping she would speak.

She, however, turned toward the sun glow again. From that glow came a voice, Neff's voice, speaking for her ears only, soft as the feathers of his breast had been. "Cruel, Pamra. Cruel to so raise up the dead, who should lie at peace."

"Remember," instructed her mother, also silently. "Remember."

And from the wrapped darkness that was Delia came a sigh.

"Cruel," Pamra said. "Cruel!" A flame-bird called as though in answer to this.

"Yes," said Thrasne, thinking she meant the man she had just seen. "Very cruel. But we can deal with that."

"It has to be stopped."

He nodded. He had already decided to stop Ilze himself, in the only way possible, but Pamra took his agreement for more than he had intended. Her eyes clouded with mystery once more; her spirit disappeared along some road he could not follow.

"We must go to the Protector of Man. He must be told. He must be told to stop it."

Her face was utterly calm. Behind her in the golden light Neff's voice seemed to breathe an assent.

And her mother's voice. "Remember!"

And for the first and only time, Delia's voice, breathing from the effulgent silence. "It is better when all the people know, Pamra. It is better not to be alone."

Pamra turned to Thrasne, smiling. He had not seen her like this before, though the novices of Baris Tower would have recognized her radiant face, her eyes lighted as though from within by rapture. Her arms went out, out, as though she would encompass the world. "We will go, yes," she breathed to him. "But we must take the people with us, all of them; to the Protector of Man."

And he, lost in her eyes from which the dark shadows had suddenly gone, stared at her in terror, seeing her flee away from him down a long corridor toward a blinding glow into which he could not see and would not dare to go.

From the shore, Medoor Babji saw them there, saw their faces, both, seemed to see an effulgency of wings hovering at Pamra's side, put her hands to her eyes and drew them away again to see only the sun glow and two people silhouetted against it.

Soon the Melancholics would be leaving the *Gift* to begin the trip to the steppes. It had been disturbing to travel aboard the *Gift*, disturbing and strange. Now she found herself glad that they would be leaving in a short time. She could not bear the expression on Thrasne's face.

· 16 ·

The lady Kesseret, Superior of the Baris Tower, former prisoner in the Accusatory of Highland Lees, now convalescent, her injuries received under the question slowly healing, leaned in the window of the library wing looking out upon an evening of early summer. Beneath the window on a narrow ledge was a flame-bird's nest, a tidily woven basket of straw and wild-pamet fiber, holding three spherical golden eggs. An additional pile of pamet fiber lay to one side, weighted down by several small stones. In a flash of orange and gold, the flame-bird itself came swooping down the wall to perch on the ledge and move restively between this pile of tinder and the nest, fluttering its wings as though in indecision whether to stay or go.

The window was in the lady's bedroom, hers at least by guest right. She had occupied this room since the laggard sun had broken winter's hold upon Highland Lees and let them all come up from the caverns. Cozy though the caverns had been, she preferred this room, windowed to the air. Through the open door she could hear Tharius Don's flat-harp virtuoso, Martien, as he flicked his hammers over throbbing strings. Behind her on the porcelain stove a kettle sang an antiphon to itself. She was warm, well wrapped in a thick robe and in Tharius Don's arms, for the moment forgetful of her pain.

"You comfort me," she said drowsily. "I am wondering why."

"Because we remember really comforting each other," he said. "When it was more than this." For a moment there was something virile and intemperate in his voice, as though for that instant his passion had been more than merely memory. His arms tightened about her, strong arms still, capable of stirring her own recollection so that her mind lusted briefly over old visions while her body lay aside, like some discarded garment.

"It isn't fair," she complained. "Why can we still feel pain so very well when all the other feelings are gone?"

"All the other feelings aren't gone," he said patiently, knowing she knew, knowing she needed to hear him say it. "Only lust. And lust is gone because the Payment is a Talker gift." He did not need to explain that. They both understood it. The Talkers died if they bred. Therefore they did not breed or value breeding. They did not lust. They had no experience of passion. Though they perceived it intellectually, their bodies rejected it, and the elixir made of their blood rejected it as well. "We could have refused the elixir, Kessie."

Refused it. She thought of having refused it, of having grown old with Tharius Don. There were old lovers in Baristown whom she had watched over the years. She had seen them, too, aged past passion, walking hand in hand in the market square. She imagined them snuggled side by side in their beds, complaining to one another like old barnyard fowl, full of clucks and chirrs, grinding the day's events in their leathery gizzards to make each one reasonable and useful to them. "My, my," they would say. "Did you see? Did you ever? What's the world coming to?"

How was it different for them, those old people? Remembering the loves and lusts of youth? Little different, perhaps, except that their twilight was brief, the memories strong enough to last that little time between age and the end, their flavor and fragrance scarcely dimmed by the years, death coming at last while the perfume lingered, making their old lives redolent of youth. They breathed the scents of childhood, a potpourri of their green years.

But for Kesseret? And Tharius? What remained?

"Dust," she whimpered. "All our love, dust."

"Not while I hold you," he told her urgently. "Not while I grieve for your pain."

The memory of pain made her fleetingly angry. "Pain and anger," she said. "Those we keep."

"And curiosity. And laughter. And determination. So you see, it isn't all hopeless."

"It seems so sometimes," she said, remembering the pincers at her fingers, the wedges driven beneath her toenails. "Ah, gods, Tharius, but it seems so."

He buried his face in her hair so she would not see his tears, thinking to himself. "Pity. We haven't lost pity. Which is why we go on plotting, always plotting. Oh, gods, when will the plots be thick enough to clot into action!"

She moved in his arms, as though aware of her pain. "You shouldn't be here," she said.

"Because of Martien? He wouldn't say a word to anyone."

"No, not because of your musician friend, love. Because you shouldn't be here. You shouldn't be showing any interest in me at all. Someone may be watching the corridor to this suite, to see if you come and go—or come and stay."

"You are thinking in township terms, Kessie. Those of us here at the Chancery no longer have the habit of thinking in terms of sexual misconduct. We are beyond scandal."

She hid her face in his shoulder, very white at his words. "I know. Stupid of me."

"Yes, my dear. Stupid of you."

"Do you ever . . . are you ever sorry?"

"Sorry to have outlived my passions? Yes. Sorry to have time, still, to do what we are trying to do? No."

She shuddered, trembling at his words, fearful of what they were trying to do. In the past, the cause had seemed the only righteous way to live, and it had not brought her pain. Now it had brought her more than she was ready to bear. "Still, love, they may wonder at your interest in me. What am I, after all? Superior of a Tower. There are thousands of those."

"I made my interest very clear," he said, folding her more closely in the robe. "I said before the questioning started that it was shameful treatment of a loyal member of the service. I've said it in the interim, several times, and I've capped it by demanding they recognize your courage by providing you with care and attention until you can be restored to duty."

"Which I could have been yesterday, or last week."

"Not true, Kessie. You may have come here the direct route, by flying. The road back is not so easy."

"Easy! By the true God, Tharius, I hope you didn't think that was easy!"

"You lived through it," he said, caressing her. "That's the important thing. You lived."

"I lived because I dragged the most ambitious and viciously self-serving Awakener in my Tower into my problem and linked his future to mine. He's one I should have rid the Tower of early on. I didn't. I saved him, for just such a need. As a stratagem it worked, but I'm not proud of it, Tharius." She trembled again, and the slow tears gathered at the curve of her eyes. She blinked, driving them back, willing that he would not see her so weakened. "Now he is loose out there, a Laugher. And I am among those who sent him."

"You lived," he said again. "That's all that matters."

She had begun to feel real pain again, but it was too soon to take more of the waters of surcease that Tharius had provided. "Tell me," she whispered in an attempt to distract herself from her pain. "Tell me how far we have come?"

He looked around carefully, being sure they were not watched or overheard, a movement made habitual through a hundred years of conspiratorial conversations. "The cause has members in over five thousand Towers," he murmured at last, like a litany, well learned, often rehearsed. "One-fifth of all Towers. Over half of them include the Superiors of those Towers. We have strong lay groups in ninety percent of all the towns. Over half the signal routes are ours, at least on some shifts. I am now informed within a day or two of things happening anywhere on Northshore."

She concentrated, remembering conversations held long

ago. "The cause is about where we planned it would be, then. Somehow I had thought it lagged."

"No. It has not lagged. The suspicions of Mitiar and Bossit were planned for. The only thing we had not foreseen was this untimely suspicion on the part of the fliers. Now there must be some kind of diversion, something to draw them away. At the moment, they are too much focused upon the Chancery."

"What are you planning?"

"I've sent an actor friend to the tents of the Noor, to visit Queen Fibji."

"Oh, Tharius, haven't those poor devils suffered enough?" Her own pain was forgotten for the moment in the pain she felt for the Noor, constant victims of the Jondarites. "Can't we leave them out of it?"

He shook his head sadly. "It will mean nothing worse for them than they already suffer, Kessie. I've sent someone to talk of Southshore, that's all. I've had him say nothing which wasn't in the palace library. There's every possibility Southshore really exists, just as I've had it described to her. If I know Queen Fibji, she'll send an expedition within the year. General Jondrigar would try to stop them, of course, if he heard of it. He would not let all those possible slaves go. He enjoys his expeditions among the Noor too much to let them escape. We must make sure he does not hear of it. The fliers will be much confused if *they* hear of it. So, we must make sure they do."

"And it will turn eyes away from us. When do you think, Tharius? Soon?"

"I think soon. If nothing else happens to upset our plans. If no other junior Awakener goes off with a pitful of workers. If no eager Riverman starts the uprising ahead of time. If there is no spontaneous religious uprising of one kind or another." He brooded over this while Kessie moved restlessly in his arms.

So much to keep track of; so much to control.

Many years ago there had been two factions within their movement. One for immediate war; one for the hope of peace.

The war faction had plotted to kill the fliers, all of them. They had planned to pick a time when the Talkers would be out of the Talons and simply murder them all.

Tharius had been a leader of the peace party. He recalled impassioned speeches he had made, phrases he had used. "We would be forever guilty of the murder of an intelligent species." He believed it. Much though he detested the fliers, including the Talkers, still he believed it. Moral men did not do such things. Not to another species with intelligence, with speech, with a culture of its own.

Some years of covert exploration into the actual attitudes of Talkers had followed. He laughed bitterly sometimes when he recalled that time. His thesis had been so simple. What the fliers were doing was immoral, unethical. They were eating intelligent beings. They were raising the dead, who were possibly aware of that fact. If they ate fish, they could continue to live, but in a moral way. Wouldn't that be preferable? Wouldn't it be a better arrangement? He had asked this of Talker after Talker during convocations. "Wouldn't it be better?"

To which they had cawed hideous laughter or turned to deposit blobs of shit at his toes, showing what they thought of the idea. Eventually he had been forced to understand. Morality was not an absolute. Theirs was not his. His was not shared even by all humans, much less by this nonhuman species.

He had quit trying to sell the idea after a time. He had been warned it wouldn't work, and it was becoming difficult to disguise his stubborn efforts as anything but what they were. He had called it research, but research was not Tharius's affair, after all. Council member Koma Nepor was Chief of Research. Questioning the fliers was not Tharius's responsibility, either. Ezasper Jorn was Ambassador to the Thraish. When it became evident Tharius's efforts were drawing unpleasant attention from both the Talons and the Chancery, what had been confidential attempts at negotiation became deeply covert. There were to be no more attempts at persuasive conversion of fliers.

Which left, he was convinced at last, only conversion by necessity. If there were no bodies to eat, then the fliers would eat fish or nothing.

And in that belief, the cause had been born. From that statement all else had followed. Agents moving among the towns, increasing the fisheries against the day when fliers would need fish to eat. Superiors of Towers sending worker crews to build more jetties. Rivermen holding themselves ready for the day when every worker pit would be emptied in the deep of the night. Even now agents moved across Northshore seeking patches of Tears to spray with fungicide, reducing the number of locations where they were found. When the day came, there would be no human bodies available, at least none treated with Tears. And when the morning of the revolution came, fliers would eat fish or die.

His arms tightened around his burden once more. The fliers would eat fish or die. And the humans in the Chancery? Those in the Towers? Well, they would eat fish or whatever else they liked, but in a little time they would die as well. When the cause struck, there would be no more elixir to keep their superannuated bodies alive. On some days, Tharius actually looked forward to that time. It was not so much that he tired of life as that he tired of the lives of others. His mouth quirked, thinking of this. Oh, to see the end of Gendra Mitiar!

"Why are you smiling?" asked the lady Kesseret, amused at his expression despite herself.

"Because what we are doing is right," he said. "Because it is right."

The flame-bird left its nest to swing out across the courtyard, the vivid circle of its flight seeming to linger on the air. Then it returned to the ledge and began to dance, wings out, legs lifted alternately as it hopped to and fro on the narrow stone, bowing, stretching, stopping occasionally to shift the little stones, sharp-edged with red in the ruddy evening light, as though bloodstained.

"Do you think it will light the nest soon?" She could ask this without crying, distracting herself.

"Probably."

"I always feel so sorry for them."

"Shh. Kessie. Don't waste your time feeling sorry for them. If you must feel sorry, feel sorry for yourself, or for me, come to that."

The flame-bird danced gravely to a music and song it alone could hear, forward on one leg, then back, on the other leg forward, then back, bowing with wings wide, pointing its beak upward as though invoking some far-off presence. In the adjoining room, Martien seemed to sense the rhythm of its lonely ballet, for the music began to accompany the performance.

"I wonder what the bird thinks."

"I'm afraid we'll never know."

Whirling rapidly, the feathered dancer picked up a stone and held it firmly in its beak to strike it against the ledge with a tiny battering sound. Sparks flew, dwindled, died. It struck again, and again.

"Oh, Tharius. Can't you stop it?"

"I could. But then the young ones wouldn't hatch, Kessie. The eggs won't break without it."

"I know." She turned her face into the hollow of his throat, not wanting to see.

A spark caught the tinder. The flame-bird picked up a beakful of burning tinder and laid it upon the nest, fanning it with her wings. Smoke rose in a white coil. The sticks and straw of the nest began to burn with tiny, almost invisible flames.

"Did it catch?" A muffled question from her hidden mouth.

"Yes. It caught."

The flame-bird began to roll one of the golden eggs about on the burning nest, charring the surface of the shell, seeming not to notice its own feathers were on fire, the flesh of its legs crisping, its bill beginning to blister.

The first egg cracked wide in the heat, the tiny nestling within it pushing out a questing beak, then thrusting the shell fragment aside with strong, infant wings as it flew upward in a wild flutter of damp feathers amid the smoke. The mother turned to the second egg, then the third. Only when this last nestling flew did the flame-bird raise itself into the air, singing, alive amidst its flaming plumage, spiraling as though in a frantic attempt to escape its own immolation.

"Oh," cried Kessie. "I hate hearing them sing like that."

"Shh. They say it sings in ecstasy, Kessie."

Above them in the sky, the singing faded into a whisper of sound, the wings stopped beating. A black speck planed away, trailing a line of misty smoke beyond the walls of the palace.

"I don't believe that," she wept, raising her stained face to look at the fading trail of smoke. "I think it sings in agony. It would scream if it could." She trembled, suddenly aware of her own pain, wanting not to think of that, wanting to forget, to think of anything else instead.

"Pamra used to use the flame-bird as a parable in recruitment homilies," she chattered, letting the first thing that came to mind flow from her mouth like water. "She tried to liken the Awakeners to the mother flame-bird, sacrificing itself for its children. It wasn't a successful parable at all. Too painful. The last year or so she'd been using one about the Candy Tree which worked better. She was a marvelous recruiter."

His mouth turned down, reminded now of the cause of all their recent pain. "Where is she, do you think?"

"Oh, Tharius, I hope she got away. I hope she's safe somewhere, if anywhere can be called safe. Perhaps there was enough time before Ilze got onto her trail for her to find safety."

"Or the River."

"I think not, somehow. There was a toughness about her. A kind of impenetrable naiveté, but tough, nonetheless."

"The last of the Dons," said Tharius. "My great-great-grandchild. I had such hopes for her, somehow. I thought she might be another you, another Kesseret. . . ."

"I know. I know you wondered about her, cared for her. That's why I kept close track of her. Though not close enough, it seems. She came very close to ruining everything."

"How could you keep track of her at all without attracting notice? Superiors don't normally interest themselves in novices or junior Awakeners. Not as I remember."

"Oh, my dear. You of all people to ask such a question, when you taught me every subterfuge I know. I kept track of her through my servant, Threnot. Threnot always goes veiled, and she goes everywhere. And sometimes it was Threnot herself, and sometimes it was me, listening to a recruitment parable or watching someone at the worker pits. I spent a lot of time watching Pamra."

He shook his head, drawing her closer. "Risky, love. But kind of you in this case. Great-great-granddaughter Pamra. Well. I hate her causing you this agony, but it wasn't the child's fault. Perhaps we can locate her, provide some kind of assistance. It would be sensible to do that. I don't want the Laugher to get her. I don't want the fliers to get her. Not alone that she's kin; more important, it would set them off again. When I heard it was she who had started all this, I thought how ironic it was—my own great-great-grandchild, without knowing it, coming close to betraying us. I'd like to help her, since she's the last. Not that the intervening generations were much to brag about."

She ticked them off on her bandaged fingers. "Your son, Birald. Your granddaughter, Nathile—bit of a fishwife, that one, so I've heard. Pamra talked to Jelane about her unpleasant grandma. And then your great-grandson, Fulder Don. . . ."

"Useless. Like a piece of fungus. All sweaty and damp. Not much of an artist, either, I'm afraid."

"And finally your great-great-granddaughter, Pamra Don. Something about that one, Tharius, love. Something more to her than to the others. A kind of shining, sometimes."

"Awakener, heretic, and now fugitive," he said bleakly. "The best of the lot, and what an end to come to."

She squeezed his hand. "Old Birald wasn't that bad, actually."

"You knew him?" He was astonished at this.

"I knew everyone in Baristown. I knew Birald before I came to the Tower. I was twenty then. He was a couple of

years younger than I, a stiff, fussy youth, always looking
over his shoulder. He ended as a crotchety old man who
carved leaves and flowers on door lintels, holding on to the
artist's caste by his fingernails. Oh, God, Tharius, but speaking of fingernails, my hands hurt. . . .''

He reached for the carafe on the table and poured a glass
of its waters for her. "Kessie. Oh, Kessie, you did get the
drugs I sent? You did get them in time.''

"You know I did.'' She drank what he had given her,
thankfully. "I've told you over and over. It was all that kept
me going. Knowing I wouldn't actually feel the pain, not in
my body, at least. Knowing you were here, doing whatever
you could to get me out of that . . . that nightmare.''

"I couldn't do anything! I saw Shavian Bossit throwing
suspicious glances my way when Gendra spoke of putting
you and the Awakener to the question. He knows I came
from Baristown, and he knows I've spoken out against this
inquisition atmosphere the fliers want to force us into. Trust
Shavian to put egg and fire together and hatch a plot.''

"You think he suspects?''

"Suspects? Of course he suspects. Everyone! Of everything! Suspicion is his standard mode of operation. He maintains the household by suspicion.'' Tharius gritted his teeth.

"I mean, do you think he suspects us? Do you think he is
convinced there really is . . . a heresy? From his point of
view, I suppose that's what it would be.''

"No. Not yet. The thing that's occupying his mind just
now is another matter. There's supposed to have been a
miracle in Thou-ne. Some idiot fished an image out of the
World River, and the people demanded it be taken into the
Temple. They're almost worshiping it, calling it the 'Bearer
of Truth.' It shines, so they say. There are people traveling
from six towns east just to visit the Temple, even though they
know they can't come home again.''

"The Bearer of Truth?'' Kesseret frowned. "An image? I
hadn't heard about that. Do you think it's connected in any
way?''

"Shavian may. He has a habit of connecting everything.

And it may be more than habit. During the last convocation, he spent an unwarranted amount of time with the Talkers. It was almost as though he were trying to usurp Ezasper Jorn's prerogative as Ambassador. He's ambitious, is Bossit.''

There was a sound from the next room, a hesitation in the music, then the dissonant fall of a hammer. In the silence they could hear a monotonous thrumming. Martien thrust one hand into the room, knocking on the open door.

"Tharius. Someone's coming down the private corridor. It sounds like the old weehar. Mitiar.''

"Damn,'' Tharius said, unwinding himself from the lady Kesseret. "That's Gendra's majordomo with that damn drone. Quick, Kessie. Get yourself into bed.''

"I really should sit up—''

"Quickly. Don't argue. Back to your hammers, Martien.'' Quickly he closed the window, pulled the chair into the center of the room, and seated himself in it, reaching a long arm toward the bookshelves. "Something dull, Kessie? An eschatological essay, perhaps?'' He leafed through the volume and began to read, his voice dry and instructional.

The thrumming came closer, a low moaning, "Whoom, whoom.'' The sound ceased outside the door to the suite. In the outer room Martien's music was interrupted once again, this time by a crash as the door opened and a loud voice cried, "Dame Marshal of the Towers, Gendra Mitiar.''

"She didn't even knock,'' Kesseret hissed between her teeth. "Your private corridor, and she didn't knock!''

"Shh, Kessie. Remember who she is.'' He smiled quickly as he leaned back in his chair and called through the open door, "Ah, Gendra! I see you do not need to be invited to come in. Have you come to tender apologies to the lady Kesseret?''

There was a bark of humorless laughter from the outer room. "I'm sure all my subordinates understand necessity.'' She came into the doorway, showing a voracious arc of yellow teeth. "We must all make sacrifices. And it is not necessary to apologize for necessity. Isn't that so, lady?''

"I'm sure it is, Your Reverence.'' Kessie lay pale upon

the pillows, not needing to play a part. At the sound of Mitiar's voice her hands and feet burned agonizingly, and she found herself remembering the flame-bird as unexpected tears flowed unheeded down her face, sudden and unstoppable as the spring spate.

"Gendra, if you will?" Tharius was on his feet, escorting the woman out, pulling the door almost shut behind them. Kesseret heard him in the outer room. "Have you no sensitivity at all? By Potipur's teeth, woman. At least let her recover!"

"I was told she was little injured," the Dame Marshal snarled, aggrieved. "The Ascertainers said she seemed to feel little pain. Had it not been for the infections, she would have been long since healed."

"Let them do to your hands and feet what they did to hers, Gendra, then tell me if you consider yourself little injured. Let your hands and feet swell to twice their size in the winter caverns, let you burn with fever! Would you have been happier if your blasted Ascertainers had broken her? Made her whimper for mercy? Made her confess to something she hadn't done in front of a roomful of fliers? Would that have satisfied you, made you sympathetic?"

"Why should I be sympathetic? It was she who housed the conspirator."

"Oh, pfah, Gendra. Conspirator! Don't talk nonsense. Only the Talkers profess to believe that, and even they doubt it. You owe the lady Kesseret your thanks. Don't you understand she protected us all by her demeanor? If it weren't for the lady Kesseret's courage, the entire Chancery might be under siege by some thousands of paranoid Talkers. By all three gods and their perverted offspring, Dame Marshal, but you've more gall than good sense." He heard himself raging and didn't care. Let her make what she would of it.

Stiffly, she answered. "I would not have come if I had thought she would not welcome—"

"She may understand the necessity of what you did to her, but for the love of Potipur, don't expect her to welcome your visits now."

This was a word too much. Gendra snarled, "She'd better welcome them if she intends to go back to the Baris Tower as Superior under my orders."

He did not relent. "Of course she goes back to the Baris Tower. And you'll let her alone until then and not harass her after she's returned. I swear to you, Gendra, you've laid an obligation for vengeance on me already. Don't make it worse."

"Why you, Tharius? Hnnn? What is she to you?" It was both a sneer and a threat.

"An old friend and my cousin—oh, yes, Gendra, my cousin. Though we must perforce set aside family relationships when we receive the Payment, those of us who have family members also receiving the Payment are blessed with kin who remember us as we were. My cousin, I say it again. Also a loyal member of the service. That's what she is to me and should have been to you, if you'd forget your damned Tower discipline for a moment and think of people. . . ."

Their voices dwindled away down the corridor. Into the silence behind them the sound of the flat-harp flowed; water music, a few tones repeated over and over in differing orders. Rippling. Lulling. Martien was covering the anger with calm, washing the pain away.

Tharius shouldn't have spoken so. He shouldn't have angered Gendra. He shouldn't ever do anything to make her angrier or more suspicious. And yet Kesseret warmed at his words, at his defense of her. For a little time she forgot the conspiracy to which her life had been given and let the waters of surcease wash around her.

After a time, the lady slept.

S ix stone courtyards separated the library wing from
the Bureau of the Towers, each succeeding each through
long, echoing corridors lit by occasional oculars that
spilt dim puddles of watery light onto the ·clattering stone.
Jorum Byne, majordomo to the Dame Marshal, led the procession, the long neck of the single-stringed viol held against
one shoulder as he plied the bow with his right hand, *whoom,
whoom, whoom.* Two functionaries followed after, laden with
documents and dispatch boxes. Then came Gendra herself,
her teeth grinding endlessly in time with the viol, and last her
personal servant, Jhilt, in a shankle, shankle of chains and
rustle of stiff fabrics. Jhilt was a Noor slave from the lands
north of Vobil-dil-go. There was no reason for her to wear
chains. Though her personal duties in providing various kinds
of pleasure for the Dame Marshal were not pleasant for
her—were, indeed, often quite painful—escape from behind
the Teeth was impossible. Still, she wore chains. Gendra
Mitiar liked the sound of them, finding them even more
pleasing in that there was no reason for them at all.

Except for the palace itself, the Bureau of the Towers
loomed higher than any building in the Chancery, its vast
hexagonal bulk heaving skyward in stark, unornamented walls
of black brick, windowless as cliffs. Behind those walls in
serried ranks were four divisions, each with six departments;
each department with ten sections, each section with a Super-

visor; each Supervisor responsible for ten Towers and thus ten townships. Each Supervisor had a deputy and an assistant. Each of these had a clerk, perhaps more than one. Some Towers, after all, were much larger than others, and the supervision of them was therefore more complex.

Deep in the bowels of the bureau lay the labyrinthine vaults of Central Files, their complexities guarded and their secrets plumbed only through the let and allowance of the Librarian, Glamdrul Feynt, who did not, as might be naively supposed, have any responsibilities at all for the library wing of the palace. There had not been any books or records worthy of attention in the library wing for generations. What was there could be cared for, if at all, by Tharius Don, cared for by Tharius Don simply because it did not matter. Such was Feynt's opinion. He had not seen the books in the library wing. He did not need to do so. He had seen what was in the files, and everything of importance was there.

So now, Gendra Mitiar, passing by the great corridor that led to her offices and reception rooms, her dining halls and solaria, elected to descend the curving stone staircase that led to the vaults below. The railing of this stair was carved in the likeness of fliers slaughtering weehar, thrassil, and an unlikely animal that was the artist's dutiful though uninspired conception of the legendary hoovar. None of the party except Jhilt—who shuddered to see the ravenous talons so bloodily employed, reminded thereby of certain habits of the Dame Marshal's—paid any attention to the railing. Gendra did not see it. She had stopped seeing it several hundred years before.

The *whoom, whoom, whoom* of the viol announced her coming. Far down an empty corridor that dwindled to tininess at the limit of its seemingly endless pespective came a faint echo—a door slamming, perhaps, or a heavy book dropping onto stone. At this, Gendra halted, snarling at Jorum Byne to stop the noise. Jhilt, too, was silenced with a gesture, and the five waited, heads cocked, listening for any defect in the dusty silence.

" 'Roo, 'roo, 'roo," came the call, softened by distance

into a whisper. "Haroo. Your Reverence. Dame Marshal. Haroo?"

"Tosh," growled the Dame Marshal. "Jorum, go find him. Bring him here. And don't lose sound of him. He's half-deaf and likely to go limping off in six other directions."

Pleased with her own wit, she chuckled, grinding her teeth together as she found a bench along the wall to sit upon, not bothering to dust it, though it was deep with the even gray coating that covered every surface in the files. The bench was in a niche carved with commemorative bas reliefs, fliers and humans locked in combat, fliers and humans solemnly making treaty. Dust softened the carving, obscuring the details. No one had looked at it for generations.

"Glamdrul Feynt is too old for this job," Gendra assured her clerks and bearers, going so far as to glance at Jhilt as though the information were so general it might be shared even with so insignificant a person as she. "Too old, and too deaf, and too crippled. Trouble is, hah, what you might suppose, eh? Trouble is, no one else can find anything! We give him apprentices, one after the other, boys and boys, and what happens? They vanish. Lost. So he says. Lost in the files, he says. Can you imagine. Hah!"

"It is said," ventured Jhilt in a whisper, "that a monster dwells below the tunnels here, coming out at night to feed upon those in the Chancery."

Gendra found this amusing. "A monster, hah? Some toothy critter left over from ages past, no doubt? A hoovar bull, mebee? Got frozen in a glacier until we built Chancery atop him, hah?" She roared with laughter, stopping suddenly to listen to the clatter of approaching footsteps, one firm, one halting.

Glamdrul Feynt was a young man by Chancery standards, only slightly half past a hundred, but he seemed to hover on the edge of dissolution, his aging unstemmed by the Payment. It had been given him tardily and with deep frustration by certain underlings of the Dame Marshal who devoutly wished him dead but were unable to replace him. It amused Glamdrul Feynt, therefore, to act even older and feebler than he was while still conveying omniscience on any matter relating to the files. Bent and gray, shedding scraps of paper from every pocket as he came, he approached the Dame Marshal with dragging footsteps and failing breath, leaning heavily upon his cane, meantime whispering his compliments in a gasp that bid fair to presage extinction at any moment.

"Oh, sit down, sit down," she snarled at him. "Jorum, make him sit down. Now get off down the corridor, all of you. I've private business to discuss." She watched them malevolently as they retreated out of earshot, then leaned close to Feynt's side and said in a low voice, "I need you to do some research for me, Glamdrul Feynt. And if you do it well, I'll see you get a dose of the Payment that'll do you some good."

"Ah, Your Reverence. But I'm too old, I'm afraid. Too late. Much too late, so they say. On my last legs, I'm afraid." He fished in a pocket for a wad of paper fragments, drew them forth, and peered at them with ostentatious nearsightedness.

"Nonsense. Play those games with those who believe them, Feynt. Now listen to me.

"There's a thing going on. The Talkers call it the Riverman heresy. What it is, it's people putting their dead in the River instead of giving them to the Awakeners. Now, it's no new thing. Seems to me I've heard of it off and on in passing for a few hundred years. There's been a flare-up of it in Baris. Maybe other places, too. There's a new thing in Thou-ne. Some fisherman pulled a statue out of the River. Now it's set up in the Temple, right under Potipur himself. Rumblings. That's what I hear. What I want to know is, where did this heresy start? And when. *When* is important, too. And could the two things be connected?"

"I can look, Your Reverence. I don't recall the heresy, offhand. Don't recall anything about Rivermen. But I can look. . . ."

"Go back two or three hundred years and look in the records of Baris. Find out who was Superior of the Tower then. Find out what was going on. Hah? You understand?"

He did not answer, merely wheezed asthmatically and bowed, as though in despair.

For her part, she took no notice of his pose but shouted for her entourage and went back the way she had come. Something within her quickened, hard on the trail of a connection she merely suspected. Tharius Don. The lady Kesseret. Hah. Both from Baris. And she seemed to recall something about Baris as a center of rebellion, long ago.

Behind her on the bench the old man peered after her with rheumy eyes, his hands busy with the scraps of paper he had drawn from a pocket, sorting them, smoothing them, folding them twice and thrusting them into the pocket once more. "Oh, yes," he muttered to her retreating back. "I'll bet you would like to know where it started, old bird." He sat there, perfectly still, until he was alone in the files once more. Then he rose and moved swiftly down the corridor, shedding scraps from every pocket as he went.

A door halfway down the long corridor opened as he approached, and a figure came halfway into the hall, beckoning imperiously.

"Well, what did the old fish want?" The question came from a mouth thin-lipped as a trap and was punctuated by the snap of fingers as long and twisted as tree roots. Ezasper Jorn was a man of immense strength and enormous patience, though this latter characteristic was not now in evidence. "Come up with it, Feynt! What did old Mitiar want?"

Behind the Ambassador the shadowy figure of Research Chief Koma Nepor stared at the file master. "Yes, yes, Feynt. What did she want?"

Glamdrul Feynt entered the room, casting a curious glance at the boyish figures that lay here and there in its corners and along its walls. These were his apprentices. They were also the materials Nepor had used in his research on the effects of Tears and blight and half a dozen other substances found here and there on Northshore. "Any luck?" he asked, purposely not responding to their questions. "Did you have any luck with that last one?"

"It talked," whispered Nepor, his pallid little face with its pink rosebud mouth peering nearsightedly at one of the forms. "It talked for quite a while, didn't it, Ezasper? I was quite hopeful there for a time."

Ezasper Jorn refused to be sidetracked by these considerations. He gripped the file master in one huge hand and shook him gently to and fro, as a song-fish might shake a tasty mulluk. "Out with it, Feynt. What did the old fish want?"

And Glamdrul Feynt, chuckling from time to time, explained what it was that much concerned the Dame Marshal of the Towers. After which came a long and thoughtful silence.

· 18 ·

Mumros Shenaz rolled out of his blankets well before dawn, awakened by the peeping of the ground birds, a repetitive, percipient cry that seemed as full of meaning as it was without purpose. There was no mating, no nest building, no food searching going on. No defense of territories. Only this high, continuous complaint of bird voice, as though only by this sound could the dawn be guided to the eastern horizon and only by these cries driven to mount the sky.

Such thoughts amused Mumros. He sat often by himself, thinking such things, and was called the Lonely Man because of the habit. He did not mind. Since all who were his had died, he was indeed a lonely man, spending his life seeing the joys of others and remembering his own that were past. One such was to be remembered this dawn time. He stretched, bent from side to side, working the kinks out of his back and legs. All around him lay the lightweight pamet tents of the Noor. Last night's campfires were hidden beneath lumps of half-dried bog-bottom. Smoke leaked upward in thin, coiling bands. He stretched again and bent to pick up the pottery flask of sammath wine laid by for his father's ghost. His father's mud grave was nearby, only over the hill, and Mumros walked away from the camp toward it, the walk turning into the distance-eating trot of the Noor as his sleep-tightened muscles loosened with the exercise.

At the top of the hill he looked back, hearing someone in

the camp call, a long-drawn cry to the new day. There was
movement there. Flames. Someone had risen as early as he
and built up the fire with dried chunks of bog-bottom cut by
some other traveling Noors, days or even months ago. Such
was the life of wanderers. Planting grain to be eaten by
others, harvesting grain others had planted. Cutting bog-
bottom for another's fire, burning bog-bottom some other
Noor had cut. "Of such small duties is the solidarity of the
Noor built," he remarked to himself, remembering something similar his father had once said. "Of our concern for
those who travel after us comes our unity as a people."

He trotted down the hill, head swinging to and fro in its
search for the mud grave. His tribe had not been this way in
several years. He could have forgotten where it was—no.
No. He had not forgotten. It stood in a slight declivity, the
sculptured face looking toward him. Rain, though infrequent,
did come upon the steppes from time to time. It had washed
the mud face, leaving it bland, almost featureless. In a way
that was a good sign, for when the mud grave fell to dust, the
spirit would move on. Some were ready to go on in only a
year or two. Others so longed for their lives and kin that they
stayed in the mud graves for many years, even a lifetime.
This grave was neither very old nor very young.

"Father . . ." He bowed, pouring the sammath wine onto
the thirsty clay that covered the bones. "I have brought you
drink. And news. The tribe has been chosen by Queen Fibji
to take part in her great plan. We go now to her tents, all of
us. Your friend Mejordu is still well, though he tires sometimes after a long day, and he asks to be remembered to
you." He had several anecdotes about Mejordu to share, for
the man had always been clownish and amusing. After this
he was still for a moment, trying to recall the last bit of
news. Oh, yes. "Your grandson Taj Noteen has led a group
of Melancholics south to net shore-fish for the Queen."

He fell silent then, thinking he had heard cries from the
camp. Well. Whether or not, it was time to be getting back.

"I take my leave, Father. I will visit you when we next
come by this way." He bowed again and turned back toward

the camp, not trotting now but running, for he did hear cries, screams.

Before reaching the crest of the hill, he dropped to his belly and writhed upward to peer over it.

Glittering figures moved among the tents of the Noor. Jondarites! Shiny fishskin helms plumed with flame-bird feathers sparkled over the huddled people of Mumros's tribe. He wriggled forward, serpentlike in the sparse grass, down the hill into a slanting gully. Over the cries of his people he heard the voice of the Jondarite captain.

"Women and children here. Men over there. All boys over ten with the men. Boys under ten with the women. Speed it up there, move! Move!"

Mumros risked raising his head. The men were herded together at one side of the camp. The women were all in the center, near the fires, surrounded by the Jondarite soldiers. Suddenly, without a word of command, the soldiers began slaughtering the women and children. All at once. Quickly. Like fishermen clubbing fish, they struck them down. Like stilt-lizard beaks, swords dipped in and out, emerged dripping, plunged in again.

The men of the tribe tried to break loose, but they had been tied. Over his own howling blood, Mumros heard their voices, crying names: "Onji, beloved!" "Creedi, Bowro, children—ah!" "Girir, oh, Girir!"

Then the voice of the captain once more.

"You men are to be taken as slaves to the mines. You will be roped together and marched there. Before we go, you are to look at the bodies, closely. Make sure all are dead. We have had men try to escape in the past to get back to their families. We want you to be very sure you have no families to come back to."

Mumros dropped his head into the grass. He could not move. There was bile in his mouth, an agony in his head. He wanted to kill but had nothing to kill with. He was one and they were many. He could go to them, but what good would it do? They would only take him with the others.

So he lay, not moving, while the chain of roped captives

was led away into the distance. When they had gone, he went into the camp. The captain had been right. None of those who had been taken away had anyone left to return to.

He lit three fires, spread them with damp bog-bottom, tended them while the smoke rose in pillars in the still air. By noon the first helper arrived. By nightfall there were several more. After several days there were many, and where the camp had been now stood the mud graves of the women, those of the children clustered at their knees.

"Come," said one of the helpers to Mumros. "There is nothing more you can do here. Join us."

"I know I can do nothing here," said Mumros. "But I will not come with you. I must go and tell of this thing to Queen Fibji." And he turned his face from the cluster of graves to begin the long march.

19

In Thou-ne, Haranjus Pandel had been expecting a visitor for over two years, since the day he had sent a signal to the Chancery announcing the finding of an image in the River and the elevation of that image in the Temple. As a matter of policy, the existence of the signal towers—or, rather, of their purpose, since the existence could not be concealed—was kept from the general populace. No one except Haranjus Pandel knew of the message he had sent or that it was possible to send a message at all. Thus, no one knew the eventual visitor had come in response to that message. The whole township saw the boat, of course, and the Chancery man getting off it, but it was all very casual.

Bostle Kerf was his full name, a Section Chief in the Bureau of Towers, sent south in all haste through the pass, thence quickly west, and then south again to arrive after a year's travel in Thou-ne after a short detour to Zendigt, two towns east. His arrival from the east would evoke less concern, he had been told, than if he had appeared suddenly, coming down from the north like a migrating Noor. It was necessary to come to Thou-ne. It was not necessary to cause more talk than had already occurred. Gendra Mitiar had been clear about that. Once safely ensconced in the Tower, Kerf had a long, troubled conversation with Haranjus Pandel.

"How did you allow this to happen, Pandel? Her Reverence is in a fury over it, I'll tell you. Bad enough to have no workers in Thou-ne, without having a miracle here as well."

The Superior nodded, sweating a little. He had never aspired to the Payment. Indeed, he had never aspired to be Supervisor of a Tower, but then, no one with aspirations would have taken the job in Thou-ne. The mountains to the east prevented any traffic from the next township that way. This meant there was little enough need for Awakeners in Thou-ne, and little enough to do for the few there were. The Tower was small, cramped, and needed only one recruit every decade or so. Since there were no workers, there was no fieldwork, road or jetty building. All the Tower really had to see to was the transport of Thou-ne's dead to the worker pit in Atter, next town west, and since Thou-ne itself was small, there was little work in that. Haranjus had been content to be what he was, letting happen what happened, and in general the people of Thou-ne had approved his stewardship. Now he sweated more than a little, wondering if he was to be blamed for what had happened despite his innocence.

"I wouldn't call it a miracle," he said now, not wanting to contradict the Section Chief but unwilling to be blamed for more than was just. "It's only some image from old times, floated up on the River, that's all."

"It shines, man. I went to the Temple. I saw it for myself. It's all wet, and it shines."

"Well, there's that, yes. But dead fish often do that, and mulluk shells."

"She shines and smiles," Kerf went on, not listening. "And holds out her hand. More attractive than the moon faces, I'll tell you."

"Oh, well, now, Your Honor, but nobody's suggested the thing's a god! No. I wouldn't have tolerated that for a minute. No. No heresy here. All they've said is the thing is an image of . . . well, of the Bearer of Truth."

"And what's that? Not a goddess? You're sure?"

"Well, nobody's said it's a goddess. I shouldn't think anyone believes so unless they've said . . ."

"If they haven't so far, depend on it they will soon."

"Well, if they do, I'll just have to pick up a few, that's all. Pass around a few Tears. Settle things down."

"Why haven't you settled things down already?"

Haranjus shrugged, a bit uncomfortably. Why hadn't he? "Well, because if I did, you know, they'd think there was something in it. Something important. Something the Tower needed to defend against. If I let it be, it's a wonder for a few years, and it brings some curious travelers to spend their money here in Thou-ne—which won't hurt, Your Honor. Potipur knows we're poor enough. And it will blow over. When it does, let enough time pass for them all to forget it, then take the thing and burn it, shine or no shine."

Bostle Kerf was no fool. He liked having his own way but wouldn't push it to the point of causing trouble. Here, he felt, the local man had the right of it. Don't fuss it. Don't make a racket. Let it die, as it would, of its own accord, without drawing more attention to it.

"How long since it was found?"

"Two and a half years. Maybe closer to three. I signaled the Chancery the very night of the day it happened."

As he had, sweating away at the handles of the signal light, clickety-clacking the coded message across all those miles to the nearest signal tower, first time he'd ever done it; first time he'd ever had anything to report. And it had taken over a year for the Chancery to decide it wanted to investigate, so why all this uproar now? Well, thought Kerf, Haranjus was probably right. Let it alone. For now.

He snarled a little, letting the local man know he was being watched. No harm in that. Keep him on his toes. When it was dark, they went to the signal room, polished the mirror and lighted the lantern while Kerf worked the shutters. He did it a good deal faster than Haranjus had done, but then, he'd had more practice. "Reported image of local interest only," he signaled. "Thou-ne Tower recommends allowing interest to die of its own accord. Kerf in agreement. Returning to the Chancery."

All that travel for nothing, Kerf thought. Not even any good food in Thou-ne. And certainly none in the lands of the steppe people, going back. Noor bread always tasted of ashes, and no one but a steppey could pretend to enjoy roasted roots. Besides, Noor hated Chancery men. Only his escort of heavily armed Jondarites guaranteed passage and food at all. Though they hadn't seen many steppeys, come to that. Fewer than he'd thought they would. Perhaps they were traveling, east or west of the route Kerf had taken.

He shrugged, setting those thoughts aside as he bullied Haranjus a bit more before leaving. It had taken him a year and a half to get to Thou-ne. It would take that long at least going back. In his eagerness to leave, he did not ask the local man if devotion to the image had increased or decreased since shortly after it was found. Haranjus had very carefully not mentioned that subject. Bostle Kerf was able, therefore, to leave Thou-ne in good conscience.

Three days after Bostle Kerf left Thou-ne, the *Gift of Potipur* arrived there with a boatload of Melancholics who intended to disembark in Thou-ne and begin the trek north to their home country. Pamra was also on the ship. She came ashore in Thou-ne. By that time, however, it was too late to summon the Chancery man back again.

20

The Queen of the Noor sat upon her carved throne, legs neatly aligned in their tall fishskin boots, eyes forward, feathered scepter in hand, dying a little more as each delegation from an outlying tribe made its appeals, thankful for the protocol that insisted upon an expressionless face. As a young Queen she had rebelled against the requirement; as an old one she realized its necessity. Had it not been for protocol she would have wept, screamed, howled in frustration, anger, and pity.

Now the last of the delegations was on his knees before her. One lonely man.

"They came on us before dawn, Highness," said the lonely man in an emotionless voice. "Most of the camp was still asleep when I left. When I heard the cries, I came back. They rounded up the women and children, even the babies, and killed them while the men were forced to watch. After the killing, they let the men see the bodies just to be sure all the women and children were dead." He went on in that same dead voice, describing the scene, the cries. "The Jondarite captain told them they had no families to return to," the man said at last, falling silent. He knelt before her, eyes on the floor, as though he expected nothing from her at all, as though he expected nothing from anyone.

Fibji had bitten her tongue in the need not to speak. Strenge had spoken for her, as he usually did, knowing what was in her heart.

"How did you escape?"

"I had gone out before dawn to visit the mud grave of my father, to leave offerings to his spirit. I was returning when the Jondarites came. I hid, watching from the hill. I should have been taken with the others, but I could have changed nothing, and someone needed to tell you, Highness."

Fibji had recently spent some time at the Chancery, going there under a banner of truce, appealing to the Protector of Man, attempting to get something from the Council of Seven, a treaty, an understanding, anything that would stop the taking of slaves and the mindless killing. She had not even seen the Protector. The council had refused to consider her request. She had failed in every effort, all the time afire to get home. Now she regretted being here. At the Chancery there might be something more she could do; there was nothing here. She could do nothing here except listen to the endless tales of slaughter and rapine, endless pleas for action against the Jondarite tax collectors and slavers and murderers, pleas that received a sympathetic hearing and no action at all. "Because they have me," she told herself. "That damned general has us all, like birds caught in a net." General Jondrigar would not mind if all the Noor were dead. He welcomed those times when the young men of the Noor rebelled against her to wage war against him, for then he could kill them more quickly. He welcomed uprisings, for then he could mount a major assault. Their only hope lay in not provoking him to a major effort, not until the plan could be put into effect. Then . . . well, then they would either live or die, but they would not go on as victims.

If the young men would hold their peace. If they could move onward with the plan. If she could have seen the Protector.

Oh, surely, surely Lees Obol would have listened. Surely the Protector of Man would not consider the Noor unworthy of his protection. Were Noor not men? But she had not seen the Protector. Only Maintainer of the Household Shavian Bossit, who had put her through half a dozen inconclusive and frustrating sessions.

"Have you seen Jondarites take your people slaves?" he had asked half a hundred times. "Have you seen it?"

No, she had not seen it. Had not seen the slavers come, had not seen the tax collectors come, had not seen the murderers come, had only heard about it afterward, from the survivors, when there were any. "Take me to your metal mines, Lord Maintainer. Let me identify the slaves there. They are my people."

"Tsk. Your Highness is misinformed. We have no slaves in our mines. Only bondsmen from Northshore. And as for those who took your people, how do you know they were Jondarites? Rebel townsmen, perhaps, in Jondarite dress? I'm sure that's who it was. Apply to the Supervisor of the Tower of whatever town they are from, Queen Fibji."

As well apply to the moons, she thought viciously. There were no rebel townsmen, only Jondarites, Jondarites who kept the depredations remote from the Queen's tents and thus could not be directly accused by the Queen.

"We will accept without question anything Your Highness has seen personally," said Bossit, smiling, always smiling, dripping politeness and courtesy as a rotten fruit drips juice. "In accordance with the treaty the Chancery has always had with the Noor," he said, showing his tiny teeth, a curve of threatening ivory, like a knife.

In accordance with the treaty! A treaty, made generations before, in an untrusting age when the Noor King had feared anyone speaking in his name and would speak only for himself. Used against them now to prevent her speaking. If she camped north of Thou-ne, the Jondarites struck above Vobil-dil-go. If she went to the lands above Vobil-dil-go, the Jondarites would take captives above Shfor. Wherever the Noor moved upon the open steppes, the Jondarites could find them. There was no stone, no tree, to hide behind. There were no chasms, no caves. There was only the steppe, open to the sky, and the tethered balloons of the Jondarite spies, who would see their quarry from miles away. And she, Fibji, would see the pain of the wounded and the mud graves of the dead—assuming there had been anyone left to bury the dead—but she would

not see Jondarites. She knew that someone reported on her
movements. Perhaps those winged demons, seeing where she
went and being sure the Jondarites knew it.

So, now, she heard the man from the slaughtered tribe. He
was alone. Without near-kin. Well, that, at least, she could
pretend to remedy. She gestured, a tiny movement, at once
interpreted, as she called out a few words in the secret
naming language of the Noor.

"Mumros, Her Highness takes you into her tribe, into her
family. She calls you *Kalja Benoor*. Adopted Near-kin."

The man who had brought the news leaned upon his hands
and wept. It was not for joy. He knew as well as she the
adoption was only a gesture. Near-kin could not be so easily
replaced, nor grief so easily stayed. Still, when he left the
tent it was with a steadier gait than that with which he had
entered.

"Your Highness?" A murmured voice at her ear.

"Yes, Strenge, what is it?" Of all her men he was her
favorite: strong, not at all servile, yet attentive to her dignity,
virile, father of two of her children.

"The delegation from the boatmen."

"Haven't there been enough delegations for one day?"
There was despair in her whispered voice. He heard it.
Among all her people he was the only one she let hear it.

"They have Glizzee spice, Your Highness." His eyes
were down, his posture dignified. If they were alone, he
would call her Fibby. They had been children together. And
lovers later. And lovers still.

"And we have no spice, is that it? And our people have
few enough pleasures, they should not have to do without this
one. And the boatmen won't deal without seeing me?"

"Your Highness sees the invisible and hears the inaudi-
ble." He gave her a secret glance, one she knew as well as
she knew the feel of her own skin.

"My Highness is dying of the agony of my people, Strenge.
Of inanition and frustration. Of the duplicity of the Chancery
and an unapproachable creature that calls itself the Protector
of Man. Put them off."

"Ma'am, one of them is the man called Fatterday. He claims to have seen Southshore."

Fatterday! Was Fatterday a real person, then? Not a mere story hero, favorite protagonist of the Jarb Mendicants' tales? Was he here, now? Bringing word of a larger world out there than this circumscribed one, squeezed between the Teeth of the North and all the little, biddable towns of Northshore, and chewed to death by Jondarites? Fatterday, who had perhaps seen what Fibji had only dared hope for, a homeland beyond the reach of the general's troops? She gasped, holding Strenge with the fire of her eyes. "Do you think he tells the truth?"

"Who could know, ma'am? However, I knew you would want to see him."

"In the small tent, then. I've a cramp in my butt from sitting on this damn thing, and I must be able to question him."

Strenge affected not to have heard her, his face impassive as he turned to bellow at the courtiers and warriors hanging about. "You have Her Highness's leave to go. The boatmen may await her pleasure outside."

They left quickly. Protocol prevented her rising until they were gone, and they knew her displeasure at being kept waiting. When the heavy tent flaps dropped behind them, she stood up, rubbing her rump, kicking off the jeweled boots and harness, handing over the holy scepter to be put in its case. Strenge was ready with a soft robe and shoes of quilted pamet embroidered with flowers. Against the white fiber her skin glowed dark, like oiled fragwood, and when she pulled off the high, feathered crown, her hair tumbled across the fabric like a thousand twining little vines, twisty and moving as though each lock had its own life. Her hawk-nosed face relaxed somewhat from its audience expression, the lines around her mouth and eyes smoothing out, dropping decades from her appearance. I'm an old woman, she thought to herself, knowing she wasn't, yet, but needing to get used to the idea. Too old for all this sitting.

The small tent adjacent was her own living space, the piled

carpets dotted with soft pillows and small tables. "Let them come in here," she said, taking one of the huge pillows for her own. "Have someone bring us some wine. I ache all over."

They came in, three of them, one lean, two stocky, brown men all, though none so dark as she. Their darkness was merely of the sun, while hers was of an ancient race, so it was said among the Northlings.

"Your Highness." Three voices, all of them muffled from being spoken into the carpet, three backs bent impossibly to prevent their eyes meeting hers.

"Oh, stand up," she said impatiently. "I have to have all that out there where people are watching, but I haven't time for it here. Which one of you is Fatterday?"

He stood forward, the leanest one of the bunch, burned almost as dark as she by the sun and with deep white lines radiating from his eyes where the sun had not reached down into squint lines, smiling irrepressibly. "Your Highness. I'm Fatterday."

"And you've truly seen Southshore?"

He bowed again, nodding assent, not speaking.

"Well, tell me! What is it like? Are there people there? Are there fliers?"

"Your Highness, we were cast ashore on a rocky coast among high mountains. From the top of a mountain I saw an endless plain under the sun." His eyes were alight, his fingers twitching as they described the outlines and dimensions of the lands, the rivers. "I saw no fliers, no people. After many days, we managed to repair the boat enough to sail northward once more. Only we three survived to bring you the tale."

"A great land." She regarded him thoughtfully, wondering if he told the truth. "For the taking, boatman?"

"From all I could see, free for the taking, Your Highness. If one could come to it. I saw no fliers."

And that was it, of course. No fliers. No Jondarites. She lusted for it. The dream required lands. Lands for the people of the north, free from fliers, free from attacks by the Jondarite

tax collectors, free from the constant pressures of the Chancery.
Lands to hold without taxation. And lands with beasts. In her
mind she saw wagons pulled as they were in the Chancery
lands, by beasts instead of by her people. Oh, with beasts
one could move, move, out of reach of pursuing armies. Oh,
why not have lands, Northlings? Why not have beasts?

"How did you come there?"

"We were prospecting among the islands for Glizzee,
Your Highness. We followed a great school of strangeys.
Came a strong, wild current in World River, and we were
driven south. Came storm and great wind driving us, days
and days, until we lost track of them. Many died. Most. Only
seven of us came to that shore, and only we three returned."
He did not say how they had lived or what they had eaten.
They could not have eaten the local animals and survived,
not without human grains to go with them. They could have
eaten fish. It was better, perhaps, not to know how they had
survived.

"So, how would we come there, if we chose to go?"

"If you chose to go, Highness, you should go well provisioned. It is a long voyage. Still, I would not hesitate to make
it again. There are wonders there."

She waved him away. That was the question, wasn't it?
How could one get better provisioned with the Chancery
taking all but a bare sufficiency. They were lucky if the
scavengers from the Chancery left them grain enough for the
cold season and a spare bit more should the warm come late.
When that was all they were allowed to assemble, how could
they put together a store for a long voyage? And how put
together the boats, come to that? Fibji's people numbered
some hundreds of thousands, not many compared to the
population of Northshore, but a great horde when one considered the size of most boats. Fifty at a time, perhaps. Hundreds of thousands of Noor, and only fifty at a time. If they
took one boat from every town . . .

She shook herself, shedding the vision of lands beyond the
River. Fatterday was still standing there, as though he had
not seen her excuse him. The man was still to be dealt with.

"You came north across the World River to Thou-ne?"

"We did, ma'am. With Glizzee spice as the whole of our property, all that was left us after the storm save the shell of our boat."

"And you brought it here because the price is better so far from the World River?"

"As Your Highness says." He grinned knowingly.

"And it would help you, now, if we bought your spice from you?"

He bowed, unspeaking. It was probably the only thing that would help him, she thought. He had likely been impoverished by his adventure. He must have had everything he owned lost on the voyage. She beckoned to Strenge, signaling him to send for the coffer keeper. They had little enough in stores of food or obvious possessions, the Noor, but the Melancholics did keep the Queen's coffers filled. So let Fatterday be paid, and let him think it was for the spice. Actually, the payment was for the news he brought her. News she could use.

When the boatmen were gone, she summoned her nearkin, not forgetting the lonely survivor most recently adopted. They drank sammath wine as they talked of Southshore, of the goddess, of themselves and the Jondarites.

"But what of the plan?" they asked, uncomfortable at the thought of giving up the thing they had been working on for so very long.

"We are not yet changing the plan," she replied. "It was too long in the making to change it unless for something far better. So far, we have only the word of an explorer. He could be lying. He could be mistaken. No, we are not yet talking of changing the plan. But let us investigate the dream. If Southshore is within reach . . ."

She did not need to complete the thought. The old plan had been fifty years in the making, thirty in implementation. Here and there across the steppes were great complexes of tunnels dug secretly by the Noor. There beneath the steppes were towns, cities. There beneath the scattered grainfields were dormitories and meeting halls and storehouses now beginning to hold some grain and roots hidden from the tax collectors. Timbers supported the corridors beneath the earth, timbers bought from the Queen's coffers, moved at night, hidden by day. Clever mechanisms brought air into the depths, mechanisms paid for from the Queen's funds. Melancholics went south into the cities and returned with goods and coin, and both went into the underground cities Queen Fibji was building. Fifty thousand of the Queen's people dwelt beneath the moors already, and more were descending every day. In twenty years more, or thirty, all would have made themselves a redoubt within the earth. Then, the scouts would watch for Jondarite balloons, would signal the approach of armies, but those armies would find no one on the open steppes, no one to enslave, no one to tax. Or if they did, they would fight tunnel by tunnel, room by room, against strong defenses.

And across the breadth of the steppes hundreds of thousands of mud graves stood mute evidence of the soil dug out in the dark hours. If any had had sense to see it. How could so sparse a people have had so many dead? But the Jondarites had not asked that question.

"And yet," she whispered to herself, "and yet, in that thirty years or fifty years, how many more will really die?" The young men grew belligerent in the underground places. If they could not fight the Jondarites, they fought one another. Queen Fibji had made a rule that boys could dwell below only until they had fathered two children; then they must return to the nomad tribes above. Which made it more peaceful below but left the children without fathers to learn from. She sighed. Thinking again of Fatterday, she wondered how many of her people might be saved if there were truly a Southshore and she could find some way to come to it.

Now her near-kin were saying the same things over and over, worrying the subject to rags. Her mind wandered, remembering.

On one particular day long ago she had walked with her father across a stretch of the arid lands, away from the tribe, free for the moment from servitors or petitioners. He had taken her on these walks sometimes, talking and talking, as though to gift her with the essence of his thought to store for some future time. She was his only child.

"The young always want to go to war," he had said. "And the old are too often eager to send them. The young revel in thoughts of battle. They think blood is wine, that it can be spilt without consequence and a new vintage bought for tomorrow's feast. And the old are sometimes willing to have young men gone, to have their exasperating numbers thinned to a biddable fraction, for they, the young men, are the source of dissent and confusion. It is among them that revolution breeds, often to no point. But what good are dead warriors, Fibji?"

He stopped, as though taken by a sudden memory. "Long ago, when I was only a youth and my father was yet King, I came upon a Jarb Mendicant sitting on a stone here on the steppe, wreathed in the smoke of his pipe. I was joyful and sanguine then. I said to him, 'Mendicant, give me a prognostication for our people.' He looked at me through the smoke, as they do, and said at last, 'I see peace and prosperity for the Noor, Prince, but only when the ruler of the Noor can answer the question, "Of what good are dead warriors?" ' "

He brooded again. "I have never answered the question, Fibji. See the mud graves of the dead as we pass. Is our way not marked with the bones of our people? And what good do the dead do themselves or us?"

He had intended it as a rhetorical question, but it had caught Fibji's attention. What good indeed? The mud tombs were scattered everywhere on the endless plains, thinly in most places, thickly around much used campsites. Inside them the bones of the dead, rolled in their robes, sat inside thick mud shells sculptured into the shapes of them as they had been in life. Children played among the clayed-over bones, thinking nothing of it. Death had no reality to children. Fibji herself had played among the tombs, knowing what they were well enough. They had no more reality for her than for other children.

Until that moment. Her father stood at her left hand, staring

off across the steppe where the sparse grass moved in a small
wind, the half-dried blades making a gentle susurrus, barely
audible. To her right was a cluster of mud graves, three
almost alike, as though of one family, two men and a woman,
their faces staring toward her from the clay. She fancied they
would speak in a moment, greeting the King, and in that
instant her mind saw into the clay to the place the bones
rested and beyond the bones to the people who had once
lived. It happened all at once, like a vision. Almost she could
have called the names of those who rested in the shells, gone
now. They stared out at her with eager eyes, those young
men, eyes anxious for battle, hungry for death. And in that
instant she knew mortality, all at once, entirely. Even she,
Fibji, would stop! She, Fibji, would cease to be!

"Of what good are dead warriors?" her father had repeated, and she had screamed, cowering against him in a
sudden spasm of fear so palpable it was like a presence, as
though death itself had touched her.

"Fibji?" he had said, looking her full in the face with total
understanding. "Daughter?" And then he had held her tightly,
waiting for the fear to pass. "I know," he said. "I know."

She had been about seven when she'd realized death.
When she had taken up the scepter, she had tried to explain
why they must not wage war. And yet there were always the
young men who rebelled against her. Young bloods, always,
in love with their concept of justice, eager to prove themselves, making it easier for the Jondarites, plunging into
battle with a scream of defiance and naked chests.

Now she was fifty-five with perhaps a decade or two left
before understanding became reality. For the Chancery there
was the elixir and an almost immortality. For the people of
Northshore, the Promise of Potipur. For the steppe dwellers,
the Noor, nothing. Seven tens of years and then the mud
grave and the cold wind. Now, though she was closer to that
end she had perceived when she was seven, she did not fear
it as much for herself as she had feared it then. She feared it
more, however, for her people and knew what her father had
tried to tell her.

"Think well," she said now, speaking earnestly to the near-kin, an interruption of their wrangles. "I remember the words of my father. We walked upon the steppe, and he told me the Noor would not have peace until they could answer the question, 'Of what good are dead warriors?' Think well, kinfolk. Let us consider the possibility of Southshore. But whatever we do, let us save every Noor we can in the doing of it."

Then she turned away from them, went into the small tent where she slept, where Strenge waited for her now. "Old friend," she said, "when Medoor Babji, our daughter, begged to be allowed to accompany a troop of Melancholics to the cities of the River, we thought it well she should see the world in which the Noor must live."

He nodded. "Those she is with do not know who she is or what she is to be."

"True, but she carries sufficient proof to command them to her service. Here, in her tent, is a cage of seeker birds kept by her servants. Send the birds south. Tell our daughter what we have heard of Southshore."

It was a daughter, not a son, selected to be Queen Fibji's heir. Her sons were too brave, too puissant, too eager for war. They disbelieved in death. "Tell our daughter," she said once again, "what we have heard of Southshore."

· 21 ·

S havian Bossit drank wine with General of the Armed Might of the Chancery Jondrigar and described the futile embassy of Queen Fibji.

"Honest as the day," he sneered, reaching down with his toe to tap the floor in emphasis. All the general's chairs were too large for Bossit, but he forced himself to sit in them, forced himself to fill whatever chair he sat in, whatever room he occupied, whatever role he chose for himself. "The Queen will not lie, General. She has not seen Jondarites herself, and she will not say she has."

"The woman's a fool."

Shavian twitched his shoulders in a quick shrug. "Perhaps. A very tortured fool, General. I would not take her honesty as her only foolishness. She may be foolish enough to attack you."

The general snorted. "Don't be stupid, Bossit. So long as she does not see what we do, she remains comfortable. She will not disrupt herself over deaths she does not see." He considered death in the abstract. To him the victims of his raids were not men, not women or children, not babes as he had once been a babe. They were simply steppe dwellers, Noor, tribesmen, proper targets for a military exercise. How else should troops be sharpened against the inevitable time of need, against the time when someone or something might threaten the Protector of Man? He used the steppe dwellers in various ways, sometimes working parties of young males up into a killing rage, then quelling them in a well-planned exercise; sometimes surprising whole tribes and taking the males captive—for the iron mines or the copper mines or to be given to the woodcutters as slaves—sometimes merely slaughtering them because Jondarites must become accustomed to killing.

"You may underestimate her," nagged Bossit, staring at the other man with frank curiosity. The general wore his helm liner, its flaps covering his head and neck. Beneath it his face was gray as lava and pitted as dust after a spring shower. No disease had caused this skin coloration or texture. Jondrigar had been born with it, born with the gray, pitted skin and the wild, iron-gray hair—now kept shaved— the massive shoulders, the long arms that let his standing figure touch his knees without stooping. He was a hideous man. He had been as hideous a child. His mother, so Bossit had been told, had screamed at the sight of him and shortly thereafter had died. Bossit, though more or less accustomed to Jondrigar's appearance, sometimes amused himself imagining what had gone through her head, that faceless woman who had given him birth. Had she thought, perhaps, of Jondrigar's father? Whoever that might have been? Had she thought of her sins, wondering whether this monstrous baby was some old sin made manifest? What had she thought? Or had she thought at all?

Bossit had had Jondrigar's antecedents looked into, insofar as that was possible. Jondrigar had been reared by his mother's sister, Firrabel. Firrabel was as resolute and dutiful as her sister had been flighty and hysterical. It was Firrabel who had taken the ugly infant, reared him, fed him, and schooled him, teaching him more of letters than nine-tenths of Northshore thought necessary; it was Firrabel at last who had sent him to the Chancery to be of service, claiming the Chancery had picked him for that service when he was still a baby, as, in a sense, perhaps it had.

If that is what had happened, it had occurred during a royal Progression. The shore had been lined with people, the golden ship of the Protector moving slowly along the Riverbank with the Protector held high above the crowd in the arms of his servitors, leaning down now and then to toss a glittering token to one of the common people.

And Firrabel, taken up with the drama of it all, had held Jondrigar high above her head, waving him like a banner, him ugly as a mud grave, all wide-eyed, reaching out with his little gray paws, grab, grab at anything. The hands caught the robes of the Protector, and the Protector had laughed and turned to someone else with a remark.

Someone had given the baby a token. "By the moons, look at the face on him," someone had said. "Send him to the Chancery when he grows, mother," someone else had said to Firrabel. "We have need of those who can frighten demons just looking at them." Had it been the Protector who had called out, saying these things? Or someone in his entourage? Who knew? Firrabel didn't remember, then.

He was a child who had had to fight for his life, many times. He learned to fight very well and to despise weakness, in himself, in others. Then, when he was a strapping youth of such horrible mien and reputation that people hastily hid when they saw him coming, Firrabel had given him the token and sent him north. "Go to the Chancery," she had said. "Ask for the Protector and remind him that he chose you out of thousands to serve him."

By this time, she had convinced herself the Protector had said it all. Actually, it had been Bossit himself who had said most of it, and it was Bossit who remembered the whole thing when Jondrigar came to the Chancery at last. The guards had laughed in his face when he'd passed into Chancery lands. They had laughed, but they had passed the word. Bossit had seen monstrousness in the child, he saw the promise of that monstrousness fulfilled in the man. Bossit had given him a spear to see what he could do with it, and he could do a good deal. Jondrigar had become a guardsman, and then the leader of a company, and then head of a battalion. And by the time the old general had died, all the guards in the Chancery were Jondarites, and no one suggested any other candidate to lead the Chancery army.

Jondrigar the gray, the scaly, the pitted, wild-haired, long-armed monster. Jondrigar the untouchable. Jondrigar, who cared for only two people in all the world: Firrabel, who had raised him and cared for him; and Lees Obol, Protector of Man, who had picked him—so he thought—out of all the world. He had never loved a woman, never cared for a child. To Firrabel he sent money and gifts and infrequent letters. To Lees Obol he gave all his devotion and his life. And to Bossit, who furnished the general with tempting morsels from time to time, the monster served as a constant amusement, a source of daily wonder.

As for the general's own feelings, he did not think he had underestimated Queen Fibji. The northlands might rise under one of the male advisers to the scepter, perhaps, but not under the Queen. She was a pacifist. She would not fight. Her young men would fight, but she would not. From what he knew of women—that is, of his dutiful aunt and some even more dutiful whores—Jondrigar believed that women put comfort above all other considerations. Fibji was a woman, and she was comfortable as she was. He, Jondrigar, would allow her just enough comfort to keep her quiescent by exercising his troops at some distance from the Queen's tents. When Noor were to be murdered, maimed, or otherwise brutalized, he would do it out of Fibji's sight or hearing. Though she might learn of it later, it would be after the blood had dried and most of the grieving done. None knew better than Jondrigar how difficult it was to work up an outrage over something that had happened a long time before. So wherever Fibji went, the balloon scouts came to tell him, and he sent the troops elsewhere. A kind of game, really, but effective. The ceaseless depredations of the Jondarites kept the steppe dwellers' population in check and prevented them from assembling the stores they needed to wage outright war: the confiscated grains and roots filled vast storehouses behind the Teeth, enough to keep the Chancery for a generation if it were ever needful.

General Jondrigar was well satisfied with Queen Fibji. If General Jondrigar was grateful for anything, he was grateful for comfortable, dutiful, compliant women.

In a hidden room off a remote corridor of the palace, Ezasper Jorn, Ambassador to the Thraish, built up the small fire in his porcelain stove and invited his guest to bring a chair closer to the warmth.

"Glad the winter's well over," he said, holding his hands to the stove. "One can find out absolutely nothing in the winter." His mighty form was close-wrapped in a heavy cloak, his pendulous ears half-covered by a floppy cap. Still he shivered, holding his huge hands almost upon the surface of the stove. Ezasper Jorn was never warm. Even at the height of polar summer, he shivered. In winter, he was almost immobile. He had fulfilled the duties of his office for many years, mostly by virtue of saying almost nothing to the Thraish and agreeing with everything they said to him. Since no action was ever taken on any recommendation made by Ezasper Jorn—indeed, he seldom made any at all—it did not matter. The position of Ambassador was filled harmlessly, and all at the Chancery were satisfied by that.

"We have to find out somehow," said Koma Nepor, purse-lipped. Chief of Research was a position lacking clear duties but implying vast and often unnameable expectations. Koma brought to the role an instinctive appreciation of mystery coupled with an inquisitive, persistent mind. The mystery over which he now troubled himself was the reported disappearance of animals from the Chancery herds of weehar and thrassil. It could have happened late last fall, perhaps.

Not during the winter, when the creatures were dug deep into the ice. Perhaps early this spring, when the first thaws came and the grass turned green on Chancery lands.

The surviving herds had been kept small at the command of Shavian Bossit, Lord Maintainer of the Household. Generations ago he had perceived the dangerous temptation large herds of weehar and thrassil might present to wandering fliers, assuming any such abrogated the treaty and flew north of the Teeth. It would have been wise, he had felt then as now, to kill the remaining beasts, leaving no cause for temptation at all.

However, the Protector of Man enjoyed red meat from time to time, and General Jondrigar, who regarded each least notion of the Protector as though it were an order given under penalty of death, had seen to it that the herds remained. The Protector received his roasts and chops at intervals, carefully augmented by certain grains and herbs. Men who ate the native animals had learned to serve them thus or risk a bewildering loss of intelligence. On Northshore the relationship between what eats and what is eaten was closer than on many worlds—or so the histories implied. There were those foods, for example, that allowed the fliers to retain their wings while others would have confined them to a life on the ground. There were foods that allowed those in the Chancery to live long, long lives, and others that would have condemned them to an early and brief idiocy. So it was that the fliers ate what they ate in order to maintain their wings, and the Chancery officials, when dining upon roast thrassil, consumed it with leguminous garnish. Which they would not do soon again if too many animals were missing.

"Bormas Tyle has investigated the report and is sure some of the animals are gone," said Ezasper. "He's told Tharius Don about it, you may be sure of that. Bormas may go his own way most of the time, but he is not derelict in his deputized duties. And Bossit won't drop the matter, you may be sure." His flaccid arms were held toward the welcome warmth of the stove, his pouchy face reddened by the heat. "Just *gone*."

"How would he know? We don't keep them on inventory, for the gods' sake. They wander. They get killed. Some of them die."

"Bormas says the two herds were small, almost household herds, kept close to the Chancery. The herdsmen had counted the young last fall, marking some to be set aside for the table of the Protector. When they went to do the butchering last week, there were only a few of the younger animals left. Up to a dozen of them gone, says Bormas."

Ezasper frowned. "Almost enough to make one remember those old legends about the monster in the main files. The one who eats all the apprentices."

Nepor giggled, appreciating this reference to the legend of the monster. "Most likely fliers," he said. "That's really what everyone is worried about. That Talker was here, before winter set in. First time ever, him and his friends. And he wasn't blind. He saw the thrassil, the weehar."

"Bormas wanted those herds killed off, long since."

"Bormas was right to urge it." Koma Nepor mused, "The general should have listened to him. Well, if the fliers have taken the animals, they haven't taken them to a Talons. Nothing for grass eaters in those rocky places. No. They'll have them on pasture somewhere. Most likely on the steppes, or in the badlands. Whichever, they'll have to be found." He scratched himself reflectively, thinking. "Bormas says we must send Jondarites. I told him no, it would be better to get the Noor to find them. Bormas asked why the Noor would bother, considering what use had been made of them in the past. To which question, of course, one cannot give convincing answer. Still, I think no Jondarites. Too much room there for conflict of an undesirable kind. Perhaps we had better consult with Tharius Don?" He left it as a question. Both of them knew what such consultation would mean—an hour's lecture on the morality of the situation. Still, better Tharius Don than Mitiar, who disliked unpleasant news and retaliated against those who brought it. Better than Bossit, who would definitely seek a scapegoat to take responsibility for the disappearance.

They postponed the decision in desultory chat. "And what of your researches?" Ezasper asked. "What new and remarkable things have you found?"

Nepor giggled again. "I've been experimenting with blight, Jorn my boy. There are, ah . . . interesting applications. Applications I do not intend to reveal to General Jondrigar. Oh, by the moons, none of us would be safe if he knew them."

Ezasper turned his wide face toward the other, held up a cautioning fist. "Careful, Koma. If you have found something like that, be very careful speaking of it. To anyone at all."

The other shifted uncomfortably. He never knew exactly what Ezasper meant. Perhaps he meant not to speak of it at all; perhaps he meant to speak to no one except Ezasper himself. Sometimes Nepor felt he did not understand what was going on. Experimental situations were very different from people. In experiment, one could control what happened—or, if not what happened, the conditions under which it happened. Results could be duplicated time after time. With people, very little was controllable. They acted quite unpredictably. It seemed wisest to let the subject go, for now. Still, it was quite remarkable what a sprayer full of blight could do to a living person.

• 23 •

The lady Kesseret prepared to depart from Highstone Lees. On the morning she would go to the top of Split River Pass and down the other side, carried in a palanquin by Noor slaves while she meditated upon the evil of their slavery. Slavery, like Awakening, would vanish on the day. Until then, she could not appear to disapprove of it without coming under suspicion. *More* suspicion, she told herself, sure that she was already suspected of much.

"Have you any word?" she asked Tharius Don.

"The man who played the role of Fatterday did his job well. Queen Fibji will send an expedition to the Southshore."

"When? How soon?"

"Probably not until late summer. Still, that is only a little time. When she does so, we will see that the fliers hear of it. It will give them something to think about besides Rivermen. Also, I've sent an envoy to ask her to search for the missing beasts. The envoy will plant the idea that such beasts should be taken on any voyage, in case there are none beyond the River. They will steal the beasts—if they find them. And this, too, will draw the fliers' attention."

She was not sure this feint would have its desired purpose. The fliers were subtle, more subtle, she thought, than Tharius realized. "When the time comes, Tharius, do you really think the fliers will capitulate? Do you really think they will give up their wings? Become like the Treeci? Legendary

Treeci, I should say. We don't even know if they really exist."

"There are books in the palace library that say they do, Kessie. Old books, which have stood on those shelves for hundreds of years, talk about the Treeci islands. Books no one looks at but me. Luckily, Glamdrul Feynt cares for nothing but his files. Strictly speaking, the books should be his responsibility, yet I thank whatever gods may be that they are where I can read them. And yes, to answer your question, I think the Thraish will capitulate. Rather than see us die or themselves. Once they have experienced the other kind of life, I think they will prefer it."

"You're so sure." She shook her head at him, smiling wanly. He had always been sure, very sure. Perhaps it had been that quality in him that she had loved. So nice to be sure, without doubts.

"They've seen us, Kessie. We don't fly. And yet we have a civilization better than the one the Thraish have. They borrow our craftsmen, they borrow our writing. They take from us constantly. They can't be unaware of the difference. It's only custom that keeps them to the treaty. A hard custom, and one tightly held, but when it comes right down to it, I think they'll be relieved. By all accounts, humans and the Treeci live very well together."

"So you've said, Tharius. I wish I were as sure as you are." She choked, oppressed by this act of leaving him. In a moment her voice came back and she went on, "Sometimes I lie awake in Baris Tower at night. Everything is very quiet. Far off in the town the crier sings out, and his voice comes gently. There is wind, perhaps. I lie there, almost at peace, my mind drifting quietly.

"Oh, Tharius, there is a peaceful place inside the head where one may wander. Like fields, new mown, green and moist and fragrant. One wanders inside oneself, at peace, unconscious of being oneself. Then, suddenly, out of nothing, a hard, hurtful thing intrudes and one cries out."

"I know." He smoothed her hair from her forehead. "I

forget, too, sometimes. I drift, dream. But I always remember again.''

"There is such peace in that forgetting! But yes, one remembers again, and the future looms up like a rocky cliff, creased with bruising edges and sharp corners, a thing which cannot be drifted over but must be climbed, hard stone by hard stone.'' She fell silent for a time, lines starring from her eyes and lips, her face for that moment incredibly ancient.

"When I remember, I start to think of the morning of the rebellion, of the day itself. Our people will have been to the pits in the night and every worker pit will be empty. All the bodies will be in the River. Weighted down. We will have killed every patch of Tears we have been able to find. The fliers will have nothing to eat. . . .''

Tharius Don took up the account. "In every town the crier will call watch against fliers who may come seeking living meat. There will be Tears in the Towers, and these must be sought out and destroyed by fire, by our friends within the Towers. By those outside the Towers, if necessary.''

"I think of Towers burning," she said.

"But not Baris Tower," he said. "In Baris Tower the Superior will tell her Awakeners of a new revelation.''

"Yes," she agreed sadly. "A new revelation, to be preached by the Awakeners to the fliers. A revelation from Potipur which demands that they give up their wings. . . . When I look at someone like Sliffisunda, though, I'm not sure he will ever accept it. There's a kind of hatred in him. For us. For all our kind.''

"Tradition. Custom. That's all. The attitude they've adopted. It doesn't mean that's the only attitude they can adopt.''

"Does the Ambassador to the Thraish agree with you on that point?''

"I don't discuss anything with Jorn. He returned from his journey some time ago, but all I've said to him thus far is 'Good evening.' Ezasper cares for nothing except that the stove be well alight and he not expected to go out on cold days. Don't seek confirmation from those like Jorn, Kessie. Don't doubt our cause. Have faith. When the time comes to

choose between wings or life, the Thraish will choose life
and life with us as . . . well, if not as brothers, at least as
kin.''

"And we, Tharius? When will the day come?''

"Soon. There are only a few more pieces to be set into
place. A few more patches of Tears to kill. A few more
Towers to recruit. A few more groups to get organized for
the night of the strike. Not many. Have patience.''

She, who had had patience for some hundred years, snorted
at this, and he joined her in wry laughter.

"Have you any word of Pamra?''

"No signals. If Ilze had found her, we would know.''

"Let us hope we hear nothing.'' She stretched, moved her
fingers and toes to be sure they had healed. "Let us pray we
hear nothing.''

He nodded. Time pressed, now. Secrecy had to be maintained. They needed some minor distractions to keep the
Talkers busy. They needed absolute quiet from those involved in the conspiracy. They needed no more upsets such
as the one provided by Pamra Don. Not too much to keep
track of, really. He kissed her on the forehead, a valedictory.
They might never see one another again.

"If I am killed while you still live, Kessie, find Pamra
then. Tell her I cared about her.''

She shook her head; a tear gathered that hung, unshed, like
a gem upon her lashes. "Better I don't see her again, love.
Better for all of us. Let us pray she has gone to ground and is
well hidden. Pray we do not hear of her again.''

• 24 •

High in the Talons above the Straits of Shfor in the aerie of Sliffisunda—the Uplifted One, by the grace of Potipur articulate, a Talker of the Sixth Degree—met with his students, newly located Talkers, still awed by their selection. The aerie, once a graceless, chilly cave, full of wind and the stench of guano, had been reshaped by the hands of human slaves. There was a privy slot in the outer wall, set in a niche covered with a heavy curtain. There was a low, broad perch, on which Sliffisunda stood to receive visitors. There were carvings on the walls, and a meat trough with an ornamental post and chains to hold the meat down until it died. Though heavily dosed with Tears, the living human bodies tended to thrash about unpleasantly while they were being eaten. Sliffisunda sometimes believed that despite the stench of carrion, he might have preferred to eat as the ordinary fliers did, in the bone pits.

The students before him, three of them, were egglings who hardly knew the meaning of the Covenant. They did not understand humiliation. It was Sliffisunda's job to teach them, to let them know how far the Thraish had fallen from their onetime communion with the gods, and by imparting that knowledge to cleave these youngsters to the doctrine of rage that governed the Talons.

"Perch," he directed them, waiting impatiently while they settled before him, wings outspread, heads carried well back on their flexible necks, foot talons stretching beyond their knees as they crouched, knees on feet, in the posture of subordination.

"I want you to imagine you are a flier," he said at last, when they were well settled. "Just a flier, a female. Not a Talker at all. I want you to imagine it is long ago, more than a thousand years." There was a snigger at this. There was always a snigger at this, but Sliffisunda waited without outward show of impatience for his own heavy regard to make their eggishness manifest. Soon they felt his disapproval and became uncomfortable, shifting from foot to foot, staring at him from lowered eyes.

Sliffisunda's voice became a monotone, a rhythmic chant. "It is spring. You have slept the winter away in the caves low in the mountains of the north. Now the time of warmth has come, and you emerge from your cave to the time of rejoicing. Your name is Shishus, flier of the Thraish. . . ."

His voice was hypnotic. They would imagine, combining what they knew in their blood with what they had learned and what he would tell them in his chanting. They would fall into a trance, and in the trance they would dream that last awakening of ancient times.

In the trance it seemed that the season of warmth had come upon the northern plains. The cold rains were over. On the endless prairies the tall grass moved like water, silver blue like the River the grass moved, breaking around the herd of weehar as the River broke on the rocks of Shfor, near the Talons. The herd whuffled nervously as Shishus's shadow fell across them, she crying, "Rejoice! Warmth is come!"

The weehar rejoiced in their own way, heads down, legs trembling. Each thing rejoiced in its own way. Even trees, doubtless. With warmth came the end of hibernation, the season of rejoicing, the season of Potipur's Promise to the Thraish.

Shishus whispered the name of her people. "Thraish." The word was a rejoicing in itself. After the lonely time of cold, she longed for Thraish, for huntmates. First the rejoicing. Then the obligatory trip to the Talons for the dancing as the moons gathered. Then mating. Then nesting, the joy of nestlings. "Thraish," she whispered, turning on her strong wings above the prairie.

Though perhaps the Talkers would suggest again that the dancing not take place. As they had at the last Conjunction. Last warm season there had been rebellious muttering against the Talkers, and Shishus had been a leader in that rebellion. In old times Talkers had been wise, settling disputes over nesting sites or huntmates. Last season—no, the season before that and before that as well—they had not been helpful. Not orthodox. Of late the Talkers seemed to doubt Potipur's Promise, the promise of ten thousand years. "Do my will and ye shall have plenty."

Thinking of it made Shishus angry. Among the free fliers there was talk of overthrowing the Talkers. Shishus had told them it was foolish talk. It was not necessary to overthrow the Talkers. They could simply be ignored!

Potipur's Promise was holy. Long, long ago the Thraish had been hungry. All the hoovar had been eaten and were gone. Then came the Talker Shinnisush, bringing Potipur's Promise to the people. "Follow me and ye shall have plenty!" And after the promise there had been great explosions in the northlands, mountains jutting fire, and endless herds of thrassil came, driven out of the north by the fire, driven from behind the great mountains. The Thraish had rejoiced in plenty once more.

But in time the thrassil also were gone, eaten. Then the world had shaken again, and the weehar had come, down in great herds to the silver-blue plains that lay between the Riverlands and the northern mountains.

Great herds.

Shishus planed in a wide gyre, peering down. One herd only. Small. Perhaps she should wait to find a larger herd. No. Cold season had been long, and soon huntmates would arrive. She threw back her head and cried loud into the sky, "Invitation! Join! Rejoice! Summer beasts are here."

Below, Shishus's shadow fell across beasts, and they began to gallop, a frenzied flight, knowing time to rejoice was near. Far on the western horizon two winged specks moved toward Shishus, crying as they came, "Rejoice, rejoice." Her huntmates: Slililan, Shusisanda.

They met in midair, wingtips caressing, beaks touching the tender sweet places behind ears, glorying in touch, in flight. Then they cried together, fell together, talons extended, crying the great invitation to the weehar. "Rejoice! Rejoice!"

The weehar rejoiced, galloping, snorting, leaping in a wild dance upon the grass, evading, skipping, falling at last beneath the clutching talons, beneath the spearing beaks. Blood ran hot into Shishus's beak.

In Sliffisunda's aerie the young shifted uncomfortably from foot to foot, beaks agape. They tasted the hot blood of the weehar, heard the cries of the huntmates. Sliffisunda chanted to them, telling them what to feel, what to experience. In the trance they heard Sliffisunda's voice:

"Rejoice! Rejoice!"

Away upon the prairie the few remaining weehar stopped running, stood trembling, the few young in the center of the group. This was how weehar prayed to Potipur. This is how the herd beasts rejoiced. Shishus stood upon one of the beasts she had killed, gorged now, beak dripping, and called to her huntmates to see the beasts rejoicing.

"Not rejoicing," snapped Slililan. Slililan did not always sound like free flier. Sometimes she sounded almost like Talker. "No rejoicing, Shishus, silly flier. Weehar scared. Only scared. Herd too small."

"Rejoice in own way," Shishus screamed. Slililan was spoiling their first feast. "Slililan makes unorthodox talk. Doubts Potipur."

Slililan flew at Shishus then, battle ready. Only Shusisanda's bulk thrust between had stopped them as they stood with wings cocked high in threat, spear-beaked and blood-eyed. "Huntmates," Shusisanda whispered. "Time to rejoice."

What had made them grow so angry? There had never been anger among free fliers before. They had fought only the mock battles of conjugation, vying for the dancing males.

They had not fought one another. Was it something in the look of the plains? In the trembling silence of the few weehar?

"Find bigger herd," Shishus demanded, lifting away from the many bodies that littered the ground. Perhaps they should not have killed so many. They could have killed only three, one for each of them, though they could have eaten only a tiny fraction even of that. Already grouped in a wide circle around the corpses were the silly fliers, those with no speech, waiting for their own time to rejoice. Shishus and her huntmates winged toward the Talons, uneasy as distances drifted by, uneasier yet when they came within sight of the peaks.

There the hunters of Thraish, free fliers, gathered in their hundreds of thousands, thick as grass, their clattering so loud it reached the huntmates when they were still far away.

They had flown half around the world, had arrived at the Talons, but there had been no bigger herd of weehar.

There had been no herds at all.

They arrived to sounds of the summoning rattle, propelled to and fro on its flexible sapling base by young fliers, telling Talkers to come out of their rocky towers. Speaker's rock was empty. No Talkers sat upon it. Rattle went on as sound of Thraish grew louder, more agitated.

Then silence, for Talker came out, old Talker, blue with age, eyes deep-pouched, beak silver and ragged-edged. He came from a dark hole in rock, perched on doorstep, peered nearsightedly at great throng there, said in a dry, uninterested voice, "Rejoice, people of Thraish."

There was only muttering from free fliers. Shishus, alone among throng, called response. "Rejoice!"

All eyes came to Shishus, fastening upon her. Muttering grew louder. Talker fixed his old eyes upon her, called to her.

"You found weehar then, flight leader?"

Shishus could not reply. This was not the way ceremony went. Talker asked again, and yet again, before Shishus could think to say, "Huntmates have rejoiced."

"How many weehar did you find?"

Shishus conferred with Shusisanda. How many had there been? Five claws? About that. Fifty.

"And when you had rejoiced, how many left?"

Three claws, perhaps. Or less.

Silence then upon Talons. A long, uneasy silence, unbroken except by rustling of thousands shifting from foot to foot in an agony of apprehension. "Promise of Potipur," one called from midst of free fliers, whining. "Promise of Potipur."

"Ah, well," cried old Talker. "If Potipur has promised, then free fliers of Thraish have nothing to worry about."

Muttering began again, angrily this time. Potipur had promised plenty, but there was no plenty. So. So. There must be fault somewhere. Evil. Sin. Talkers, most likely. Their fault. Their sin. Doubting.

The old Talker might have read their minds. "Who told you free fliers last warm season not to eat weehar?"

Muttering. It was true. Talkers had told them that. Talkers had said weehar were too few. Free fliers had told Talkers something different instead. Free fliers had told Talkers to keep quiet. Had told them, "Promise of Potipur."

"Last warm season, who told males not to dance? Who told free fliers not to breed last Conjunction? Who told the fliers to break their eggs?"

The Talkers had told them. Talkers said to eat fish. Foul fish that softened beaks, made feathers fall, which made free fliers unable to fly at all. Talkers said not to nest. Not do Conjunction. But flight leaders had cawed laughter. Promise of Potipur. Shishus had cawed laughter with all free fliers. Do will of Potipur! Breed. Grow more numerous. Have plenty!

"Who told fliers to eat, breed?" Old Talker had a voice like rocks rubbing together in flood. "Flight leaders said eat, breed. Flight leaders, like Shishus there. She called shame on Talkers. Told you Potipur would provide plenty. So. Ask flight leaders where is rejoicing Potipur will provide."

The Talker had gone then, quickly, down inside the stone, where it would be safe against Thraish, for Thraish were very angry at Talkers.

At first.

Anger was there. But Talkers were not there. Free fliers could not attack them. Could not spear beak, wing buffet. Talkers were different. Males who would not dance. Males who changed, instead. Knew more. Used more words. Had different thoughts. Lived down in stone, somewhere deep where Thraish could not get to them.

So, wrath turned against others.

Against flight leaders.

Against Shishus, flying, flying, hiding among stones, in grass, walking along streams to hide, not flying, huntmates lost, pecked to death, only Shishus living, eating stilt lizards, eating worms, living, while all around Thraish died by thousands, thousands. Starving.

In the towns along the River lived the two-legged outlanders, humans. Despicable nonfliers. Good smelling. Full of hot blood. Weak. Slow. Some fliers hunted this meat. Some fliers ate this meat, died. Screaming, insides burning, they died. Human meat was poison to the Thraish.

Some ate fish. Feathers dropped out for a time. Bones changed. Couldn't fly. Treeci, meaning "crawler." Fish eaters. Filth. Betrayers of Potipur.

Some, like Shishus, ate lizards, worms, bodies of dead fliers. Only those few like Shishus lived, eating dead fliers, smaller birds, not eating the poisonous humans, not eating fish as the foul Treeci did, who forsook Potipur's Promise, giving up their power of flight. It was a test, a test. Potipur testing. Soon would come Potipur's Promise.

Of the Talkers, only a few lived. Of the fliers, only a few, like Shishus, survived.

In the aerie, the egglings woke from their trance, gagging, no longer full of giggles.

"Attend," said Sliffisunda. "Some survived. Shishus, whose story you have heard, survived. And many of us, the Talkers, survived. It was one of our number, Thoulia, who learned that the flesh of the humans could be softened by Tears of Viranel and then safely eaten by us. We took them, the soft, weak humans, took them to eat.

"We chose not to eat fish, not to become flightless, not to betray the Promise of Potipur.

"But the humans fought us. Many of them died. Many of us died. Thoulia said to us, 'They will never let you take them without fighting. And if you kill them all as you did the weehar, what will you eat? And if they kill us all, who will keep Potipur's name alive?'

"We chose rather to arrange matters in order to assure ourselves a sufficiency of human flesh.

"We made treaty with humans. We offered some few of them the elixir of the Talkers in return for the flesh of other humans. Dead flesh for the fliers, who are many. Live flesh for us Talkers, who are few. We gave some few of them the elixir if they would worship our gods. We offered some of them long, long life if they would become Awakeners, build the Towers, let the Thraish feast in their bone pits and live upon those Towers. One Tower at first, then two. Then four. Then many. Few free fliers at first, then more. Not many, about eighty thousand. Living on Towers of life. Towers."

The young ones shifted on the floor. They had not yet had time to take in what they had learned. They looked at him with baffled eyes, one, bolder than the rest, whispering, "But we despise the Towers?"

Sliffisunda nodded his approval. This one would go far.

"Yes, egglings," he said in a grating whisper, lifting his tail to deposit a symbolic dropping on the subject under discussion. "Never forget it. We despise the Treeci, our own kind, who betrayed the Promise of Potipur and gave up their wings. We despise those who are consumed by us, made into shit by us. We despise those among them who will sell their kindred for a few years of stinking human life.

"Yes, egglings. We despise the Towers, and the Chancery. We despise all humans in the world of the Thraish. We allow mankind to live only that we may live winged as Potipur commands. If we could not live as our god commands, we would die. And every human would die with us, for we despise them all."

When the egglings had gone, he left the wide perch to go

to one of the openings in the stone. The humans called them windows and put glass or oiled paper over them. The Thraish called them spy holes and hid them behind hangings or piers of rock. This one looked toward the north.

The north! Behind the great mountains. Sliffisunda had seen thrassil there, and weehar. Though he had not yet been hatched when the great beasts were last seen, he knew them when he saw them, as he knew his own wing feathers. He already knew the taste and smell of them. And he knew filthy humans had them and would never give them to the Thraish voluntarily.

Which did not matter. Now that the Thraish knew they were there, it would not take long to get them. A few strong fliers had already been instructed to go through the pass in the deep night, find young ones, carry them out. Indeed, the task might already have been accomplished.

A dozen young ones would grow up, become a herd. A herd would become a great, great number in time. And when there were enough of them . . .

"Now, egglings," he imagined himself saying at some not-too-distant time. "Now, egglings, every human shall die, because Potipur our god commands that we kill them all."

• 25 •

Once Pamra had heard the voices clearly, her doubts and fears left her. Rapture and joy had returned. The rapture that had abandoned her at the worker pit when she had found Delia; the rapture that she had thought forever gone; the joy she had felt in Neff's company; the joy she had thought eternally lost; now they had returned, both, so that she walked encircled by peace and sureness, unable to remember a time when she might have doubted.

Thrasne watched her and hated what he saw.

Before Strinder's Isle she had begun to talk with him, begun to care about the *Gift*, begun to take part in the daily life of the River. He had begun to plan for their future together. He knew of a carpenter in Darkel-don who would rebuild the owner-house into a fit place for Pamra, Pamra and their children. He thought of a weaver he had met in one of the little towns past Shfor. From her he would buy covers for the beds and hangings, for the colors she used were the colors of sunset and dawn, warm as light itself. He would buy gowns for Pamra herself, gowns of that long fiber pamet grown only in the bottom lands near Zephyr, soft as down. She would respond to these gifts with affection and approval. They would plan together for their future. It was all there, in his mind, how each thing would happen in its time.

Now she had left him, gone elsewhere, become as remote as the girl he remembered outside the Tower in Baris, tolerating his presence, perhaps. Perhaps not noticing he was there. She spoke to him of voices, gently, as though to a child, as though he should be able to hear what she heard. She nodded, smiled, as though in conversation. Sometimes she sat upon the deck of the *Gift* with Lila on her lap, pointing to something Thrasne could not see, but which he suspected Lila did see. At least the child's eyes followed Pamra's eyes, followed and fixed in a kind of concentration that was not childlike.

Seeing Pamra like this, he began to be afraid she would leave him, though for the time being she seemed willing to stay on the River. He saw her sometimes murmuring to herself, as though rehearsing words she would say, but when they stopped at Trens and Villian-gar, or any of a dozen other small townships, she made no move to go ashore.

Once, she had shared in his life, at least a little. She had chatted with him of the sights along the shore, sometimes gone to the market with him in the towns where they stopped. She had cooked for him, appearing to enjoy it. He had told himself it was only a matter of time, of patience—both of which he had in seemingly unlimited quantity.

Now, since Strinder's Isle, all his plans seemed moved into some future so remote he was not sure there was enough time after all. For the first time he thought of himself growing old, still without her. Old, still alone. No children to roll about the owner-house floor and learn to be boatmen in their turn. No woman to share the everlasting voyage, no Suspirra. What right had she to destroy his hopes? When he had watched over her, sought her out, saved her?

He found himself growing angry at her. What right had she to change in this way! And for what? Some Treeci who had died. Some dream she had had. When compared with his hopes, what was that? Nothing!

Nothing, he assured himself, going to the room he had given her and entering it without asking her leave. He took hold of her before she quite knew he was there, his arms tight around her, his lips on hers, forcing her lips apart, tasting her mouth, pressing her beneath him onto the bed.

And she did not move, did not seem to breathe. When he drew back to look into her face, it was like looking into the face of an image he might have carved from pale wood, then smoothed until its reality was blurred into mere shape. So she was, mere shape, eyes wide and unseeing, not Suspirra, not Pamra even, not anything.

"Pamra!" He shook her, slapped her. She fell against the bed, slumped, limp.

Slowly her eyes focused, saw him. "But you must help me, Thrasne. Don't you see? You were meant to help me. That's why you came for me. Mother sent you, don't you see? To help me?" Her eyes filled with hurt tears, and his heart churned within him, creating a vertigo, a sick dizziness. "Help me, Thrasne."

Her face cleared then. The tears dried. The rapture came into her eyes once more, and she nodded, hearing something he could not hear.

He stood up unsteadily and left her, feeling a deeper loneliness than he had felt since long, long ago in Xoxxy-Do.

Medoor Babji saw him leave the cabin, saw the unsteady walk, the drunken demeanor. He leaned over the rail as though he might be sick or readying himself to leap into the water, and she moved up beside him to lay a hard, small hand upon his back.

"Thrasne owner," she said, risking everything for his pain. "It doesn't take a Jarb Mendicant to tell us the woman is mad." Jarb Mendicants had a reputation, not often undeserved, for treating mental troubles of one kind or another, and it was in the Jarb Houses that the truly mad found refuge.

For a time he seemed not to have heard her. "Mad?" he asked at last, as though he did not know the meaning of the word.

"Mad, Thrasne. Though she has not tasted jarb to see visions, still she has visions of her own. She is not your Suspirra because the Suspirra you dreamed of was not mad and this woman is. Your Suspirra is an ideal, Thrasne owner. Not a real creature of this world. This woman, Pamra, she is only a semblance of your ideal, and she is real. Of this world. Therefore, imperfect.''

"No, not of this world," he disagreed simply. "But I love her with all my heart."

She shook her head, tears forming at the corners of her eyes. She, Babji, hardened by the marketplaces of a half hundred towns, to cry so for this man. She shook her head angrily, letting the tears fly away. "Then love her if you must, Thrasne. But you must look somewhere else for the things you dream of." She left him and went to her bedding where it lay upon the deck. Long into the night she lay there, alternately angry and sorrowful, picturing herself and Thrasne, together, without realizing she was doing it. He was not Noor. Given only that, he was not her equal, for the Noor were what they were only to others of their kind. To mate with one outside the Noor was to diminish oneself. She had no right to consider him at all, but consider him she did. Finally, just before dawn, she said to herself in an ironic voice, "Well, love him if you must, Babji; but look elsewhere for the things you dream of."

The morning brought them to a mountainous region, a place of towering peaks and precipitous cliffs; a Talons. Upon the stony peaks they could see the clustered forms of fliers, and high above were their spread wings, floating in great circles. Thrasne kept the *Gift* well offshore, away from the cliffs and the treacherous currents that swirled around the tumbled stone at their feet. Pamra stood at the rail, peering forward, shifting from foot to foot, speaking aloud, as though to a company of friends, pointing to the fliers far above in increasing agitation. Thrasne watched her, telling himself he did not care what she was doing. He had not spoken to her since the night before except in passing, as he might speak to any member of the crew. Now she acted as though she had been told to go or do something she was uncertain of, for she asked something again and again, almost plaintively. Whatever answer she received was eventually enough, for when night came she went to her bed with a calm face. They would come into Thou-ne on the morning tide.

When they tied up at the jetty and edged out the plank, he
was not really surprised to see her leaving the boat. He
wrestled with himself for a moment, deciding not to follow
her, then deciding that he must. He had promised to keep her
safe. He had made no conditions then; it would not be fair or
proper to set conditions now. Still, he was hard put to it to
follow her as she went through the town, one foot in front of
the other, as sure as the wind. She had a cloak drawn over
her head, but when she reached the public square she drew it
back, hair floating wildly free as the drowned Suspirra's had
used to do. She mounted to the steps of the public fountain
and turned, arm outstretched, face glowing like a little moon.
"People," she cried in a voice like a flute, softly insinuating.
"Is it not better when the people know?" Those in the
marketplace turned to see her, astonished, drawing close and
staring as she stood there, gathering them in with her hands.

And from some little fellow at the edge of the square came
a scream, almost hysterical, a treble cry as from a child but
with the force of a trumpet blown, announcing war. "She has
come, in flesh, the Bearer of Truth!" It was Peasimy Flot,
alert to the coming of light as he had always been, always
remembering the dark, the lies.

(Peasimy, remembering following the Awakeners when
they took his father to the next town east and then just threw
him in the worker pits in the dark, as though they didn't care;
Peasimy remembering when the body fixer told him it wouldn't
hurt, what they were going to do to him that time he broke
his arm, and it did hurt, a lot; Peasimy remembering the
shining face from beneath the water, and it was this face.)

"She has come," he cried again, like a call to battle.

A shout went up then. It was half surprise, half recognition, from a hundred throats. Thrasne had lingered at the
edge of the square and was suddenly at the back of a crowd,
all watching her. Pamra's eyes opened very wide, as though
to take this in. Then she nodded, answering their shout as a
sigh went through those gathered by.

"I have come," she agreed, beckoning to the thin, hectic-
looking young fellow who had called out. "I have come

bringing the truth. You have been expecting me, and I have come.''

Thrasne turned back to the docks, sick at heart.

He went to a tavern, where he drank among a crowd of doubters and nay sayers, then returned to the *Gift*. Medoor Babji stood on the deck, reading something while stroking the feathers of a large, dun-colored bird. When she saw him coming, she tossed the bird into the air, then put the missive in her pocket as she came toward him. She was the only one there. She had stayed behind when her fellows had left the boat to buy stores for their journey. Perhaps she had known he would return.

"Medoor Babji," he croaked. "You were right. She is mad. Mad or possessed. Or something else I have never heard of. What shall I do?''

His agony was manifest. She held out her arms, and he fell into them as into a well. She held him, kissing his sun-browned face where the hair grew back, tasting the sweat of his forehead along with his tears. What could he do?

"I have kept her hidden, but she is in the square now, where anyone can see her. The Laughers will find her! Or the fliers. I think she will preach revolt against the fliers.'' So much he had inferred from her soliloquies over the past days.

"If she is surrounded by people?'' Medoor asked abstractedly. She was still thinking of the message the bird had brought, a letter from her mother, Queen Fibji. A letter commanding her to a great exploration, a voyage. How could she think of something else just now? Yet she did, seeing in the agonized face before her all agonized faces, Noor and shore-fish alike. "How can the Laughers take her if she is surrounded by a multitude?''

"If the Laughers cannot take her, they will send Jondarites. Jondarites to put down a rebellion.'' Thrasne had seen this happen once or twice in the past. He was sure of it, hopelessly sure.

Jondarites.

Holding him in her arms, close against her girl's breasts, Medoor felt the chill of the word. Jondarites. Now, now she

SHERI S. TEPPER

began to realize what was really happening here. It was not a matter merely of a madwoman and a man. There was more to it than that.

Jondarites.

Jondarites and the Noor.

Queen Fibji, far to the north, bearing greater burdens than anyone should have to bear. The endless depredations of the Jondarites. The great plan. And now this word of an even greater possibility, which the seeker bird had brought. If the Jondarites were sent in great numbers to Northshore, to put down a rebellion, there would be fewer to prey upon the Noor. And if there were fewer depredations among the Noor, then the Noor might better do what was best for them.

"Come," she whispered at last. "Let us go see what Pamra is really doing."

Pamra had gone to the Temple, together with half the town. Thrasne and Medoor Babji pushed their way into a corner of the crowded sanctuary, where they could kneel with the others before the image of the glowing woman. At first Thrasne did not recognize his carving of Suspirra, for it shone with a light he had never seen. Only when Pamra stood before it and claimed it as a precursor, divinely meant, sent to announce her coming, did he become truly aware of what it was. He wanted to laugh. He would have laughed except for the ominous stillness in the place. Precursor? Yes, but from his knife and a lump of fragwood, nothing more than that.

Afterward he scarcely remembered what she had said. There had been something in it of love and something of righteousness. She had spoken of being misled. Of a conspiracy to keep the Protector of Man unmindful of the evil that flew upon the winds of the world. She spoke of the worker pits and of the great lie of Sorting Out. She told them truth, that the true Sorting took place in another realm, beyond the world, and what happened in this world was a blasphemy. She called the fliers Servants, not of Abricor, but of their own pride. She said all that, over and over, in different words, making them laugh and weep and cry out. Someone called to her, asking how she knew these things, and she said her voices had told her to stand before them and tell the truth, at which many had shouted out they would follow her in the telling.

"Crusade," she cried. "Let all who can, join me in crusade. We will carry the word of this injustice around the world. And when we go to free the Protector of Man from those who hold him in ignorance, we will be many, a multitude, a great tide to sweep away the evil of the world." Lila lay in her arms as she said this, looking out at the crowd with great, wide eyes, reaching out her baby arms toward them all.

The strange little man who had first hailed her called out again, "The Mother of Truth," and others echoed these words. His face and theirs were shining with devotion.

Thrasne thrilled to her voice, as did everyone within sound of it. He could not stop himself. His flesh responded even when he told himself it was all foolishness. There were others there, Awakeners among them. They, too, looking at her with an expression of alert surprise and wonderment, nodding their heads as though she had been Viranel herself.

Not Viranel. No. Viranel's face carved on the wall behind Pamra was only an image, crude and somehow horribly inhuman. One could not worship a god that was a stranger. Not Viranel. Something finer than that. Holier than that.

And even then, he wanted her still. The impossibility of that wanting struck him like a blow, and he leaned forward on his knees and wept as Medoor Babji regarded him thoughtfully, fingering in her deep pocket the message she had received.

And Peasimy crouched at Pamra's feet as she went on teaching, lit from within as though by flame. He crouched there, cheeks red with the fire of her talk, eyes burning also, all of him lit up as if from within by that hot, plasmic vapor, as though he were liquid, without form except as her words gave him form and meaning, shaped by her with that shape crystallizing in every instant to something more refined, simpler, with keener edges and corners to it. "Light comes," he murmured to himself, a litany, an obligatto to her speech. "Light comes, light comes."

But then, his eyes lighting upon the tall, dark-cloaked Jondarites, who made a shadowy enclosure about the sanctuary, unable in their uncommanded state either to attend to what Pamra was saying or prevent her from speaking, held in abeyance as the dammed River holds itself, full of force and power that is for the moment unused, not out of conviction but out of simple inability to act—seeing these, their high-plumed helmets nodding as they craned their necks to observe all who came into that throng, Peasimy spoke again.

"But first, night comes. Night comes."

The story of Pamra Don,
Thrasne, and Medoor Babji
is concluded in
Southshore: The Awakeners, Volume II.

1

When Pamra left Thou-ne, moving westward along the River road, some thousand of the residents of Thou-ne went after her. Most of them were provisioned to some extent, though there were some who went with no thought for food or blankets, trusting in a providence that Pamra had not promised and had evidently not even considered. Peasimy Flot, for all his seeming inanity, was well provided for. He had a little cart with things in it, things he had been putting by for some time. The widow Flot would have been surprised to find in it items that had disappeared from her home over the last fifteen years or so. There were others in Thou-ne who would have been equally surprised to find their long-lost belongings assisting Peasimy in his journey.

The procession came to Atter, and though some of the Thou-neites dropped out of the procession, many of Atter joined it. Pamra preached in the Temple there, to general acclaim. Then came Bylme and Twarn-the-little, then Twarn-the-big—where the townspeople made Pamra a gift of a light wagon in which she might ride, pulled by her followers—then a dozen more towns, and in each of them the following grew more numerous, the welcome more tumultuous. Peasimy himself began to ap-point "messengers" to send ahead with word of their coming. It was something that came to him, all at once. "Light comes," he told them. "That is what you must say." As time went on, the messages grew more detailed and ramified, but it was always Peasimy who sent them.

It was on a morning of threatening cloud that they left Byce-barrens for the town of Chirubel.

The storm did not precisely take them by surprise; the day
had brought increasing wind and spatters of rain from very near
dawn until midafternoon. Still, when in late afternoon the full
fury of the wind broke over them and the skies opened, the
multitude were in nowise prepared for it. Some stopped where
they were, crawling under their carts or pitching their tents as
best they might, to cower under them out of the worst of the
downpour. Others fled into the woods, where they sought large
trees or overhanging ridges. Pamra, high on her wagon, simply
pointed ahead with one imperious finger, and the men who
dragged the wagon, half-drowned by the water flowing over
their faces, staggered on into the deluge. It was not until they
stumbled into the outer wall of the Jarb House that they realized
she had pointed toward it all along. Pamra came down from the
wagon, and the dozen or so of them, including Peasimy Flot,
struggled around the perimeter of the place looking for a door.

It opened when they pounded, warmth drifting out into the
chill together with a puff of warm, dry air laden with strange
smells and a haze of smoke. Peasimy coughed. Pamra pressed
forward against the warding arm of the doorkeeper, the others
following, gasping, wetter than fish.

They passed down a lengthy corridor into the main hall to
stand there stunned at the scale of the place. It was like standing
in a chimney. At one side stairs curved up to a balcony that
spiraled around the open area, twisted up, and up, kept on going
around and around, smaller and smaller, to the seeming limit of
their eyes, where it ended in a dark glassy blot, a tented skylight
black with rain. It was, Pamra thought, like being inside the
trunk of a hollow tree with an opening at the top and all the
tree's denizens peering down at you. Heads lined the balconies,
went away to be replaced by others, and throughout the whole
great stack of living creatures came a constant rustle and mum-
ble of talk, a bubbling pulse of communication that seemed to
be one seamless fabric of uninterrupted sound.

From some of the balconies nets hung, littered with a flotsam
of clothing and blankets. From other balconies long, polished
poles plunged to lower levels. A brazier was alight at the center
of the floor, its wraiths rising in dim veils in this towering,
smokestack space.

"Come in," said the Mendicant ironically. "So nice to have you."

"It is raining out there," announced Pamra evenly, no whit aware of the sarcasm. She drew back the cloak that had covered Lila to disclose the child, not at all discomfited by the soaking she had received.

"Wet," affirmed Peasimy. "Dreadful wet. A great flood out of the skies. Mustn't let *her* drown. Too important."

"Ah," assented the Mendicant. "And you are?"

"The crusade," said Peasimy. "We are the crusade. Light comes! She is the Bearer of Truth, the very Mother of Truth."

"Ah," said the Mendicant again, frowning slightly. He had heard of this. All this segment of Northshore had heard of this, one way or the other. As one of the Order's more trusted messengers, he had more interest in it than most. A message had come through Chiles Medman, Governor General of the Order, from Tharius Don asking the Order to assist in procuring information.

"Trale," he introduced himself. "Mendicant brother of the Jarb. What can I offer you by way of assistance?"

"Towels," said Pamra simply. "And a fire to dry ourselves. Something hot to drink if you have it conveniently by." She stared around her, up at the endless balconies where people came and went, staring down at her, leaving the railings to others who stared in their turn. Pale blots. Mouths open. Hands moving in beckoning gestures. Something distressed her, but she could not identify it. Something was wrong, missing, as though she had forgotten to put on her skirt or her tunic. She looked down at herself, puzzled. She was damp but fully dressed. Why, then, this feeling of nakedness?

Trale led them across the hall, through an arch beneath the balcony and into a wide, low room that curved away just inside the outer wall. A refectory. Pamra shivered. It was not unlike the refectory at the Tower of Baris. The smells were not unlike those smells. Cereals and soap, steam and grease, cleanliness at war with succulence. Trale beckoned to them from an angled corner, a smaller room opening off the large one, where a fire blazed brightly upon the hearth.

"I'll return in a moment," he murmured, leaving them there.

Those who had drawn the cart stood back, waiting for Pamra to approach the fire. She gestured them forward. The room was warm enough without baking herself. She took off her outer clothing and spread it on a table. Her knee-length undertunic was only damp, clinging to her body like a second skin. The men turned their eyes away under Peasimy's peremptory gaze, one of them flushing.

Trale was back in a moment with towels and a pile of loosely woven robes over one arm. He did not seem to notice Pamra's body under the clinging fabric but merely handed her one of the robes, as impersonally as a servant. Behind him came a man and a woman, one bearing a tea service, the other a covered platter at which Peasimy looked with suspicion.

"Jarb," said Trale. "It is our custom."

"We won't—" Pamra began.

"No. It is *our* custom. With any visitor. Call it—oh, a method of diagnosis."

"We are not ill."

"The diagnosis is not always of illness. Do take tea. This is a very comforting brew. It has no medicinal qualities aside from that."

They sat steaming before the fire, moisture rising from them and from their discarded clothing in clouds. Rain fell down the chimney, making small spitting noises in the fire. The wall at their side reverberated to the thunder outside, hummed to the bow-stroke of the wind. In the great hall the voice murmur went on and on. Beside the fire Trale knelt to scrape coals into a tiny brazier. Beside the brazier lay three oval roots, warty and blue, each the size of a fist. Jarb roots, Pamra thought. Trale peeled the roots carefully, dropping the peels into a shallow pan. When all three were peeled, he laid the roots into the ashes and began to dry the peels over the brazier, stirring them with a slender metal spoon. The woman who had brought in the tea buried the peeled roots in the ashes and turned to smile at Pamra.

"It is only the peel which has the power of visions. Jarb root itself is delicious. The Noor eat it all the time. Have you ever tasted it?"

Pamra shook her head, oppressed once more by the sense of something missing. "No." She ate less and less as the crusade wore on. Hunger seemed scarcely to touch her. Now, for some reason, however, she felt ravenous. Perhaps it was the smoke. Perhaps the smell of food. "I am hungry, though."

"They only take a few moments to steam. Some scrape the ashes off, but I like the taste." She drew a pipe from her pocket and handed it to Trale, who filled it with the powdery scraps from the pan. All three had pipes, and in a moment all three were alight, seated before the fire, the smoke from the pipes floating out into the room, into the refectory, away into the chimney of the great hall. The fragrance was the same one that already permeated everything. Sweet, spicy. Pamra folded her arms on the table and laid her head upon them, suddenly both hungry and tired. She had not felt this hungry, this tired, in months. Why was she here? She thought briefly of the *Gift of Potipur*, wishing she were aboard, translating the murmur of Tower talk into the murmur of tidal current, the thunder outside into the creak of boat timbers. She could be there. With Thrasne. Instead of here. Beside her Lila chortled and said, clearly, "Over the River. Thrasne went over the River."

Peasimy turned, his little ruby mouth open, cheeks fiery red with the drying he had given them. "She talked!"

Pamra nodded sleepily. "She does, sometimes."

"I hadn't heard her before."

"She talks about the River a lot. Mostly that." She rubbed her forehead fretfully. The sweet smell of the Jarb had soaked into the top of her nose and was filling it, like syrup. She turned to find the three smokers knocking the dottle from their pipes onto the hearth. The immediacy of the smell was dissipating.

The woman raked the baked Jarb root from the fire, brushing it off and placing it upon a little plate. This she placed before Pamra with a spoon. "Try a little."

Pamra spooned off a bite, blowing on it to cool it. The root was sweet, too, but delicious. The slightly ashy taste only complemented it. She took another spoonful, then hesitated.

"Go ahead, eat it all," the woman said. "There are people bringing plenty of food for you and for the others."

By the fire, Trale sat, rocking back and forth.

"Did you have a vision?" asked Peasimy curiously, studying the man's face.

"Oh, yes."

"What was it of?"

"Of you, Peasimy Flot. And of Pamra Don. And of what is to come."

"Oh!" Peasimy clapped his hands, delighted. "Tell us!"

Trale shook his head. "I'm afraid it can't be told. There are only colors and patterns."

"Red and orange and yellow of flame," said the woman. "Black of smoke."

"Red and orange and yellow of flowers," said the man. "Black of stony mountains."

"Red and orange and yellow of metal," said Trale. "Black of deep mines."

"That doesn't sound like much of a vision," pouted Peasimy.

"Or too much of one," said Pamra, one side of her mouth lifted in a half smile. The Jarb root had settled into her, making some of the same kind of happiness Glizzee spice often made. Not rapture. More a contentment. Warmth. It had been a sizable root, and her sudden hunger was appeased. She smiled again, head nodding with weariness. "I'm so sleepy."

"Come with me," the woman said. "We'll find a place for you to rest."

They went out into the great hall again and up the spiraling balcony. A twist and a half up the huge trunk, the woman pointed into a room where a wide bed was spread with gaily worked quilts. The door was fastened back with a strap, and the woman loosened it now, letting the door sag toward its latch.

"Sleep. When you've slept enough, come back down to the place we were. I'll be there, or Trale. Will the baby be all right, here with you?"

Pamra nodded, so weary she could hardly hold her head up. She heard the latch click as she crawled into the bed, felt Lila curl beside her with a satisfied murmur, then was gone into darkness.

Outside the room people moved to and fro, some of them pausing to stare curiously at the door before moving away to be replaced by someone else. Inside the room, Lila squirmed out of Pamra's grasp, turned to let her feet drop off the edge of the bed, then stagger-crawled to the door to sit there with her own hands pressed to its surface, smiling, nodding, sometimes saying something to herself in a chuckling baby voice, as though she watched with her fingers what transpired outside the wooden barrier.

Below in the firelit room, the three Mendicants crouched before the fire, staring into the flames. Peasimy had fallen asleep where he sat, as had the men with him.

"Mad," said Trale at last. "There's no doubt."

"None," agreed the woman. "She hasn't eaten for weeks or months. She's all skin and eyes. She's an ecstatic. A visionary. The fasting only makes it worse. The minute the smoke hit her, she felt hungry. She's half starved herself."

"How long do you think we can get her to stay?" the man asked.

"No time at all. Tomorrow morning, perhaps. If the storm goes on, perhaps until the rain stops."

"Not long enough to do any good."

"No."

"It's too bad, isn't it?"

Trale nodded, poking at the fire. "Well, a time of changes is often unpleasant. I don't see the Jarb Houses seriously threatened. Or the Mendicants."

"There will be a need for more houses." The woman made a spiraling gesture that conveyed the wholeness of the edifice with all its murmurous inhabitants.

"Perhaps some of the people in residence will be able to leave," the man said. He sounded doubtful of this.

"Some are ready to leave as Mendicants." Trale sighed. "Taking their pipes with them, as we do. The others—if they go, they go into madness once more. More houses will be needed, but it's unlikely we'll be able to build them."

"We could keep her here."

"By force?" It was a question only, without emotion. But the woman flushed deep crimson. "I thought, persuade her, perhaps."

"Try," Trale urged her. "By all means, Elina, try. It has not a hope of success, but you will not be content unless you try."

Late in the day a bell rang and people began filing down from the chimney top toward the refectory. Children leapt from the railings into nets and from these into other nets below. Some whirled down tall poles. A train of whooping boys came spinning down the spiraling banister, loud with laughter. The tables filled, and there was a clatter of bowls and spoons. Out in the chimney hall, Elina pared Jarb-root peels onto the brazier, renewing the pale wraiths of smoke which filled all the space to its high, blind skylight. Pamra opened the door of her room and came out onto the balcony to look down, Lila held high against her shoulder. Elina beckoned to them, and Lila squirmed out of Pamra's arms, over the railing, plunging downward, arms spread as though to fly. Elina caught her, without thinking, only then turning pale with shock while the child chortled in her arms and Pamra, above, put hands to her throat as though to choke off a scream.

"All right," said Lila. "You caught me."

"Did you know I would?" the woman asked in an astonished whisper.

"Oh, yes," said Lila. "The smoke is nice."

Pamra was coming slowly down the twisting ramp, her eyes never leaving the child below. Lila squirmed to be put down and staggered toward the foot of the ramp, face contorted in the enormous concentration necessary to walking. She did not fall until the ramp was reached, and Pamra scooped her up.

"Lila, don't ever do that again." In her voice was all the anguish of every mother, every elder sister, all imperiousness gone. She smiled at Elina, shaking her head, and they shared the moment. Children! The things they did! It lasted only a moment.

"I should be getting back to my people," Pamra said. "They will be wondering what has happened to me."

"They know you are here," the woman responded. "It is still raining. They will be more comfortable if they believe you are comfortable. Do not add your discomfort to their own by going back into the wet."

"You're right, of course. And it will not hurt to have a warm meal." Pamra was amazed at herself, but she was hungry again. She looked around her curiously. "I got only the general impression before. Are all Jarb Houses built this way?"

"Yes. So the smoke can permeate the whole structure."

"The smoke? I see it does. But why?"

Elina took her by the arm, drawing her close, as though they had been sisters, used to sharing confidences. "The Jarb smoke is said to give visions, you know? But in reality, Jarb smoke erases visions and restores reality. For those disturbed by visions of madness, the Jarb smoke brings actuality. You see that woman going into the refectory? The tall one with the wild red hair? On the outside, she is a beast who roams the forests, killing all who pursue her, sure of their ill will and obsessed by the terrors of the world. Here she is Kindle Kindness, a loving friend to half the house."

Pamra peered at the woman, not seeming to understand what was being said.

"Outside, she has visions of herself as a beast, of herself hunted. In the house, the smoke wipes those visions away. In here, she is only herself."

Pamra stared at her, awareness coming to her suddenly, her face paling. "Neff," she cried. "Neff!"

"Shhh," said Elina. "Shhh. There is no need to cry out."

"Neff! Where is he?"

Trale came from the refectory, joining them, taking Pamra's other arm. Wearily, pointedly, with a resigned look at Elina, he said, "Your visions wait for you outside. They cannot come into a Jarb House."

Pamra drew herself up, regally tall, becoming someone else. "Truth cannot exist in this place, can it, Mendicant? Light cannot come here? Only darkness and smoke?"

He shook his head. "All your—all your friends are waiting for you. Come now. There is food waiting, also."

She shook her head at them, pityingly, but allowed them to take her to the place where Peasimy stood impatiently with the others, all standing beside their chairs, waiting for her to be seated; then all waiting until she began eating. She nodded at the others, saying, "Eat quickly, my friends. We must leave this place."

"Dark comes?" asked Peasimy, glaring at the Mendicants. "Pamra?"

She shook her head. "They are not evil, Peasimy. They are only misled." She had been hungry, but now she began to toy with the food before her, obviously impatient to be gone. Elina laid a hand upon her shoulder, tears in the corners of her eyes. "Pamra! Courtesy! 'Neff' is not impatient." Pamra took a bite, chewed it slowly, watching them with that same pitying gaze. Now she knew what had been missing since she had entered the house. Neff, and Delia, and her mother. Them and their voices. Gone. As though they had never been except in her memory. Did these poor smoke-blinded fools think she would let them go? Though she could not see them in this smoky haze, the center of her being clung to what she knew to be true. They—they were true. Neff was true. She took another bite, smiled at Peasimy and encouraged him to eat.

From the side of the room, Trale watched, eyes narrowed in concentration. Elina came toward him. "She did not make the connection with her own condition at all."

"Oh, yes. She knows what we tried to do. But she has rejected it."

"Why, Trale?"

"Because her madness is all she has. Whatever else there might have been once has been taken away. Whatever else there might be in the future seems shoddy in comparison. Who would wed a man when one might wed an angel? Who would live as a woman when one might rule as a goddess?"

"We could keep her here by force."

"Setting aside that we would break all our vows, yes. We could."

"In time, she would forget."

"Ah."

"She would grow accustomed."

"Elina."

"Yes, Trale."

"Clip the flame-bird's wings if you must, Elina. Set it among your barnyard fowl. Tell yourself you do it to save the flame-bird's life. But do not expect it to nest, or to sing."

She bowed her head, very pale. At the table behind her, Pamra rose, her hand shaking as she wiped her mouth with the napkin. "Where are my clothes?" she asked.

Peasimy found them for her, beside the fire, and she put them on. They were warm and dry.

"Won't you stay until it stops raining?" Elina asked her. "Only until morning."

"No," Pamra said, her eyes darting from place to place in the high dwelling, marking it in her memory. Another time—there might be converts to be had in places like this. "No. Neff is waiting. Mother and Delia. They're waiting. We have set our feet upon the road and must not leave it. This is a bad place, Elina. You should come with us. You can't see the road from in here, Elina. Come with us. . . ." Her face lit from within, glowed, only for a moment, but for that moment Elina felt herself torn, wrenched, dragged to the gate of herself. Fear struck at her and she drew back.

"No, Pamra. It is safe here. The people here find much joy and comfort."

"Joy," said Pamra. "Comfort!" The scorn in her voice was palpable, an acid dripping upon those words. "Safety. Yes. That is what you have here."

Peasimy was suddenly beside her, swallowing the last bite of his supper. Then they were moving toward the entrance, out across the open chimney, through the hallway, pulling at the great doors. They went into the night, a night miraculously cleared of storm, with the moons lighting the sky. Potipur, half-swollen and sullen above them to the west; Viranel a mere sickle dipping beyond the western horizon; Abricor a round melon, high in the east.

"You see," said Pamra. "Neff has arranged it. Here he comes now." And she turned her radiant face to the woods, from which some invisible presence moved to join her. Elina, in the doorway, gasped, for she saw it, for that moment saw it, a towering figure of white light, golden wings outstretched, its breast stained with red.

Trale was behind her. "Come in, Elina."

"Trale, I saw . . ."

"Saw what she sees. As do all those who follow her. Come in to the fire, Elina."

Behind Pamra and the others, the doors of the Jarb House shut with a solemn clang. From the forests came the multitude, and Pamra's heart sang. "Crusade," she called. "Let us go on."

2

Thrasne thought of what he was about to do somewhat as he might have regarded taking the axe to himself if he had been touched by blight. He would have rejected the intention to lop off his own leg with horror, yet he would have done it because the alternative was more terrible still.

So, he fell in with the plan to go with a group of Medoor Babji's Melancholics on a voyage of exploration to find Southshore without enthusiasm, with a kind of deadly reluctance. He resolved upon it because staying anywhere near Pamra was more horrifying than leaving the world in which she moved. If he stayed, he would have to follow her. And it would be terrible to watch Pamra, to hear of her, to be told of the crusade. Any of these were more repugnant to him than risking his own life. He told himself he would welcome death if it meant he need not realize the danger Pamra ran and go in apprehension of that terror.

"I love her," he said to Medoor Babji. "Whether she is mad or not. I love her." And he did. His loins quivered at the thought of her. He knew every curve of her body, and he dreamed of that body, waking in a shaking sweat from agonies of unfulfilled passion.

And Babji, having observed his obsession over the days that had just passed, was wise enough to hold her tongue, though she thought, Stupid man, at him, not entirely with affection. How could she blame him for this unfulfillable desire when she had a similar one of her own?

Here, in the city of Thou-ne, on the same day Pamra cried crusade in the Temple of the Moons, Medoor Babji came to Taj

Noteen and gave him the tokens she carried with few words of explanation about the seeker birds, watching his face as it turned from brown to red to pallid gray, then to brown once more.

"*Deleen p'Noz,*" he said, sinking to one knee. "Your Gracious Highness." The secret Noor language was used these days only for names and titles, little else.

"We need none of that," she told him firmly. "This is not the courts of the Noor. I do not need to hear '*Deleen p'Noz*' to be recalled to my duty. We are not in the audience tent of the Queen. Though I am the Queen's chosen heir, we are here, Noteen, in Thou-ne, as we were this morning when you whacked me with your whip stock. I've told you what we are to do. I want you to pick me a crew to go. Thrasne will need his own boatmen, and we cannot expect to live on the deck if there is storm or rough weather. We must limit our numbers, therefore, to the space available. Thrasne kindly offers us the owner-house. There are three rooms for sleeping, with two bunks in each room. There is an office and a salon. Not large. We can have none among us who will cause dissension."

"Not Riv Lymeen, then," he mused. "How about old Porabji?"

"He has a good mind," she assented. "Which we may need far more than a young man's strength. Yes."

Noteen thought about it. "Do we need a recorder? Someone to keep an account? A journal of the voyage?"

She thought a moment, then nodded. Queen Fibji had not commanded it, yet it was something that should be done.

"Then Fez Dooraz. He was clerk at the courts for ten years as a younger man. He looks as though a breath would blow him over, but he's the most literate of all of us."

She suggested, "Lomoz Borab is sound. And what about Eenzie?"

"Eenzie the Clown?"

"I'd like one more woman along, Noteen. And Eenzie makes us all laugh. We may need laughter."

He assented. "Six, then. Porabji, Dooraz, Borab, and Eenzie. You, Highness. And me."

"You, Noteen?"

"I will send the troupe back to the steppes. Nunoz can take them."

"I had not thought of you, Noteen."

"You object?" He asked it humbly enough.

She thought of this. He had not bullied her more than he had bullied anyone else. She could detect no animosity against him in herself. "Why not. And I have a thought about it, Noteen. You will command our group. So far as they are concerned, Queen Fibji's message came to you."

He thought on this, overcoming his immediate rejection of the idea as he confronted her thoughtful face. It might be better, he thought to himself, if no one knew who Medoor Babji was. "It might be safer for you," he murmured.

"I was not thinking of that," she said. "So much as the comfort of the voyage. We have done well enough with me as a novice. Why complicate things?"

"Thrasne owner doesn't know?"

"I told him we were ordered to go. I didn't tell him the seeker birds came to me, or what words they carried."

"Do you have enough coin to pay him?"

"Strange though it may seem, Taj Noteen, he isn't doing it for coin, or at least not primarily for coin, but yes. I have enough." Among the tokens she carried was one that would open the coffers of money lenders in Thou-ne. The Noor had accounts in many parts of Northshore.

"We'll need more yet for stores. How long a voyage do we plan?"

"Queen Fibji commands us to provision for a year. A full year. We will need most of the hold space for stores. Thrasne knows that."

"Well then, I'll get Dooraz and Porabji ready. They're good storesmen, both of them."

And it began.

Thrasne talked to the crew. He didn't give them his reasons, just told them they'd be well paid. Several of the men told him they'd go ashore, thanks for everything but they were not really interested in a voyage that long. Thrasne nodded and let them go. The others chewed it over for a time.

"You'll want me to replace the ones that left," Obers-rom said at last. "We'll need full crew, Thrasne owner. I don't suppose those blackfaces will be up to much in the way of helping on a boat."

"I don't suppose so. And we'd better get in the habit of callin' 'em by their names, Obers-rom. Or just say 'Noor.' They count that as polite."

Obers-rom agreed. He hadn't meant anything by it. Boatmen weren't bigoted. They couldn't be. They'd never make a copper if they couldn't deal with all kinds.

And it was Obers-rom who worked with Zyneem Porabji and Fez Dooraz—they were Obbie and Zynie and Fez within the day—to fill the *Gift of Potipur*'s holds. From the purveyors and suppliers they ordered dried fish and pickled fish and salted fish, grain in bulk, grain in dry cakes, and grain in flour, dried fruit, jam, hard melons, half barrels of slib roots—ready to sprout salad whenever they were wet down, even with the brackish River water. They ordered smoked shiggles, procured by Fez from some unspecified source along with kegs of Jarb roots. They bought sweetening and spices and kegs of oil, both oil for cooking and for the lanterns and stove. They paid for bolts of pamet cloth and coils of rope, extra lines for fishing, and bags of frag powder. They sought a pen of fowl for the rear deck with snug, watertight nesting boxes, and the cooper began making an endless series of kegs for fresh drinking water.

They ordered spices and medicines, a set of new pans for the cook, and supplementary tools for the carpenter's locker.

Not all of this was available in Thou-ne. Some of it was mustered mysteriously by the Noor and arrived as mysteriously on other boats coming from the east. This meant delay, and more delay, but the Noor were patient, more patient than Thrasne owner, who wanted only to put some great challenge like an impenetrable wall between himself and the way Pamra had gone. The harder he worked, the less he thought of her, yet he could not give up thinking of her entirely and went each day to the marketplace, asking for news of her, unable to tell truth from rumor when news was given.

And in between times he sat in his cubby or alone in his watching place and distracted himself by writing in his book. Though, as it happened, sometimes the things he wrote were not a distraction at all but led him deep within himself to the very things he would rather not have thought of.

• 3 •

Talker of the Sixth Degree, by the grace of Potipur articulate, Sliffisunda of the Gray Talons perched in the entryway of his aerie waiting for the approach of the delegation. He had asked for a report on the herd beasts, and the keepers had told him they would send a delegation. From the northlands somewhere, wherever it was they kept the young animals they had taken. So, let them send their delegation and be quick about it. Sliffisunda was hungry. They had brought him a new meat human just that afternoon, and he could hear it moving about in his feeding trough. It made him salivate disgustingly, and the drool leaked from his beak onto his feet, making them itch.

Rustling on the rampway. Wings at far aperture. So, they were assembling. Now they approached. Stillisas, Talker of the Fifth Degree. Two fours, Shimmipas and Slooshasill. He knew them, but then . . . he knew all Talkers. There were only some fifteen hundred of them in the whole world, divided among the Gray, Black, Blue, and Red Talons, the only four that had not been allowed to fall into ruin at time of hunger. Well.

"Uplifted One." Stillisas bowed, tail tucked tight to show honor. The others, one on either side, bowed as deeply.

"So," Stillisunda croaked. "Stillisas. You have something to report to me."

"About young thrassil and weehar, Uplifted One. We have six of each animal. One male, five females of each. They are carefully hidden. I have just come from place. By next summer they will be of age to breed. Slave humans say we must capture other males, next year or year after, if herds are to grow strong. No more females are needed.''

"And how long, Stillisas, before we may dispense with shore-fish?'' Many of the Thraish had adopted the Noor word for the human inhabitants of Northshore. It conveyed better than any other word his feelings for humans. Shore-fish. Offal. To be eaten only when one must.

"Realistically, Uplifted One, about fifteen years. And then only under most rigid controls. There is already some trouble with fliers assigned to me as help. Fliers must be prepared for restraint. Fliers must be sensible!''

Sliffisunda twitched in irritation, depositing shit to show the extent of his offendedness. "You may leave that to Sixth Degree, Stillisas. To those of us who no longer share meat.''

Stillisas flushed red around his beak. It was true. Stillisas did share meat with others, one wriggling body for four or five Fifth Degree Talkers instead of having one for each of them. Only the Sixth Degree could eat in dignified privacy, without the stink of others' saliva on their food. He should not have spoken so. He abased himself now, crouching in the female mating position while Sliffisunda flapped twice, accepting the subordination.

"If all goes well, there will be herd of some sixty to eighty thousand in thirteen years, Uplifted One. Weehar females often throw twins, according to *sloosil*, captured humans. At Thraish present numbers, fifty thousand animals will be needed annually to feed Thraish people. In fourteenth or fifteenth year, that many may be slaughtered.''

"Enough if *horgha sloos*, sharing meat,'' sneered Sliffisunda. He shat again. "And if Thraish do not share?''

"Many years longer, Uplifted One. One and one-half million animals each year would be needed if all are to have fresh meat, without sharing.''

"At Thraish present numbers.''

"Yes, Uplifted One.''

Sliffisunda hissed. There were only seventy some-odd thousand of the Thraish. Only fifteen hundred of them were Talkers. At one time there had been almost a million fliers. But it would take two hundred million weehar and thrassil slaughtered a year to support that many. Dared he dream of that?

Power. Power over many. What power was it to be Talker over this pitiful few? He dreamed of the ancient days when wings had filled the skies of Northshore, when wings had flown over the River, perhaps to the fabled lands of the south, in the days before the fear came to prevent their flying over the River at all. But why not? There had been that many once. If the fliers had stopped breeding when the Talkers suggested it, all would have been well. So, somehow the fliers must be brought under control. It would require some new laws, some new legends. The opaque film slid across his eyes as he connived. *An elite order of fliers to carry out will of Talkers. Breeding rights given as awards for service. Eggs destroyed if flier did not obey. Number carefully controlled. And yet, that number could be larger than at present. Much larger.*

He came to himself with a shudder. Those crouched before him pretended not to notice his abstraction, though he glared at them for a long moment, daring them to speak.

"Tell me of disturbance among the *sloosil*," he asked at last. "I hear there is disorder among humans, near Black Talons, in places called Thou-ne and Atter."

"It is same person as before," murmured Slooshasill. "Uplifted One sought same person in year past. Human called Pamra Don."

So. Human called Pamra Don. Human who emptied pits in Baris. "Rivermen!" Sliffisunda hissed. It took him a time to recognize that the three before him had not replied. Contradiction? "Talkers do not agree?"

"Pits are full," ventured Shimmipas. "Full. Fliers gorge."

"Not Rivermen." Sliffisunda almost crouched in amazement, catching himself only just in time. "Tell!"

"Procession." The Talker shrugged. "Many humans walking. At sunset Pamra Don speaks to them."

"Words?"

"Tells of Holy Sorters in sky. Tells of Protector of Man. Says humans must know truth. Says will tell Protector of Man."

"*Shimness*," snorted Sliffisunda. It was the name of a legendary Thraish flier, one who had always accomplished the opposite of what he tried. In common parlance it meant "crazy" or "inept," and it was in this sense Sliffisunda used it now.

"Pits are full," Shimmipas repeated stubbornly. "If procession goes on, more pits will be full."

Sliffisunda looked narrowly at the others. They dropped their eyes, appropriately wary.

"See with eyes," Sliffisunda said at last. It was all he could do. In the room behind him the chains in the meat trough rattled, reminding him of hunger. He drooled, dismissing the delegation, and returned to his own place. They had brought him a young one this time. Soft little breasts, tasty. Tasty rump. The Tears had softened it nicely, and the mindless eyes rolled wildly as he tore at the flesh. It screamed, and he shut his eyes, imagining a weehar in his claws. It, too, would scream. Why, then, did these human cries always annoy him? He tore the throat out, cutting off the sound, irritated beyond measure, no longer enjoying the taste.

He went to his spy hole and looked out upon the sky. The delegation was just leaving, three Talkers and three ordinary fliers, flying east along the River against a sky of lowering storm. *Foolish to fly in this weather. They could be blown out over water.* Sliffisunda postulated, not for the first time, where the fear had come from that prevented the Thraish from flying over water at all. *Survival*, he told himself. *During Thraish-human wars, many Thraish ate fish. Other Thraish killed them. Only Thraish who did not eat fish survived. Perhaps reason some Thraish did not eat fish then was fear of water.*

It was possible. Anything was possible. Even this thing in Thou-ne and Atter was possible.

He would go to Black Talons. He would see for himself.

• 4 •

The Council of Seven was gathered in the audience hall of the Chancery, the round council table set just outside the curtained niche where Lees Obol lay. By an exercise of willful delusion, one could imagine the Protector of Man as part of the gathering. The chair nearest the niche was empty. Perhaps the Protector occupied it spiritually. Or so, at least, Shavian Bossit amused himself by thinking.

As for the other six, they were present in reality. Tharius Don, fidgeting in his chair as though bitten by fleas. Gendra Mitiar, driving invisible creatures from the crevasses of her face with raking fingers. General Jondrigar, his pitted gray skin twitching in the jellied light. Koma Nepor, Ezasper Jorn. And, of course, Shavian himself. A second ring of chairs enclosed the first, occupied by functionaries and supporting members of the Chancery staff. So, Tharius had invited Bormas Tyle to attend, though Bormas was a supporter of Bossit's and Tharius knew it. Gendra had her majordomo, three district supervisors, and her Noor slave to lend her importance, though Jhilt squatted on the floor behind the second ring of chairs, conscious of her inferiority in this exalted gathering.

Koma Nepor and Ezasper Jorn supported one another. And Chiles Medman, the governor general of the Jarb Mendicants, was there—supporting whom? Shavian wondered. The Jarb Mendicants were tolerated by the Chancery, even used by the Chancery from time to time, but they could not be considered a part of the hierarchy. So what was Medman here for? Supporting some faction? There were three factions, at least. Tharius, the enigma, who would do the gods knew what if he were in power.

Gendra, advocate of increasing the elixir supply and the power of the Chancery with it, and of increased repression. She enjoyed that. And Bossit himself, practical politician, who plotted enslavement of the Thraish and no more of their bloody presumption. And old Obol, of course, behind the curtains, lying in his bed like a bolster, barely breathing.

The general had no faction. His Jondarites stood around the hall as though carved of black stone. The scales of their fishskin jerkins gleamed in the torchlight; their high plumes nodded ebon and scarlet. Their axes were of fragwood, toothed with obsidian. Only their spear points were of metal. From time to time the general pivoted, surveying each of them as though to find some evidence of slackness. He found none. The soldiers in the audience hall were a picked troop. If any among them had been capable of slackness, that tendency was long since conquered.

"Let's get to it," Shavian muttered at last, tapping his gavel on the hollow block provided for it. It made a clucking, minatory sound, and they all looked up, startled. "We are met today to consider the matter of this 'crusade'—preached and led by one Pamra Don. I might say, this person is the same Pamra Don who caused us some difficulty a year or so ago." He stared at Gendra, letting his silence accuse her.

She bridled. "You know we've set Laughers after her, Bossit. Including that Awakener from Baris. Potipur knows he would give his life to get his hands on her. His search must have been out of phase. Evidently she has been behind him the whole time."

"Behind him, or on the River, or hidden by Rivermen, what matter which," Shavian sneered, annoyed with her. "The fact is, she avoided him, him and all the others who were looking for her. She came to surface in a town where no Laughers were, a town from which your representative had only recently departed, a town ripe for ferment because of some damned statue the superstitious natives had found in the River."

"The Jondarites should have stopped it," growled Gendra through her teeth, glaring at the general. "Why have Jondarites in all the towns otherwise. . . ."

"The Jondarites have no orders concerning crusades," said the general in an expressionless voice. "They are ordered to put down insurrection. There was no insurrection. They are ordered to punish disrespect of the Protector of Man. No disrespect is being shown, rather the contrary. They are told to quell heresy. There has been no heresy they could detect. The woman spoke of lies told to the Protector, of plots against the Protector.'' His eyes glowed red as he spoke. Who knew better than he of the lies that surrounded Lees Obol. Who knew better than he of the actuality of conspiracies. Scarcely a day went by that Jondrigar did not uncover a plot against the Protector. The mines had their share of Chancery conspirators he had unearthed.

"Enough," rapped Shavian. "Recriminations will not help us."

"Where is the crusade now?" Tharius Don asked, knowing the answer already but wishing to get the conversation away from those around the table and onto something less emotionally charged. He was rigid in his chair, yet twitchy, full of nervous energy. New adherents to the cause were being reported almost daily. For reasons he could not admit even to himself, he had been delaying the strike for months, and it could not be put off much longer. With every week that passed, the fear of discovery grew more imminent and compelling. In his heart he thanked the gods for the crusade, even though it had put Pamra Don at risk. It had drawn the Chancery's attention, for a time. "What's the name of the town?"

"A few days ago, she was in Chirubel," Bossit answered in a weary, irritated voice. He did not want the fliers stirred up any more than they were, and though this matter had not yet seemed to upset them, who knew what it might mean in the future. And with Lees Obol failing so fast . . . though he had only the Jondarites' word for that. No one else could get nearer to him than across the room. He shook his head and rasped, "A watchtower relay brought word. The pits in Chirubel are full. There was a great storm there, and many of her followers died."

"Died?" Tharius had not heard this.

"Old people, mostly. The great mob of them have no proper provision of food or shelter. The towns have been instructed to put their own surplus foodstuffs under guard, and the Jondarites have been ordered to prevent looting. So, there is a good deal of hunger. Which begets a regrettable tendency to eat off the land, as it were.''

"Violence?''

"Some. Fights break out. Mostly the deaths are old people dying of lung disease brought on by cold and hunger. Some younger ones, too, through accidents or violence. Some children and babies, the same.''

"So, the pits are full,'' Gendra mused. "Well, the fliers wanted the quota of bodies increased. They should be happy.''

"Ezasper Jorn,'' queried Bossit, "what mood are the fliers in?''

Jorn, huddled in his chair wrapped in three layers of blankets, blinked owlishly at them from his cavern of covers. "Voiceless as mulluks. They may not understand what's going on so far as a crusade is concerned. They don't seem curious, but then they've seen these little skirmishes before. We've had intertown wars; we've had rebellions put down by the Towers. That kind of thing has filled the worker pits from time to time over the centuries, so they might not think much of it. In short, they do not seem to be concerned. It's a local phenomenon, after all.''

"They'll scarcely change their reproductive habits on the basis of this temporary glut, which, at most, affects ten or a dozen towns.'' Koma Nepor was using his best pedant's voice, reserved for meetings such as this where chortle and giggle would not serve. "I agree with Jorn. They'll stuff themselves for a time; then the movement or whatever it is will fizzle out as these things always do; and they'll go back to normal.''

"Hungry normal,'' commented Gendra with a vast grinding of teeth. "In those towns, at least. With all the oldsters gone, the death rate will be low for a time.'' She reflected upon this. There was no reason the average lifespan should not be somewhat shortened. For parents, say, fifteen years after the birth of the last child. Or even twelve. For nonreproducers, earlier, unless they filled some important niche in the town economy. She would send word to the Towers. Fuller pits around the world would please the fliers, and if she could start currying the favor of the Talkers even now . . .

"So, the Talkers will tell the fliers to move across town lines and share.'' Shavian was heartily weary of the entire discussion.

"The point is not what the fliers will or will not do, though it may come to that later. The point is, what are we to do?"

Tharius stirred uneasily. He had been arguing the proper course of action with himself for days now, first yes, then no, both sides with reasons that seemed equally good. Now he must choose.

"Have her brought before me," he said firmly, nothing in his voice betraying either how little faith he had in his own recommendation or how deeply he was invested in its success. "Have her brought here. We know where she is. We do not need to wait for Laughers to find her. They were instructed, had they found her, to bring her here, so let us get on with it. Send word to the Jondarites in—what's the next town west, Gendra?" He knew perfectly well. Pamra Don had surfaced in a hotbed of the cause. The dozen towns west of Thou-ne were all rife with rebellion, and their Towers were full of Tharius's men.

"Rabishe-thorn," she responded absently, even as she peered at him with searching eyes. What was he up to? "Rabishe-thorn, then Falsenter. If we send word now, they should be able to intercept her in one or the other."

"Send word she is not to be harmed," Tharius went on in an emotionless voice, praying the quivering of his hands clasped in his lap could not be seen. "As Propagator of the Faith, I need to know everything she knows, and I won't get it if she's too frightened or abused or—forbid it—dosed with Tears. It will take months for her to reach us overland. During that time, the crusade will be effectively stopped since she will not be there to lead it." And this was the bait he hoped would bring them. Though he was thankful for the distraction she had provided, he wanted Pamra safe. With the day of the strike approaching, with his own inevitable mortality close at hand, he wanted to know she was well. I want to leave something behind me, he told himself, as though talking to Kessie. Kessie, I want to leave a posterity—silly though that may seem. I want it.

None of this was the business of the gathering. He pulled himself into focus and said again, "The crusade will dissipate while she is on her way here."

Gendra would have liked to find something wrong with his reasoning, but she couldn't. Gendra wanted Pamra Don killed,

both because it was her nature to dispose of wild factors in that
way and because some instinct told her it would be a very good
idea. Pamra Don and Tharius Don. And the lady Kesseret. An
odd group, that. An untrustworthy group. When she, Gendra,
became Protector of Man, her first order to the Jondarites would
be to do away with certain of the Chancery staff. And certain
Tower Superiors. And others. She smiled, a rare, awful smile,
showing her teeth.

Shavian, his eyes darting between them as though watching a
game of net-ball, nodded in approval. The general glared but
did not object. Why would he? He would sooner believe in plots
than in no plots.

Ezasper Jorn and Koma Nepor simply watched, listened, said
little. Having plans of their own, they didn't care about these
things. And as for Lees Obol, his voice came to them plaintively from the curtained niche behind them. "Somebody get
me my pot."

The Jondarites outside the niche moved to the Protector's
service. Gendra stood up and ordered tea in a loud voice, at
least partly to disguise the sounds emanating from the curtained
room. There was general babble for a few moments, for which
Tharius Don was very grateful. A Jondarite brought the Protector's teapot into the hall and set it upon a distant table, over a
lamp, ready when the Protector asked for it. Behind it, the
curtain glowed red as blood in the light of the warmer. Tharius
found his eyes fixed on it, as though it were an omen.

He joined the babble, adding to it. When they came to order
once again, his suggestion would be remembered, but his own
connection with it would be somewhat overlaid by later conversation. A subtlety, he felt, but nonetheless acceptable. Even
subtlety was welcome.

And yet, except for his own emotional needs, why bother?
He had asked himself this more than once in the preceding days
and weeks, ever since the first word of the crusade had come
via seeker bird and watchtower. Servants of the cause had
passed the word along, knowing Tharius Don would want to
know. Mendicants of the Jarb had passed the word along, for
Chiles Medman had asked them to. The Jarb Houses were firm

supporters of the cause, to Tharius's amazement, though Chiles had explained why.

They had met by chance on one of the outer walls of the Chancery compound, brought there by a day of inviting sun and more than seasonable warmth, encountering one another quite by accident and remaining together because not to have done so would have looked suspiciously like avoidance or disaffection. Avoidance was as suspect as propinquity. There were always watchers. They had fallen into conversation, the first they had ever held outside the context of the conspiracy. They had spoken of the nature of fliers.

"Look at a flier through the smoke sometime, Tharius Don." Chiles Medman had held out his pipe, as though inviting Tharius to do it then and there. There were no fliers closer than Northshore that anyone had reported, though there might have been a dozen of them spying from the high peaks for all anyone knew.

"What do you see, Medman? A differing reality?" Tharius was touchy about this.

"We see them stripped of our own delusion, Tharius Don. Through the smoke they look like nothing much except winged incarnations of pride."

"Pride?" He had not really been surprised. Everyone knew how stiff-necked the Talkers were.

"They would be happy to see every human dead if they did not need us for food. They would rend all intelligence but their own. They kill, not out of bloodthirstiness, but out of pride. They have a word for sharing, *horgho*. It means 'to abase oneself.' Their phrase for sharing food, *horgha sloos*, means also 'dirtying oneself.' Did you know they call us *sloosil*?"

Tharius Don could not help snorting at the word. "No. What does it mean?"

"Meat. Simply that, in the plural. Meat. I met one of the Fourth Degree Talkers at a convocation once. His name was Slooshasill. 'Meat manager.' He was responsible for providing bodies for Fifth and Sixth Degree Talkers."

"So you don't think they respect us?"

Chiles Medman had shaken his head, lit his pipe, and considered Tharius through the smoke. "Why should they?"

"They've borrowed our craftsmen. They've learned writing

from us." Why shouldn't they? his hope had insisted. Why shouldn't they respect us?

"Well, they don't. If they didn't need us for food, they would slaughter us all tomorrow. They would not even keep us for slaves, because we remind them of *horgha sloos*. We remind them of abasement. They had an oral tradition and adequate housing for thousands of years before we came. Why do they need our writing? Or our craftsmen?"

Tharius had glanced around, assuring himself they were alone, then said softly, "And yet you support the cause? Not, seemingly, because you share my dream of sharing this world in dignity?"

"You know I don't, Tharius. I support the cause because I believe it's the only chance for humanity. The track we are on is madness. We're a flame-bird's nest, waiting for the spark. Our self-delusion grows greater every generation. We are moving farther and farther from our own truths."

"We have twenty-four hundred townships. Every township has about forty thousand people in it. There are almost a hundred million of us and fewer than a hundred thousand of them," Tharius had said in a mild voice.

"There are a hundred million blades of grass, and yet the weehar graze upon them all. The fliers could double their numbers in one year, Tharius. They're keeping their numbers down by breaking their eggs. They only incubate seven or eight a year in any given township, and they could incubate fifty or more. There's fifty percent mortality among the chicks. When the population grows too large, the Talkers kill the male chicks. If they could breed as they like, there would be a million of them in four or five years. All young. In fifteen years, when those came to breeding age, there would be hundreds of millions, all at once. The young may not be able to breed, but they can fight. They're carnivores, for gods' sake."

"Necrovores, rather."

"Not the Talkers. And none of the Thraish like eating dead meat."

"How do you know all this about them? Their numbers? Their habits?"

"We look, Tharius. We listen. We pay kids to climb rocks

and spy on their nests. We send spies into Talons and listen to what they say.''

"In contravention of the Covenant?''

"Oh, shit, Tharius. Come off it. Don't go all pompous on me. Who else is going to do it? Who except the Jarb Mendicants could be trusted to do it?''

Tharius's face had reddened. "I get sick, sometimes, of your assumptions of omniscience, Medman. You see everything through the smoke, and that's supposed to be reality. It is not necessarily my reality, which I tend to believe has an equal right to exist!''

"We've never said it was the only reality,'' Medman had said, putting away his pipe. "We've only said we see without delusion. Without preconception. Without prejudice. The Jarb pipe does that for us. For some of us.''

"But only for you madmen.'' It was unkind, and Tharius had repented of it at once.

"Yes.'' Softly. "Yes, Tharius Don. Only for us madmen. The smoke only works for those of us who are capable of alternate visions.'' Chiles Medman had left him then, a little angry, only to return, speaking in a vehement whisper.

"Tharius Don, you have not been among the people of Northshore for a hundred years. When I am not here in the Chancery—which I am not, most times—I see them every day. I see those who are told to believe in Potipur and Abricor and Viranel. Potipur the Talker. Abricor the young male Thraish. Viranel the female Thraish. Three gods, Tharius Don, made in the likeness of their creators—the Thraish. Who eat humans. And I see mankind trying to believe in that. . . .

"I see them trying valiantly to believe in the Sorters. Virtually every human knows in his heart it's a lie. They have seen the workers. You think boys don't sneak into the pits and look at the dead ones, just on a dare? You think people don't follow the Awakeners out to the pits sometimes, spying on them? You think people don't know? Aren't aware? Even those who believe the most, you think they don't suspect, down deep, that something is awry, that they are being fed on lies?''

"The Awakeners tell us most people believe,'' Tharius had answered. It was lame, and he'd known it.

"The Awakeners tell you most people believe, and they tell the people the Holy Sorters exist, and they tell their colleagues one thing and their Superiors something else. I only knew one Awakener in all my years who would tell the truth. He's a man named Haranjus Pandel, from Thou-ne. He's a cynic, Tharius, and an honest man.

"But as for the rest of Northshore, it's a tinder pile, as I said. People have no hope for the future. They are ready to immolate themselves if it would hatch that hope. We have more Jarb Houses now than we had a hundred years ago, and we need twice as many. People see the workers shambling around, and something—perhaps the way one of them moves or the tilt of a head—makes them think maybe Mother is under that wrapper, or Daddy, or sister or daughter or son. Or they think of themselves there, not peacefully laid away but staggering around, stinking, hated by everyone. Then madness, Tharius Don. Madness. And only the pipe gives them any hope then."

"Your hallucinogenic pipe." Tharius had smiled a little bitterly.

"The inverse of that," Chiles Medman had replied. "An inverse hallucinogenic, Tharius Don. A pipe that lets them see the dead for what they are, and the moons for what they are, and the fliers for what they are, so that they need not struggle to believe what their eyes and noses tell them is ridiculous. It is the struggle to believe which maddens, Tharius Don. The wildest of the Jarb House Mendicants come from the most devout homes. . . ."

Something had happened then to interrupt their conversation, and Tharius had not talked with him since except for the odd word at ceremonial events. Still, and despite Tharius's own rudeness on that occasion, he counted on Medman's support. When the time came.

"If the time comes," he said to himself bitterly. "If the time comes." The strike was as prepared at this moment as it would ever be. He was making excuses these days to delay it as he had been for months. He knew it. He didn't know why. "When the time comes," he said again, not convincing himself.

The council members resumed their places, now with tea steaming before them. The niche was silent. Shavian rubbed his forehead, reminding himself. "Ah, what were we saying? Yes. Pamra Don to be summoned to the Chancery. Any comment?"

Chiles Medman rose, was noticed, said, "I would support a meeting with Pamra Don here in the Chancery. The fact that this crusade has moved the people with such fervor indicates a level of dissatisfaction among them we should be aware of. For our own sakes, as well as theirs." He sat down again, having started them off like hunting birds after a swig-bug, darting here and there.

"Dissatisfaction," bellowed Gendra Mitiar. "I'll give them dissatisfaction!"

"Hush," Bossit demanded. "The governor general of the Jarb Mendicants has not said there is an insurrection. He has said 'dissatisfaction,' and I agree we should know of any such. What do you hear of dissatisfaction, Mendicant?"

"Murmurings," Chiles replied, as though indifferent. "The 'disappearances' seem more noticed of late. Taken more account of."

"They have been no more than usual," Gendra said stiffly. "About two a month from each township. Mostly old people."

"They used to be mostly old people." Chiles nodded. "Of late, there have been many young ones. When old people vanish, it is a short wonder. When young ones go, people grieve longer. And talk longer."

"The Towers have strict orders . . ." She fell silent, suddenly suspicious. Indeed, the Towers had very strict orders concerning those recruited for Talker meat. And yet, if the Talkers offered . . . if the Talkers offered a sufficient reward directly to the Superior of a Tower, might not that Superior be bought? The idea was shocking, and terrible and inevitable. Her eyes narrowed.

"Do you allege malfeasance?" she challenged Chiles Medman. "If so, where? What Tower?"

He shook his head, took his pipe from his pocket, and lit it to peer at her through the smoke. What he saw evidently reassured him, for he smiled. "I have no knowledge, Dame Marshal of the Towers. Only murmurings. Which is why I suggest bringing Pamra Don to the Chancery. Let us ask her."

Gendra subsided, her teeth grinding. Shavian looked from

one to the other of them, awaiting further comment. Koma Nepor assented, Ezasper Jorn nodded. The general merely pivoted, keeping his eye on his men. "No objection to that?" Shavian asked. "Then let it be done."

Now, Tharius thought to himself, let us send them off yet again in some other direction. "Has any word come from the herdsmen? When last I spoke with you, Jorn, you said it was thought that fliers had made off with young weehar and thrassil. Is it still assumed that fliers have stolen a breeding stock? And did I hear there were herdsmen missing as well?"

Shavian reddened with chagrin. He could not fault the question, but it reflected upon his own purview. As Maintainer of the Household, the household herds were his responsibility. "Yes," he grated. "There are herdsmen missing as well. Three of them, and among them the best men we had for understanding of the beasts."

Tharius mused over this, looked up to catch Chiles's eye upon him through a haze of smoke. "What do you see, Mendicant?" he asked.

"Herds," the Jarbman replied. "Stretching over the steppes of the Noor, in their millions."

Koma Nepor snorted. "From ten beasts? Hardly likely, Governor. The Talkers may guard a small herd. They will not be able to keep the fliers from depredations upon a large one. Eh, Jorn? Am I right?"

Ezasper Jorn nodded from his cocoon. "Likely. They are voracious beasts, the fliers. Not sensible of much, according to the Talkers. I have been told that before the time of Thoulia they were warned to curtail their breeding and yet ignored the warnings until all the beasts were gone. What sensible beast would outbreed its own foodstock?"

"And yet," brooded the Mendicant, "I see herds."

"And Noor?" asked the general, suddenly interested. "If there will be herds, where are the Noor?"

The Mendicant put out his pipe, shaking his head. "I see no Noor, General Jondrigar. None move upon the steppes in my vision. But then, who is to say when my vision will come true? In a thousand years, perhaps? Or ten times that."

Tharius Don cleared his throat. "It would be wise, General,

to ask your balloon scouts to keep their eyes open for weehar and thrassil. If they are found upon the steppes, they should be slaughtered, at once. And I suppose a guard has been set upon the herds here behind the Teeth?''

Shavian gnawed his cheek, asserting to this without answering. Did the man think him a complete fool? Of course a guard had been set. Not only upon the household herds, but upon every herd in the northlands. All were being driven here, close by, where they could be watched.

"Have we anything more?" he asked, hoping fervently that what had already been discussed was enough.

"Hearing none," he said, tapping the gavel perfunctorily once more, "we are adjourned."

"Somebody," came a plaintive voice from behind the curtain. "Bring me my tea." The Jondarite across the room picked up the pot he had placed there and brought it forward. Ceremoniously, he entered upon service to Lees Obol.

They left the audience hall to go their various ways. Gendra Mitiar took herself off to the archives to harass old Glamdrul Fcynt. The master of the files had not been diligent. When the time came, soon, she wanted proof or something that looked like proof, some reason for doing away with Tharius Don. Self-righteous prig! Staring at her as though she were less than nothing! She would show him who was nothing. Him, and his pretty cousin Kesseret, and his descendent, too, that Pamra Don. . . .

Shavian Bossit went to his own suite and sent a messenger to Koma Nepor. It was time to talk seriously about what could be done to keep Talkers alive, but passive, while the elixir was made from their blood—not in these piddling quantities, but by the gallon! His spies told him Koma had been experimenting with the blight. Perhaps . . . He grinned in anticipation, a wicked mouse grin, then sat himself down to wait. . . .

And Tharius Don took himself to the tower above his own quarters in the palace and brooded. He felt caught in a wrinkle in time, a place in which time was both too long and too short. Too short to do all his raging imagination told him he should have done long since; too long to wait, too long a time in which too many obstacles might be thrust up before the cause to inhibit the last great rebellion. . . .

"Rebellion," he whispered to himself. "Since you were only a child, Tharius Don, you have dreamed of rebellion." And yet, what else could he have been?

He could have been nothing else, born into the family Don with its strong tendencies toward both repression and ambition. There had been many old people in the household. His mother's parents, the Stifes. His father's parents, the Dons. His own parents. An aunt. Seven of them, all artist caste. And against the seven of them, only Tharius and an adored, biddable younger sister who was happy to do whatever anyone said, at any time.

And they did say. Continually; contradictorily; adamantly. The Stifes were at knife's point with the Dons. The Stifes were clawing away at one another. The Dons elder were at the throats of the Dons junior, and the alliances among the seven swung and shifted, day to day. There was only one thing that could be depended upon, and that was that young Tharius would be both the weapon they used on one another and the battleground over which they fought. He was petted, praised, whipped, abused, slapped, ignored, only to be petted once more. He was of their nature, if not of their convictions, and at about age nine or ten—he could not remember the exact year, or even the incident that had provoked it—he had repudiated them all. He remembered that well, himself rigid against the door of the cubby in the attic which was his own, his face contorted as he stared into his own eyes in the mirror across the room, his utter acceptance of his own words as he said, "I renounce you all. All of you. From now on, you can fight each other, but you will not use me." Or perhaps those words had only come later, after he had had time to think about it. The renunciation, though, that had happened, just as he remembered it.

And from that time he was gone. An occasional presence. A bland, uninteresting person, hearing nothing, repeating nothing, unusable as a weapon because he did or said nothing anyone could use or repeat to stir up enmity or support. Useless as a battleground because he did not seem to care. Not about anything at all.

As for Tharius, he did not care about them anymore. He had discovered books.

There had always been books, of course. There always were books, in the shops. Holy books. Accepted books. Bland histories in which there was never any violence or deviation of opinion. Devotional books in which there were never any doubts. Even storybooks, for children, in which obedient boys and girls obeyed their elders, learned their lessons, and became good, obedient citizens of their towns.

Life wasn't like that. Looking around him, Tharius saw hatred and violence, pain and dying. He saw workers. Awakeners. Grim, stinking fliers in the bone pits. Men and women vanishing, as though swallowed by evil spirits. None of that was in the books. Not the accepted books.

But there were other books.

A few days before Tharius's repudiation of his kin, the poultry-monger's shop across the alley was raided by the Tower. A great clatter of Awakeners and priests of Potipur came raging into the place, all blue in the face with their mirrors jagging light into corners. Tharius Don was on the roof above the alley when it happened, hiding from his grandmother Stife. There was noise, doors slamming, some shouting, some screaming, people moving around in the attics opposite him, barely seen through the filthy glass. Then the Awakeners burst through the back door and began throwing books into a pile. They were screaming threats at the poultry-monger and his wife, both of whom were protesting that they had only bought the house a year ago, that they'd never looked into the attic, that they didn't know the books were there. It was likely enough true. Tharius had never seen lights in the windows opposite his own.

"It's only that saves your life for you now, poulterer," snarled an Awakener. "That and the dust on these volumes. Don't touch them. There'll be a wagon here in an hour or so to haul them away for burning."

They left a blue-faced priest of Potipur at the head of the alley to keep watch, but he got bored with the waiting and fell asleep. Most priests were fat face-stuffers anyhow, half-asleep on their feet a good part of the time. Tharius had stared down at the pile of books, silent as a stalking stilt-lizard, judging how many of them he might take away and how long he had. His own attic room was at the top of a drainpipe, and getting them back would be a difficulty. . . .

Inspiration struck him, all at once. He found a sack, put all his own books in it, hung it over his shoulder, and climbed down the protruding drainpipe, his favorite road to freedom. The exchange was quick—his dull books for the ones in the alley—and he was back up the drainpipe again, sweating and hauling for all he was worth, hearing the creak of the wagon wheels even as he slid over the parapet onto the roof beside his own window.

When the wagon arrived, the books were loaded by some flunky who did not even look at them. From the roof, Tharius watched him as he took them down to the stone wharf at the Riverside and burned them. Everyone pretended not to notice, even one old man who was choked by the smoke and had to act as though it were from something else. So. There were books, and books. The forbidden books went on the shelf in the corner, just where the others had been. No one ever came up here except Grandmother Stife, once a month or so, to peek in the door and then shout at him to sweep the place out.

Tharius was hooked, confirmed in rebellion. The books were real ones. Stories of people as they were. A history of Northshore. A little book about the arrival, called *When We Came*. Tharius had been taught certain things as true, but they had always seemed senseless. Now, suddenly they began to connect.

Time went. Tharius became a book collector. Hidden in the attics of the Don home was a collection that would have condemned all the family to death had an Awakener got wind of it. Tharius found them in other attics, entering from the roofs, prowling dusty spaces by lantern light, old, shut-up places where no one came anymore but where books were sometimes found. In corners. Under floorboards. He found them in houses where people died, before the Awakeners or the kinfolk came to take inventory. He found them in the rag man's yard, buried at the bottom of stacks of old clothes. Fragments more often than whole volumes, but of whole volumes, three or four a year, perhaps. By the time he was eighteen and subject to the procreation laws, he had almost thirty of them.

Which was bad enough in itself. Worse, so far as Tharius was concerned, was the fact that in these thirty books were references to hundreds of others. Somewhere on Northshore there were, or had been, more!

Sometimes late at night, when the moons lit the alleyway, Tharius Don had a waking dream of all those books. More and more. All the answers to all the questions anyone had ever asked would be there in the books.

And the books, he was convinced, were in the Towers. Why else would the Awakeners be so agitated about books, if it were not some kind of secret knowledge only they were supposed to have? Knowledge about how things really were. How things used to be. How they had been in some other place before humans had come here.

Influenced by a bit too much wine, Tharius broached that subject at dinner one night, hearing the words fall into a horrified silence.

"Before what?" his father snarled. "Before what?"

"Before humans came to Northshore," Tharius stuttered.

"Where did you get an ugly idea like that?"

"I just—I just thought we must have come from somewhere else, you know. Because there are so many things we can't eat." Even in his half-drunken surprise at the words that had come from his own mouth, he was wary enough not to mention the books. "It seemed obvious. . . ."

He was sent from the table, in disgrace. Doctrine was clear on that point. Humans had always lived on Northshore and had always been governed by the gods. His bibulous remark was occasion for a loud, screaming battle among the Dons and the Stifes. Two days later when he returned home from a foray, he found a young woman named Shreeley at the table. He had seen her before. Not often. She was the daughter of a friend of his father's, a pamet merchant from the other side of Baris.

"Your wife-to-be," his father said in a stiff, unrelenting voice. "You have had entirely too much time on your hands to sit around dreaming up obscenities."

Tharius Don was more amused than anything else. The girl wasn't bad looking; she had a sweet, rounded body, and Tharius

Don had had some experience with sweet, rounded bodies. It would not be a bad thing to have one of his own to play with.

What he had not foreseen was the sudden loss of privacy. No more attic room. He had only time to hide the books before all his belongings were swept up and reinstalled in a room two stories below, one he would share. And after that, he found it difficult to be alone for a moment.

Shreeley made sure of that. She slept with him. She rose with him in the morning and walked with him to the job his grandparents Stife had obtained for him. "You show none of the family talent for art, Tharius Don," said Stife grandfather. "We have apprenticed you, therefore, to Shreeley's father, the pamet merchant."

"I thought it was custom for young people to choose their own professions," Tharius complained.

"Had you done so in your fifteenth or sixteenth year, as is also customary, we would have acceded to your choice, Tharius Don. Since you did not do so, you lost that opportunity."

Shreeley came to walk home with him after work. She ate with him. She sat with him or walked with him after dinner. Went to bed with him. He tried to read one of his books only once, but Shreeley caught him at it. "Read to me," she begged sweetly. "Read to me, Tharius Don." He made up something about Thoulia, and she fell asleep while he was reciting. He hid the book away, sweat standing on his brow.

Still, for a time it was not impossible. Sex was more than merely amusing. Tharius had a great deal of imagination about sex, and Shreeley was compliant. Until she became pregnant, at which time everything stopped.

"No," she said. "It might hurt the baby."

"It won't hurt the baby. And you like it."

"I don't like it. I only did it to get pregnant and comply with the laws, Tharius Don. I hope you don't think I *enjoyed* all that heaving about."

"Shreeley's father says you have been neglecting your duties," his father admonished. "With a baby on the way, you'd better start attending to business."

It was that night Tharius Don went to the Tower of Baris and begged admittance as a novice. When the family learned of it, they never spoke of him again. When Tharius's son was born, they named him Birald. When Tharius heard of it he uttered a heartfelt wish for the boy's sanity, but without much hope considering that he, Tharius, might be losing his own.

He had sacrificed everything in hope of books, and there were no books in the Tower except those of a shameless falsity and unmitigated dullness. There were no books, and there was no leaving the Tower. For a time Tharius considered killing himself, but he could not think of any foolproof way to do it. And as time wore on, one factor of Tower existence saved him—the rigid, unvarying discipline which allowed much time for thought. Tharius was in the habit of thought. And as the months wore away, he began to find links in the behavior and beliefs of the Awakeners to things he knew from books.

And he saw early on a thing that many in that place never saw. He saw that the seniors did not believe what the juniors were told to believe.

It was evident, once the first piece fell into place. There was knowledge here. Not among the juniors. Not taught to the juniors. Withheld from them, rather. Given to others, later on.

With a grim persistence that would have astonished all factions among the warring Stifes and Dons, he persevered. Years went by. He achieved senior status, learned what he could, learned there was more yet that could be learned, in the Chancery!

He was thirty-eight, a cynical member of the trusted circle that actually ran the Tower of Baris, and a personal friend of the Superior, when he was responsible, all unwitting, for bringing Kesseret to the Tower.

One of his duties was the enforcement of the procreation laws. Women over the age of eighteen who were not readying for marriage or were not already mothers, whether married or no, came under his jurisdiction. A wealthy man—whose wealth did not exceed his age, decrepitude, or hideous ugliness—presented a petition together with a generous gift to the Tower. Tharius Don signed it as a matter of course. It ordered the nineteen-year-old woman named Kesseret to marry the merchant at once or present herself to the Tower as a novice. It was routine. Rarely did anyone come into the Tower as a result. Sometimes the one under orders made a generous gift and the petition was revoked for a time. Sometimes not. It was simply routine.

Except in this instance. Kessie had been unable to buy herself free. She had been unwilling to submit. She came to the Tower.

To the Tower, to Tharius Don, who asked for and received mentorship in her case. She was older than most novices, as he had been. It was harder for her than for most, as it had been for him. She rejected much of what she was taught, as he had done.

So he told her the truth. From the beginning. Comforting her, urging her, meeting her in quiet places away from the Tower, keeping her away from worker duty as much as possible. And one day she had said, "You can protect me all you like, Tharius Don. That doesn't make it right, what we do."

He had agreed. And from that the cause had been born. Not right away, not all at once. They did not know enough yet.

"I'm told the answers are at the Chancery," he said. "I'll have to get there."

"How long?"

He shrugged. "Twenty years, minimum, I should think. I'm in line to be Superior when Filch dies or moves up. If they don't give him the elixir pretty soon, there'll be no question about his moving up. Say five years there, either way. Then I have to make some kind of reputation for myself. In something."

"Something safe," she whispered. "Apologetics, Tharius. The apologetics they feed us juniors is awful. It's dull. It's ugly. It wouldn't convince a swig-bug. Make your reputation in defense of the faith, Tharius. In scholarship. It takes only cleverness and a way with words. It's all mockery, all lies, but we can do it. I'll help you."

And she had helped him, and he her. They had been lovers for twenty years, sometimes impassioned, never less than fond. Kessie was forty when she took Tharius's place as Superior of the Tower in Baris and he moved on to the Chancery. They had not known then that it was the last time they would make love to one another. Once at the Chancery, Tharius had advanced rapidly. He had been given the elixir. And after that was no passion, only the remembrance of their coupling, their ecstasy, though that remembrance had been full of nostalgic longing.

The books he had sought were at the Chancery. The palace

was full of books, very old books. No one cared except Tharius. He read his way through centuries of books. Of all those at the Chancery, only Tharius knew the truth of the Thraish-human wars in all their bloody, vicious details. He rebelled against that viciousness. Only Tharius knew of the Treeci and dreamed of that gentle race—for so he interpreted what he read—as an answer not only for the Thraish, but for man. From these books came the cause, and in that long, long remembrance the cause had grown.

And now, now he had delayed long enough, and it must all soon come to pass. He leaned his face into his cupped hands and evoked the memory of Kessie. Kessie as he had seen her last, carried away over Split River Pass, smiling bravely back at him. Her life had been given to this thing. This secret thing. His own had been given, also.

For the two of them there could be no future, but perhaps he could save Pamra Don for some better fate. Perhaps she could live the life he and Kessie had not been able to live. Perhaps she could find someone to love; perhaps she could bear children as he and Kessie had never been allowed to do.

With such simple hopes he comforted himself, believing them. He would give up everything, the world itself, for this cause. But even while doing that, he would try to save Pamra Don.

• 5 •

Midday in the Temple on the first day of first summer, the year's beginning. In the wide, carved sand urns, sticks of incense burn away into curling smoke, gray-white wraiths, rising into the high vaults of blackened stone. On the floor the murmuring multitude shifts from foot to foot with a susurrus of leather upon rock. All is muted, the color leached away, all sharpness of sound reduced to this soft, formless whisper which runs from side to side of the Temple, like liquid sloshing in a bowl. "Truth," it says, "Light," lapping at the walls of the place like surf, returning again and again, tireless as water.

A pale blur of faces, staring eyes, gaped mouths, nostrils wide for the heaving, phthisic breath, indrawn by bodies that have forgotten to breathe for a time. Wonder piled on wonder as the crusaders parade with their blood-bright banners to the rumble-roar of the drums, rhythmless as thunder, rhymeless as pulse. Oh, Peasimy Flot has an eye for spectacle and an ear for the wry, discordant sound to set teeth on edge and wrench the ears away from ordinary concerns. See what drums he has manufactured from kettles and hides, what robes he has managed to scrounge from what can be begged or stolen; see what gilded crowns and jeweled scepters he has set in the followers' hands to confound and amaze the multitudes. Glass and shoddy may glitter with the best in the dim Temple light, as they do now, among the hundreds half-drunk on fragrant smoke.

And Peasimy himself, now mounting the steps of the Temple to stand as he always stands, as Pamra always stood, before the carved moon faces, turning in his high coronal and rich-appearing vestments to call into that breathing silence.

"Thou shalt follow no creature except the Bearer of Light," he calls in his little piping voice, from the Temple stairs in the twentieth town west of Rabishe-thorn. "Thou shalt not earn merit except by crusade. Thou shalt not give to the Temple and the Tower what belongs to the Protector of Man."

His voice is shrill, the high treble sound of a whistle. It cuts through the crowd murmur like a knife, leaving a throbbing wound of uncertainty behind. The voice is not of a piece with the display. They had expected other than this.

"Where is she?" someone brays in a trumpet voice. "Where is the Light Bearer?" They have heard of her. Every township on this quadrant of Northshore has heard of her, and though the entertainment thus far has been better than expected, some few are irritated that she has not come herself, that this pumped-up little creature has come in her stead.

"Gone to the Protector of Man," Peasimy replies, irritated to be so interrupted. "Long ago. With many following after her to testify to truth." He pauses, trying to remember his place in the usual speech, counting the thou-shalts in his head. "And those who have gone will be first in her kingdom, and those who come later will be last, but even to the last will gifts be given which are greater than any gifts these devils have ever pretended to give." His gesture at the carved moon faces is almost like Pamra Don's gesture, and these words are almost exactly something Pamra Don has said. Most of what Peasimy says is almost what Pamra has said. She has never referred to "her kingdom," though she has spoken of the kingdom of man. Peasimy points to the carved moon faces, flier faces, and waits until the babble dies down.

"Thou shalt not revere the Awakeners," says Peasimy. "Thou shalt not walk in darkness."

"What does he mean?" a rugged, doubtful man grumbles to one of the followers. "What does he mean about walking in darkness?"

"It's symbolic," whispers the follower. "At night, when the lanterns are lit, you must walk in the patches of light as though splashing them into the darkness. It's symbolic of the Light Bearer."

"What the hell good does it do?" the doubter persists.

"It's pious," snarls the other. "The Light Bearer does it. To concentrate her mind on the truth." So Peasimy has said, and they have had no reason to doubt him. Perhaps. Or maybe what Peasimy said was that the Bearer of Truth had been found in that way. The follower can't remember. It doesn't matter.

"Oh." The other subsides, twitching. None of this sounds like good sense to him, and he wonders what all the fuss has been about.

"Thou shalt love the Protector of Man with all thy heart," Peasimy shouts. "Thou shalt keep him safe from lies."

"That's what the Light Bearer is going to the Chancery for," the follower instructs. "To advise Lees Obol of the lies which are done in his name." The doubter grunts, unconvinced, though in this case the follower has quoted correctly.

"Thou shalt give generously to the followers of truth, in order that the world may be enlightened," Peasimy goes on, ticking the commandments off on his fingers. Sometimes he remembers ten, sometimes more than that. Tonight the crowd is restive, he will only give them ten. "Thou shalt not withhold food from those on crusade." He is hungry, very tired, and his throat is sore from all the shouting. Tomorrow they will go on to a new town, and his voice can rest. He takes a deep breath. "Thou shalt not make fuk-fuk."

An embarrassed titter runs through the Temple, a break of laughter, like light coming suddenly through clouds to astonish those beneath with a benison of gold. "What the hell?" the doubter growls, doubled with laughter. "Baby talk. What the hell!"

"The Mother of Truth commands it," the follower says through gritted teeth, embarrassed himself by the word Peasimy always uses and weary of having to explain it. "If you want to be really Sorted Out, you don't do *that*."

"Well, if we didn't do *that*, there wouldn't be any of us to be Sorted Out." The man laughs in genuine amusement. "Where the hell does he think babies come from, pamet pods?"

In which he is closer than he knows to Peasimy's true belief. The widow Flot had never found it necessary to tell Peasimy other than the pleasant myths of childhood, and Peasimy, who has discovered the facts beneath other myths by following and spying through windows, has never found the facts of this one. He has never seen a baby born. He would not believe the connection between that and the other were he told. Pamra Don, Mother of Truth, has said the strange, frightening act he has so often observed through windows at night is a mistake. It is therefore a perversion. A darkness.

The follower, elderly enough to have forgotten the urgencies of passion and much puffed up by his new position as expositor of truth, defends the revealed word. "There's a lot more fucking going on than necessary for babies. That's what the Light Bearer means. The Mother of Truth says we don't do it, so we don't do it. Not and be a follower of hers."

The questioner laughs himself out of the Temple, his healthily libidinous nature rejecting all of it. But in the vast echoing hall, there are others to whom the ideal of abstinence appeals. There are disenchanted wives who can do well without a duty that seems to consist mostly of discomfort, grunting, and sweat. There are husbands who consider it an onerous and sometimes almost impossible performance which seems to be demanded—in pursuance of the procreation laws—too frequently and at inconvenient times. There are young ones, drawn to a life of holiness like moths to a flame, easily willing to give up something they know nothing of. There are spinsters being forced into marriage or pregnancy by the procreation laws, and men being forced into unwanted associations by the same. There are those who resent the Tower saying yes and therefore choose to follow the Bearer saying no. For every lustful lover there is at least one juiceless stick, anxious to have his lack made into virtue. Thus, in the departing footprints of each mocker, a follower rises up, and Peasimy Flot leads them on to the next city west while a trickle of the formerly recruited ones move northward, then west, where Pamra Don has gone. The crusade has steadily been approaching Vobil-dil-go, the township through which Split River runs, the most direct route from Northshore to the Chancery.

"How long do we carry the word before we follow the Bearer?" one of the followers asks Peasimy. He is one of the dozen or so who have accumulated the status of leaders in the crusade, those to whom Peasimy habitually talks, those who know what is going on.

"Pretty soon now," Peasimy answers him, though somewhat doubtfully. "Pretty soon now I'll take some and go after the Bearer, and you must take some and go on." He has dreamed this. The Bearer had gone a way, then turned north. Now Peasimy must go a way and then turn north. And so on, and on, like a chain. As he says it, he begins to like the idea. "A chain," he repeats. "Like a chain. One, then another one, then another one."

The follower to whom Peasimy speaks is an excellent speaker who has often itched to take Peasimy's place upon the Temple stairs. He has a loud, mellifluous voice, and, since he finds both women and sex utterly repugnant, he has wholly adopted Peasimy's doctrine. He will have sense enough not to speak of his repugnance directly to the multitudes, as he knows he must include women among his followers if he is to acquire the kind of power—and service—he desires. In his satisfaction at considering this not-so-distant future, he forgets to answer Peasimy's suggestion.

"You will do it if I tell you," Peasimy asserts, interpreting the man's silence as unwillingness. "Yes, you will."

"If the Bearer of Light commands," the man says, silently exulting. "When you leave us, how will you know which way to go?"

"North, until we see the mountains. Great tall mountains," Peasimy replies proudly. The Jondarites had told him that, when they had taken Pamra Don away. Now he quotes them in a singsong voice, certain of the way he will go. "Keep the mountains on the right." He pats the arm on which he wears his glove. That is his right arm, Widow Flot had told him. "The arm with the glove is your right arm, Peasimy. You eat with your right hand." So he pats it now, quite sure. "Keep the mountains on the right. Until we come to a big river with some high places with flat tops. That's Split River Pass, where we go through, to the Chancery."

Joal makes note of it. He has no plans to lead the crusade anywhere but where he wants it to go, and at the moment that does not include going anywhere near to the Chancery.

• 6 •

Sometimes I wonder what I'm doing when I write these things down. I read what I wrote about what happened, and then I try to remember what happened, and sometimes I can't remember whether I'm remembering what really happened or only what I wrote about it. The words have a way of doing things on their own. They sneak around and say things I'm not sure are real.

I wrote something the other day about an order of food that came in from the east, and later I heard Taj Noteen talking with Medoor Babji about it as though it had been some other thing entirely. I always figured me and the men saw things pretty much the same way, but now there's others here who seem to look at this world as though they had eyes different from mine. If I hadn't written it down, I wouldn't have thought again about it, figuring I'd just missed something about it at the time. But I did write it down, and what I wrote wasn't what the Noor were saying at all.

Of course, I'm only an ignorant boatman. Maybe priests and Awakeners are taught to do it better, but words written down seem to me could be very dangerous things.

From Thrasne's book

While the *Gift* and the Noor waited for stores, Thrasne passed the time by doing things to the *Gift*. A new railing on the steering deck. A small cabin below for himself since the Melancholics would be using his house. Reinforcement between the ribs in the fore and aft holds. And, though it cost him much thought and argument with himself, a tall mast mounted on the main deck, just behind the owner-

house. This was decided soon after Obers-rom hired three new
men who knew about sail.

"Used to run back and forth among the islands out there,"
one of them told Thrasne. "There's chains of islands out there,
out of sight of Northshore, farther out than the shore boats go,
Owner."

"You ran *up*-River?" Thrasne asked in astonishment.

"Well—what I'd say about that would depend who I was
talkin' to."

And thus did Thrasne owner learn of whole tribes of boatmen
who paid the tides no more attention than they paid the little
pink clouds of sunset.

"You don't know how the tide works as far out as you plan
to go, Thrasne owner," the man said. "You don't know and I
don't know. You'll never row this flat bottom across World
River, that's for sure, and I'm suggestin' it would be a good
idea to have another way to move it."

Thrasne regarded the mast with a good deal of suspicion, but
he could not argue with what the man said. They surely couldn't
row the *Gift* across the World River.

By the time they were ready to depart, Pamra had been gone
for months. Still, word of her came to Thou-ne. The Towers
evidently had a way of getting information, and Haranjus Pandel
had conveyed certain information to the widow Flot, who conveyed it to half the town.

"She was in Chirubel," Thrasne said to Medoor Babji in a
carefully unemotional tone. "There were thousands and thousands following her when she got there. I wonder how all those
people are fed?" He wondered how Pamra herself was fed, but
he did not mention it. Thoughts of her were like a wound which
he knew could not heal unless he quit picking at it.

"Way I hear," said Medoor, "some aren't fed. Many dead,
Thrasne. The worker pits in the towns between here and Chirubel
are full. Some of the Towers are recruiting extra Awakeners, so
I hear it."

"I'll bet the old bone eaters love that," Thrasne said, turning
his eyes to the wide wings that circled above the town.

"Well," she said abstractedly, watching his face, "if there

are more dead people, there could be more fliers hatched, couldn't there? Probably the fliers like that idea.''

"You're not saying they think?'' Thrasne objected. ''You mean more of their little ones would survive, that's all.''

"Did you ever hear of fliers who can talk?'' she asked.

And he, driven into memory, remembered a time when old Blint had said something very much like that. Just before he died. He mentioned it to her, wondering.

"Talk to the Rivermen sometime, Thrasne. They know things.''

It was all she would say at the time, but it gave him something else to concern himself about. What was Pamra doing? Hadn't that Neff been a flier—well, sort of? Was she doing the will of the fliers? Without even knowing it!

These concerns were driven away in the flurry of departure.

It was almost at the end of first summer. The mists and breezes of autumn were beginning. Alternate days were chill and windy, and it was on one such that the *Gift* left the docks at Thou-ne. So far as the standabouts were concerned, the boat had been hired by the Melancholics for a Glizzee-prospecting voyage among the islands. It departed properly downtide, and only when it was out of sight of the town did it turn on the sweeps and press away from Northshore. Once well away, the new boatmen—sailors they called themselves—put up the bright, unstained sails and the boat moved on its own, cross-current, the wind pushing at it from up mid-River and yet somehow moving it across. It was the way the sail was slanted, the new men said, and Thrasne paid attention as they lectured him.

In the weeks that followed, he learned about tacking, though the new men laughed at the lumbering *Gift*, calling her ''fat lady'' and ''old barge bottom.'' When Thrasne objected, they offered to show him the kind of boat that skipped among the islands, and he gave them leave to stop at a wooded isle they were passing at the time to spend two days cutting logs for ribbing and planks. It was to be a small thing, one that could be put together on the top of the owner-house. Thereafter the voyage was livened for all of them by their interest in the new boat.

Once they had passed the braided chains of islands, it was livened by little else.

Except for the sailors, none of them had ever been out of sight of land. Even the sailors had experienced this seldom and briefly, for the islands were thickly scattered in their chains, few of them isolated enough to require long sailing without a few rocky mountaintops or rounded hills in view. Now, however, they were beyond the last of the islands.

Each day at dusk, the winds began to blow from behind them, from Northshore. Then the sails would be set to take the wind almost full while the rudder slanted them against the tide, and all night long the watch would stand, peering ahead into nothing but water. In the mornings, the wind would reverse, blowing toward them, and the sailors would curse, setting the sail to let them move slightly forward and downtide. Thus they moved always away from Northshore, sometimes a little east, sometimes a little west, cleaving to a line that led southward—southward into what? None of them knew.

"This man who saw Southshore—Fatterday? Why didn't the Queen of the Noor hire him for this voyage?" Thrasne asked after a particularly frustrating bout of tacking.

"When they sought him, to send him to us, he was gone, Thrasne. Noor scouts looked everywhere for him. All the Melancholics were sent word to watch for him, but he has not appeared."

"Sounds like a madman. Perhaps he is in a Jarb House somewhere."

Medoor Babji shook her head at him. "Then he will never come out, except as a Mendicant."

"You won't know him then, if he does. All dressed up the way they are, with those pipes in their mouths most of the time."

"Only when madness is about, Thrasne owner. So they say. They smoke the Jarb root only when madness is about, for they are vulnerable to visions."

"The Mendicants? Truly? I thought they were supposed to be the only certifiably sane ones."

Medoor Babji perched on the railing, teetering back and forth with a fine disregard for the watery depths below, setting herself to lecture, which she often enjoyed. "The way I have heard it is this: There are two types of people in the wide world, Thrasne owner. There are those like you, and me, and most of those we know, who see the world the same. I say there is puncon jam on the bread, and you say it, too; we both taste it. Then there will be one who says there is an angel dancing on the bread, and another who says there is no bread at all but only starshine in the likeness of food. Those are the mad ones. So, the mad ones go to a Jarb House and live in the smoke, and they become like you and me, eating puncon on their bread. But if they come out of the house, they see angels again, or lose their bread entirely. But some of them come out with pipes in their mouths which they light when madness threatens. And they go throughout the world selling their vision of reality to those who are not sure whether they are mad or not.''

"And with the money they build Jarb Houses," concluded Thrasne, amused despite himself. It was the first time he had been amused in a very long time.

"Don't laugh! It's all true. Moreover, those who come out as Mendicants can see the future of reality as well as the present. That's what they are paid for. So it is said. Now, I said don't laugh."

"I wasn't laughing," he said. "I was wishing Pamra could come into a Jarb House, somehow."

"No." Babji shook her head, sending her tightly twisted strands of hair into a twirling frenzy around her back and being sure he heard what she said. "That is a vain hope, Thrasne. She would not stay. It is not our world she wishes to see."

Upon the River day succeeded day upon the *Gift*. At the end of the first week they had made a modest festival, and this habit continued at the end of each week that followed. On the morning after one such celebration, a hail from the watchman brought them all on deck.

The creatures came out of the oily swell of the water like hillocks, lifting themselves onto the surface of the River to lie staring at the *Gift of Potipur*, a long row of eyes on a part of each one of them, that part lifted a little like a fish's fin, large eyes down near the body of the strangey and smaller eyes out at the tip. They blinked, but not in unison, those eyes, so that the people gathered at the ship's rail had the strange notion they were confronting a crowd, a committee rather than one creature. One of the oily hillocks swam close to the *Gift*, dwarfing it, and spat strangey bones onto the deck. "A gift," it sang in its terrible voice, turning onto its back and sinking into the River depths with a great sucking of water and roil of ivory underside, like a bellying sail of pale silk.

"What is that?" asked Medoor Babji, seeing how quickly the crew of the *Gift* moved about picking up the strangey bones.

"Glizzee spice," said Thrasne. "It grows within them. They spit it onto ships, sometimes, or into the water near where ships are floating. Old Blint said they mean it as a gift. Strangeys watch ships a lot. Sometimes if a man falls overboard, a strangey will come up under him and hold him up until the boat can get to him, or even carry him downtide to the boat if it's gone on past."

"They don't look like fish."

"Oh, they aren't fish, Medoor Babji. Not shaped like them, not acting like them, not the size of fish. One time when old Blint was still alive, I saw one the size of an island. The whole crew could have gone onto his back and built a town there."

"I never knew Glizzee was strangey bones."

"Most people don't. They think it grows somewhere on an island, and that's why the boatmen have it rather than some land-bound peddler. And you know, there's some ships a strangey will not come near. Strange in look, strange in habit, strangey by name. That's what we say, we boatpeople."

"How marvelous," she breathed. "And probably it isn't bones at all."

"Likely," he agreed. "But it is something they make in their insides or swallow from some deep place in the River."

He knew there was more to it than that. When night came, he wrote in his book, all his wonderings about it, but he said nothing of these to Medoor Babji.

Baris Tower shone in the light of first summer sun, its stones newly washed by rain. About its roof the fliers clustered, perching on the inner parapet, keeping watch as they had been commanded to do. Something about Baris had been doubtful for a considerable time now. From faroff Chancery to the Talons, word had come. Baris was suspect. The one called Gendra Mitiar had sent the word. So much all the fliers knew. What was suspected, they did not know, except that it was something to do with the Superior of the Tower, with the human called Kesseret.

And yet it was Kesseret who had told them of the expedition over the River, to Southshore. "It's only the Noor who are going," she had said. "And they are of no use to you, anyway. However, it might give other people bad ideas. You had best take word to the Talkers of this. . . ."

This word had gone to the Talons, Black Talons and Gray, Blue and Red. In each it had led to much screaming argument on the Stones of Disputation. If a human was guilty of heresy, surely she would not have given such important information? If she had given such important information, then could she be guilty of heresy? Such nice distinctions, though they were the stuff of life to Talkers, were beyond fliers' comprehension or interest. They had been told to watch. Unwillingly, they watched.

Kessie, well aware of their constant surveillance, paid no more attention than was occasionally necessary. The story about the expedition of the Noor had done its planned work of distraction. She saw fliers constantly at the Riverside, spying on the boats that came and went. Reports would be going back to the

Talons; speculation among the Talkers would be rife. So, their attention was where Tharius Don had wanted it. Now she had only to hang on, letting time wear by, praying he would not delay much longer, trying to figure out why he had delayed so long. Did he fear death that much? Surely not; surely not the idealist, Tharius Don. She could not answer the question that came back to her, again and again. Why had he delayed so long?

The business of the Tower crept on at the pace of a tree's growth, slow, unobservable. She tried to keep up appearances, with everything as it had been before. She let herself become a bit negligent in recruiting, but that could be laid to her experiences with the traitor junior, Pamra Don. Her servant, Threnot, seemed to spend more time than ever walking around Baristown in her veils and robes, but if the Superior wished to gather information, no one would question that too strongly. The Superior herself looked unwell, old, somehow, which might be explained by the strain of the long journey that had returned her to Baris.

Or could be explained by the fact that the elixir, sent from the Chancery through the office of Gendra Mitiar, was not efficacious. It seemed to have been adulterated. Kessie sent frantic word through secret routes. She did not mind dying, but she did not want to do it until after the strike. Her life had been given to the cause. She must see its fulfillment.

In time, another vial of elixir arrived from Tharius Don, but the damage had been done. She looked in the mirror at the lines graven around her eyes and mouth, the fine crepe of her skin. No pretense would convince her ever again that she was young. She regretted this. When the end came, she had wanted both of them to appear, at least for a time, as they had when they loved one another so dearly. It had been a culmination, a picture in her mind. A honeymoon. Ah, well; ah, well. She offered it up to the cause, along with her twisted fingers and toes.

"How long, lady?" begged Threnot. She was an old woman, eighty at least. She wished to live long enough to see the end, to see the Thraish confounded, to see the pits emptied. She was glad to see the lines around Kessie's eyes. They were like the lines around her own, confirming them sisters grown old in the cause.

"Soon, Threnot. Tharius Don tells me that Pamra Don is only a few weeks' journey from the Chancery. He admits to selfishness, but says he wishes to have her in his protection before the strike. There are one or two other things he's waiting on. If possible, he wants to locate the stolen herd beasts and eliminate them from consideration. He thinks if the Thraish have any beasts at all, they may place great weight upon some impossible future and delay acceding to reality." And when he has done that, she thought despairingly, he will find some other reason for delay.

"They would." Threnot nodded. "Those filth bags would rather do anything than what good Tharius Don expects them to do." Threnot had never met Tharius Don, but she had long been Kessie's confidante.

"When they are Treeci, they will not be filth bags anymore," Kessie admonished, surprised that she had come to believe this. She had longed for this faith, the faith of Tharius Don, and perhaps it had come as a reward for her suffering. "When they have become Treeci," she said again, rejoicing in the calm confidence of her voice.

· 8 ·

In the Tower at Thou-ne, Haranjus Pandel reflected on transiency. The sun was far sunk in the south. First summer had gone, and the rainy winds of autumn gathered about the tower, making the shutters creak and cold drafts creep through the stone corridors. Thunderheads massed over the River and surged over Northshore, sailing away into the north in mighty continents of cloud. Ill luck gathering, he thought. Like fliers. Dark and ominous. For days, weeks, fliers had been gathering upon the Black Talons to the east of the town, coming and going. He had never seen so many, not even at Conjunction when they came, so he believed, to breed. It was not the only strange thing to have happened recently.

A few weeks ago had come a Laugher, down from the northlands, cut off from further travel east, so he said, by the towering height of the Talons.

"I demand your assistance, Superior."

He was like all of them, hot and bitter, his eyes like burning coals in the furnace of his face.

"How may I assist the servant of the Chancery?" Haranjus had asked, taking refuge in formality. It would not do to be indiscreet to a Laugher. It was not smart to relax convention or ritual. "The Laugher's need is my command."

"I need to get word to the Talkers, up there," and he had pointed to the heights of the Talons, looming at Thou-ne's eastern border.

"I . . . I can summon a flier," Haranjus had stuttered. He had expected anything but this, anything at all. "What is it you wish me to say?"

"I will say it myself. Just take me to the roof and summon one of them, however it is you do it."

There was a way, of course. Twice each month, Haranjus was expected to provide a living body for the Talker's meat. He saw that these bodies were taken, almost always, from among the travelers through Thou-ne. The town was too small to accommodate the loss, otherwise. Certainly it was too small to accommodate it without comment. Now that the Temple attracted so many travelers, it was no trick to abduct one here, one there, as they traveled on westward. His few trusted seniors had become expert at the exercise.

And when the living bodies were ready, they were trussed up on the roof of the Tower and fliers were called. At evening. In the lowe of sunset, so the fliers might return to the Talons with their burden well after dark.

"Yes. There is a bell," Haranjus said. "But I don't have . . . I mean, there's no reason to call them. They may be very angry."

"Leave their anger to me," said Ilze. "They will be more angry yet when they hear what I have to tell them."

He went with Haranjus to the roof, not unlike the roof at Baris, surrounded by a low parapet, fouled with shit, littered with feathers, and reeking with the musty, permeating smell of Thraish. They waited there, not speaking, Ilze because he had no inclination to speak, Haranjus because he was afraid to. When the blaze of sunset was at its height, Haranjus struck the bell.

The plangent tone stole outward, away from the Tower, rising like a bird, lifted upon the air, winging to the Talons tops, a reverberation now softly, now loudly feeding upon itself, intensifying its own sound with echoes. When the blaze of the west began to dim, dark wings detached themselves from the distant peaks and came toward the tower. When those wings folded upon the tower top it was almost dark. The flier croaked, "It is not time for meat."

"This man asked for you," Haranjus said. "I have brought him at his command, as I am sworn to do." He turned then and left the roof. Whatever it was, he didn't want to be involved in it. Nothing could have stopped him from listening at the door, however. He leaned there, ear applied to the crack, holding his breath.

"I have a message for Sliffisunda of the Talons," Ilze said. "There is heresy abroad upon Northshore, and Sliffisunda of the Talons must be told of it."

The fliers gabbled, croaked, not sure of whether they would or would not.

"Sliffisunda will command it if you tell him I am here," Ilze said at last. "He knows me. Return and ask him."

Sliffisunda, it appeared, could be asked. He was at Black Talons. He had come there fairly recently. The fliers would return and ask him, albeit unwillingly. Sliffisunda was evidently in a temper.

"Tell him to send a basket for me!" shouted Ilze as the great wings lifted from the Tower. He stumped to the door and down the stairs, finding Haranjus somewhat out of breath in the study at their foot.

"Give me food," Ilze commanded. "And something to drink. They'll be back within the hour."

"You're going to the Talons?" He could not help himself. Despite all promises to himself not to ask questions, his traitor tongue did it for him.

"One way or the other," Ilze sneered. "It was here the crusade started, wasn't it. I shouldn't wonder if you were involved in it."

"Oh, no. No. A man came from the Chancery. He said I did right to ignore it. . . ."

"Fools! What do they think is happening here? The roots of our society are being nibbled away, and they say to ignore it?"

"It seemed very—innocent."

Ilze barked. It could have been a laugh. Like a stilt-lizard, ha-ha, ha-ha. "When all the fliers are dead and the elixir gone forever, then tell me how innocent it was, fool." Ilze, like many of the lower ranks of the Chancery staff, was naive enough to suppose that all Tower Superiors received the elixir. Haranjus Pandel did not disillusion him. Belatedly, firmly, he shut his mouth.

In an hour the fliers arrived with a large basket clasped in their claws. Moments later, the Laugher was gone, carried away in that same basket. Shortly after that, Haranjus sent a full account of his visit, via the signal towers, to Gendra Mitiar, knowing it would reach others as well.

• 9 •

Ilze was unceremoniously tumbled from the basket to sprawl upon a high, dung-streaked shelf of stone. Half a dozen fliers stood about, shifting from foot to foot and darting their heads at him as though he were prey. Ilze drew his knife and made a darting motion in return, at which there was a great outcawing of mockery. This, in turn, brought a Talker, who dismissed the fliers—to their evident annoyance—and escorted Ilze through a jagged opening in the cliffside along a rough, narrow corridor that appeared to be a natural cleft in the stone only slightly improved by artifice. A number of small rooms opened from this cleft, rooms with smoothed floors and blackened corners showing where fires had been laid in the past. Rough hangings closed each of these niches from the corridor, and piles of rugs along the walls made it clear the rooms were for the use of human visitors. Or slaves, Ilze told himself. Or meat.

He was left alone here, the Talker taking himself off without a word. Ilze was content with this. If they were interested in what he had to say, they would listen to him sooner rather than later. Though he feared them, it was worth the gamble to find and hold Pamra Don. He could not go on living until that was done.

A scrape at the doorway drew his attention, and he regarded the pallid man who entered with suspicion.

"Who are you?" They both asked it, at once. It was impossible for both of them to answer, and there was an itchy pause during which each waited for the other.

"You!" grated Ilze with an impatient gesture. "Who are you?"

The pallid man answered, words tumbling over one another as though long dammed up behind the barrier of his throat. "My name is Frule. Which tells you nothing much. I am a scholar. A student, you might say. I live here. I study the Thraish."

Ilze snorted. "And they allow that?"

"They might not, if they knew that's what I was really doing. However, I am an acceptable stonemason and a fair carpenter. The Thraish have a need for both."

"For what?" Ilze stared around him, making an incredulous face. "Do they live better than their guests?"

"Differently." The other shrugged. "Who are you?"

"I am Ilze, formerly of the Tower of Baris. I've come to bring the creatures news of something that much affects them," he said in a challenging voice. "In return for which I hope they will help me with my business."

"Which is?"

"Finding and avenging myself on one Pamra Don."

"Oh. The crusade woman." The pallid man nodded wisely. "We've heard of that business, even here. What has she done to you?"

"That's my business." Had he tried, Ilze would have been unable to answer the question. It was one he had never asked himself. Pamra had been the cause of pain and unpleasantness. She was, therefore, fit subject for vengeance, no matter that she had done nothing at all to Ilze. "My business," he repeated abstractedly.

"Let it be your business, then," said Frule. "I only asked because it helps to know what brings humans here. The Thraish have few human visitors. I have seen only one or two. There are a few others like me, who pretend to be craftsmen. And a few who really are craftsmen, not that the Thraish can tell the difference."

"Stupid animals," Ilze snorted.

"No," said the other in a calm, considering voice. "Not, I think, stupid. Simply not very interested in most of the things humans are interested in. Though I can understand much of what they say to one another, when one has been here a time, one longs for human speech. And yet, as I remember it, we humans spend much time talking of sex or politics—that may not be true in the Chancery, of course." This was a polite aside with a little bow to Ilze. "The Talkers have no sex, and their politics are rudimentary. They do not talk of things most of us would find interesting. They talk of philosophical things. The nature of reality. The actuality of God. How Potipur differs in his essential nature from Viranel. Whether perception guarantees reality. Things of that kind. . . ."

"I find that hard to believe," Ilze said with a sneer. "They do not look or behave like philosophers."

"But then, how should philosophers look or behave? We cannot expect the Thraish to behave as if they were human. If human philosophers perched on high stones, engaging in screaming matches, shitting on each other's feet the while, they would be discredited, but for the Thraish that's ordinary enough behavior."

"And they talk only of philosophy."

"And food, of course. They talk a great deal about food."

"Dead bodies," snorted Ilze.

"No. They scarcely mention what they eat now. All their talk is of what was eaten long ago, when there were herdbeasts on the steppes. They recall the taste of weehar with religious fervor. There is something deeply and sincerely religious among the Thraish, and it wells up from that belief they call the Promise of Potipur." The man nodded to himself, reflecting. "Do you know that promise? 'Do my will and ye shall have plenty.' That seems to be the core of it. And the will of Potipur involves breeding large numbers of themselves, too many for this world to sustain, which destroyed their plenty before. I think sometimes how hard it must be for them to keep to that belief when there have been no herdbeasts on the steppes for centuries. But, I understand, there may be beasts soon again.."

Ilze had not heard this rumor. Frule enlightened him, telling him what had been overheard. "They don't seem to care what we overhear. Sometimes I don't think they believe we are sentient," he commented, shaking his head. "They don't seem to consider what we might tell other humans about them when we leave here.''

"Perhaps they have ethics which would make such a thing impossible," Ilze suggested with a sneer.

"Possibly." The man shrugged. "It is true that the Thraish cannot conceive of a nest sibling giving anything of value to others outside that nest, and that would probably include information. They cannot conceive of it because no Thraish would do it, for any price. Perhaps they consider us human workers as a kind of next sibling because they feed us. Perhaps they consider us an emotional equivalent to nestlings. On the other hand, there is a kind of scavenger lizard, the ghroosh, which lives in Thraish nests, feeding on the offal that is left there, and perhaps they consider us in that light. Perhaps we are merely tolerated. Ah, well, whatever the truth of that may be, it is interesting to meet you, good to see a new face."

"How many humans are there here? And what do you eat?"

"Oh, we bring some food with us. And the fliers catch stilt-lizards for us, or we climb down to the River to catch fish. Though we have to eat it there. The Thraish will not allow it in the Talons. As for how many of us? A dozen or so, sometimes more, sometimes fewer. I've been here two years myself, building perches and feeding troughs, mostly. Though it's interesting, I've stayed long enough. It's getting time to go."

"Go where?" Ilze was suddenly very interested. Did the Chancery know of these human lice, creeping among the feathers of the Thraish?

"Back home," the scholar said with a vague gesture. He peered closely at Ilze, not reassured by what he saw in the Laugher's face. "You wouldn't be of a mind to make trouble for me with the fliers, would you, Laugher? For my saying I'm studying the Thraish."

"Is it in accord with doctrine?"

"I've never been told it's forbidden."

"Which is not the same thing," Ilze sneered. "I've other stuff on my plate just now, *student*. I will remember you are here, however, when my current task is done." He turned away in contempt, and when he turned again, the man was gone. Ilze threw himself down on the piled rugs and waited, not patiently.

When the day had half gone, a flier pushed into the room, perhaps the same one who had led Ilze here.

"Sliffisunda of the Talons will see you, human. Follow me."

Which Ilze was hard-pressed to do. Twice he had to be lifted in the claws of the fliers before he was deposited at last on an elevated ledge above a yawning gulf. A jagged hole led to a space among the stones where Sliffisunda stood before a curtained opening. Ilze was not invited to enter, and he shivered in the chill wind of the heights.

"You wish to report heresy," it croaked at him. "Heresy, Laugher?"

"There's that woman, Pamra Don," Ilze snarled without preliminary chat. "She's guilty of heresy. This crusade of hers is a heresy. The Talkers—all the Thraish—will soon learn to regret it."

"We have listened to what she says, Laugher. It is nothing much. Meantime, pits are full. Fliers find much meat."

"You have listened to what she says in the public squares, Sliffisunda. You have not heard what she says in the Temples."

"Tower people tell us, nothing much."

"Then Tower people lie."

Sliffisunda hissed, head darting forward as though he would strike. "Why would they lie?"

"Because they have been corrupted, stolen from the faith. They are not believers in Potipur. They dissemble, Talker. Pamra Don is a heretic, and she leads a band of heretics."

"And yet pits are full."

Ilze gestured impatiently. "Of course. For a little time. Until she gains strength. Then there will be no more bodies in the pits at all."

Ilze had expected rage. There was no rage. The Talker hissed once more, then turned his head away. For a time there was silence. "How long, Laugher, before this crusade does, as you say, 'gain strength'?"

"Years," Ilze admitted. "It moves slowly, true. And yet, not many years. It will get all the way around the world in twelve or fifteen years, if it continues at its current pace."

"And in that time, we may expect pits to be full?"

"Probably. But that's temporary, and purely local. Only where the crusade is passing at any given time."

"Ah." The Talker turned away again, hiding his face so the human would not see his expression. One might let the crusade alone. In fifteen years, when it had rounded the world, the Thraish would be ready to strike at them all. In the meantime, many humans would have died and been eaten, the fewer to fight later. However, Thraish numbers could not be increased on the basis of purely local plenty, and if some accident happened, if breeding stock were lost to winter cold, then fifteen years might be too soon.

On balance, it might be better if the crusade were stopped. On balance, it might be better if things were as usual for the next few years. Peaceful. The humans kept biddable and quiet. It was something for the Stones of Disputation, something he could discuss with his colleagues of the Sixth Degree.

"You wish to stop this thing, Laugher?"

"I can stop it, yes."

"How?"

"Pamra Don is being taken by Jondarites to the Chancery. You Talkers must demand she be turned over to you. It was she, after all, who emptied the pits at Baris. You have just ground for complaint. Demand she be given to you. Then give her to me!"

If Sliffisunda could have smiled, he would have done so. Transparent, this one. And still as fiery as when the Talkers and Accusers had done with him, before he was made a Laugher. Set on the trail of Pamra Don, nothing would stay him, not even his fear of the Talkers.

"Do you not fear us?" he asked now. "We gave you much pain."

"Necessary," Ilze said with an angry flush. "It was necessary. Not your fault. Pamra's fault." There was a little fleck of foam at the corner of his mouth. He felt it there, wiped it away, struggling to remain calm.

"And if we took this Pamra Don, but did not give her to you?"

"You owe her to me," Ilze whined, the words vomited out unwillingly in a detested, shameful tone he could no more

control than he could withhold. He willed himself to silence and
heard his own voice once more. "You set me looking for her.
You owe her to me."

"Perhaps," soothed Sliffisunda, chuckling inwardly. "Perhaps we do. We'll see, Laugher. Remain with us for now, while
we discuss this matter."

"If you will provide for me." Sulkily, this.

"Oh, we will provide." This time chuckling audibly,
Sliffisunda turned away through the heavy curtain. In time some
fliers came to take Ilze back to his room.

In a high, narrow shaft cut into the bones of the mountain,
Frule edged himself away from the hole leading to Sliffisunda's
aerie. It had taken him a year and a half to open the cleft wide
enough that he could climb it. It was hidden on three sides and
from above. Only the fourth side gaped toward the north, and
Frule braced himself against the stone as he withdrew a small
mirror from his pocket, breathing upon it, then polishing it
vigorously upon his sleeve. He cocked an eye at the sun, then
tilted the mirror to catch it and fling the dazzling beam into the
empty northlands. Flash, flash, again and again, long and short,
spelling out his message. After a time he stopped, waiting.
From a distant peak came an answering flash, one, two, and
three.

Frule sighed, hiding the mirror once more in his tunic. He
had had more excitement in this one morning than in the last
two years put together. Gratifying, in a way. There had been
very little to report to Ezasper Jorn since the Ambassador to the
Thraish had recommended him to Sliffisunda as a competent
workman, luring his spy, Frule, to take the job by promise of
much reward when the duty was done.

Much reward.

There could be only one reward. The elixir. Something of
that magnitude was what it would take to pay him for these two
cold, comfortless, stinking years! And yet, it would have been
difficult to argue for such a reward had there been no results, no
juicy, blood-hot information.

He shivered, half anticipation, half cold, drawing his cloak
more closely around him. It would be some time before his
message could be received at its ultimate destination and new

instructions transmitted. Still, better wait where he was. Getting into the cleft required a hard climb up a rock chimney with his shoulders and feet levering him upward in increments of skin-scraping inches. He had managed to get into position today barely in time to hear the conversation between the visitor and the Talker. Better stay where he was. He lost himself in dreams of fortune, eyes glazing with thoughts of the elixir. He dozed.

He did not wake even when the claws dragged him out of the cleft and over the cliff to bounce upon a hundred projections before his pulped body came to rest far below.

"A spy," said Sliffisunda mildly. "I knew he was there, somewhere. I heard him breathing. And I smelled him. He was very excited about something."

• 10 •

Looking at my carvings today, wondering which ones I ought to give away, I came across the little boat I'd carved, oh, fifteen years ago, maybe. The Procession boat. Always meant to get some gold paint for it, but never did.

I remember that Procession. I saw the Protector of Man with my own eyes. I don't know where I was when he came around before—I'd have been old enough to remember if I'd seen him, so I suppose I didn't. The golden boat was as long as a pier, and it shone like the sun itself, all full of Chancery people in robes and high feathers. It was a wonderful thing to see, and all the shore was lined with people chanting and waving. But when I saw it, I remember wondering what it was all those people did, there in the Chancery, there in the northlands. No farmers among them, that's for sure, nor boatmen, either. Soft hands and pale faces, all of them, so they aren't people who work. So I said to Obers-rom, what do you suppose they do with their time, those people? And he said, whatever it is, it won't help you or me, Thrasne. And I suppose that's right.

But I still wonder what they do.

From Thrasne's book

Word reached Ezasper Jorn late in the evening, carried down endless flights of stairs, through door after door, shut against the cold of polar winter, the message carefully transcribed onto handmade paper, the missive properly folded and sealed. Jorn liked these little niceties, the sense of drama conveyed in folded, sealed documents, ribbons dangling from the wax, the color of the ribbons betokening what lay within. These ribbons were red. Something vital. Something bloody, perhaps. He played with the heavy paper for a moment, sliding his thumbnail beneath the seal, teasing himself.

So, Frule had at last acquitted himself well! Ezasper Jorn had almost given up hope of receiving any sensible information from the man, not that it was his fault. Ezasper had visited an aerie in the Talons, once. They were not made for two-legged spies, and Ezasper had no source of winged ones. Frule must have carved himself a spy hole somewhere. Ezasper grinned, for the moment almost warm enough in the flush of his enthusiasm.

Now. Now. Where could the information best be used? He peered into the corridor for a long moment before slithering along to Koma Nepor's suite, knocking there for an unconscionable time before the Research Chief heard him and let him in. Ezasper gave him the letter, reading it again over his shoulder, jigging with pleasure.

"I think we'll give it to Gendra, don't you? Part of a package? Later we'll get old Glamdrul to tell her there's heresy all right, started in Baris. She'll like that. She's dying for a reason to get rid of the Superior in Baris, dying to rub Tharius Don's face in it, too. Then we'll suggest it would be a good idea if she went there herself."

"She won't leave the Chancery," Nepor objected. "She won't leave the center of power when the power is looking for a center, old fish. No. Never. She won't."

"Ah, but might she not go in order to obtain the support of the Thraish for her candidacy?"

"How would she do that?"

"Read what's in front of you, nit. She will gain the support of the Thraish by delivering Pamra Don into their claws. In return for supporting her, of course. All other things being equal, it's a strategy which just might work. The assembly likes things peaceful between us and the Thraish. It would get her some votes, if she were around to get them—which she won't be."

"Because while she's gone, we'll do away with Obol and see that you, old fish, that you're named Protector, is that it?"

Nepor rubbed his hands together, jigging from foot to foot in his excitement. "Oh, that will be a turn."

Ezasper Jorn sat down ponderously, pulling his cap firmly down to cover his ears and stretching his legs toward the fire. Even in these vaults, far below the earth, the cold crept in as the winter lengthened. "Well, Tharius will vote for himself, you may be sure of that. Obol will be dead. Gendra will be gone. That's three."

"Bossit will vote for himself. You and I will vote for you, Jorn. That's six, and two votes for you."

"Leaving Jondrigar."

"Oh, that's a difficult one. I should think the general will not vote for anyone."

"Ah, ah, but you see, I have this letter."

"A letter? What letter, Jorn?"

"This letter from Lees Obol. To the general."

"When did Lees Obol last write anything? Come now, Jorn. Would you try our credulity?"

"Nepor, if you ask the general, 'Can the Protector of Man write a letter?' what will the general say?"

"He would say the Protector could write a letter, or ride a weehar bull over the pass, or thump down a mountain with his fists. He would say the Protector could do anything at all. I think he believes it, too."

"He does, yes. He has that happy faculty of never confusing reality with his preconceptions. General Jondrigar will believe in the letter, leave that to me."

"And the letter will say?"

"That Lees Obol, feeling himself fading away, chooses to recommend to the general that he vote for Ezasper Jorn as the next Protector of Man."

"That's three of you," said Nepor admiringly. "And only two against."

"But a very strong two," Ezasper mused, holding out his hands to the fire. "Bossit. And Tharius Don. Perhaps I can find some reason that Tharius Don would consider it wise to support me. . . ." He stared into the dancing flames, lost in contemplation. Koma Nepor, familiar with this state of reflective trance in his companion, snuggled more deeply into his chair to consider which of the several strains of blight he had available to him would be best to use in ridding themselves of Lees Obol.

Ezasper Jorn carried the message to Gendra Mitiar the following morning, wending his way through endless tunnels from the roots of the palace to the roots of the Bureau of Towers, finding Gendra Mitiar at last in a room warmed almost to blood heat by a dozen braziers, ventilated by the constant whir of great fans turned by her slaves. Gendra was undergoing a massage at the hands and feet of Jhilt, the Noor. Though Jhilt was sweating and panting from her exertions, the sheet-covered heap that was Gendra's ancient body showed no signs of perceiving her exhaustion.

"Message from the Talons," he said, trying to fit his words between the slap, slap, slap, wrench, crunch, grunt that Jhilt continued.

"Ahum," Gendra responded.

"Important, Gendra. You should listen."

"Don't care about the stupid fliers."

"Don't care about being the next Protector of Man, perhaps?"

"Enough, Jhilt," Gendra said, slapping the woman's hands away. "Get out of here." She sat up, wrapped in the sheet, her ravaged face peering from the top of it like the head of an enshrouded worker, looking no less dead than many did. "What was that you said?"

"I merely asked if you were not concerned with the possibility of being our next Protector. Koma Nepor and I have talked it over. In return for some arrangement which we can undoubtedly agree upon, we two would be willing to support you for that position. Entirely quid pro quo, Gendra. You know me well enough to know I am not altruistic." He made a long face, appearing both shamed and somehow ennobled by this admission, sighing deeply the while. She regarded him suspiciously, and he made a disarming gesture. "I have no chance at the position myself, and making an arrangement to support you would be more profitable for me than seeing Tharius Don as Protector." He turned away, watching her from the corner of his eye. It was not necessary to see her, for she ground her teeth at the mention of Tharius Don. He went on, "Of course, this is all somewhat premature. I have every reason to believe Lees Obol will live for two or three years yet. Still, it is not too early to plan. Proper planning will, I am sure, assure your nomination. However, nomination by the council is only a first step. Election by the assembly is necessary. As Ambassador to the Thraish, I feel it would be important to convince the assembly you have the endorsement of the Thraish as well."

"And how is that happy eventuality to be achieved?"

He handed her the message, its open seal still dripping red ribbons across the words. "My spy, Frule, has overheard a conversation between the Laugher Ilze and our old friend Sliffisunda."

She took the paper from his hand, screwing her eyes into it, pulling the content of the words out of the paper like a cork from a bottle, weighing, evaluating. When she had read it once, she cast Ezasper Jorn a suspicious glance and read it again.

"What here can be used to my advantage, Jorn? I don't see it."

"If you were to deliver the woman to them yourself, Gendra? Having made somewhat of a bargain with them? Their support for yours. Tharius Don won't let this Pamra Don go easily, you know. He wants her in his own hands. So much was clear at our last meeting."

"True. He has some unexplained interest there. I've asked Glamdrul Feynt to look into it, but the old bastard dithers and forgets. Still, I'll threaten Feynt a bit and see what emerges. So. So. You think my turning the woman over to them would gain their favor, eh?" She had quite another reason for wanting the favor of the Thraish, but she did not intend to discuss that with Ezasper Jorn.

"Something for something, Gendra. If you want our support, Nepor's and mine, you'll have to offer something. We'll talk again." He left her chewing on that, figuring how to outwit him in the long run, so taken with her own cleverness she couldn't think for a moment he had already outwitted her.

The corridors of the Bureau of Towers were long and echoing, the stairs even longer. When he came to the bottom of the sixth flight, three levels below winter quarters, smelling the opulent dust of the files, he was too out of breath to summon Glamdrul Feynt for a time. He contented himself with leaning on a table while his heart slowed, then banging the nearest door in its frame three or four times, hearing the echoes slam down the endless corridors, ricocheting fragments in an avalanche of sound.

When the sound died it was resurrected, coming from the opposite direction, another door slammed somewhere far away, and the sound of Feynt's voice, "Hoo, hoo, hoo," as he stumbled nearer. When he saw who it was, he straightened and stopped limping. "So, Jorn. What's on your mind?"

They sat on a filthy bench, staring at dust motes like schools of silver fish in a slanting beam that struck from a high lantern into the well of the files, talking of Gendra Mitiar, of fliers, of this and that.

"So you've got it all planned, have you?"

"If you'll tell her there's heresy in Baris, yes. That'll do the trick. She'll trot off to the fliers with Pamra Don, and she'll keep right on going. Oh, she can't wait to set her claws into that woman in Baris."

"And you'll be the next Protector, then?"

"Sure as can be. We count three votes for it, against two at the council. Of course, the assembly's something else, but we can manage that."

"And what's in it for old Feynt, Jorn? Oh, I know you've talked dribs of this and drabs of that, but what's in it for me, I want to know?"

"Elixir, Feynt. All of that you want. What else can I do for you? Some other job? No reason you have to stick down here, is there?"

"Nobody else knows where anything is, you know that, Jorn." It was said with a kind of belligerent pride.

"Does it matter?" It was said all unheeding, Jorn so drunk with his own plotting he didn't think. He was watching the dust motes, thinking of himself on the royal Progression, dressed all in gold and held up by the Jondarites to the acclaim of the mobs. He did not see the wrinkle come between Feynt's old eyebrows or the hateful gleam that winked once across his eyes. *Did it matter?* Did a man's life matter? Over a hundred years spent on these files, and did it matter?

When Ezasper Jorn left in a little time, he did not know he had made an enemy of what had been, at worst, a malicious but disinterested man.

Among the more respected followers of the crusade were several scribes, including a light-colored spy sent by Queen Fibji and at least one adventurer from the island chain. Night found these assigned recorders, among others who kept records for their own various reasons, hunched over their individual campfires or crouched into the pools of their lantern's light, scribbling an account of the day's sayings. Some of them had not seen Pamra Don herself, so they wrote what others said of her, of her and Lila.

"She shines with a holy radiance," some wrote, confusing the shining statue that had appeared in Thou-ne with the woman it had likened. "The child is a messenger of God, sent into her keeping, an unearthly being, of an immortal kind." In which they were more accurate than they realized, though Lila's unearthly nature came from a source closer to them than the God of man.

"The Noor are personifications of the darkness," they scribbled. Queen Fibji's spy gritted his teeth as he made note of this particular doctrine. It was a new teaching. Peasimy Flot had been stopped by a troop of Melancholics in a town market square as they were passing through. Unwisely, the Melancholics had suggested the crusaders be whipped for holiness's sake. Peasimy had peered into their dark, grinning faces and had turned away with revulsion, shivering. "These are devils," he cried. "The darkness creeps out of their skins." The word had spread rapidly through the following, and since that time, the crusade had gone out of its way to surround and brutalize troupes of Melancholics, beating them with their own whips.

When the spy for Queen Fibji had written it all down, he rolled the account into a lightweight tube made of bone and attached it to the legs of a seeker bird. The Queen would soon have this news to add to her many burdens. The writer considered it more ominous than most information he had provided.

After sending the bird off, he went back into his little tent and shaved his head. His skin was light enough not to appear Noorish, but nothing could have disguised the long, crinkly strands of Noor hair. He would follow yet awhile. The whole movement had a feeling about it, as before a storm when the quiet becomes ominous. He slept badly, dreaming of that storm but unable to remember its conclusion when he wakened.

· 12 ·

Out here, on the water, I think about things a lot, things that didn't bear thinking of when we were closer to shore. The nights are bigger here, and the daytimes, too. Space is bigger. I feel as though the inside of me—what's in my head—is bigger out here than it was on Northshore. Perhaps because it's quieter, here. Perhaps the quiet entices the shy thoughts out, ideas that never come out when there are people around. . . .

Like the truth of what I felt . . . feel for Pamra Don. When she came, it was like there was a woman-shaped hole in my life, just waiting. Like a flower waits for a beetle to come along and land on it. Not doing anything, you understand. Just blooming, all that color around an emptiness. The emptiness has to be there, ready for something to move into. That's the way it was with me; all my bloom surrounded this Pamra-shaped hole. When she came along, that was the space that was empty. I guess things always nest or build or roost in spaces that are unoccupied, so that's where she roosted. You can't expect the beetle to love the flower or the bird to love the branch. The branch and the flower are just there, that's all. Does the flower need the bug? Maybe so. Maybe the branch needs the bird, too. But the bug and bird don't know that. Or care.

Maybe what happens between people, men and women, is often like that, one having a certain place that needs filling and another coming along who seems to fill it—for a while, at least.

From Thrasne's book

When Pamra Don arrived at the Split River Pass it was the beginning of second summer, the seventh month. Behind the Teeth of the North, polar winter had given way to thaw and the promise of spring. On the steppes, the rains of autumn made room for the balmier days to follow. Pamra went crowned with flowers, for each day some one among her followers created a chaplet for her, a task begun as one follower's happy inspiration and continued thereafter as custom. Each night the faded wreath was taken away by its creator to be pressed between boards and kept forever. Or so it was thought at the time.

The Jondarite captain, commander of her escort, had orders to bring her only so far as the cupped, alluvial plain at the foot of the pass. No one had known how long the journey would take, and it had been thought possible they might arrive during polar winter when the road to the Chancery was impassable. He sent word, therefore, upon arrival at the edge of Split River, and set up camp to await a reply. Pamra's followers, who had been strung out in a procession many days long upon the road, began to agglomerate on the banks of Split River and around the tall, flat-topped buttes that dotted this stretch of steppe with brooding, sharp-edged cliffs. Soon the vacant lands had the look of a settlement, with tents springing up like mushrooms, fishermen and washerwomen at the waterside, children climbing rocks and chasing birds, and small groups constantly coming and going from their search for food in the surrounding foothills and valleys.

When word came to the Chancery of the arrival of this mob, Tharius Don, after some deliberation, sent word for the Jondarite captain to see that the multitude was fed from the Chancery warehouses at the foot of the pass, "for the prevention of disorder, and lest hunger lead large numbers of people to attempt an ascent of the pass."

Not that the Jondarites weren't quite capable of killing several thousand of them, but disposal of the bodies would be a problem, and there was no sense in letting scavengers ruin the

326

surrounding countryside. So Tharius Don said, at some length, whenever anyone was inclined to listen.

Only then did he send a litter for Pamra Don, instructing the Jondarite captain to escort her to him, at the palace, as soon as might be. This order was countersigned by General Jondrigar. The captain would have ignored it, otherwise.

"What're you going to do with her?" the general wanted to know. "Stirred up a lot of trouble, evidently, and showed up here with a mob. Better let me have the lot of 'em put down." He said this with a flick of his curiously reptilian eyes. "Save trouble."

Tharius shook his head. "No! We need to know many things about this crusade, General. We will not find them out by violence. Just get the young woman here, safely into my hands, please. As Propagator of the Faith, this is my province, and I have Lees Obol's instructions to take care of such matters." As indeed he did, though the last such order had been issued fifty years before. Still, none of Obol's orders had ever been re-scinded, and the least word of the Protector was supposed to be considered a command forever. Tharius used the Protector's name now in order to assure obedience from Jondrigar, knowing that unless Lees Obol himself contradicted what Tharius had just said, Pamra Don was as good as in his hands.

In which intention, Tharius succeeded better than he had planned. The general was so impressed by the use of the Protector's name—little enough referred to in recent years—that he decided to go over the pass and fetch the woman himself.

He set out upon the morning, riding a weehar ox, his plumed headdress nodding in time with the slow stride of the beast, as unvarying a pace as the sun's movement in its ponderous half circle above the mountains, from twilight to twilight. Soon this half-light would pass, and the Chancery lands would lie beneath a sun that did not set, but the general was content to relish this season of spring dusk. In it his accompanying men moved like shuffling shadows, their individuality lost, becoming one multilegged beast which tramped its way up the long, winding road toward Split River Pass. At such times the general knew the immortality of now. There was no past, no future, and he was content to let time fade into nothing. There was only this plod, plod, plod, his own pulsebeat magnified into something mighty and eternal. Armies, he thought, turning the word over in his mind as though it had been the name of God. Armies. Mighty, inexorable, obdurate. It was as though his own body had been multiplied a thousand times, and he felt the multiplied strength bursting through his veins at each beat of the footfall drum. It was better, even, than battle, this slow marching, and in the dim light below the plumed helm, the general could have been seen to be smiling.

Behind him in the palace, Tharius Don supervised his servants in making ready the suite Pamra Don would occupy, vacant since Kessie's departure. It was chill from the winter, dusty from disuse. Out the window he could watch the slow snake of Jondarites as it wound its way up the pass. A day to the top, a day down the other side. A day there, changing the guard, seeing to the warehouses. Then two days to return.

"The cover on this chair is split," he said to the housekeeper. "Have it recovered and returned here within three days. Oh, and Matron, the paint on that window needs to be redone." The window frame was blackened by fire. The ledge below, also, where the flame-bird's nest had burned. As he stood there, a flame-bird darted down the wall, the first bird of summer, shimmering across his sight like a vision, blurred by tears. "Stupid," he cursed at himself, wiping the moisture away. "Stupid." He had been thinking of Kessie.

Someone else at the Chancery also thought of the lady Kesseret. In her high solarium, still too cool for real enjoyment, though the view was, as always, enthralling, Gendra Mitiar stood peering out at the marching Jondarites. Shifting from bony buttock to bony buttock on a bench nearby, Glamdrul Feynt pretended a lack of interest. A litter of paper scraps around the bench testified to the fact he had been there for a time he considered unnecessary and unconscionable.

"I have to get back to the files, Mitiar," he whined. "Things are stacking up."

"Oh, hush," she snarled impatiently. "I'm thinking."

"Well, I can be doing my filing while you're thinking."

"I want you here!" She ran her fingers down the crevasses of

her face, once, twice, then scratched her balding pate vigorously, as though to stimulate thought. "Tell me again, Feynt.
You found evidence of heresy in Baris. . . ."

"Some evidence there may be a hotbed of heresy in Baris,
yes. I've said that. Go back a few generations and you find all
sorts of things happening in Baris that spell unorthodoxy. Dat-
ing from the time of Tharius Don, when he was Superior of the
Tower there. That was before you were Dame Marshal." As it
had been, though not by much, and Tharius had continued in
that job for some time after Gendra had acquired her current
position. Glamdrul Feynt did not dwell on that. Suspicion thrown
on Tharius Don was merely lagniappe, thrown in for effect.

"Aha," she muttered for the tenth time. "Aha. And you
have documentary evidence?"

"Sufficient," he said. "Sufficient." He did have. Or would
have, if he decided it was necessary, though chances were it
would never be needed. Gendra was lazy. She wouldn't ask to
see it. She was content to let underlings do the work, at risk of
their heads if she was later displeased.

"All right," she snarled. "You can go."

He closed the door behind him emphatically, then crouched
to peer through the keyhole. Inside the solarium Gendra Mitiar
was flinging her ancient body from side to side, jigging wildly,
as though something had gotten inside her clothes and was
biting her. It took him a moment to figure out what she was
doing.

Gendra Mitiar was dancing.

The master of the files stumped away, limping ostentatiously
until he was around the corner and a good way down the hall.
The servant he had left there was sitting dejectedly on a bench,
staring at nothing, and he snapped to attention when the old
man struck at him.

"Wake up, you stupid fish. What do you think this is, your
dormitory?" He fished in his clothing, shedding paper like
confetti, finding the folded, sealed packet at last in the bottom
of a capacious pocket. "Now, you take this to Tharius Don.
Now. Not five minutes from now, but now. Got that? Then you
come tell me you've done it or bring me an answer, one."

He watched the man scurry off, then took himself below.

"So, Ezasper Jorn," he snarled happily. "So, Gendra Mitiar.
So and so to both of you. Old shits. Old farts." It became a
kind of hum, te-dum, te-dum, and he sang it to himself as he
went down the endless stairs. "Old shits. Old farts. So and so."
Occasionally he interrupted this song to mutter, "Does it matter?" to himself, screwing up his mouth in a mockery of
Ezasper Jorn's usual speech. "Does it matter, old fart? Does it,
eh?"

Glamdrul Feynt was on his way to keep a very important, and
secret, appointment with Deputy Enforcer Bormas Tyle, and
with Shavian Bossit, Lord Maintainer of the Household.

When Feynt's servant arrived, Tharius was still at the window. Somehow he had not been able to leave it. He did not
leave it when he opened the sealed packet, putting it before his
blind eyes but not seeing it for long moments.

"Today Gendra Mitiar sends word to Jondarites in Baris for
the arrest of Kesseret, Superior of the Tower at Baris." He saw
it without seeing it, and then it blazed into his consciousness all
at once. *Arrest. Kessie.* Unsigned. He whirled. The man had
gone. He ran to the door, looked down the hallway. Gone. He
couldn't remember the man's face. Not one of his own servants.
Whose? The packet was anonymous.

It was from someone in the Bureau of Towers, then. Someone Gendra had antagonized, perhaps. What matter who?

He left the room hastily, setting all thoughts aside but those
of the message he must send. "Highest priority, immediate
attention, to Kesseret, Superior of Tower at Baris, Jondarites
have order for your detention. Go at once to Thou-ne." The
message would be sent through his own secret channels, of
course.

And then another. "Highest priority, immediate attention, to
Haranjus Pandel, Superior of Tower at Thou-ne. Provide secret
refuge for Kesseret, from Baris. Patience. Soon. Tharius Don."

Only when these messages were sent did he sit down to try
and figure out what was going on. The only message to reach
Gendra lately, he assured himself, was one from Thou-ne saying
that Ilze, the Laugher, had gone to the Talons. All messages
from Haranjus Pandel—as from any member of the cause—

were surreptitiously obtained and copied to Tharius as a matter
of course. What other messages? What other messengers? In
winter? None he knew of.

Ezasper Jorn was thought by Tharius—indeed, by everyone—to be so complete a fool that Tharius did not even consider him in passing.

At the top of the pass, General Jondrigar dismounted his
beast and let the handlers take it away. Now that it was assumed
the fliers knew there were weehar and thrassil behind the Teeth
of the North, the general chose to ride an ox whenever he liked.
Since last year's depredations on the herds, he had had
crossbowmen stationed with the herdsmen, ready to bring down
any flier who presumed to try such theft again. Making off with
a weehar calf wasn't something that could be done quietly. One
flier couldn't lift the creature, unless it was newborn, and the
newborns were now carefully guarded. It would take two or
three fliers, together with straps or some kind of basket, to carry
a young beast, and that meant a certain amount of noise. The
crossbowmen were alert. The general was fairly confident the
fliers would get no more.

As for the beasts already gone, Koma Nepor had provided
some clear flasks filled with a clinging liquid. Whenever the
abducted herdbeasts were found, this liquid was to be thrown
among them. "It contains a special strain of . . . ah, let us say
biological material? Eh? No matter what, exactly. It will do the
job on the beasts. Additionally, it will infect any of the fliers
who come into contact with them."

Which, being a derivative of the blight, it would do. Nepor
had not been successful in determining the life cycle of the
blight. Something in it escaped him and his ancient micro-
scopes. He had been able, however, to make from blighted fish
a long-lived distillation that was very effective. This distillation,
modified in various ways, had remarkable effects on people,
and Koma Nepor had no reason to believe it would not work as
well on weehar and thrassil.

Seeing the clutter on the plain below, the general's hand
twitched as he considered using the flasks upon the herd humans
gathered there. "Trash," he muttered, reassuring himself with a

glance at the expressionless Jondarites around him. "Trash." Indeed, the multicolored splotches at the foot of the pass could as well have been fruit rinds, paper scraps, shells, bones, and chips. It heaved like a garbage pit, too, alive with human maggots squirming along the River and among the buttes. "Where is the woman?" he asked the messenger who awaited him. "Pamra Don?"

The messenger pointed, offering his glass. On a slight hillock overlooking the River a wagon stood with a tall tent beside it. All around the hill, banners bloomed like flowers; red, green, blue, and Jondarite tents surrounded the whole. "There," said the messenger.

Through the glass, General Jondrigar stared into Pamra Don's face. At this great distance he could see nothing but the pale oval. A woman, carrying a child. Why was it, then, he asked himself in irritation, that she seemed to be looking directly into his eyes?

He did not hurry his trip down the pass. At the bottom of the pass there were warehouses to inspect. He received a report that worm had gotten into one that stored dried fish as well as roots and grain captured from the Noor. He specified the materials in that particular warehouse be used to feed the multitude. He was told what the spy balloons had seen from on high, a great number of approaching Noor, also crusaders, the steady trickle rising from Northshore into the northlands and thence to the place they stood.

"And a war party of young Noor, General. Just above Darkeldon. We could have a troop there in two days."

The general shook his head. "Not now, Captain. Not with all this nonsense going on. I want a battalion here, spaced out around this mob. I want crossbowmen stationed on the slopes of the Teeth and on some of those buttes. You'll have to scale some of them and let rope ladders down. No threats, mind, Tharius Don doesn't want this flock of nothings injured. Nonetheless, we won't take chances," and he grinned his predator's smile, hard as iron, his gray, pitted skin twitching as though insects were crawling on it.

Only when all that business was attended to did he go on out onto the plain and to the tent his aides had set up at the foot of one of the buttes, protected from the wind. Evening was drawing down, and the cookfires were alight. They bloomed around him like stars, many nearby, fewer farther away, only a scatter at the far horizon and beyond, showing where the stragglers were.

A large fire marked the hill where Pamra Don's tent stood. He looked at it for a time, scornfully, then sent word to the commander of the troop guarding her. He wanted the woman brought to him tonight. As soon as he had eaten.

He had not finished when they brought her, carrying the child. He pointed with his chin at a chair across the tent, far from the fire. The soldiers escorted her there and stood at either side, calm and alert. General Jondrigar stared at her over his wine cup, waiting for her to say something. Prisoners always said something, started pleading sometimes, or offering themselves. Pamra Don said nothing. The child stared at him, but Pamra was not even looking at him but at something else in the room. The general swung his head to follow her line of vision. Nothing. A bow hung on the tent pole. His spare helmet. His spare set of fishskin armor, with the wooden plates. She wasn't looking at those, surely. Nodding in that way. Seeming to murmur without actually making a sound. He went on chewing, suddenly uncomfortable.

"You can go," he muttered to the soldiers. "Wait outside." For some reason he did not want them witness to this . . . this, whatever this was. Not rape. Even without Tharius Don's command, he would not have done that where anyone could see or hear him. Not good for discipline. When the men had gone, she still did not seem to see him.

"Do you know who I am?" he asked her at last.

She turned toward him eyes that were opaque, almost blind. They cleared, very gradually, and she focused upon him. "I . . . they said you were General Jondrigar."

"Do you know what I am?"

"You . . . no. I don't know."

He rose to walk toward her, leaning forward a little, thrusting his face into hers. "I am Lees Obol's right arm, his protection, leader of his armies. . . ."

Her face lit up as though by fire. She leaned forward, across the child, to take him by the shoulders, and by surprise. He could not remember a woman ever having touched him willingly. Aunt Firrabel, of course, but only she. And now this one. Where she touched him burned a little, as though he were pressed against a warm stove, and he could not take his eyes from hers.

"General Jondrigar," she said, "the Protector of Man has need of you. Lees Obol has need of you."

Of all the things she might have said, only this one could have been guaranteed to draw in his whole attention, focused as by a burning glass upon a radiant point. He lived for nothing but to meet the Protector's needs. Who could tell him what those needs were better than his own eyes, his own ears? Still, her eyes burned into his own with a supernatural glow. Perhaps some messenger had conveyed something to her. Perhaps the soul of Lees Obol had spoken to her.

"What need?" he gurgled, barely able to speak. "What need has the Protector?"

"The Protector has been misled by evil men," she said, fulfilling all his fears and hopes at once. Had he not suspected plots against the Protector? Had he not prayed to forestall them all? "They have told him that the fliers are more important than men, have told him some men are more important than others. They have made his great title a trivial thing."

"No," he croaked. "They would not dare."

"They have," she asserted, her face radiant with truth. "I tell you they have! What is the Protector of Man if any man is nothing? Have you thought of that, General? If even a single man is nothing, of what value is the Protector of Man?"

"Man?" he asked, uncertain how she had meant it.

"Northshoremen," she whispered, "Jondarites. Chancerymen. Noor. Yes. Even the Noor. For if the Noor are made less, then their Protector is made less. A blow at the Noor is a blow at Lees Obol. . . .

"And the workers, too, General. Were they not once men? If they are used and eaten, is not Lees Obol minimized by that?"

"Who does these things?" he asked, still a little uncertain, his slow, ponderous mind finding its way among the things she had said. Part of it had been clear the moment she said it. If a treasure was of no value, then he who guarded it was of no value, either. He could grasp that, all at once. It needed no explanation. "Who?"

"You know who. Who here in the Chancery treats with the fliers, General? Who here in the Chancery maintains the Towers? Who goes ravaging among the Noor?"

"We?" he asked, uncertain, in growing horror. "I?"

"You have said." She nodded to him. "You have said, General. All of you, here in the Chancery. You have betrayed Lees Obol!"

He roared then, striking her hands away, glaring at her with red, righteous eyes. How dared she? How dared she? And yet. Yet. The roar died in his throat. She stood there still, glowing, totally unafraid, looking at him with pity.

"It's not your fault," she whispered. "You didn't know. Not until I told you."

"I know now," he growled. It was a question, but it came forth as a statement of fact. "I know now."

"Yes." She waited for a time while he stood there, immobile, the child on her shoulder, then turned and left him, without another word, walking out through the tent flaps where the soldiers waited. One of these men called, uncertainly, "Shall we take her back to her tent, General?"

He muttered something affirmative, unable to form words, standing there in silence, brooding beside his fire, slowly building the edifice his nature demanded, the structure that must properly house the Protector of Man. It could have no window or door to admit error. Monolithic, it must stand forever. Lees Obol must be better served, and he could be better served only if man were better served.

What had she said to him? There were only those few words. He said them over to himself, again and again, seeking more. There must have been more. And yet, had she not said everything?

Late, past midnight, he sat there, getting up from time to time to add a stick to the fire, sitting down again. Very late in the night he rang the bell that summoned his aides. When they came, he astonished them with the messages he gave them, each signed with his own seal.

When only one was left, he said, "That woman, the prophetess. She is a warrior for Lees Obol."

The man, not knowing what to say or if it was wise to say anything, merely nodded, attempting to look alert.

"She needs armor. A fighter needs armor. Tell my armorer. A helmet for her. Made to her measure. And a set of fishskin body armor, such as we wear. And boots. Have him plume the helmet with flame-bird plumes, like mine, and make her a spear."

The man presumed to comment, "Can she handle a spear, General?"

"No matter. Someone can carry it at her side. Let it bear a pennant. Tell the armorer. He will know. And bring one of the weehar oxen over the pass for her to ride, one of the young ones."

The man went away, shaking his head, puzzled, wondering what the prophetess would think of all this.

She, when the armorer came to measure her the next morning, thought it another sign. Neff from his shining cloud approved, and the radiance and the shadow both nodded.

· 13 ·

Tharius Don's frantic message came to Baris at first dark. Each evening at this time, Threnot went for a walk along the parklands. From time to time on such forays she encountered wanderers who might, perhaps, have been accounted a little furtive if anyone had been inclined to care who a servant talked with during her frequent strolls. The wanderer encountered this night was less furtive and more in a hurry than most. Threnot returned swiftly to the Tower. Only an hour or so later, she might have been seen to leave once more, going down to the town on some errand, her veils billowing in the light wind. The flier detailed to watch such comings and goings nodded, half-asleep. When Threnot was later seen to leave the Tower yet again that night, the flier scratched herself uncomfortably, for she had not seen the woman return from her second trip. Three trips in one night was not unheard-of, but it was rare. Perhaps she would mention it to the Talkers. Perhaps not. The ancient tension between Talker and flier had in no sense been changed by recent history.

Actually, only the first and third veiled women had been Threnot. The second had been Kesseret herself, fleeing to the house of a Riverman pledged to the cause. Threnot joined her there some hours later, and when dawn came, both women were on a boat halfway to the next town west. In the hours between Kessie's leaving the Tower and Threnot's leaving it, word had been spread in the Tower that the lady Kesseret was ill of a sudden fever, that she would stay in her rooms until healed of it, keeping Threnot with her to nurse her. Kesseret's deputy had been told to take charge of Tower affairs and asked not to bother the Superior for five or six days at least.

"I have taken water and food and all things needful to her rooms, Deputy," Threnot had said in her usual emotionless voice. "The Superior is anxious the Tower should avoid infection." "Infection" was a word generally used to mean any of several nasty River fevers that were occasionally epidemic and frequently fatal.

"She asks to be left alone until she is well recovered, which I have no doubt will occur in time." Threnot looked appropriately grave, and the deputy—not an adherent of the cause—entertained thoughts of a possible untimely demise and his own ascension to the title.

Therefore, on the morrow when Jondarites came bearing orders for Kessie's arrest (emanating from Gendra, but countersigned by the general), the officious deputy told them of the Superior's illness in such terms as did not minimize the likelihood the sickness might prove fatal. The word "infection" was used several times again, at which the Jondarites had second thoughts and departed. They would return, they said, in a week or so. Nothing in their instruction had indicated sufficient urgency in the matter to risk infecting a company of troops.

On board the *Shifting Wind,* the lady Kesseret, Superior of the Tower of Baris, became simply Kessie, marketwoman, one of the hundred thousand anonymous travelers on this section of River and shore. Her hair was not braided in the Awakener fashion; her clothes were ordinary ones long laid by for such a need; when she looked in the mirror, she did not see the lady Kesseret. If Gendra had looked her full in the face, she would not have seen Kesseret, either.

And Kessie amused herself bitterly, hour on hour, wondering whether Tharius Don would recognize her if he ever saw her again.

• 14 •

Rumor spread through the palace like a stain of oil on water, at first thick and turgid with unbelief, becoming thinner and brighter with each retelling, until at the end it was a mere rainbow film of jest, an iridescent shining upon the surface of the day.

The general, accompanied by a woman? The general's weehar ox harnessed with another? His banner companied with another banner? Laughter burst forth at the thought, jests abounded, giggling servitors lost their composure when confronted by glum-faced Jondarites, themselves privy to the rumor but unable, because of the exigencies of discipline, to show any interest in it.

"True," the palace whispered, cellar to high vault, "it's true. The crusade woman has converted Jondrigar. She has put flowers on his head!"

Tharius Don shook his head, incredulous. Typical, he thought. The more outrageous the rumor, the more quickly it would spread in the Chancery, where excitements were few and urgencies infrequent. Any titillation was worth its weight in metal, and a laugh at the expense of the general was worth ten times even that. Flowers on his head, indeed. Tharius made his way to the high Tower, his powerful spyglass in hand, wanting to judge the progress of the procession now coming toward Highstone Lees, along Split River from the pass.

The drummers first, then the spearmen. Then the banner carriers—with two banners. And then . . .

Then, Tharius Don's eyes told him, then the general on a weehar ox with flowers on his head.

They came marching through the ceremonial gate, drummers, spearmen, banner carriers, then the general and Pamra Don, walking side by side while the weehar oxen were led off to be fed hay and groomed for another such occasion. Tharius Don so far recovered himself as to put on hierarchical garb and come out to meet them. While nothing had prepared him for this unlikely event, he had managed to survive the political climate of the Chancery for a hundred some years by reacting quickly to events no less improbable.

"General." He bowed, waiting some explanation and trying not to stare at the chaplet of flowers that both the general and Pamra Don wore around their helms. Pamra Don carried a child. The child stared at him, smiling.

"Tharius Don," boomed Jondrigar, "Propagator of the Faith. This young person is a strong warrior for the faith, Tharius Don. She is a great soldier for Lees Obol!" This said, he peered intently at Tharius Don to see how it was received. The general had already determined that his view in the matter was to be the only one permitted.

From a window above them in the palace, Gendra Mitiar and Shavian Bossit stared down, Gendra's nails raking her face in agitation; Shavian, as usual, was inscrutably calm. Behind them in the room, Bormas Tyle strained for a glimpse of the ceremonial group assembled in the square, but his line of sight was obscured by the fountain which threw a curtain of spray across the assemblage. He grimaced, his knife sliding ominously in and out of its sheath as he stared at Gendra's back. No matter. Soon things would be arranged differently. Soon enough, no one would place himself so impolitely relative to Bormas Tyle, so carelessly respecting his dignity. Shavian Bossit turned from the window and winked at him, only a twitch in that impassive face, but enough for Bormas Tyle to understand. He took his hand from his knife and went to find another window. Soon it would not matter. Meantime, he, too, would observe the spectacle.

In the square below, Tharius Don blinked away the spray of the fountain and replied, "I know she is a soldier for Lees Obol, General. Pamra Don cares greatly for the Protector of

Man." He stared at the child. It looked deeply into his eyes, making him uncomfortable.

The general shifted from foot to foot a little uncertainly. His imagination had carried him no further than this formal declaration, though he now felt that something more was warranted. He had feelings inside himself for which he had no name, feelings of anxiety, perhaps even of fear, as though recent events presaged dangers that would be inevitably derived from them, yet which he could not foresee.

"What is she to do here?" the general demanded, coming to practical matters.

"She is to be my guest," said Tharius Don. "She and the child. I have had a suite prepared for her . . . them. We will talk of her crusade. Perhaps she should meet with Lees Obol."

"Yes." The general nodded, his face clearing like a lowering sky after storm. "Oh, yes, she should meet with Lees Obol." Thus relieved of responsibility, he stepped back, satisfied for the moment, though Tharius Don knew his natural and chronic paranoia would overtake him before much time had passed.

Tharius Don offered his hand, courteously. Pamra Don took it, shining-faced. She turned to bow toward the general. "Thank you for my armor, General Jondrigar. We will talk again of this great war we fight together."

In the guest suite, high above the courtyard, Pamra Don went immediately to the windows to fling them wide. Neff had not followed her through the corridors, as her mother and Delia had, but he stood at once on the ledge outside the window, smiling through it at her, his radiance lighting the room.

"Would you like to put the baby down and put on something a little more comfortable?" Tharius Don suggested.

"I didn't bring any clothes," she said simply, not seeming to care.

He opened the armoire, showing her a rack of soft robes and shoes. "These would fit you, Pamra. They belonged to the lady Kesseret, of Baris. She wore them when she was here."

"The Superior!" Her eyes flashed and her lips twisted. "Liar!"

Tharius sighed. He had wondered whether Pamra held some such opinion. "When did Kesseret ever lie to you, Pamra?"

"The Awakeners lied. About the Holy Sorters. They lied."

"When did Kesseret ever lie to you?"

"Full of lies and filth about the workers, none of it true. I have come to appeal to Lees Obol, the Protector of Man. It is better if man knows the truth."

"When," Tharius repeated patiently, "did Kesseret ever lie to you?"

The glaze left her eyes and she looked at him uncertainly.

He said it again. "When did Kesseret ever lie to you?"

"She was Superior."

"When did she ever lie to you?"

"Not she," Pamra admitted, "but . . ."

"Kesseret would never have lied to you," he concluded. "Ilze lied to you, I have no doubt. But it is unfair of you to blame the lady Kesseret, my dear friend, your cousin."

"Cousin?" She had not expected this, this homely word from a long-ago childhood, before the Tower. "Cousin."

"Cousin, yes. Can you remember your grandmother?"

Pamra's lips twisted again, but she nodded, yes.

"Her father was my son. And Kesseret is my cousin."

She did not make the connection at once. It came only gradually, almost against her will. "You are—you are my great-great-grandfather?"

"Say merely 'ancestor,' it is easier. Yes. Which is one of the reasons I have brought you here. We are family. Indeed, we are the only remnants of the family. Your half sisters are dead, so I am told. Without children. You and I, Pamra, are all the Dons." He did not want to talk with her about her crusade. He did not want to talk with her about the lies told in Towers or the obscene stupidity of the workers. He did not want to defend the status quo or to tell her the truth about the cause, for she might blurt it all out, unwittingly, even angrily, and then where would they be? He wanted to talk to her about the Dons, about Baris, about easy, sentimental things. It was a need in him.

But Pamra did not help him. She turned to the window where Neff blazed in the air, hearing his voice ringing in her ears. "I must see Lees Obol," she said, putting aside everything Tharius had said as though it had been wind sound, the chirping of swig-bugs, meaningless. "Since you are family, you will help me see him."

"Of course." He sighed. "Tomorrow. He is a very old man; he sleeps much of the time. Tomorrow morning, very early." If one was to get any sense out of Lees Obol, the very early morning was the only possible time, though in recent months even that was unlikely.

"Not now?" She was disappointed, but not angry at the delay. She had come almost to welcome delay, so long as it was inevitable. Things had gone at such a pace, such a headlong plunge, that at times she felt she could not encompass all that was happening. Delay gave a space. Inevitable delay could not be questioned, not even by the voices. Sighing, she sat down.

"Would you like to take off your armor?" Tharius Don asked again. "Put on one of these robes, Pamra Don, and we will have something to eat together. It is time you and I spoke, don't you think?"

Yet still she looked past him to the window, not seeing him, and he gave it up, sending in one of the servants instead, a heavy-bodied woman who would peel Pamra out of the tight fishskin armor and the high helm at Tharius Don's command. As she did, coming grim-lipped from the room.

"That's no dress for a woman. What kind of heretic is this? What's the matter with that child?"

"Never mind, Matron. Just see that the luncheon I've ordered is sent up promptly." The thought of food made him slightly ill. He had not eaten for days, perhaps for weeks. His body refused food, even though he was light-headed sometimes from hunger. He told himself it was only the imminence of the strike, the ultimate victory of the cause, but even telling himself this could not make his tongue enjoy the taste or his throat want to swallow. He had always felt his vision was clearer while he was fasting. Perhaps he fasted instinctively now, desiring the resultant clarity. Still, Pamra had to eat. The child had to be fed. Pamra seemed to be mostly skin stretched over slender bones. He did not look into the mirror to see how this description suited himself as well. "Send up the luncheon," he repeated to the servant's departing back.

She was gone with a fluster of skirts and a tight-lipped grunt.
To spread more rumor, no doubt, thought Tharius. Rumor, the
blood of the Chancery. Which we suck together, more, and yet
more.

They sat together at a small table set by the window. The
child drank water. Pamra ate almost nothing, and that little
without any indication of enjoyment.

"What is the child's name?" he asked her.

"Lila," she answered. She told him about Lila. He understood about one-tenth of what she said, and disbelieved most of
that. The child was very strange. Its expression was not childlike. The way it moved was not childlike. It could not be her
sister, and yet it could not be what she said it was, either.
Tharius turned his eyes away to poke at the food without tasting
it, watching this year's flame-bird as it built its tinder nest on
the ledge, flying back and forth across the window with beakfuls
of fiber from the pamet fields.

"Do you see him?" she asked suddenly, her eyes fixed on
the open window.

"The flame-bird, yes."

"Flame-bird," she said. Yes. Neff was a flame-bird, born
from the flame of his funeral pyre. How clever of this man, this
ancestor, to have known. She reached out to take his hand,
wanting to share with him what she knew, what she felt, about
Neff, about Delia, about the God of man. Words poured from
her, a spate of words, tumbling over one another in their haste
to be spoken.

"Tell me," he asked finally, marveling at what he thought
she was saying to him, "is Neff in the keeping of the God of
man?"

She nodded urgently. "Yes, oh, yes."

"But he is not a man. Neff, I mean. Treeci, didn't you say.
Not human at all." Treeci! His heart pounded. The Treeci
existed. They really did. Just as the books had said, just as they
needed to be. Beautiful. Civilized. As the Thraish would be,
too. "Neff was a Treeci. Not human?"

"Not then, no," she said. "But now, now he is . . ." She
had not thought of this before, but of course he was. She saw

him, radiantly winged, not the Neff of Strinder's Isle, but Neff with arms to hold her and a mouth that spoke to her, kissed her gently through the flames. "He's a man now. Not like I am, or you, Tharius Don. Something finer than that."

"An angel, perhaps." He was trembling, awed, feeling himself in the presence of something exalted and marvelous.

She considered this. "Angel" was a very ancient word, but one that every Northshoreman knew. A kind of beneficent spirit. Without sex or identity or kind. Suddenly she knew that was exactly what he was. "An angel, yes," in a tone of ringing rapture that made him want to weep.

"And the general saw all this, when you explained it to him!"

She tried to explain this as well, and Tharius Don's soul, ever eager for proof of his thesis, took it in like water upon sun-parched earth. Even in this unlikely soil, goodness would grow! Oh, if Pamra Don could find a soul in Jondrigar and warm it to thaw, what might she not do for the Thraish! He longed for someone to discuss this with. Kessie. Kessie had told him the girl had this talent. Why had he not understood what Kessie meant? She had called it "recruiting," but it was so much more than that! Oh, if Kessie were here. But she was not! No one was. Only himself, and Pamra Don, and the world out there waiting a message from him.

Which he had dreaded to send. Which he had put off sending for some little time. The cause had been ready for a year or more, ready as it would ever be, and yet he had not sent the word. Why? He had asked himself this, morn and evening, wondering whether his own dedication was as great as it once had been. Was it failing purpose? Or did he fear his own inevitable death when the elixir was no longer available?

Or was his delay, his procrastination, foreordained, perhaps, in order to allow this thing, this miraculous thing, to happen.

"You told the general the truth," he urged, "and the general accepted that?"

She nodded. That was what had happened.

He shook his head, awestruck into silence. She had told the truth, and the general had accepted it. Tharius Don had never doubted the existence of the divine, and her statement confirmed his belief. Yes. He had delayed in ordering the strike because something greater than himself had chosen that he do so. Perhaps the Dons had indeed been chosen for something marvelous, for some great purpose. But it might be Pamra Don, not Tharius, who was to accomplish this great thing. He stared at her, watching the glitter of her eyes as though it had been stars, moving in the heavens to spell out a command.

There was a knock at the door, a knock too soft to break through his reverie, which was then repeated until he heard it.

A messenger with a letter from Shavian Bossit.

He broke the seal and read it, read it without really seeing it. "The Jondarite captain at Split River Pass has received a delegation of Talkers, and they bear a written message as well. Sliffisunda demands Pamra Don be sent to him. The Thraish want her at the Talons for questioning. Gendra and I are inclined to agree it is a good idea, and Gendra offers to escort her and oversee her safety."

Pamra was saying something, but he didn't hear her. He read the message again. At first it made no sense, but then its purpose bloomed in him like some gigantic, fiery flower, its perfume enwrapping him, spinning him in a sudden delirium. Pamra Don was wanted at the Talons, by the Thraish. Pamra Don, who had done a thing for the cause that Tharius Don had never thought of doing. Pamra Don, who had converted the general in one day. Pamra Don, who saw the souls of Treeci and people reborn as angels.

And yet, how could he know? How could he be sure? He turned to her with a fierce and longing love to demand the answer.

"If you were to speak to the Talkers—to the fliers, Pamra. If you were to tell them the truth, would they believe?"

She looked at him uncertainly, past him at the glowing figure of Neff, outside the window. Radiant. Breast stained with red, nodding to her as he always did. Yes, yes, anything was possible, anything was conceivable. Yes.

"Talkers?" she asked.

"The fliers. The fliers who talk. You know."

She did not know. Still, anything that talked should be told the truth. "It's better to know the truth," she said. Neff would know. Wasn't he kin to the fliers? Wouldn't he know?

"If I send you to them, Pamra? Can you convert them as you did General Jondrigar?"

"It's better when people know the truth," she said again, a thing she often said when nothing else seemed to fit, for that is what Neff often said to her. Her voice was calm, her face serene, still colored by the rapture that often came over it. "It's better to know the truth."

He took it for affirmation.

"Rest," he told her with an exultant glad smile. "I'll come back and talk with you more later."

He went down to the council meeting, where Jorn and Mitiar, with their arguments for sending Pamra to the Thraish well rehearsed and arranged, were amazed to find such disputation unnecessary.

"I agree Pamra Don should go to the Thraish. Take her," Tharius said. "Keep her safe, Gendra, but take her along. Take her, and the child, but be sure she talks to Sliffisunda himself."

"I think Sliffisunda will require that," Shavian interjected in a dry voice. "There will be no problem." He wanted to ask Tharius what had happened to him. The man was dizzy with joy, like a child on festival morning when the Candy Tree had grown in the night. Like a young Chanceryman at his first elixir ceremony. Full of light. Buoyed up. It was almost tempting to delay the meeting a little in order to find out why, but Gendra's offer to leave the Chancery was too much a godsend to risk losing. Easier on everyone if she's away for a while, he assured himself. Gives us time to get ready for it. And he glanced at the chairs against the wall where Glamdrul Feynt and Bormas Tyle huddled together, exchanging occasional whispered words. The perfect picture of conspirators, Shavian thought, shaking his head at them warningly.

The three of them had only the bare outline of a plot as yet. It would require three deaths: that of the general, that of Gendra Mitiar, and that of Lees Obol. One, two, three. Like a starting chant for a race. One to get steady, two to get ready, three to go.

Since Glamdrul Feynt was to end up as Lord Marshal of the

Towers, he would dispose of Gendra Mitiar. Bormas Tyle wanted to be General of the Armies, which meant Jondrigar was his meat. Since Glamdrul and Bormas had charge of the elixir, nothing should be easier for them than a little selective adulteration. One, two. And then Lees Obol, with Shavian Bossit to take his place as Protector of Man—three votes in the council guaranteed: Bormas, Glamdrul, and his own—and the assembly already primed to vote for him.

Shavian started from agreeable visions of this future and was brought to himself.

"It's decided, then," Gendra Mitiar intoned. "I'll take her to Red Talons."

"That's closest, yes," Tharius Don approved.

"You'll keep her safe?" asked General Jondrigar, his voice heavy and obdurate as iron, oily with suspicion. "You, Mitiar, you'll keep her safe?"

Gendra smiled maliciously. "Of course, General. Of course I will. That's why I'm going."

The smile made Tharius wince, but only for the instant. Of course the old fish was up to something, but it didn't matter. What did she think of Pamra Don? Did she think anything at all? How could she know that Pamra Don was the divine intervenor, the peace bringer, the messenger of God, sent to mitigate violence and death? The messenger sent to Tharius Don to say he had been right in holding his hand, right to delay the strike. It would not be needed. The Thraish could be converted. The cause might be fulfilled without violence.

"It's settled, then," said Gendra Mitiar. "We'll leave in the morning." She cast an enigmatic look at Ezasper Jorn, who had been silent throughout the meeting. He and Koma Nepor had exchanged two or three carefully casual glances, nothing more, though inwardly they were jubilant. The old crock had fallen for it. She thought she was going to gain support for herself. By the time she got back—it would be too late. If she got back at all.

So, the Council of Seven adjourned. Both they and their ancillary personnel rose to move about the room. Shavian Bossit rang a small bell, its sound hanging in the hall like a strand of tinsel, a bright shivering of metal. Through the high doors came screeching carts bearing tea; a dozen soft-footed servitors in gray livery to tend the tall silver and copper kettles with handles worked into nelfants and gorbons and other mythical animals, the charcoal stoves below them emitting a pungent smoke. Plates of cakes were passed: puncon tarts, nutcakes, sweetbean, and mince. The council members floated upon an ebullience that was infectious, every member of it assured that his or her own ambition was shortly to be fulfilled.

Ezasper would be Protector. Shavian would be Protector. Gendra would be Protector. Each of them knew it, was certain of it, glorying both in the absolute sureness of it and in the fact that no one else knew.

Koma Nepor would be Marshal of the Towers. Glamdrul Feynt would be Marshal of the Towers. They chatted with one another, laughing, each glorying in the other's eventual discomfiture.

The general would use his position to rectify distortions and lies. He thought of this as he listened to Bormas Tyle, who was certain he would soon become general. The two of them stood together in a window aperture with their cakes. General Jondrigar even made a little jest about the flower chaplet he had worn. They laughed.

And Tharius Don stood alone, happier than he had been in fifty years.

From behind the curtain a querulous old voice exclaimed, "What's everyone laughing about? Tell me the joke. Tell me," and several Jondarites went to busy themselves within.

To the assembled council, Lees Obol's command only seemed amusing, and even the general smiled. How could any one of them explain his joy? Each, knowing the reason for his own, thought better to pretend it was inexplicable.

The euphoria passed. Voices died down. The babble gave way to whispers, winks, nodded heads. Cups were set down on the waiting trays. Servitors scurried about with napkins to brush up the crumbs. The carts went screeching away, complaining into the vaulted silences. Ezasper Jorn hesitated in the doorway long enough to whisper to the Chief of Research, "As soon as she's well gone, Koma. As soon as she's well gone." And they, too, departed in good humor.

Above, in his guest suite, Tharius Don sat down with Pamra

before the fire while Lila waved her hands at the flames and chortled in words he could not understand.

"Let me tell you about the Talkers," he said gently, watching her face to be sure she paid attention.

But she, nodding and making sounds as though she were listening, heard very little that he said. She was far away, in some other world.

• 15 •

At the end of each month those aboard the *Gift* celebrated riotously on the extra day. Eenzie the Clown juggled hard melon and eggs on the main deck, discovering the eggs in the ears of the boatmen and losing them again down the backs of their trousers. On this occasion, Porabji brought out a great crock he had had fulminating in the owner-house and poured them all mugs of something that was almost wine and almost something else, cheering as Glizzee, though in a different way. Thrasne himself had taken a generous amount of the gift Glizzee from the locker and given it to the cook for inclusion in whatever seemed best. They played silly games and sang children's songs and ended by pouring wine on the new boat and naming it the *Cheevle,* which, said Eenzie, was the name of the delicious little fish that thronged the streams of the steppe. She mimed taking bites out of the new boat, making them all laugh. They took the canvas cover off the boat and sat in the hull, wrapped in blankets against the night chill, singing River chanteys and old hearthside songs. By the middle of the night they were all weary but wonderfully pleased, and most of them wandered off to their hammocks or bunks.

Thrasne came to himself atop the owner-house, staring at the stars, humming tunelessly, almost without thought. Medoor Babji found him there, came to stand beside him at the railing, leaning so close her bare arm was against his own and the warmth of them both made a shell around them.

"Babji," he sang, more than half-drunk. "Ayee, aroo, Babji, Babji." He smiled at her, putting an arm around her.

She did not answer, only pressed closer to him, knowing

what would happen and willing that it happen. When he put his
lips on hers, it was exactly as her body had anticipated. His
mouth was sweet, wine smelling, his lips softly insistent. He
cupped her bottom in his hands, pressing her close to the
surging hardness of him. When he moved toward the *Cheevle*,
toward the blankets piled in the bottom of it, she did not resist
him. When he laid her down, himself above her, and found a
way through their clothing, she did not say no. She cried out,
once, at a pain that quickly passed, then all thought ceased.

It was a long time later she opened her eyes to see the stars
again. She was cradled on Thrasne's shoulder, his right arm
under her and around her, blankets piled atop them like leaves
over fallen fruit. No sound on the ship except the water sounds,
the creak of timbers, the footsteps of the watch on the forward
deck, the rattle of ropes against wood.

"Babji," he said again, not singing, in a voice totally sober
and a little disconsolate.

"What?" she said, knowing he had been awake while she
slept. "What are you thinking?"

"I was thinking about what you said the other day, Medoor
Babji. About the two kinds of people in the world. Those like
you and me, who see puncon jam on our bread, and those others
who see other things. I have been thinking about that. Those of
us who see jam are the most numerous, I know. But does that
mean the jam is really there?"

She stared at the silhouette of his face against the night sky.
"Does it not, then?"

"I don't know. After a great, long time thinking of it, I could
tell myself only that. I don't know."

He brought her closer to him, reached down to arrange the
blankets against the night's chill. The wind was cold, his voice
was colder yet. "It was Pamra's madness made me think of it.
She does not see the world as we do. As you and I see it. As the
boatmen see it. As your people see it. And so we call her mad.
She will not come into the world I wanted for her, so I call her
mad. She will not love me and bear my children, so she's mad.
She talks with dreams and consorts with visions, so she's mad. I
was thinking of that as I lay here, listening to you sleep."

She did not reply, halfway between sobbing and anger, not

knowing which way to fall. After what had just passed between them, and it was Pamra in his mind still! She took refuge in silence.

He went on, "The Jarb Mendicants could come with their blue smoke to sit beside me and tell me, 'Yes, she's mad.' But what would it mean, Medoor Babji? It would mean only that they see the same dream I see, not that the dream is real. So—so, if I were to share her dream, couldn't that be as real as my own?"

"How?" she asked him, moving from sadness to anger. "Your good, sensible head wouldn't let you do that, Thrasne."

"If the Jarb root gives one vision of reality, perhaps other things give other visions. Glizzee, perhaps."

"Glizzee is a happy-making thing, truly, Thrasne, but I have never heard that visions come of it."

"Then other things," he said thoughtfully. "Other things." He looked down at his free hand, and she saw that he held a jug of the brew old Porabji had made. "Other things."

She moved away from him, less angry now, though he did not seem to care that she went, for he began to lace up the canvas cover of the little boat. In the owner-house she undressed and braided the long crinkles of her hair into larger braids to keep them from tangling while she slept. Perhaps tomorrow she would cry. There was a bleak hollow inside her full of cold wind. Perhaps she would not get up at all.

Eenzie stirred. "Doorie? Where've you been? Up to naughty with the owner, neh?"

"Talking," she said tonelessly, giving nothing away.

"About his madwoman, I'll wager," Eenzie said with a yawn, turning back into sleep. "He has nothing else to talk about."

The morning found many less joyous than on the night before, with Obors-rom leaning over the rail to lose all he had eaten for a day or more.

"It's that brew of old Zynie's," he gasped. "I should have had better sense than to drink it."

"Perhaps," Thrasne suggested, "you should only have had better sense than to try and drink it all." Medoor Babji was passing as he said it. He saw her and looked thoughtfully at her, half remembering he had done something unwise, perhaps un-kind. He needed to apologize to her for whatever it had been, if he could only have a moment to remember. She stared through him, as through a window.

"It is never wise to drink too much of old Porabji's brews," she said. "I have had a word with him." She passed Thrasne by, not stopping, and he stared after her in confusion. The night before was not at all clear to him. Part of it, he thought, he might have dreamed. And yet something was owed because of it, he thought. Something needed to be done.

• 16 •

L ate that afternoon came wind. It was no small breeze. At first they welcomed it behind them, but the sailors soon began to shake their heads. They reefed the big sail, leaving only a small one at the top of the mast to maintain way. Later the wind fell, but the sailors did not put the sail out again.

"Storm," said one of them to Thrasne. His name was Blange, a laconic, stocky man who looked not unlike Thrasne himself. "Last time I remember the clouds lookin' like that"—he gestured to the horizon, where a low bank of cloud grew taller with each passing hour—"last time we were lucky enough to get behind an island and ride it out. Five days' blow it was, and the ship pretty battered when it was over. I don't like the looks of that."

Certainly if Thrasne had been near Northshore, he would have tried to get behind something. He didn't like the looks of it, either. The sky appeared bruised, livid with purpling cloud, darted with internal lightning so that sections of the cloud wall glowed ominously from time to time, a recurrent pulse of pallid light that was absorbed by the surrounding darkness as though swallowed.

The River surface looked flat and oily in that light, full of strange, jellylike quiverings and skitterings, as though something invisible ran across the surface. Swells began to heave at the *Gift*, lifting and dropping, lifting and dropping.

"What's it likely to do?" Thrasne asked.

"It's likely to give us one hell of a beating," Blange replied.

"Then let's get that little boat off the owner-house roof," Thrasne commanded. "We don't need that banging around."

They lowered the *Cheevle* into the water, running her out some distance from the *Gift* at the end of a stout rope. The two boats began a kind of minuet, bowing and tipping to one another across the glassy water between.

The wall of cloud drew closer even as they worked, still pulsing with intermittent light, muttering now in a growl that seemed almost constant. Obers-rom and the other boatmen were busy tying everything down that could be tied down and stowing everything else in the lockers and holds.

"Best take some of the spare canvas and nail it over the hatches," one of the sailors told Thrasne.

"Surely that's extreme?"

"Owner, if you want to keep your boat and our lives, I'd recommend it. I'm tellin' you everything I know, and I don't know half enough."

Thrasne stared at the wall of cloud. Perhaps the man was one of those doomsayers the River bred from time to time. On the other hand, perhaps he wasn't. Blange wasn't a young man. He had scars on his face and arms—from rope lashes, so he said. His hands were hard. One thing Blint had always said: "You pay a man for more than his strong back, Thrasne. You pay him for his good sense if he's got any."

So. "Tell Obers-rom what you need, Blange. I'm going to see what's going on in the owner-house."

What was going on was a card game among four of the inhabitants and naps for the other two.

"Thrasne," burbled Eenzie the Clown. "Come take my hand. I'm being beaten, but you could fight them off. . . ."

"Yes, Thrasne," Medoor Babji said in a chilly voice. "Take Eenzie's cards and we'll do battle."

He shook his head at her, scarcely noticing her tone. "No time, Medoor Babji. The sailors tell me we are probably going to be hit by a storm. They say a bad storm. Anything you have lying around should be put away." The sound of hammers came through the wall, and old Porabji sat up with a muffled curse.

"What're they doing?" Eenzie asked, for once in a normal tone of voice.

"Nailing canvas over the hatches to keep water out."

"Waves?"

"I don't know. I've never been in a bad storm. Rain, I suppose. Waterspouts, maybe. I've seen those." Thrasne was suddenly deeply depressed. The *Gift* was about to be assaulted and he had no idea how to protect her. "If things get violent, you might rig some straps over the bunks and strap yourself in. Less likely to be hurt that way, I should think." He turned and blundered out, needing to see what Blange was up to. Surely there would be something he could do.

When he emerged from the owner-house door, he was shocked into immobility by the wall of black that confronted him. The *Gift* rocked in a tiny pocket of clear water. Straight above them Potipur bulged toward the west, pushing his mighty belly toward the sunset in a tiny circle of clear sky. Elsewhere was only cloud and the ceaseless mutter of thunder. At the base of the cloud lay a line of agitated white, and Blange pointed this out, his face pale.

"There's the wind," he said. "Those are the wave tops, breaking up. It will be on us soon." He turned away, shouting for men to help him cover the other hatch.

"The ventilation shafts," Thrasne cried suddenly. "We have to cover the ventilation shafts."

"I'll help," said a small voice at his side. Medoor Babji. "Taj Noteen and I will help you. We can do the front shaft." Indeed, she knew well where it was, for she had sat there many an hour during the voyage, watching as Thrasne himself had once watched. Birds. Waves. The floating stuff that the River carried past.

"Get tools from Obers-rom," Thrasne said, hurrying away to the aft shafts, one eye on the rushing cloud.

Obers-rom gave them a hammer, nails—worth quintuple their weight in any nonmetal coin. "Take care," he growled at her. "Don't drop them, Medoor Babji. These are all we have." He sent one of the other men to carry the cleats.

She and Taj Noteen scrambled across the owner-house roof and dropped onto the grating above the shaft. They would have to squat or lie on the grating and lean downward to nail the cleats across the canvas. There was not room for two of them.

"Get back up," she grunted. "You can hand me the cleats as I nail them." She spread the canvas beneath her, holding it down with her body, pressing it against the outside of the square shaft, reaching behind her to take the cleat.

The wind struck. The *Gift* shuddered, began to tip. Medoor Babji cursed, thrust the hammer between her body and the canvas, and held on. Above her, Taj Noteen shouted, but she could not understand what he was saying.

The wind got under the canvas, lifted it. Her hands were clenched tight to it, her eyes shut. Only Taj Noteen saw her lifted on the bellying sail, lifted, flown, over the side and down into the chopping River. The water hit her and she screamed then, opening her eyes, seeing the loom of the *Gift* above her. Under her the canvas bulged like a bubble, air trapped beneath it, floating her. She was moving away from the boat. Away. She screamed again, soundless against the uproar of the sudden rain.

Then something struck the canvas, brushed it, away, brushed it again. The *Cheevle*. It bowed toward her once more, and she grabbed the side, lifted by it as it tilted away from her, pulling herself in. The canvas was tangled around her legs. It followed like a heavy tail, and she rolled onto the cover of the *Cheevle*. The wind stopped, all at once, and glassy calm spread across the waters.

Medoor Babji shouted. There were figures at the rail of the *Gift*, staring at her. Blange shouted at her. "Get under the cover, Babji! Get under it and lace it up. The wind is coming back. There's no time to pull you in. . . ."

She had scarcely time to comprehend what he had said and obey him, hurriedly loosening the lacing at one side of the little boat enough to crawl beneath it. She lay in the bottom of the boat, on the blankets tumbled there, and tugged at the lacing string with all her strength, pulling it tight again only moments before the wind struck once more. It was like being inside a drum, then, as the rain pounded down upon the tight canvas, and she clung to the lacing strings, flung this way and that by the wind, protected from battering only by those tumbled blankets and the wet canvas that had almost killed her, then saved her from drowning.

There were sounds of thunder, muttering, growling, sharp cracks like the sudden breaking of great tree limbs. After one such crack her ears told her the *Cheevle* was moving, racing, driven by the wind. She imagined the *Gift* also driven, wondering briefly if one of them preceded the other or whether the wind sent them on this journey side by side. After a time the violent rocking stopped. The rain continued to fall in a frenzy of sound. Lulled by the noise, by the dark, by her fear and the pain of her bruises, she fell asleep, still clinging to the lacing strings of the cover as though they held her hope of life.

Aboard the *Gift*, darkness fell like a curtain, rain-filled and horrid. Wind buffeted them. The old boat creaked and complained, tilting wildly on the waves. They had seen Medoor Babji crawl beneath the cover of the *Cheevle*. They had no time to worry about her after that. In breaks in the storm they managed to cover the forward ventilation shaft. The hammer and nails were caught between the shaft and the forward wall of the owner-house. Except for Thrasne, and for the steersmen, struggling mightily to keep them headed into the waves and wind under only a scrap of sail, the others went into the owner-house and cowered there, waiting for something to happen. Thrasne lashed himself to the rail and peered into blackness, seeing nothing, nothing at all, rain mixed with tears running down his face. He could feel the pain in the *Gift*, and he was awash with guilt for having brought her on this voyage.

After an endless time, the wind abated. The rain still fell in a solid curtain of wet. Men went below and came back to say there were leaks—none of them large, but still, water was seeping into the holds. They set up a bailing line, using scoops to clear the water, chinking the seep holes with bits of rope dipped in frag sap. Night wore on. The rain softened to a mere downpour, then to a spatter of wind-flung drops. Far to the west the clouds parted to show Abricor, just off full, descending beneath the River. In the east, the sky lightened to amber, then to rose.

Thrasne untied the knots that held him to the railing, coiled the rope in his hands, and staggered up to the steering deck to relieve the men there and give orders for repairs. He was half through with it, Obers-rom busy in the hold, Blange and a crew restacking the cargo to make room for caulking, when he chanced to look over the railing to the place the *Cheevle* swam along in their wake.

Should have swum. The rope that had tied it lay frayed on the deck, broken in the storm. Of the *Cheevle* itself, or of Medoor Babji, there was no sign.

· 17 ·

To most of the crew on the *Gift*, it seemed that Thrasne owner had gone mad. He was determined to search for the *Cheevle*. No matter what they said, he would not hear them. "She'll be downtide," he said, again and again. "We have to look for her downtide."

Taj Noteen had his own reasons for wanting the *Cheevle* found. He did not want to go to Queen Fibji and tell her the chosen heir had been lost upon the river, lost with no attempt made to find her. Still, looking about him at the measureless expanse of heaving water, searching seemed ridiculous and was made to seem more ridiculous still by the advice of the sailors, those men who had plied the island chains throughout much of their lives.

"Thrasne owner," they begged. "Making great circles here in the midst of the water will do no good! The *Cheevle* was blown as we were blown. The tide moved it as it moved us. If it is not near us now, and if it cannot be seen from the top of the mast, anything we do may merely take us farther from it."

Thrasne would not hear it. Why it meant so much to him, he did not bother to figure out. Why his eyes filled at the thought of Medoor Babji alone, possibly injured upon the deep, he did not wonder. Why his gut ached at the idea of her lost, he did not put into words. He spoke often of finding the *Cheevle*. What he really longed to find was Medoor Babji herself, though he never said her name to himself. The name he had attached for so long to this feeling was Pamra. He had not brought himself to replacing the name, though her image had been replaced by another in his imaginings. In his sexual fantasies he would have

whispered Pamra's name, though the woman in his mind would
have been dark and fringe-haired, fire-eyed and silk-skinned as
only Medoor Babji was. If he had realized this, he would have
accounted this as being unfaithful to his dreams, his hopes, his
vows, and therefore he did not admit to any change. If someone
had asked him he would have said he loved Pamra Don as he
always had, as Suspirra, as herself.

"She is as a member of the crew," he wrote in his journal, in
yet another of those many books he had filled over the years
with *Thrasne's Thoughts*. "We would not abandon a crew
member until all hope was lost; so we may not abandon her."
As he wrote this, he was conscious that it was not quite the
truth, but he could find no other words that satisfied him. "It
may be," he continued, "as the sailors say, that it is already
hopeless."

And yet he would not cease searching for the *Cheevle*.

They spent some days tacking, circling, up and down, back
and forth, the sailors trying to keep some record of the way they
had gone, shaking their heads and snarling at one another from
time to time. During the storm several of the great water casks
had been broken. Thrasne set the carpenter to repairing the
casks, a job that did not take them long, but he either did not
notice or did not see the implications of the fact that the casks
were now empty. In this he was quite alone. The crew and the
Noor saw well enough that the remaining water would not last
them long. One could drink the brackish River water for a short
time, a day or two, perhaps, the sailors said. Longer than that
and people drinking the water doubled in cramps and fits and
died.

On the evening of the fifth or sixth day of this aimless
searching—during which every available pair of eyes had been
stationed at the rail or on the steering deck or even aloft, at the
top of the mast, the watchman having been hauled up there in a
kind of swing—Taj Noteen made his way to the place Thrasne
brooded atop the owner-house.

"Thrasne owner," he said. "Would you dishonor Medoor
Babji?"

Thrasne turned on him, lips drawn back in a snarl. Then,
seeing the quiet entreaty on the man's face, he subsided, won-

dering what ploy this was. "I would not," he growled. "As you well know. Medoor Babji is my . . . friend." He heard himself saying this, liked the sound of it, and repeated it firmly. "My friend."

"Then if you would honor your friendship, you should do as Medoor Babji would wish, Thrasne owner."

"I would presume she would wish to be found," he growled, becoming angry.

"Any of us would," agreed Taj Noteen. "Unless we were on a mission to which we would willingly sacrifice our lives. In that case, we might feel our mission more important than being found." He sweated as he said this, and his mouth closed in a hurt, bitter line, for he revered Queen Fibji, as did most of the Noor. Blame for the loss of the Queen's daughter would fall on the leader of the group. Who else could be asked to bear it?

"So you say," Thrasne argued. "You, who lead this group. Perhaps those who follow you feel differently. Perhaps to them the mission is not more important than their lives."

"We go at the Queen's command," Noteen said softly. "You have been told this."

"I have been told. Yes." It meant nothing to him.

"Medoor Babji is the Queen's daughter, her chosen heir. Medoor Babji is the real leader of this expedition, boatman. I speak with her voice when I tell you to give up this fruitless search."

"How can you?" Thrasne cried. "You know her! How can you?"

"Because there are ten thousand Medoor Babjis among the Noor," he replied, gesturing wide to include all that world of suffering humanity. "Ten thousand to be killed by Jondarites and taken slave in the mines. Ten thousand daughters to weep, ten thousand sons to die. We do not go to Southshore out of mere curiosity, Thrasne. We go because we must. The Noor are being slaughtered, day by day, week by week. Medoor Babji knows this! How do we honor her death if we perish of thirst here upon this endless water and the mission comes to nothing? Then she will have *died* for nothing! Would you dishonor her, Thrasne owner?"

Thrasne did not give up easily. Still, Noteen's words burned in his head. He went below to his airless little cubby and anguished to himself, thinking that everything he cared for was always reft from him, surprised at the thought, for it was only then he admitted to himself that he cared for Medoor Babji. Realizing it made his grief the worse, and he spent the night attempting to assign that grief some cause and function or to find some reasons in his own life for his being punished in this way. It was no good. He could not really believe in such punishment, though the priests and Awakeners taught it as a matter of course. It was nothing in his own life which controlled the lives of Pamra or Medoor Babji. They, too, were creatures who moved of their own will. He could only touch their lives a little, share their lives a little, if they would give him leave.

And Medoor Babji had given him leave where Pamra had not. The thought fled, like a silver minnow through his mind, elusive and yet fascinating.

Still, when morning came, he gave in to Taj Noteen's entreaties. The sailors turned the *Gift* toward the south, praying they would find water before many days had passed.

Despite his decision, Thrasne kept at the rail every hour of the light, or had himself hoisted to the top of the mast, or stood on the steering deck peering into the quivering glow of sun upon the waves for endless hours. He would resign himself to the need of the Noor to go south, he could not resign himself to the fact that she was gone. Something within him cried continuously that he would see the *Cheevle* dancing in the sun, beyond the next wave.

• 18 •

I remember when Blint first brought me aboard the *Gift*,
sometimes at night I would wake from a dream of being lost
upon the River. I was only twelve or thirteen, I suppose. Not
a man yet, or anything near it. Perhaps they were a child's
dreams, just as children dream of falling or flying but grown-
ups seldom do. At least, I suppose that is true. I used to
dream of falling all the time but don't anymore. I don't
dream of being lost on the River anymore, either, but sometimes I dream of swimming—as though I were one of the
strangeys. . . .

From Thrasne's book

Medoor Babji woke to the slup-slup-slup of wavelets on
the side of the boat, to the heat of the sun on the
canvas above her. The air was stifling. She lay in a
puddle of wet blankets, cozied into them like a swig-bug into
water weed. It took her some minutes to extricate herself and
untangle the lacing strings from fingers that were stiff and
sticklike. "Blight," she cursed at herself, attempting cheer.
"My fingers have the blight."

Her head came out of the *Cheevle*, bleary eyes staring around
at the sparking wavelets on all sides, taking some notice of the
clear amber of the sky and the high, seeking scream of some
water bird before realizing, almost without surprise, that the
Gift was gone. It was as though part of herself had been
prepared for this eventuality—aware of it, perhaps, when the
rope snapped, even during the fury of the storm—even as some
other, less controlled persona prepared for panic.

"Now, now," she encouraged herself, quelling a scream that
had balled itself tight just below her breastbone and was pushing
upward, seeking air. "It may not be the *Gift*'s gone. Maybe I'm
gone. Separated, at any event. Oh, Doorie, now what?" Her
insides were all melting liquid, full of confusion and outright
fear, but the sound of her own voice brought a measure of
control.

The persona in charge postponed answer of this question,
postponed thought while she unlaced half the drum-tight covering of the *Cheevle* and folded it over the intact half. She wrung
out the blankets as best she might and laid them over the loose
canvas, seeing steam rise from them almost immediately. Her
clothing followed. There was water in the bottom of the boat,
though not much, and she sought the bailing scoops the sailors
had carved, still tight on their brackets beneath the tiny bow
deck. She postponed thought still further while bailing the boat
dry, and further yet by turning and returning the blankets and
clothing so that all were equally exposed to the drying rays of
the sun.

And when all this was done, when she had dressed herself
and taken a small drink of water from the River, brackish but
potable—so Thrasne had told her, though one should drink very
little at a time and not for long—there was no change in the
circumstance at all. The *Cheevle* still bobbed on the wavelets,
alone on the River, with no rock, no island, no floating flotsam
in view.

"And no food," she murmured to herself. "And no really
good water." The taste of the River on her tongue was mucky,
a little salty. It had done little to reduce her thirst.

The mast lay in the bottom of the boat. She had slept between
it and the sharp rib corners all night. Now she considered it with
a kind of fatalistic resignation. She had paid some attention
when the sailors had demonstrated how the mast was to be
stepped. It had, as she recalled, taken two of them to get it up.
Still. If she had the wind, she might go somewhere. If she went
on bobbing here, like some little wooden toy, lost in immensity
by a careless child, she might float forever.

The mast was heavy. After using her strength to no purpose
for a time, she stopped fooling with the thing and thought it

through. She took the lines loose from the canvas cover, maneuvered the butt of the mast into position against its slanting block, then attached a line halfway up the mast, running it under and over two of the lacing hooks and using a third to take up the slack. She heaved, sweated, cursed, saw the mast rise a little. She tied it off and recovered, panting, then tried again. By alternately heaving and cursing at this primitive pulley arrangement, she managed to get the mast almost upright, at which point it slid into its slot with a crash that made her fear for the bottom of the boat. She felt around it gingerly, praying to find no water. There was water. Was it left over from bailing or from a new leak? She had no idea and spent several anxious moments measuring it with eyes and hands to see whether it got any higher.

When she had convinced herself—deluded herself, her other persona kept insisting—that the hull was sound, she restored the lacing to the cover and relaced half of it, folded the now dry blankets under this shelter, remembered to drop in the wedges that held the mast erect, and set about trying to recall what Blange had said about sail.

"If you cannot remember what you are told," Queen Fibji had told her more than once, "you must use trial and error. The thing to keep in mind about trial and error is that some errors are quite final. Therefore, it might be wise to listen carefully to the instructions of those who have experienced what they are trying to tell you about."

"People are always telling me things," Medoor Babji had complained. She had been about twelve at the time, coming as inevitably into rebellion as a flame-bird chick into its plumes. "They don't even ask me what I think."

The Queen had nodded, brow wrinkled a little at this. They were in the Queen's own tent, and her serving women were redoing the Queen's hair as well as Medoor Babji's. It was a long process, though infrequent. Each strand was carefully combed out, washed and rinsed, one by one, then rewound and decorated at the bottom with a bead of bone or faience. The serving women chatted between themselves, politely, pretending that the Queen and Medoor were not present, thus allowing the mother and daughter the same freedom.

"Ah," Queen Fibji had said. "Well, let us suppose you have broken your leg. Chamfas Muneen is sent for. Chamfas says to you, 'Hold fast, this is going to hurt,' and then sets your leg and binds it up. Do you want Chamfas to ask you what you think before doing it?"

"Chamfas is a bonesetter!"

"So?"

"So of course he won't ask me what I think! I don't know anything about bonesetting."

"Well, let us suppose it is Aunty Borab. Suppose she tells you to eat your breakfast."

"Yes, that's what I mean. She doesn't ask me if I want breakfast. She just tells me."

"And what is Aunty Borab?"

"She's just an old woman."

"Ah, no, Medoor Babji. There you are wrong. Aunty Borab is a life liver. She is a survivor. She is a power holder and a health giver. She is no less expert at what she does than is Chamfas Muneen. But you call her an old woman and disregard what she says."

"She's bossy!"

"So is Chamfas, when he knows what is best for you. So am I when I seek to save my people hurt. And so is Borab when she knows it is best for you to eat your breakfast."

The Queen's expression had been mild, but there had been obsidian in her eyes. Hard, black, and questioning. *Is this one to be my heir, or shall I choose some other?* After a pause, she continued. "Instead of thinking of older folk as bossy persons with whom you must contend for control, Medoor Babji, think first what they are trying to tell you, or save you. Indeed, they may only be attempting to assert the privilege of age, but it does no harm to listen, even to agree. They will die before you, and you will have time to do it your way."

Medoor Babji had not wanted Queen Fibji to choose some other heir, so she had begun to save the rebellion for other targets and pay attention to Aunty Borab.

Now she wished she had paid as much attention to Blange and the other sailors.

"My fault," she said, putting the rising sun on her right hand

and bowing her head in the direction she assumed was north, toward the Noor lands, toward the Queen. "I called them common sailors in my mind. I should have called them expert boat handlers and learned from them." She closed her eyes in meditation. One had to meditate on mistakes when they were discovered. Otherwise, the opportunity to learn from them might pass one by. Another of the Queen's axioms that Medoor had adopted as her own.

When the meditation was over, she had remembered a few things. Other details came to her as she worked. There was a line to haul the triangular sail on its boom up and down the mast. There were lines to move the trailing end of it right or left. In the morning, they kept the wind behind them. That she remembered, for Thrasne had said it over and over. "Morning wind to take us out, evening wind to bring us back." After a time she got the hang of it, even remembering to steer a bit east of south. Then there was nothing to do but sit hot under the sun, watching a far bank of cloud in the west retreat below the horizon and disappear while other clouds formed out of nothing, fled away into shreds, and vanished. Around her the River heaved and pulsed, clucking against the boat's side. She grew half-blind from sun glimmer. She thought she saw things, strange winged figures larger than people, riding upon the waves. She blinked, and they were gone.

When the sun was directly overhead, something huge moved beside the boat. She felt the planks quiver and shift, not a natural, water-driven movement. Fish broke the surface of the water, leaping high to escape whatever was below. Two of them fell into the boat, flapping there with high-pitched squeals. Medoor Babji was not squeamish. She grasped them by their tails and banged them against the side of the boat. Her folding knife was in her sleeve pocket with her other essentials. She gutted the fish and filleted them, laying most of the strips of yellow flesh on the canvas to dry in the sun, eating the others slow mouthful by slow mouthful, grateful both for the sweet flesh and for the water in it.

"Strangey below," she told herself. What else could be that size? Some monster of the mid-River? Had the provision of the fish been accidental? Somehow she didn't think so. What was it

Thrasne had said? Sometimes strangeys picked up boatmen who had fallen overboard and returned them to their boats. Perhaps they fed stranded River wanderers as well.

By midafternoon she knew one thing more. Sometimes strangeys took small boats where they wanted them to go. In the lull after the morning wind had failed, Medoor Babji had attempted to set the sail as she remembered the sail on the *Gift* being set in the afternoons. She had accomplished this more or less and was headed westward once more when the boat shuddered, the sail flapped, and she found herself moving in a slightly different direction. Perhaps a bit more west of south than she had intended.

"When things are moving inexorably in a given direction," Queen Fibji had told her, "only foolish men attempt to move against the flow. And yet, those men who give themselves over entirely to the movement may also be foolish. The wise man works his way to an edge, if he can, and waits for opportunity to get ashore. From there he can observe what is happening without personal involvement."

Having no other occupation, Medoor Babji meditated upon this saying of the Queen's. She had some time in which to do it. At sundown she ate some of the sun-dried fish. It was well after dark when the movement of the boat changed from one of being towed to a mere floating once again. Against the stars she saw the bulk of hills crowned with trees. The tidal current washed her onto a shelving beach, whether of sand or rock she could not tell, and all motion ceased. She crept into the blankets beneath the canvas cover and fell asleep.

Morning came with a twitter of birds, a bellow of lizards. By the shore stilt-lizards walked, their narrow heads darting into the shallows to bring up bugs and fishes, stopping now and then to utter their customary cry, "Ha-ha, ha-ha," without inflection. Stilt-lizard meat was edible, Medoor Babji told herself, coming out of sleep all at once, fully conscious of being somewhere new, different, unknown. This place could not be too foreign, she thought, if there were stilt-lizards. Edible. Yes. Hunger pinched her stomach and brought a flood of saliva into her mouth. She sat up in the boat, unwrapping herself. The lizards fled at the sudden motion, then returned to stalk the shore once more, meantime keeping a wary eye on her.

The boat was halfway up a narrow beach, less sandy than stony, cut by a streamlet that bubbled down a shallow channel into a little bay. Contorted protrusions of black rock jutted from the beach and from the smooth surface of the bay, culminating in two writhing shapes, like a mighty arm and hand at each side of the entrance, reaching toward one another, braceleted with colonies of birds. Outside that embrace the River swept by, empty and endless.

Now the immediate danger was past. Now there was food and good water. Now that persona who had wished to cry for some time could cry.

It was some time before she realized what she was crying about, where the grief came from, boiling up from some deep well within her. It was not being lost, not being fearful for her life. It was being separated from Thrasne, lost from him, fearful for his life. And with that realization, she dried her tears, laughing at herself. The *Gift* was a strong, heavy boat, one that had plied the World River for generations. She thought of Thrasne fussing over it, repairing it at every opportunity, and of his crew of experienced men. Why had she assumed at once that he had met with some disaster? She was far more likely to have perished in the tiny *Cheevle*, and yet she lived. And if she lived, she could find the *Gift* again, somewhere, if not on Southshore or mid-River, then on Northshore when it returned.

"If the strangeys allow it," she told herself with some asperity, trying to give herself something else to think about. It was a cheerless thought, yet it had the same strengthening force as one of Queen Fibji's lectures. "Settle," the Queen had said to her often. "Settle, daughter. Consider calmly what you will do. Cry when it is done with, when you have the luxury of time."

"How did you get to know absolutely everything?" Medoor had asked, somewhat bitterly.

There had been a long silence, then a humorless laugh. Medoor had looked up at her mother, startled, almost frightened. She had not heard that laugh before.

"I'll tell you a secret," the Queen had said with a faraway, angry look on her face. "I don't know. Much of the time I don't know anything. However, my not knowing will not help my people, so I must know. And I do. It is easier to correct a mistake than to be caught doing nothing. It is easier to beg forgiveness for a mistake than to beg permission to act. People will forgive you, child, but they will not risk allowing action. Go to a council and say, 'Let me do this thing.' They will think of ten thousand good reasons you should not. It could be wrong. Or it could be not quite right. Or it could be right, but of a strange rightness they are unfamiliar with. Oh, daughter, but they will talk and talk, but they will not say, 'Do it.' That is why I am Queen and they are my followers. Because they cannot risk anything nor take part in others doing so. They are herdbeasts, daughter. And yet I love them. When I speak to you of trial and error, Babji, whose experience do you think I am speaking of? . . .''

"So," Medoor Babji told herself. "If the Queen can prevail in such a way, so her daughter can also prevail."

The resolution did not help her much in deciding what to do next. Securing food seemed most logical, and this decision was helped by a cramp of hunger that bent her in two. Fish was well and good, but it left one empty between meals.

It was important she not lose the *Cheevle*. She tugged it farther up the beach and tied it firmly to a tree. A tidal bulge might come by; the presence of beaches argued for that probability. As she faced the bay, the sun was rising on her right hand, so the bay faced northward. Could this land be Southshore? Had the strangeys brought her to her journey's end? The beach extended on either hand as far as she could see, riven with tormented rock outcroppings here and there but interrupted by no headland, curving slightly outward at its western extremity to vanish in the River haze. She had come ashore in the only protected place within sight, though the haze prevented her from being sure she was on the only land in the vicinity.

The forest was made up almost entirely of one variety of tree, one unfamiliar to her, a short, thick-trunked tree, rather twisted in habit, with two or three main branches, also short and stout, with many graceful twigs bearing lacy clusters of pale green leaves that seemed almost pruned, so gracefully they barely overlapped one another, allowing each leaf its measure of sun.

Some of these trees carried large, waxy blooms of magenta and azure blue, fringed with silver. Others bore seed heads, drying, almost ready to open. Among these strange trees were other, more familiar ones. She found a puncon tree—a larger one than she had ever seen on Northshore—with fruit almost ripe. Not far from the fruit tree was a small grove of fragwood, and beyond that, inland, stood a gawky, feathery tree that looked and smelled almost like the thorn trees of the steppes. The leaf was more divided than in the trees she knew, and the fruit was larger. The scent pulled her halfway up the tree, stretched along a branch as she fumbled for ripe ones among the cluster, finding them sweeter than she was used to and more welcome for that. She ate a few bites, filling a sleeve pocket with more. She would stuff herself later, if she didn't get sick or die in the meantime.

Returning to the boat, she robbed it of enough line to make snares. By noon there were three stilt-lizards caught, killed, gutted, and drying in the smoke of a small fire. There were patches of white on many of the rocks, River salt dried by the sun, and she sprinkled this on the lizard meat. She had bought River salt in the markets of half a hundred towns but had never seen it in its natural state before. There had been no unpleasant result from eating the thorn tree fruit, so she ate a bit more, chasing it down with roast leg of lizard. The water in the streamlet was chill and pure. She felt less inclined to weep. "Full stomachs," Aunty Borab had been fond of saying, "make calm judgments." Or the reverse, sometimes. "Hunger makes haste."

It was time, she felt, for a slightly longer exploration. The boat could always be found so long as she kept the River within sight or hearing and went out with it on the one hand and returned with it on the other. The boat was safe enough. She piled brush over and around the lizard carcasses to let them dry a while longer in the smoke of the smothered fire, then strode off into the forest as far as she could without losing sight of the River through the trees, walking westward at a good pace, taking note of what she saw but making no effort to examine any aspect of the landscape in detail. There were more and more of the lacy-leafed trees interrupted by occasional groves of other

kinds, some fruit bearing. She gathered the ripe fruit, filling her
sleeve pockets as instinctively as a bird might gather seed. The
Noor had been gatherers for generations. They did not pass
bounty by.

Occasional outcroppings of the black stone broke the flatness
of the land, peculiarly fluid-looking piles of it, as though it had
been poured and then hardened. Medoor Babji found herself
staring at it, trying to fathom what it made her think of, and
realized it was like sugar candy poured out upon the slab, before
it was worked and pulled. There were places on the steppes of
the Noor, places near the Teeth of the North, where similar
glossy stone was found. The wise men among her people said it
came from the center of the earth, out of fiery vents, with great
noise and plumes of ash. If so here, it had been long ago. Green
lay over all, blanketing and softening.

There were many tiny streams. Once or twice she stopped,
thinking she had heard something moving off in the woods
among the recurrent bird noise. Once she looked shoreward
between two groves to see a winged figure standing upon a
rocky point, ready to dive into the sea. She blinked, and it was
gone. It had not looked real, even at first, she told herself. Sun
dazzle and weariness and being alone caused people to see
things. The Noor were well aware of that. "Steppe visions,"
they called them. Well, these would be "River visions." When
the sun had fallen before her, she turned to put it at her back,
moving closer to the shore for the return trip.

Her mind was set on the outline of the boat, the stack of leafy
branches she had placed over the fire. So it was she almost
passed her campsite by, not recognizing it. The boat was shattered, great holes bashed through the planking as though by
some heavy missile, a great spear, perhaps, thrust and withdrawn, thrust and withdrawn again. The fire was scattered into
gray ash. The stilt-lizard meat was gone. All around the site and
in the stream lay small blobs of guano, white and reeking.

Their footprints crosshatched the shoreline, coming out of
nothing. Fliers. They had ruined her boat. They had stolen her
meat. They had fouled her campsite and the stream. Two of
them, she thought, who had walked side by side to do their
hateful damage.

Worse, they had laid a trap for her. She put out her hand to coil some of the rope. She had almost touched it when a familiar glisten on the rough twist caught her eye. She put her hands behind her and bent forward, peering. A Tear of Viranel. Oh, hadn't the Noor learned long and long ago to watch for that glisten as they walked the steppes? The Tears could not kill them, but they made nasty sores where they touched, sores that were painful for a long time and took weeks to heal. Tears would grow anywhere, sometimes here, sometimes there. The Noor spread wood ashes on any patches they found, but the danger was always there. Medoor cursed, briefly, suddenly aware of danger from an active intelligence, out there, somewhere. They hadn't seen her except at a distance. They didn't know she was a Noor.

There were other Tears at the site. Not many she could find in the failing light. The destroyers had not bothered to rip the canvas cover away from the boat; the blankets were untouched. She took them. The light was too poor to do more than that. Tomorrow she would return to see what else could be salvaged. She stepped carefully away from the place, watching where she put her feet, scraping them again and again through the dry sand to remove any Tear that might have clung to her shoes.

Then she was back among the trees, looking up through the boughs into an empty, amber sky. They had spied on her, without doubt, seeing her easily on that barren beach. Now perhaps she could return the favor. Medoor Babji's lips parted in a snarl, an expression her mother would have recognized. When darkness came, she was well hidden in a copse of thick foliage, well wrapped against the night's chill, reasonably well fed on the fruit she had gathered during the day, and perhaps unreasonably set upon vengeance.

Inside her, shut away, someone grieved anew for Thrasne, for the near-kin, for all old, familiar, and much loved things. She had no way to repair the boat. Without it—without it her whole life might well be lived upon this shore. She shuddered with tears that she would not allow herself to shed, summoning anger instead.

In the earliest light of morning she went to the beach and salvaged all the rope she could lay hands on as well as all the

canvas. They had been fairly clever in placing the Tears where
she might have been expected to put her hands. She dragged her
salvage through the ashes of her fire again and again, meantime
protecting her hands with canvas strips cut from the boat cover.
She would not cut the sail. Not yet. Morning and calm showed
only four planks of the boat actually splintered. Perhaps, somehow, she would think of a way to restore them.

Heavily laden with her salvage, she went back into the woods
and sought a cave, thrusting a long stick into every opening she
found until she located a bottle-shaped hole in one of the
black-rock outcroppings. The neck was almost too narrow for
her to wriggle through, but inside it opened out into a comfortable shape, smooth-walled. Here she stored the blankets, the
rope, the canvas, her snares. The opening was hidden behind
freshly cut branches. She brought out the snares to set them
among the rocks where a streamlet rattled out of the forest onto
the beach, hiding them with branches cut from the nearest tree.
It trembled oddly when she cut it, but Medoor Babji had no
time to pay attention to that. She picked fruit once more, filling
her sleeve pockets. Then she went back to the shore to keep
watch.

From a horizontal branch halfway up the largest tree in a
small grove of frag trees, she could see the wrecked boat, the
scattered ashes of her fire.

It was after noon when they came, spiraling down to land at
the edge of the sand, their feet just above the waterline, as
though fearful of it. They stalked into the campsite, examining
each step of the way with nodding heads, peering eyes. One
was of an unfamiliar type, taller and more slender than the
other, better-groomed, with a shine to his feathers. The other
was fusty and scurfy, feathers awry, and yet of the two, this one
appeared the stronger and more vital.

"It came back," croaked the taller one in harsh but understandable human language.

The other answered, making sounds Medoor Babji could not
understand.

"Speak in meat talk," the first croaked again. "I don't
understand your flier talk."

"*Horgha sloos,* something-something," the second said in a

hideous, screeching tone. Then, in recognizable speech, "Meat-talk soils my mouth."

"Then let your mouth be filthy," commanded the first. Though the shorter being croaked its speech, as though words were seldom used, the taller creature's words were clear and understandable. From her perch above them, Medoor Babji named it a Talker, unaware it was the name the whole class of creatures had chosen for themselves. It went on, "At least I can understand meat talk. You barbarians from the wild lands talk like savages."

The shorter flier deposited a blob of shit and held its wings at a threatening angle. "Fliers not savages. Fliers important. We keeping meat animals in our care. Your highmost Talker commanded. We do. You, Slooshasill, nothing but Talons servant, do nothing, blat, blat, blat. Share meat. Dirty yourself."

"Stop your words," screamed the Talker in a rage. "All that is unimportant. Do not speak of what is true on Northshore. We are not on Northshore. Thraish cannot fly over water, but storm can blow where Thraish cannot fly. Storm brought wind; wind brought us here. Now is only one importance. Food to keep us alive. Living or not living. Human meant much food, but human is gone."

"Maybe got Tears on it. Maybe wandered off." The flier opened its wings. For some reason, Medoor Babji thought it might be a female. Something in the way it moved, like a crouching barnyard fowl.

"No. Rope is gone. Cloth is gone. Ashes are spread around. Human took those things. Human saw and avoided Tears."

The other cocked its head, took quick steps toward the waterside, then darted sideways with a hideous, serpentine stretch of the neck to snatch an unwary stilt-lizard that had poked its head from among the rocks. Medoor Babji watched in horrid fascination as the flier tossed the lizard up, caught it, tossed it again, each time cutting it as it struggled and shrieked, gulping it down at last while it still wriggled feebly, all its bones broken.

"Not enough of those, Esspill," said the tall flier in a bleak tone. "Not enough to keep us alive long."

"Enough for me," replied the other one. "Enough for unimportant Esspill. Savage Esspill. Not enough for Slooshasill, important Slooshasill, Fourth Degree, that one can eat fish.''

The Talker darted his beak at the shorter bird, bloodying its head just above the beak. Dust rose around them as they fought, screamed, beat at one another with their wings. Then was silence. The dust settled. Medoor Babji could see them crouched across from each other, panting. The taller one had had the worst of it. Hungry, her mind said to her in Aunty Borab's voice. That one's half-starved.

"Only filth eat fish," the one called Slooshasill said at last. "Only ground crawlers eat them."

"Then catch lizards for yourself!"

"I am Talker." In her hiding place, Medoor Babji's mouth twisted in amusement. She had named the creature correctly. "You are flier. You are supposed to catch them. Fliers are supposed to bring food for Talkers. Females are to serve males!"

"Males," the flier screamed in scorn. "At mating time, Esspill will serve males. Talkers not males. And Slooshasill not even Talker now. Slooshasill nothing."

They still crouched. "When we get back to Northshore, Slooshasill will again be Talker. You will be punished, then, Esspill."

"How get there? Cannot fly over water."

"Did," said the other in a hopeless tone. "Did fly."

"Didn't. Wind carried. Couldn't stop. Wind brought. Wind will have to take back again. Can't fly over water."

A long silence. At last the Talker asked, in a tone that could only be the Thraish equivalent of a whine, "What we do now, Esspill?"

"What you do, don't know. What I do is get more Tears. Then find human. Put Tears on. Eat it. I be strong then. Fly back. Fear or not." It was an empty threat. Even to Medoor Babji, unused to the sound of flier talk, it came across as mere bluster. The wings came down in a hard buffet, throwing sand into a quickly falling cloud. Medoor dodged behind the trunk of the tree, afraid to be seen. When she came out again, both pairs of wings were above her, above the land, one in the lead, the other following. She watched them as they circled low above the forest, low above the beach, searching. Never, not even for a moment, did they fly out over the open water.

It seemed unwise, she felt, to stay in the vicinity of the boat, though she did not want to risk losing it. She climbed higher in the tree and took a sighting. It was likely this small bay was unique. The bay lay midway on a line between two tallish hills, one crowned with a monstrous frag tree grove. There seemed to be no other hills within sight.

She came down the tree in a chastened mood, her desire for vengeance chastened by reality. Esspill, the flier, was as large as she. Lighter, perhaps, but with talons and a sharp, hooked beak. Likely those talons could hold Tears without danger to Esspill herself. Herself. Medoor Babji would have been sure of it even without the verification of their speech.

But then what was the one called Slooshasill? A male? Not according to the other one. Not male or female. A kind of neuter thing. A Talker.

Who would have thought the fliers could talk? Queen Fibji had never spoken of any such thing. Of course, there were few fliers seen upon the steppes, but still it was odd that none among the Noor had known. If, in fact, they had not known.

And now? What?

She could hide indefinitely. She was confident of that. She had fruit to eat and would eat fish, which the flier creatures would not. Even if Esspill caught every stilt-lizard on the place, which wasn't likely, Medoor Babji could be sure of food. But it would have to be a covert, sneaky kind of existence.

Or, she could fight. Reason said that the odds against her would be reduced if she waited a while. That tall Talker creature was half-starved. The flier wouldn't feed it, and it didn't seem able to catch food for itself. Given only a little time, it would be dead or too weak to threaten her. So, patience was called for.

Still, it would be a difficult, nervous business, surviving with an eye in the sky looking for her. She went back to her cave, stopping at the snares on the way. Two stilt-lizards, not bad. She would smoke them. . . .

She wouldn't smoke them. Medoor Babji cursed. Smoke would bring the damn feather mops on her in a moment. Smoke could be seen at great distances on any clear day or moonlit night. She would have to salt and sun-dry the meat. She could eat raw fish with resignation, perhaps even with a modicum of pleasure, but she could not face the idea of raw stilt-lizard. Hot bile stirred at the back of her throat. She needed a smoke oven. Perhaps one of the caves. . . .

Smoke. She thought about·that. It might be worth the effort, just to get the creatures away from here. Otherwise they would be haunting her. She thought about it for an hour and then decided upon it. She would begin today. There was no reason to wait.

One blanket and some food made a small pack. She headed east through the forest, moving as rapidly as possible while still keeping a fairly good watch on the land around her. When darkness came, she stopped on the beach to stack a large pile of wood with a smaller one next to it and then returned to the forest to build a small, smokeless fire of driftwood under cover of a stone outcropping. She cooked a lizard over it, putting the fire out at once when she had eaten.

At early light, she lit the smaller pile of wood, connecting it to the larger one with a line of thin, dried sticks and shavings. Over the larger woodstack she laid leaves and grasses. By the time it caught and smoked, she should be some miles away to the east.

An hour later she climbed a tree and peered back the way she had come. A pillar of smoke rose straight into the windless sky, where two black dots swung and circled toward it. She allowed herself a brief moment of self-congratulation, then climbed down to walk east once more.

After the third smoke on the third morning, she went deeper into the woods and turned back the way she had come. If the fliers were not cleverer than she thought they were, they would go on east, looking for her there. The line of smokes had led them in that direction. There would be no smoke on the follow-ing morning, but they might think she had seen them and was hiding from them. If they kept on moving in that direction, she might be free of them for a very long time.

She slept in the woods for the two nights it took her to return, each time awakened by stirrings and rustlings as though something or someone wandered in the leafy spaces. She was not foolish enough to call out. Her campsites were well hidden. She saw no evidence that anyone had wandered nearby when she woke. Still, it made a small itch of apprehension at the back of her mind.

When she returned to the boat, she unstepped the mast, laying it among fallen logs in the forest, half covering it with branches. The hull she drew deep into the woods, tugging and hauling with much smothered cursing in between. It left a clear and unmistakable trail, one she took great pains to eradicate. She raked away all the ashes of her earlier fire, gathered up the bits of charcoal, and built another fire half a mile down the beach, scattering it when it had burned out. If the fliers had not paid particular attention to the landmarks, they might assume that was the place the boat had been. She scattered some broken wood in that place and drew a heavy timber down the beach into the River. Now it looked as though she or someone had returned, had made some hasty repairs, perhaps, and then pulled the boat out into the water.

"Where it promptly sank, drowning me," she said with a hopeless look at the carcass of the *Cheevle*. Two of the holes were small. They could be patched with wood whittled to size and pounded in, caulked with—well, caulked with something or other. Frag pitch. She knew where there were frag trees, and gathering the pitch was merely a matter of cutting the bark and collecting the hardening sap when it gathered in the scar, then melting it in—in something.

The remaining two holes, however, were sizable.

"When faced with a number of tasks," Queen Fibji had said, "so many that the mind balks at getting them done, pick one or two small ones and begin. When those are done, move on. Never consider all that must be done, for to do so is quite immobilizing. . . ."

She began. Repairing the two small holes took five days, from dawn to dusk. She had caulked the wood with fresh frag sap, learning that it did quite well if applied in many thin coats and allowed to dry between. Using melted resin would have been quicker. It would also have been impossible. She had nothing she could use for a vessel and could find nothing that would serve. There were no gourds or hard-shelled nuts. Clay could be made into pots, of course, but that would have taken still longer.

While working, however, she had decided how to mend the larger holes. She would cut flat pieces of wood, glue them to the outside of the boat with frag sap, then cover the entire outside of the boat with the canvas boat cover.

It took five days more to complete the repairs. She dragged the hull back to the beach and into the water, where she managed to get the canvas under and around it, lacing the rope across the boat to catch the hooks on the opposite side. The mast was up, raised the same way she had raised it when on the River, with panting and grunts and a good deal of helpless cursing. She looked at the thing where it floated, shaking her head. It had a deck of rope, almost a net, where the lines laced across to hold the canvas. She would have to worm her legs between the ropes to sit at the rudder. She would have to wriggle herself beneath them to lie down at night. If there were another storm, she would probably sink.

In all that time, she had not seen the fliers. In all that time, she had almost forgotten them.

In the morning she could forget them completely, for she would be on the River once more, where they could not follow. Westward. To the end of this land, if it had an end. Then south. And if it had no end, then northward once more. Back to Northshore. She had a plentiful supply of dried fruit stored in canvas sacks, an almost equal supply of sun-dried lizard meat. The last two days she had spent digging edible roots, which lay in well-washed succulence among the other provisions. She had raveled some rope to make a fishing line and carved some fragwood hooks. Even if the strangeys had forsaken her, she should be able to manage. She would not be out of sight of land unless she came to the end of this land and turned north or south once more.

So she built her small, smokeless fire under cover of the rocks, ate fresh fruits and roots, freshly roasted meat, curled into sleep in satisfied exhaustion. There would be plenty of time to rest on the River.

During the night there was a tidal surge which washed the

canvas-girdled *Cheevle* half back onto the shore. Medoor Babji, wanting an early start, was on the beach when the sun had barely risen, struggling to get the boat back into the water. Its canvas bottom did not wish to slide on the rough sand, and she swore at it fruitlessly, knowing she would need rollers to get it moving, which meant another day before she could leave.

The screech that came from behind turned her around, bent her backward over the *Cheevle* as though to protect it, before she even saw the fusty, raddled form of the flier stalking toward her over the sand. It carried a leaf-wrapped bundle in one set of rudimentary wing fingers. Without asking or being told, Medoor Babji knew they were Tears.

"So, human," said Esspill. "You tried to trick us." It cawed laughter. "You did trick stupid Talker. He went that way, long ago. Looking for you."

"You weren't tricked?" she asked from a dry throat, the words croaked almost in the flier's own harsh tone.

Esspill shook her head, a mockery of human gesture. "Oh, no. Was no meat in those fires. No bones. No reason for them."

"You're very smart," she gasped. "Smarter than I thought."

"Oh, fliers are smart. Smarter than Talkers think. Talkers think . . . think they are only smart ones. All words. No faith."

"Faith?" She edged to one side, trying to get the boat between her and the flier.

"Stand still," it commanded. "Don't try to run. Tears won't hurt much. After that, humans don't feel." It clacked its jaw several times, salivating onto its own feet, doing a little skipping dance to wipe the feet dry.

"Faith?" asked Medoor Babji again, thinking furiously. "What do you mean, faith?"

"No faith in Promise of Potipur. Potipur says breed, grow, have plenty. Talkers say not breed, not grow, live on filth. Now Thraish have herdbeasts again. Soon have many. Then all humans will die. No more filth. No more *horgha sloos*."

"But if you breed, your numbers will grow, and you'll eat all your animals and go hungry again."

"Promise of Potipur," it said stubbornly. "Promise. You hold still now. For Tears."

"Tears don't work on the Noor," she cried. "They don't work on blackskins."

The flier stopped, beak agape. "Noor. You are Noor?"

"I am, yes. Medoor Babji. One of the Noor."

"No. Dark from sun. Humans turn dark from sun."

"I am not dark from the sun, Esspill. I was born dark. Look at my hair. The Tears won't work on the Noor. It won't grow inside us."

"Try," the flier snarled. "Try anyhow."

She edged away again, feeling in her sleeve pocket for her knife. "I'll fight," she threatened. "I may kill you."

"Fight!" it commanded. "Do that!"

Wings out, claw fingers stretched wide, talons lifted, beak fully extended, Esspill launched herself at Medoor, who dived in a long, flat dive into the River. It was instinct, not reason. It was the best thing she could have done. She came up in the water, clinging to the bowline of the *Cheevle*, began tugging at it, frantically working the boat into the water beside her. On the shore the flier danced up and down, pulling the boat away from her, screaming its rage.

Then it was gargling, its beak wide, eyes bulging. A long wooden shaft protruded from the flier's breast. She turned around, staring. Through the rocky arms that embraced the bay came another boat, no larger than the *Cheevle*. In it sat a man. In it stood a . . . a flier? Not a flier? Something very like, and yet not?

It had a bow in its wing fingers, an arrow nocked, the arrow pointed at the shore where Esspill still staggered to and fro, falling at last in a shower of dark blood onto the sand.

"Hello?" called the person. "We saw your smoke. We've been looking for you for over a week."

"Thraish," cried the other, drumming his keeled breast with his wing fingers to make a hollow thumping. "I have killed a Thraish." Thumpy-thump, delight in that voice. "Look, Burg, I've killed a Thraish!" It turned toward Medoor Babji, bowing. "Happy day, woman. I have saved you."

"We're called the Treeci," he told her, working the sculling oar as they moved down the coast, westward, the *Cheevle* in tow. "Have you heard of us?"

"I have," she admitted. "There are Treeci on a place called Strinder's Isle."

"Oh, there are Treeci on half the islands in the River," he said, making an expression that was very smilelike with a cock of head and flirt of eyes.

"That's possibly an exaggeration," said the human person. He was a stout, elderly man with white hair that blew around his head like fluff.

"Possibly. Or possibly an understatement, so far as that goes. What was that Thraish trying to do to you, eat you?" The Treeci turned to Medoor Babji once more.

"She had Tears of Viranel wrapped up in a leaf. She wanted to put them on me and then eat me. Tears don't work on the Noor, though. Our skins are too dark."

"I've heard that. Had you heard that, Burg?"

"Oh, it's probably written down somewhere. In the archives over on Bustleby. It's probably written down there."

"You know about the Noor?"

"We have histories, young lady," said Burg. "We aren't savages. We're literate, human and Treeci both."

"But where—where did you come from?"

"The same place you did, originally. Probably for the same reason. Trying to get away from the senseless conflict over there." He jerked a thumb to the north. "Long ago. At the time of the Thraish-human wars. They were eating humans then. It's a wonder they haven't eaten them all by now."

Medoor Babji shook her head. "No. No, we have a—they have what my mother calls a detente. An agreement. They eat dead people. Northshore dead people, not Noor dead people."

The Treeci spat. "Carrion eaters," he gasped. "So I have heard, but I find it hard to believe, Medoor Babji."

"Oh, come, Saleff, the Thraish were eating human dead during the wars. You know that."

"Out of desperation, yes, but . . ."

"I presume they are no less desperate now."

"They could do what we did."

"We've talked about this a thousand times," the human said

irritably. "The ones who could do what you did, *did* what you did. The ones who were left *couldn't* do it. They had offspring who also couldn't do it. The Thraish could no more eat fish and become flightless today than they could become sweet-natured and stop shitting all over their living space. It's called selective breeding, and they've done it."

It was only argument, not even addressed to Medoor Babji, but the words rang inside her, setting up strange reverberations. Why? Something fled across her mind, trailing a scent of mystery and marvel. What? She tried to follow it, but it eluded her. She concentrated. Nothing. At least she would remember the words. *Selective breeding. Those who could do it, did it.* She would think about those words later.

"You know all about them?" Medoor Babji asked. "How do you know all that?"

"Oh, some of us human islanders sneak back to Northshore every now and then. Young ones of us, boys with time on their hands and adventure in their blood. Some of them go and never return, some go and come back, enough to give us an idea what's going on. One of the more recent returnees was a slave for the Thraish for five years."

"And they didn't eat him?"

"Would have, I suppose. He didn't give them a chance." Burg spoke proudly, almost boasting. "My son."

Silence fell, except for the sloshing of the sculling oar. After a time, Medoor Babji asked, "You came to find my smoke?"

"You could have been one of ours," said Burg. "Lost. We use smoke signals. It looked like that, one fire each day for three days. We do that sometimes. Or sometimes three fires all at once."

"Where are we going?"

"Down to Isle Point. West end of the island. You can look across the straits to the chain from there."

"Who lives there?"

"Treeci, mostly. About a dozen humans, too. Most of our folk are down the chain, on Biddle Island, and Jake's."

"How many?"

"A few thousand in this chain. The islands aren't that big. We have to spread out. Otherwise we'd overfish the River, kill off all the edible animals, the way the Thraish did during the hunger.''

''What edible animals?''

''The ones there aren't any more of on Northshore, girlie. Did you ever see an espot? Or a dingle? Little furry things? 'Course not. Thraish ate 'em all. They're extinct on Northshore. From what I understand, you've no mammals left at all on Northshore.''

''That flier, Esspill, she said they had herdbeasts again. I didn't know what she meant.''

The white-haired man pulled in his oar and stared at her, mouth working. ''Is that possible?''

''A few might have survived,'' the Treeci responded. ''Somewhere. Perhaps behind the Teeth.''

''If they have herdbeasts again, it's the end of humans on Northshore,'' the man snarled. ''You can depend on it. The Thraish will kill them all.''

Medoor Babji shook her head at him. ''I don't think the humans would let them do that,'' she said. ''I think it might be the Thraish who would end up dead.''

''Hush,'' said the Treeci. ''Don't upset yourself, Burg. Northshore is none of our business. Don't we always say that, generation on generation? Northshore isn't our business.''

''How about Southshore?'' Medoor Babji asked. ''That's what we were looking for.''

''Over there,'' said Burg laconically, pointing over his shoulder. ''That way. About a month's travel or more.''

''It's really there?''

''Was the last time we looked. Bersdof's kids sailed there last year, just for the hell of it.''

''Is it empty, Burg? Is there room there for the Noor?''

''Room for the Noor and anybody else, far's I know. Nothing there but animals and plants. No human grain over there, though. You'd have to plant that.''

''Why? Why is it just sitting there? Why hasn't anyone gone there?'' She tried to imagine an empty land, one without Jondarites. It was impossible.

''Well, those of us who fled with the Treeci landed here on the island chain first. Seeing what the Thraish had made of their world, we took it as kind of a religious thing to behave differently. We don't expand much. Small societies in small places. Closeness. That's why we haven't gone to Southshore. As for other people, I don't know. Maybe the place was just waiting for the Noor.''

The Treeci Saleff interrupted them with a long-drawn-out hooting call. There was a response in kind from the shore. "There's Isle Point," he said, turning to her with his cocked-head smile. She looked shoreward to see the water moving around the end of the island, and a little way westward another island, the long line of land broken only by this narrow strait. A village gathered itself beneath the trees, small wooden houses, curling smoke. A mixed group of humans and Treeci stood on the shore, old and young.

"Will you be my guest?" Saleff asked. "Burg would ask you, I know, but he has a houseful just now. New grandchild."

Medoor Babji bowed as best she could in the tilting boat. "I would be honored, Saleff."

"You'll be better off," Burg snorted. "Saleff's mama—Sterf, her name is—she's a finer cook than my wife is, that's honest."

"My mother will welcome you. As will my nest sister and the younger siblings."

Medoor Babji bowed again. She was already lost. She had already told them about her need to find the *Gift*. It would seem rude and ungrateful to mention it again so soon. And yet their invitation had had an air of complacency about it, as though there could be no refusal nor any limit to her stay. She cast a quick look at the horizon. Where was Thrasne? And her people? She swallowed, smoothed the lines out of her forehead, and set herself to be pleasant. The boat was rapidly approaching the shore, and half a dozen people of various kinds were wading out to meet her.

Blint told me once there are fliers who can talk, or at least that some people say they can. At first this seemed a silly thing to believe, but as I got to thinking about it, I wondered if it wasn't sillier to believe that talk was something only men could do. I've heard the strangeys calling, and the sounds they make are so large and complicated they must be words of some terrible, wonderful kind. But the sounds the fliers make, if those are words, they are short words and hard words. And I wish I'd heard the Treeci talk, those Pamra spoke of, for if they can talk, then surely the fliers can, too, and all we've thought about them for all our lives must be lies.

It would be interesting to talk with fliers, and strangeys. Except their words may not mean what our words mean at all, and it would be worse to misunderstand them than to just have them a mystery.

From Thrasne's book

At Isle Point, the house of Saleff squatted beneath a grove of stout trees with ruddy-amber leaves that filtered golden light into the rooms and onto the many porches where Saleff's kin moved about like orderly ghosts. Medoor Babji was at first amused by and then solicitous of the silence.

"We have a habit of quiet," Saleff's mother, Sterf, told her. "Originally adopted, I'm sure, out of rebellion against the cacophony of the Thraish. Later it became our own, particularly satisfying trait. The children tend to be a bit loud, of course, and must learn to go into the woods or out on a boat if they wish to shout or yodel or whatever it is they do."

There were three children in the house, three young ones, at first alike as puncon fruit in Medoor's eyes, each then acquiring a mysterious individuality that she found difficult to define. Mintel was the serious one, the quietest. Cimmy was graceful, with a lovely voice. Taneff was the most delightful, curious, always present, full of whispered questions, ready to run quick errands, even without being asked. The three soon named her Cindianda, which meant in their language, they said, "little dark human person." Medoor Babji thought they might be fibbing to her, that the name might mean something very disrespectful, though Sterf assured her not.

"How old are they?" she asked, watching them cross the clearing with amazement. They moved like darting dancers, lithe as windblown grass.

"Oh, just fifteen," Sterf said, a little wrinkle coming between the large orbs of her eyes. It was one of the things that made Treeci so like humans, the way their faces wrinkled around the eyes. If one looked only at the eyes, not at the flat, flexible horn of their beaks, they could have been humans in disguise, got up for some festival or other. "Just fifteen." There was something vaguely disquieting in her tone, and Medoor Babji thought back to everything Pamra had told her about the Treeci. Hadn't there been something? She shook her head, unable to remember. During that time Pamra Don and Medoor Babji had known one another—a misnomer of sorts, Medoor felt, since she did not feel she knew Pamra Don at all—Medoor had been so busy wondering what it was about Pamra that held Thrasne in such thrall she had paid too little attention to what Pamra had said.

"Trial and error," she murmured to herself, being contrite. When Queen Fibji learned how many times Medoor Babji had remembered that particular lesson on this trip, she would no doubt be greatly gratified.

Also in the house was the mother of the young ones, Arbsen, who was also Sterf's daughter and Saleff's nest sister. Of them all, Arbsen was the most silent, the most withdrawn. Some days she sat on one of the porches, her eyes following the children, broodingly intent. Other days went by during which Medoor Babji did not see her at all. She seemed to spend a great deal of time shut up in her own room at the top of the house, carving things. They were not Thrasne kinds of things, not definable images, but rather strange, winding shapes which seemed to lead from the current and ordinary into realms of difference, strangeness. Several of these articles decorated the walls of the house, and seeing them, Medoor Babji thought of Jarb Houses, wondering if the Treeci had such things. "Though I don't suppose Treeci ever go mad," she commented.

"Of course we do," said Saleff, amused. "We are in all respects civilized."

"You mean primitives don't go mad?"

"I mean they don't consider it madness. They would probably consider it being possessed by the gods, or in thrall to ghosts. Something of that kind."

"How do you know all this? You've never seen a primitive."

It came out as more of a challenge than she had intended, but Saleff did not take offense. "The humans have books, Medoor

Babji. There is a printing press on Shabber's Island. There are archives on Bustleby. There are men on Jake's Island who spend all their time collecting information and writing things down. During the hunger—that is, the period before and during the Thraish-human wars after the weehar were all gone—the humans who came here brought many things with them. Books. Musical instruments. Equipment for laboratories where they make medicines. It was part of the reason they came, to preserve their knowledge. The humans called what was happening on Northshore a 'new dark age.' You understand that? We have learned from men, but we have also taught them. It has been an equitable exchange.''

Medoor Babji had that flash of elusive thought again, as though someone had just told her the answer to a long-asked question, but it was gone before she could grasp it, leaving her shaking her head in frustration.

She walked in the groves with the children. ''Cindianda,'' Taneff begged, ''tell us stories of Northshore.''

''What do you want to know?''

''Tell us of the Noor. Tell us of the great Queen.''

So, she invented, spinning incredible tales into the afternoon. Taneff was insatiable. Whenever she stopped, Taneff wanted more, more and more stories, and she began to look forward to these sessions under the trees during which she could let her imagination spin without fault. Nothing hung upon her stories but the day's amusement, and she relished that.

Each morning when she woke, she resolved to get the boat repaired and set out in search of Thrasne. Each evening, she resolved it anew. Still, the days went by in placid grace, full of quiet entertainment.

One morning she rose early, conscience stricken or dream driven, determined to go to the shore and examine the *Cheevle*. She was amazed to find it had been almost entirely repaired. Only one of the planks remained to be replaced. Saleff had said nothing to her of repairing her boat, and she felt shamed that so much had been done without her help or thanks. She looked up to find him beside her, head cocked in that smiling position.

"Soon," he said. "Some of the young people will want to go journeying soon, and they can go with you to find your friends."

"When?" she begged, suddenly aware of how many days had passed.

He pointed skyward. "After Conjunction. Not now. The tides will be treacherous for a time. When Conjunction passes, they will fall into a manageable state."

She examined the moons, surprised she had not noticed how near to Conjunction they were. It would be weeks before she could go. "I'll never find him," she said hopelessly. "Never."

"Oh, we think you will. We've sent word by island messenger to all the settlements, east, west, south. The word is spreading among the island chains. Even the strangeys know we're looking for it. The *Gift of Potipur* will be spotted somewhere, don't fear."

She went walking with the children. Cimmy and Mintel ran off into the woods, saying they smelled fruit ripening. Taneff stayed with her, leaping into the path, then out again, whirling about, seizing her by the hand to drag her, protesting, to the top of a pile of rocks.

"Ouch!" She bit the word off. "Damn it, Taneff, that hurt." There was a long graze on her arm where it had been dragged against the black stone. "I'm bleeding."

Taneff stood, looking at her stupidly, saying nothing, shifting from foot to foot, a dark shadow moving behind the eyes, utterly unlike their usual expression. Then the eyes cleared, and Taneff smiled, a little uncertainly. "Sorry. I am sorry, Cindianda. I got carried away with the running and leaping, I guess. Everything in the village is so—so . . . ."

"Circumscribed," she offered with a wry laugh. "Orderly."

"Well, yes. Lately it just seems to irritate me." Legs stamping, wings held slightly away from the body, Taneff began to gyrate, a mockery of a dance. "I need to get it out of my system."

Medoor Babji repeated this to Saleff with a laugh. "I'm glad to know it isn't only among the Noor that young people get tired of order."

Saleff received it in silence, with only a few murmured words of apology for Medoor Babji's injury. "Yes. The young people need some excitement,'' he said at last. ''We'll have some dances.''

They had one two days later, drumming and a lot of very elegant prancing on a dance floor, all the young mixed in together, leaping and jostling. Among the crowd were half a dozen who were magnificent dancers, the feathers around their eyes flushed a little with the unaccustomed noise.

''Cimmy and Mintel are going to visit some kinfolk,'' old Burg announced one morning, apropos of nothing. ''Next island over. Would you like to go along?''

Medoor Babji allowed that she would. They left early in the morning, Sterf, Burg, Cimmy, and Mintel in a little, light boat with Medoor Babji perched in the stern like an afterthought, trailing her fingers in the water and humming to herself.

''I need to see some of my colleagues over on Jake's,'' Burg told her. ''The Treeci are better with boats than I am, so I hitch a ride whenever anyone is going.''

''There are a lot of boats going,'' she answered him, pointing them out, counting them off. Six boats from Isle Point, all setting out in various directions, all with young ones aboard.

''Bringing home the brides,'' said Cimmy in a depressed little voice, at which Sterf said something sharp in admonition. Medoor Babji started to ask, but Burg shook his head at her. A taboo subject. Very well, she would not ask.

On Jake's she went with Burg to meet the humans on the island, spent the day, the night, and a greater part of the next day doing so. They were many, garrulous, and eager for new faces and new information. Every word Medoor Babji uttered about Northshore was soaked up by an eager audience, and by afternoon her voice had given out.

Burg gave her puncon brandy and let her sit in a corner of the laboratory while he talked shop with his kinfolk. She dozed, warmly content after a night with almost no sleep.

''Arbsen was here last week,'' someone was saying to Burg.

''Arbsen? She hardly ever leaves her room, except to walk with Taneff in the woods.''

''She was here, Burg. She wanted the blocker hormone.''

''That's illegal. Unethical, too.''

''It's only illegal for Treeci to use it, not for us to give it.''

"Don't be silly. We live with the Treeci; of course we obey the spirit of their laws. Have you told Saleff? Have you told *any* of the Talkers?"

"Not yet. I was waiting for you to come over. You know the family."

"I'll talk to him. What did you tell Arbsen?"

"Just what you said. It's illegal."

In her corner, Medoor Babji stirred uneasily. This was evocative of something she had heard before, something Pamra Don had said. Something.

Burg roused her sometime later, and they walked together to the shore. There was a strange youngster waiting with Sterf, wide-eyed and frightened looking.

"Treemi," Sterf introduced her. "Coming back with us to Isle Point."

"Will Cimmy and Mintel be staying here long?" Medoor Babji asked. "Will I have a chance to see them before I leave?"

The question somehow went unanswered in their bustle to load the boat. She did not ask it again. Taneff met them back at Isle Point. Taneff was carrying flowers for the visitor and was unwontedly silent. He did not even answer Medoor Babji's greeting.

There were other visitors. All the youngsters seemed to be paired off, one local and one visitor, the locals wandering around a good part of the time with the visitors in attendance. Taneff, who had not let Medoor Babji alone in his demand for stories, now seemed almost to avoid her.

"All right, Burg," she asked, seeking him out and peering around to be sure they were alone, human to human. "What's going on?"

He shook his head at her, making a taciturn, pinch-lipped face.

"No, don't give me that. I know it's a taboo subject, but you've got to tell me what's going on or I may transgress. I don't want to do that."

He sighed. "I suppose you're right, Medoor Babji. It's Conjunction, that's all. Conjunction in a year in which some children in the community reach mating age."

"Breeding age?" she asked, suddenly remembering something Pamra Don had said. "Couldn't they put it off a few years? Gods, they're only children."

He shook his head. "No, actually, they're at exactly the right age. Biologically speaking, that is. Or so my friends over at the lab on Jake's tell me."

"So the visitors are what? What was it Cimmy said, 'brides'?"

"Yes. Cross-island mating, to prevent inbreeding. Do you know anything about that, Medoor Babji?"

"I know you breed champion seeker bird to champion seeker bird if you want the traits passed on. I know if you breed too close for too long, though, sometimes the chicks don't live."

He nodded. "It's the same for all creatures. Inbreeding intensifies characteristics, both desired and undesired. With seeker birds, you can destroy the faulty ones. The Treeci wouldn't approve of that, so, Cimmy and Mintel went over to Jake's Island to meet a couple of the young roosters over there, and little Treemi came back here to meet Taneff. That's really all there is to it."

It was not all there was to it. There was a great deal more to it than that, but someone came to the door of Burg's house, and the conversation ended.

As she was walking back to Saleff's house, she met Taneff on the path.

"Hear you've got a new friend," she called, teasing him a little.

He looked at her, head down, wings slightly cocked. "Friend," he said. His eyes were glazed, dull, as though a film lay over them. The visitor, Treemi, came out of the woods and took him by the wing, her fingers caressing him as she cast a quick, warning look at Medoor Babji.

"I've got fan fruit for you, Taneff," she said. "Fan fruit."

"Fan fruit," he said, turning toward her, feet dancing, wings lifting.

"Fan fruit," she sang, leading him away, half dancing. Arbsen came out of the wood and followed them, at some distance, her eyes wild and haggard.

Medoor Babji stood looking after them, more troubled than she could explain. Of the three children, Taneff had been her favorite. Taneff, as he was, not this strange, withdrawn creature who talked in monosyllables. She shook her head, annoyed at herself.

That night she was wakened by voices. She rolled from her mat on the floor and went to the window to close it, only to stop as she recognized the voices coming from the room below her.

"I want you to give it to Taneff." Arbsen's voice, husky with pain, anguish. "Saleff, you've got to."

"Arbsen, you've been eating Glizzee, haven't you."

"What difference if I have? Glizzee is the only thing keeping me sane. That has nothing to do with what I asked you. I asked you to give the hormone to me. For Taneff. He's my child, Saleff. I can't let him die."

"Arbsen. You, of all people, should know the folly of that. Remember Kora? Kora and her son, Vorn. Remember them?"

"Taneff isn't in the least like Vorn. I think Taneff's a Talker. Vorn wasn't."

"No, Vorn wasn't. And Taneff isn't a Talker, either, Arbsen. I've been testing him myself, the last time just yesterday. Do you think I wouldn't do that, carefully, with a member of our own family?"

"You made a mistake," she wept. "I know you did. He's a Talker. I just know it."

"If he were, my dear, I would know it. Can't you resign yourself, Arbsen? Go to Sterf. She'll help you."

"How could she help me! She never had this happen to her. She had a *damn Talker*. She had you!" The sound of wild weeping erupted into the quiet glade. In the houses, lights went on. Silence fell below.

Medoor Babji shut the window, hideously uncomfortable. There were things she felt she should remember, things she wanted to ask Burg on the morning.

And on the morning, she could not. Burg had gone to Jake's for a time, she was told, taking his family with him. He would be back for her after Conjunction. There were only two human families left in Isle Point, neither of them with young people. Despite her affection for Saleff's family, Medoor Babji felt abandoned.

The whole settlement seemed to be under emotional strain. There was a sense of communal anguish which kept her from asking Saleff any questions. Several times over the succeeding days, she met Taneff and Treemi in the woods or on the beach paths. Taneff scarcely seemed to know her. His voice was only a croak, though the rest of him was becoming glorious, frilled with feathers, flushed with rose. Always, Arbsen followed them at a distance. She had grown gaunt, almost skeletal. Almost every night there were dances somewhere nearby. Medoor Babji was not invited to attend, but no one could hide the sound of the drums.

And Arbsen was suddenly much in evidence, a hectic flush around her beak, very talkative. Both Saleff and Sterf watched her with a worried grimace, and Medoor Babji wondered if she should not absent herself from the Treeci house.

Which point was decisively answered by Sterf herself. "Mating time is difficult for us," she said. "Emotionally, you understand. Some of our loved children are far away, and we worry whether they are treated well. You are self-effacing and sensitive, Medoor Babji, but being so tactful is hard on you and us. Burg's house is empty. Would you mind using it for the next few days?"

To which Medoor Babji bowed and made appropriate expressions of sympathy and concern, all the while afire with curiosity.

There were drums that night, a fever in the blood. There were drums the night following. And on the third night, Conjunction came. Mindful of the laws of hospitality, Medoor Babji kept herself strictly within the Burg house, whiling the long, sleepless hours away by reading books. Burg had more of them than Queen Babji had, and Queen Babji had a good many. The drums went on most of the night, trailing away into a sad emptiness a few hours before dawn.

She woke late in the morning. The village was still silent, empty as a sucked puncon peel. Away in the woods somewhere, smoke rose, a vast, purposeful burning. The reek of it made the hairs on Medoor Babji's neck stand up—smoke, but more than smoke. Incense, too. And something else which the incense did not quite cover. There was a feeling of sadness, a smell of bittersweet horror. She sat on the porch with her book, drinking endless cups of tea, waiting for something to happen, half-afraid that something would.

What did happen was that Burg returned, with his family, grim-faced and white. Medoor walked down to meet him at the shore. "Have you seen anyone today, Medoor Babji?"

"Not a soul, Burg. Forgive my trespassing on your home, but Sterf asked me to . . ."

He shook his head. "Of no matter. I told her to send you over if things got tense. Which they have. Worse than I thought."

He turned away to supervise the family—son, son's wife, daughter, grandchild, baby—as the boat was unloaded.

"Turn it over, wash it out, and leave it here," he told his son. "Sterf will want to be taking Treemi home tonight or first thing in the morning. I'll go with her." He said this as though he did not believe it, like a courtesy phrase, said out of habit, not out of conviction.

He trudged up to his house, pausing on the porch to feel the pot Medoor Babji had left there, pouring himself a cup when he found it still warm. She held her tongue, not wanting to distress him more than he obviously already was.

"Arbsen stole the stuff," he said at last, looking over her shoulder into the woods. "The stuff we give young Talkers to get them through mating season without dying."

"I—I don't understand." And yet, she did. She remembered things Pamra had said. About Neff. Holy Neff. Her vision, the one that spoke to her all the time. Burg went on, confirming her recollection.

"Male Treeci—male Thraish, the whole species—they die after they mate. The breeding cycle triggers a kind of death hormone. Among the Thraish, the Talkers have learned to make an antidote from their own blood. They locate young Talkers before the breeding season, sequester them, give them the antidote, and it inhibits the breeding cycle." He rubbed his forehead, rubbed tears from the corners of his eyes.

"When we first came here the technique had been lost or something. When young Talkers were born, they just died, along with all the rest of the males. A rare tragedy. Only about one in a thousand males is a Talker. Still, it was always a pity. Talkers don't lose their intelligence, you know, not like the others. The ordinary males—they go into it in a kind of anesthetized ecstasy. Not Talkers. Whatever it is that makes them different also makes them victims. So, we created an antidote in the labs, to save the Talkers. Ones like Saleff. It doesn't inhibit the breeding cycle as the Thraish medication did. It just inhibits the death hormone.''

"Then they can all live?" Medoor Babji said. "Taneff can live! That's what Arbsen wanted from Saleff."

"No. No, they can't. We tried that, out of compassion, a long time ago. It was a horrible mistake. But Arbsen was so crazy with grief, she stole the stuff. Now I have to find out what she did with it. . . .''

"Why, she gave it to Taneff," said Medoor Babji. "What else would she do?"

"Oh, sweet girl, I pray you're wrong," he said, the tears now running down his face in a steady stream. "I know you're right, but I pray you're wrong."

At the fall of evening, Treeci began to trickle back into the village, silent as shadows. Somewhere far away a bell began to ring, measured stroke after measured stroke. No one needed to say it was a mourning bell. The sound alone did that.

Saleff came to the house. "Return to us, Medoor Babji. We need the distraction of your presence." He was carefully not looking at Burg.

Burg would not allow the evasion. "Arbsen stole the hormone, Saleff. Took it from the lab when she was over there a few weeks ago." Burg was blunt, demanding a response.

Saleff didn't reply.

"Is Treemi all right?"

"We haven't found her," the other said in a bleak, shattered voice. "Tomorrow we will begin to look."

"Is Arbsen around?"

"Not Arbsen, no. Nor Taneff."

"Why wait until morning, Saleff? He has had them a full day. They could still be alive. If we look tonight, we may save Treemi's life. Otherwise you'll have blood guilt to pay her family, which will mean another life. You want to risk Cimmy, too? Or Mintel?"

The other looked up, an expression of despair on the strange, withdrawn face. "If there is any chance she is alive, we will look tonight."

They searched by torchlight, moving outward from the village, all the Treeci and all the human occupants, all but the youngest children.

They found Treemi first. Alive, but barely. Body bloodied, sexual parts ravaged and mutilated. Burg gathered the body into strong arms and carried it back toward the village, Sterf close behind him, weeping.

Later, down a long, leaf-strewn gully, they found Arbsen. Her body was broken, as though she had been buffeted with heavy clubs, but her eyes opened when they spoke to her.

"Arbsen, why?" Saleff murmured in a heartbroken voice. "Why? You knew. You knew."

"I didn't believe it," she whispered, blood running from the corner of her mouth. "He is my child. He loves me."

"Oh, Arbsen, they only love if they die in the loving. If they live, it isn't love." He leaned across her, weeping, not seeing her eyes, glazed and staring forever at the darkness.

It was dawn when they found Taneff at last, a golden dawn, gloriously alive. They heard him first, crowing at the sunrise. They saw him then, tumescent, flushed red as blood, eyes orbed with triumph, dancing upon a small elevation above the forest floor. Around him the trees were shredded; beneath his feet the earth was a ruin.

Medoor Babji was among the first to see him, all disbelieving. It could not be Taneff. She called his name in her disbelief, careless of her safety. When he turned toward her, she saw that it was he. Taneff as she had never seen him. He saw her, knew her, spoke her name with a kind of brute inevitability.

"Come," he called. "Come!"

He danced on the mound, beckoning.

She stopped, horrified at the sight of him. There was blood on his talons, blood on the wing fingers, which twitched and snapped.

"Why?" she cried, unable to contain it. "Why did you kill Arbsen? Why did you kill your mother?"

"Told me to stop," he crowed at her. "Told me to stop. The young one said stop! Nobody tells Taneff to stop!"

He leaped high, rushed down the slope at her without warning. He attacked her, wings out, fingers clutching, sex organ

SHERI S. TEPPER

bulging and throbbing. He did not see the torch she held; she had forgotten she held it; her Noor-trained reflexes did the rest. It was not Taneff who blazed as he fought. It was horror.

Then there were men and Treeci all around. Someone had a spear. There was a long, howling struggle, and a body at the end of it. No one she knew. No one she had ever known.

"Why?" she sobbed on Saleff's breast. "Why?"

The Talker stroked her as though she had been one of the Treeci young. "Because they are meant to die, Medoor Babji. They are meant to die."

He took her back to the house where Treemi lay, barely breathing, Burg working over her. They built a pyre on the shore for the other two, and somehow the night and the day following passed.

A few days later, Burg showed her the *Cheevle*, mended, as sound as when it had been built. "Word has come," he told her. "We can lead you to the *Gift*. You will find it east of here, nearby a great island where our people do not go, but where the strangeys have brought your people."

"Will someone go with me?" she asked, feeling suddenly very lonely at the thought of leaving them.

"Cimmy and Mintel are taking a boat out. They wish to be gone for a time. It is hard—hard for nest mates to lose one of their number at the time of mating. It is harder still to lose one as they lost Taneff."

"He was mad," she said sadly. "Mad, Burg. The whole experience broke his mind."

"Is that what you think?" He laughed harshly. "Oh, Medoor Babji, you are far from the mark. No, no. Listen, I will tell you a little story. Something men have pieced together from tales told by the Treeci and excavations made long ago, before we left Northshore.

"Evidently in the long-ago, the males did not die when they bred. The male Thraish, that is; there were no Treeci then. They lived. As you saw Taneff, they lived. After the first mating their blood boiled with the desire for power. They took females, more than they could possibly need, held them as slaves; they took territory and held that. And they fought. You saw. That is how they fought, competing with one another. Male against male. Tribe against tribe.

"In their violence, they didn't care whom they killed. In or out of season, they raped and mutilated. They killed infants. They killed females. Because the Thraish can lay large clutches of eggs, they managed to hang on for a long time, but in the end so many females died that those tribes could no longer survive.

"I have visions of them sometimes, the last few of those prehistoric Thraish, fighting one another in the skies of Northshore, already dead."

"But the Thraish are not extinct," she objected. "What you are telling me is only a story."

"No. It's the truth. Among all those wild, violent tribes there were some few, even then, in which the death hormone functioned. The males mated and died. There were no wars. Among these tribes was no rape, no slavery, no abuse of the young. And those groups survived. Such is their history. It is what we call a survival characteristic."

After a time of silence, she asked, "Treemi? What of her?"

"She will recover. She has blessedly forgotten what happened. She will even have young this season. There will be no blood price. Arbsen is dead. There can be no retribution."

Medoor Babji nodded, overcome by sadness. Everything he had said was a heavy weight in her head, on her heart. She did not think she could bear the burden of it. There were lessons here she had not been taught by Queen Fibji, words she needed, instruction, comfort. And there was something more, fleeting like a silver minnow in her mind, something she herself could tell the Queen.

"Burg, you told me Southshore lies a month over the River. Do you swear it?"

He was startled. "Why, I will swear it if you ask, Medoor Babji. Why do you ask?"

"Because I do not want to spend more time away from my own kin. Because we were sent to find if Southshore is there, and if you will swear to me that you have seen it, with your own eyes, then I can go back and say so to the Queen."

"I swear it, Medoor Babji. It is a great land. Empty, so far as we know, of any people, human or Thraish or Treeci. There are beasts there and familiar trees. I swear it. I have seen it with my own eyes.''

She surprised him by kissing him, then. It surprised her, as well. She was afire to reach Thrasne and the others. They would turn back now, racing home, home to the Noor. Something within her told her that only speed could prevent some hideous thing from happening. She remembered things Queen Fibji had said concerning the survival of the Noor, the lusty young warriors, the difficulty of holding them in check. She thought of the strutting Jondarites, their plumes nodding on their helms, as the plumes had nodded on Taneff's head when he'd plunged into the spears. She thought of the mud graves of the warriors, and she longed to be home with every fiber of herself.

• 20 •

It was thirty days after the great storm, according to the journal of Fez Dooraz, that those on the *Gift of Potipur* saw the new island.

Though they could see no end to the land, yet they assumed it was an island, for it loomed up west of them like the prow of a great ship with the water flowing on either side. Behind that mighty rock prow the land fell away west into lowlands and forests, with hills and mountains behind, seemingly limited to north and south but with no end to it they could see to the west, a long, narrow land where they had expected no land at all. Far off to the east a cloud hung over the water, and the sailors said this meant there was land there, as well. "An island chain," they said. "It has been rumored there are island chains in mid-River."

"Do we go ashore?" Obers-rom asked Thrasne. "Is it possible this is Southshore?"

"Southshore or not, it is certainly a great land. And we have no choice if we are to get water." Thrasne felt a bit doubtful, but with their need for water and with all the crew and the Noor hanging over the side, looking at the place, how could they go on by? They needed something to divert themselves from the thought of Medoor Babji. Even Eenzie the Clown was depressed, and Thrasne could not explain the feelings he had had since the storm. Now that she was gone, he realized who she had been. Not merely a queen's daughter—"merely," he mocked himself. More than that. To him, at least.

They lowered a man over the side to swim a line to the land. When the light line was made fast, ropes were hauled in, tying them fast to trees ashore, and then the winch tugged the *Gift* in almost to the land's edge. The island fell sharply at this point, and the mooring was deep enough for the *Gift* to come very close. They built a small raft of empty kegs and planks to get back and forth, the sailors muttering meantime about the loss of the *Cheevle*.

Thrasne left a three-man watch aboard and went ashore with all the rest. He was heartily sick of the *Gift* himself, though the emotion made him feel guilty. The longest he could recall having traveled before without coming to land was a week or two, and that had been when sickness had struck a section of towns near Vobil-dil-go and all the boatmen had been warned away. Years ago, that had been, and then he had had the airy owner-house to live in. Now the little cabin he had squeezed himself out below was cramped and airless. He had considered slinging a hammock among the men a time or two, and would have except for the danger to discipline. It was hard to take orders from a man in his underwear, or so Thrasne had always believed.

At any rate, he was glad to walk on land again. He strolled along the narrow beach, really only a rocky shelf between the River and the cliffs, with a few hardy trees thrust through it. As he walked west, however, the shelf widened, dropped, became a real beach with sand on it, and the cliffs on their right hand also became lower, spilling at last into hillocks edged with dune grass and crowned with low, flat trees. The men of the *Gift* scattered toward the hills, into the woods, searching for water.

The Melancholics had dropped behind to poke among the tide pools at the island's edge, where they were finding brightly colored dye mulluks and flat coin fish. Thus it was only Thrasne at first who saw the carved man, buried to his knees in the sand.

"Ha," Thrasne said, a shocked sound, as though he had been kicked in the stomach. "That looks like old Blint." He stopped short, knowing what he had said was ridiculous and yet filled with a horrible apprehension.

The carved man began to turn toward him, as though he had heard Thrasne speak. As though he had heard his name.

He turned so slowly that Thrasne had time to measure every familiar line of him, the undulating sag of the belly, the little hairy roll of fat at the back of the neck, the wiry ropes of muscle on the legs and arms where old rope scars still showed, the slant of the shoulders. When he was turned full toward him he saw it was Blint, Blint as though carved in dark fragwood, Blint with his mouth opening slowly, so slowly, to give him greeting.

"Thraaasneee," the carved man said.

"Blint?" Thrasne bleated, terror stricken. What was this? His arms trembled, and the world darkened around him, shivering in a haze of red.

A voice in his mind said, "Remember Suspirra, Thrasne. You were not afraid of Suspirra!"

For a time this was only mental noise with no sense to it. After a time his vision cleared, however, and he turned toward the strange figure in astonishment. Yes. He had taken Suspirra from the River, still living—in a way. She, too, had seemed carved. Now Blint—Blint, who had gone into the River that time long, long since, with weights tied to his ankles.

"I put you in the River," Thrasne cried to the motionless figure.

"I know," the carved man said, each word stretching into an infinitely long sound, fading into a silence more profound than had preceded it, as though other sounds upon the island stilled to allow this speech room in which to be heard. "The blight, Thrasne. The strangeys came. Now I am here."

"Where?" Thrasne begged. "Where is here?"

"The Island of All of Us," the carved man replied, his lips twisting upward into the ghost of a smile, the lids of his eyes moving upward also, the face lightening for that instant almost to a fleshy look. "You have come to the Isle of Those Who Are Becoming Otherwise. . . ."

Behind Thrasne the shouts of the searchers stilled. Before them on the long, pale beach there was movement. Lumps and piles that Thrasne had assumed were flotsam or clumps of grass stood up, turned, became men and women. On some, fragments of clothing still hung, as irrelevant as wind-driven leaves clinging on a fence. Though it was possible to tell that some were male, some female, there was nothing sexual about them, as there had been nothing really sexual about Suspirra. In many, breasts or penises had dwindled into a general shapelessness. Or shapeliness, Thrasne thought half-hysterically, his artist's eyes assuring him that the shapes of those least human in appearance were also the most beautiful. As he thought these things, clinging tight to his sanity, willing himself to show no fear, the carved people approached him, slowly.

"Is he frightened of us?" one asked, the question seeming to take up most of the afternoon.

"Does he think we are ghosts?" asked another.

"What are they?" asked Taj Noteen from just behind him, his voice strained and shaking. "I told all the others to get back to the boat."

Thrasne responded calmly, betrayed only by the smallest quiver in his voice. "They are the dead, Taj Noteen. Those whom the Rivermen have consigned to the River. Blighted then. And, seemingly, given a new life by the blight, as the workers in the pits are given life by the Tears of Viranel."

"But these . . . these can talk."

"Talk, yes," said one of the carved people in long, slow syllables. "And observe. And hear."

"Cannot taste," said one. It was a chant, an intonation, perhaps an invocation.

"Not smell," said another.

"Not feel," said Blint. "Not much."

Thrasne's immediate terror had begun to subside, and he looked closely at Blint. There was no fear or horror on that face. There was none on any face he could see. There was calm. Expressions that might betoken contentment. A kindly and very moderate interest, perhaps, though no excitement. With this analysis, his heart slowed and he swallowed, conscious of a dry throat and scalp tight as a drumhead.

"Are you well, Blint?" he found himself able to ask, almost conversationally.

"Oh, yes, Thrasne. I am well."

"Are all the River dead here, all of them?"

"Here. Or on some other island."

"How did you get here?"

"The strangeys brought us. They bring us all."

Throughout this last exchange the carved people had turned

away and begun moving slowly back to the positions they had occupied before. There, they faded into the landscape once again, becoming mere manlike hillocks along the sand. Only Blint remained.

"Blint-wife is well." Thrasne bethought himself that Blint might like to know this.

Blint did not seem to care. "I'll leave it in your good hands," he said, each word drawn into a paragraph of meaning. "Thraaaasneeee." Blint's eyes were fixed on some more distant thing. They followed his gaze out across the waters to a swelling beneath the waves, a heaving, as some mighty creature rising from the depths, the great, glassy shells of its rising flowing with a tattered lace of sliding foam.

"The strangeys," said Blint once again, his hands folded before him as though he had been in Temple. Though they spoke to him several more times, he did not answer. At last Taj Noteen tugged Thrasne away, back across the sands to the edge of the forest. By the time they arrived there, Thrasne was shaking as with an ague.

Taj held him, clasped him tightly, until he stopped shivering. Taj was as shaken as Thrasne. Among the dead he had seen were some he thought he knew, one he had known very well indeed.

"Come," said Thrasne at last. "We will explore a little." He knew himself. In a moment his eyes would start to function, his fingers itch for the knife. In a little time, he would start to think. This shock had come only because he had known the old man, known him almost as a father. So, let him move to let the shock pass. "Come." He moved away down a forest path.

They walked. Here and there along the way were others of the dead. Some, evidently the more recent, looked up as they passed. One or two of them spoke. Others did not seem to see them. And some, those who had been longest upon the island, Thrasne thought, were rooted in place like trees, stout trees with two or three stout branches, small tendrils of growth playing about their heads and shoulders and from their fingertips.

Thrasne stopped before an ancient tree, twisted and gnarled by a century's growth. "The leaves are the same," he said, pointing first at the tree, then at one of the dead a small distance away. "The leaves. And see! It blooms." At the tips of the twigs were blossoms like waxen crowns, magenta and sea blue, with golden centers.

"We bloom," corrected a voice from behind them. "And the seeds blow out upon the River and sink down. And grow there into a kind of water weed. Which grows, and after a time takes fins and swims. To become the blight. Which seeks a body to house it. And brings it to life again. And comes to the islands. To grow. To bloom. . . ."

She who spoke had been a woman once. Now she fluttered with leaves, and her feet were deeply planted in the soil.

"And you," Thrasne whispered, needing to know. "Are you well?"

"Oh, yes. I am well."

"There is no pain?"

"No pain."

"Memories?"

"Memories?"

"Your name? Who you were?"

"I am," the tree-woman replied. "I am, now. It is enough." She did not speak again.

"This tree does not grow on Northshore," said Thrasne. "You'd think somewhere, in the forests there. Some of them . . ."

"The strangeys probably don't take them there," said Taj Noteen. "Probably they bring them only here, or on other islands."

"Why? How?"

"You will have to ask the strangeys, Thrasne," he said. "Those, swimming there in the deeps, with the foam around their faces."

For they did swim there, south of the island, shining mounds lifting great, eyed fringes, sliding through the waters like mighty ships of flesh, calling to one another in their terrible voices, deep and echoing as caves.

"Come," Taj Noteen urged him. "Come back to the *Gift*, Thrasne. It will seem less strange tomorrow." And in truth, he hoped it would, for his soul cowered in terror within him.

*   *   *

None of them felt they could leave on the day that followed, or the day after that. Thrasne did not find Blint again, though Taj Noteen found the woman he had once known, spoke to her, and returned to the *Gift* dazed and uncomprehending. On the third day, they wished to leave, tried to set sail, and were prevented from moving. Around them the strangeys moved, pushing the boat back against the shore each time they tried to move away. They had refilled all the water casks. Here and there among the strange trees on the island were some familiar fruiting kinds, and they had gathered all the fruits that were ripe. There was nothing more they could do, but the strangeys would not allow them to leave. It was time, Thrasne felt, to ask some questions.

What Thrasne wanted to know he could not ask from the crowded deck of the *Gift*, with all the crew clustered about thinking him crazy. He did not want to talk to the strangeys at a stone's throw, with old Porabji's cynical eye upon him. He wanted—oh, he wanted to be close to them. Close as their own skins or fins or whatever parts and attributes they had. He wanted to *see* them!

"Pull the raft around to the Riverside," he ordered. "And rig some kind of oarlocks on it."

It was not a graceful craft. Still, it was sturdy enough, and he could maneuver it with the long oars in the high oarlocks, standing to them as he plied them to and fro.

Once he knew well enough what he was doing with the raft, he thought to sneak off at dawn, when the strangeys usually surfaced. He set his mind to wake himself early, a skill most boatmen had, and rose in the mist before the sun. As he slipped over the rail, he did not see Eenzie the Clown standing in the owner-house door watching him, wrapped tight in a great white robe over which her hair spilled in a midnight river of silken strands. As he left, she came to the railing to watch the raft heave away, clumsy as a basket.

It was dead slack tide with the moons lying at either horizon. Only a light wind blew into Thrasne's face from the south, laden with scents strange to him. "There is more land there," Thrasne breathed, assured of it for the first time. "I smell it!"

He sniffed deeply, recognizing components of the odor as

resinous, humusy, fecund smells. Swamps and forests. On the
island the closer trees were only dark shadows against the mist
behind them, a ground fog that rose only slightly above their
tops to leave the taller trees outlined against the dawn. This
retreating sequence of river mist, shore trees, mist again, taller
trees, and yet again mist rising from some valley and the tallest
trees on the hills behind it lent an appearance of great distance
to the island, as though it had stretched away from him in the
night, becoming a place in dream in which no distance could be
measured. The far, hilltop trees were an open lacework against
the opal sky, motionless in the morning light, with only an
occasional flutter of wings among them to let one know they
were not painted there, or carved.

He sculled through the rising fogs into the deep channel on
the south side of the island. Behind him on the *Gift* the watchman raised his voice in a plaintive call, like a lonely bird.
Moving through the shore mist, the dead men and women
walked like an orchard come up from scattered seed. Though
most of them stood or walked alone, there were a few twos and
threes of them who seemed to stay together. As though they had
been friends or kin in life? Thrasne wondered, then gave up
wondering as the River surged about him, belling upward in
huge arcs of shining water.

Upon that swelling wave were winged things, smaller than
strangeys, peering at him from myriad eyes. Then they were gone.

"Perhaps they are strangey children," said Thrasne in a
conversational tone to himself. "And here are the adults."

They were all around him, their long, eye-decked fringes
suspended above the raft, peering at it through the mists, mon-
sters from dream.

"I need to talk with you," Thrasne called. "I want to ask
some questions."

A rearrangement took place among the fringes. Eyes were
replaced by others. Water swirled, and from the top of a belled
wave a comber of lace slid toward him, foaming around the
boat. "Yes," said a terrible strangey voice. "We will talk."

"You are preventing our leaving the island," he called. "If
we have offended you in some way, we wish to make repara-
tion. We cannot stay here. We must go on. Southward."

"No," the strangey boomed, diving under the water to leave Thrasne bobbing above it, then emerging a little distance off. "Your other one is coming to you."

"Other one?"

"The one you lost. The one you have yet to find. Babji."

"Coming here?" His heart swelled within him, suddenly joyous, leaping like a flame-bird chick from the nest. "Here? Medoor Babji?"

"The Treeci are bringing her."

This baffled him. It could not be the Treeci of Strinder's Isle. Some other Treeci. Before him the strangeys sank from sight, except for one.

"Do you have other questions?" it asked.

"Yes." He licked dry lips. "A long time ago, it was almost twenty years ago. A woman drowned herself off the piers at Baris. She was pregnant."

There was no sound but the River sound, yet Thrasne had a feeling of colloquy, a vibration of the water beneath the boat, a great voice asking and answering in tones beneath his ability to hear them. "Yes," said the strangey voice at last. "Her name was Imajh."

"I don't know what her name was. I called her Suspirra. I thought she was only wood, you know. But she wasn't. She was alive."

"She was alive in a way," assented the voice. "If you had not taken her from the River too soon, we would have brought her here and she would have been alive here, in a way. As the others are."

Thrasne slumped. "I killed her?"

Swirl of water. Sound as of what? Not laughter. No. Amusement. Something like amusement, but of so huge a kind that one could not call it that. Thrasne tried to identify the tone as the strangey spoke. It seemed important to know what the strangey felt as it answered. "She was already dead, boatman. What she was given after that was the blessed time. Perhaps she used it better for her where she was than if she had come here."

Thrasne, remembering, was not sure. "She had a child. Suspirra did."

"Yes. Our child. We want our child returned."

Thrasne had meant Pamra. After a moment he realized it was Lila they spoke of. "Why do you say Lila is your child, strangey? I meant her other child, Pamra Don."

"Lila is our child because she carries our seed. We know of Pamra Don. . . ." The voice trailed away in a sadness too deep to bear, the anguish beating at Thrasne's flesh like hammers.

Thrasne cried out against it. "Don't. Oh, don't. Strangey! Don't you have another name I may call you for courtesy's sake?"

Again that indefinable emotion, the trembling of the water. And then, "The name you call us does well enough. We are strangers, strangers to you and to this place. Aliens. Explorers. Though we were already here when your people came, you will remain here when we go. When our examination—our crusade— is done."

Strangers! Aliens? And yet, why not? If humans had come to this place, why not others, others with their own labyrinthine ways of thought, their own arcane judgments? It should have made no difference, yet it made all the difference. He tried to remember the questions he had wanted answers to. They did not seem so important now. The tone they had used in referring to Pamra Don closed that subject away. He did not want to hear Pamra's name spoken in that voice. There remained only one mystery, and stubbornly he asked about it.

"Why do you bring the blighted ones to these islands?"

Again that gigantic emotion that Thrasne could not identify. A troubling. A monstrous disturbance that had both laughter and tears in it. "Blight is your word, Thrasne. We call it rather 'extension.' It seems a good thing. The human people do not live long; their ends come suddenly. They . . . look beyond too much. Or they refuse to look beyond at all. This gives them time. . . ."

"The blight—you brought it?"

"We created it. Our gift. Just for you."

Again that vastness, rolling around him. He could feel it without understanding it at all. He bent forward, trying to protect the core of himself from whatever it was. He did not understand anything they had said. The words they used were insufficient to explain what they had meant. The vast, rolling emotion came closer, overwhelming him, but he could not apprehend the content of the wave in which he drowned. It passed. He lay gasping on the raft, unsure he was alive.

They spoke again, sadly.

"Bring us our child, boatman. In payment for receiving your lost one back."

Then the water flattened, all at once, as though oil had been poured upon it. There was no reaching swell, no tattered carpets of foam. Only silence, the flap of the sail, and from the distant *Gift*, muted by the mist, the sound of excited voices.

He steered toward it by sound. The cook banging on a pan. Taj Noteen's voice raised. Obers-rom, giving an order. The clatter of wood and the loose flap of the sail. The sound of laughter, cries of joy. Then he saw it, saw the little boat with the *Cheevle* tied at its stern. He called out, in a great, hoarse voice, and saw Eenzie and Medoor Babji waiting at the rail.

"Have you finished with the strangeys? Come aboard, have your breakfast, then let us sail for home!"

He gaped at her, staring into her face, unbelieving. There was a lively intelligence there, a self-interested concern. She reached down and lifted him upward with a strong arm, and his skin woke at the feel of her own against it. He was aware of nothing but this as he took her hand and let her lead him toward the cooking smells, thinking only of what was at that moment and not at all, in that moment, of the strangeys or of Pamra. He had come to a place within himself where he could no longer bear to go back or to stay where he was, unchanging, and yet he hesitated to go forward. With that mighty, enigmatic emotion of the strangeys still washing through him, he hung upon the moment, poised, unmoving within himself, aware of a stillness within himself and at the core of all the liquid shifting of the River's surface, all the windblown agitation of the island, becoming part of it for a time, rather than choose—anything.

Two days later, after Medoor Babji had walked upon the Island of the Dead until she had seen what they had seen, they set sail for home.

No matter what I start out thinking about, I end up
remembering what the strangeys said, and what they said
seemed to me to be about sadness. The sadness of men—
mankind, I guess you'd say. It's that we never have time to
be what we know we should be, or could be. And it's not
because of the time itself, the gods know we waste enough
of it not doing anything at all, but because of what we are.
And we don't have time, no matter how old we get, to be
anything else. So they've brought this gift, so they called it,
to let us be something else for a while. Something that
knows, but doesn't care so much. It's caring so much that
keeps us from being what we could be. Caring so much.
About the wrong things, maybe. But still, if we didn't
what would we be?

From Thrasne's book

Word was sent to Sliffisunda that Pamra Don would be
delivered up to the Thraish. In the Red Talons, Ilze
danced his victory, a wild, frantic prancing upon the
rocky height, then sat down upon a shelf of stone to wait, his
eyes like polished pebbles, scanning the horizon for the first
glimpse of those who would come from the Chancery. Though
the message had said clearly that Gendra Mitiar would accompany the girl, Ilze cared nothing for that. It was Pamra Don he
would see shortly; Pamra Don he would get into his own hands
at last. He thought of her as he had used to think of her: tied to
the stake, his whip falling across her shoulders as his caress, her
voice rising up in screaming prayers to the empty sky. His body

shook, twitched, spasmed with this thought, and the fliers on the rocks around him cast looks at one another, wondering what ailed him.

Sliffisunda was content to wait. There was no hurry about this business. His fliers told him the crusade went on, more massively than before, with great clots of people moving west and north. Wherever they moved, the pits were full, so he cared not whether they moved or not. In a hidden valley of the steppes known only to fliers, the herdbeasts were growing with each day that passed. Already the expedition to steal other young bulls had been planned. More than an expedition, almost an invasion, with enough surprise and numbers to succeed no matter what the humans did. It might prove expedient to stop this crusade; or again, it might not. It was a thing worthy of much screamed discussion, many loud sessions on the Stones of Disputation. Sliffisunda wiped his beak on the post of his feeding trough and was content.

And on the plains, moving southward and a little east, Pamra Don was content as well. "A journey of a week or two," she had been told. "To the Red Talons. To meet the Talkers." There were Jondarites and Chancery people escorting her. Once she felt a fleeting sadness that Tharius Don was not among them. There was scarcely room even for that emotion. She rode the weehar ox the general had given her, refusing to ride in the wagon pulled by Noor slaves. She abjured Gendra Mitiar with great passion to free these men as Lees Obol would require of her. Gendra listened, raked her face, ground her teeth, and said she would consider the matter. In truth, she found Pamra Don amusing in the same way Jhilt had been amusing during the early days of her captivity. So naive. So childishly convinced that her feelings mattered to anyone besides herself. So interestingly ripe to be disabused of that notion.

One day the escort paused on a low hill to let a procession of crusaders pass in the valley, banners, a wagon, a gorgeously robed figure in the wagon. Pamra looked down at it in wonder, not recognizing Peasimy Flot. Peasimy had decided to join Pamra Don at Split River, but he did not even see her riding in her bright armor in company with the Jondarites.

And as for the rest, it was merely travel. Creak of wheels.

Plod of feet. Crack of whip. Wind in the grass. Murmur of voices. Fires at night gleaming like lanterns in the dark. Walking out into the grasses to pee, staring up at the moons which seemed to stare back in wonder, or threat, or admonition, depending upon one's point of view.

The slave Jhilt, walking each day away in a soft chinkle of chains. The Jondarites striding along, their plumes nodding over their impassive faces, their hands upon the butts of their spears, resting at night beside the fire, polishing their fishskin armor with oil. The captain himself, on orders from Jondrigar, polishing the armor of Pamra Don. Gendra Mitiar seeing this with amusement, but not interfering. Time for that. Time for everything.

In fact, Gendra Mitiar felt herself growing strangely weary from the journey, victim of an unaccustomed lassitude. She went to her strongbox and unlocked it with the key she carried around her neck to get at her reserve supply of elixir. Though it was a full season sooner than she had planned to take more of the stuff, she dosed herself liberally with the thick, brownish ichor, at which Jhilt smiled behind her hands and jangled her chains. On those chains, among a hundred other dangling charms and coins, hung a duplicate key to the strongbox. It had taken Jhilt over a year to file it to fit, but once it was done, it had taken only a minute to open the box, months ago, and taste the acrid stuff. When they set out upon this journey, it had taken only another minute to substitute for the elixir a vial of half-burned and diluted puncon jam. Who knew better than Jhilt that Gendra's aged mouth knew no savor, her aged nose knew no scent? "Have some jam, old one," she tittered to herself to the soft chankle-chankle of the chains. "Live a little."

Though she had sometimes forgotten it during her captivity, here on the steppes Jhilteen Nobiji remembered she was Noor. If the Noor could not have justice, they would have vengeance. The key to the strongbox was not the only key that hung upon her chains, and her presence with this troop outside the barrier of the Teeth was one she had hoped for over many years.

There were twelve days like this before they sighted the Talons, looming redstone obelisks, contorted towers that broke the line of the steppes amid a dark forest. This outcropping of redstone ran all the way from Northshore to the Teeth of the North, somewheres mere edges along the land, elsewhere squat cliffs lowering over the plain. Here the stone had been eaten by the wind and rain, chewed into monuments as full of holes as a worm-gnawed pod, and here the Talkers maintained one of their four strongholds. Black Talons, so they said, for strength; Gray Talons for wisdom; Blue Talons for vengeance; Red Talons for blood. Sliffisunda had come from Gray to Red, and the significance of that had not escaped him. "From thought to action," he cawed to himself when the human train was sighted. "So, now we will have something interesting, perhaps some satisfaction."

The Jondarites made camp some distance from the foot of the Talons, yet close enough that the Talkers might come to them without exertion. The tents were set in a circle; the Jondarites took crossbows from their cases and placed quarrels for them ready at hand, the heavy, square-headed bolts most efficacious against fliers. Though there had been little opportunity to use weapons against the Thraish in some hundreds of years, the stories of the last Thraish-human conflicts were well remembered among the soldiers of the Chancery, and the general had told them to be ready for any eventuality.

When all these preparations had been completed, Gendra Mitiar sent a messenger to the foot of the Talons with a letter for Sliffisunda. He might come, she said, to their camp. To question Pamra Don. And to discuss certain matters with her, Gendra Mitiar.

Sliffisunda did not come, himself. He sent a Fourth Degree underling and the human, Ilze. It amused him to do this, setting the humans one against the other. He did it sometimes with slaves or craftsmen, making one's safety dependent upon betrayal of the other. So, now, he thought Ilze might work against Gendra Mitiar to obtain the person of Pamra Don.

But she, remembering Ilze in the Accusatory, was disinclined to pay him attention.

"I must speak with the Talker," she said. "I don't know what he was thinking of, sending you." She sniffed, raking her face, staring at him as though he had been some kind of bug. Her teeth ground, and he tensed in every nerve, expecting pain.

That sound had accompanied pain before, and he wanted to scream at her.

"Sliffisunda wants to see her," he grated.

"Fine," Gendra said. "Let him come to see her. Talk with her. Question her, if he likes. I need to talk with him, too, and I'll not be hauled up there like some sack of laundry."

Taking a quick look at the alert Jondarites, Ilze retreated, quelled for this time. He had not laid eyes on Pamra Don. For all he knew, she was not even with the group. She, however, spying through a slit in the tent side, had seen him very well; seen him and disregarded him as an irrelevancy. He would hurt her if he could, but he would not be allowed. The Chancery folk would not allow it. Her great-great-grandfather, Tharius Don, would not allow it. She explained this to Neff and her mother and Delia as all of them nodded and smiled.

Back at the Talons Ilze's failure was reported to Sliffisunda, who cawed laughter. "I did not think he would do any good!" The Fourth Degree Talker who had reported on Ilze kept his beak shut, wisely. Sliffisunda shuffled back and forth on his perch, darting his head from side to side. "Well, I will go talk to this old human. Tomorrow, perhaps. Or next day."

He let two days pass before going to the camp. Gendra, who had studied the fliers for some time, was not concerned about the delay. The lassitude that had bothered her on the journey had not yet abated, and she remained in her tent, ministered to by Jhilt. Pamra, meantime, preached to the Jondarites. They, remembering how their general had responded to her, varied in their response from polite to enthusiastic.

And at last Sliffisunda arrived. The Talkers had lately taken to regalia, a tendency borrowed from humans, and Sliffisunda wore a badge of degree slung about his neck as well as various sparkling ornaments on his legs, feet, and wing fingers. Warned of his coming, Gendra had Pamra brought out of her tent, fully accoutred in her Jondarite armor, and set in a chair beside the fire with Jondarites at either side. If the old rooster wanted this one, Gendra thought, he would have to give something significant in return, though nothing of this appeared in her face or voice as she first greeted the Talker.

"I am honored," she said. "We grant the request of Sliffisunda to talk with—even question—the woman, Pamra Don."

"She was to have been sent to us," the Talker cawed, depositing shit on Gendra's words.

Gendra's fingers twitched toward her face, then stilled, knotted. So, it was to be a battle of insults. "One pays little attention to what Talkers demand," she replied in a bored voice. "Unless one is given reason to listen."

Sliffisunda almost crouched in surprise. So, the humans could engage in Talkerly disputation! Almost always the humans were like spoiled eggs, stinking soft. This one was not. He turned away from her, showing his side—not quite a fatal insult, though close. "What reason would humans understand?" he cawed.

"More subtle reasons than a Talker could ascertain, perhaps," she replied, turning her shoulder toward him to signal the Jondarites. "The Thraish have not been noted for good sense."

He stretched his wings wide and threatened her. She gestured again at the Jondarites. He looked up to see a dozen crossbows centered on his chest. He laughed and subsided. "So. So, Gendra Mitiar. What have you to say?"

"I have to say your interest and mine are the same, Sliffisunda. Do you speak for the Talkers?"

"I speak to Talkers," he boasted. "And they listen."

"Ah," she murmured. So, he could not commit the Talkers to anything, but he could argue a case. If she succeeded in acquiring an alliance with him, she would buy an advocate, not a potentiary. Still, what matter? Those in the assembly would accept a Talker's interest as representative of the Thraish. They would not know the difference.

She turned full face toward him and said, "I have a case to put to you, Uplifted One. . . ."

She spoke of her desire for the post of Protector of Man. She spoke of her intentions, once that post was hers.

"There is no reason the Thraish cannot increase in numbers. Human numbers can be increased to feed them. The Noor are no good to you because the color of their skins will not allow the Tears of Viranel to grow properly within them. Let us eradicate the Noor. Let us replace them with settlers from Northshore.''

Behind the tent flap, Jhilt quivered in shock. This she had not heard before.

"How will you convince the Chancery to do this?" Sliffisunda asked, interested despite himself. Even though none of this would be needed when the herdbeasts multiplied, it was still an interesting concept.

"If your numbers are increased, the amount of elixir can be increased. More humans can receive it. Those whose votes are needed in the Chancery assembly will be promised elixir. A simple thing, Sliffisunda.''

"How will you wipe out Noor?''

"War." She shrugged. "General Jondrigar needs opportunity for war.''

"Not enough Jondarites." This was said as mere comment, not as objection.

"True." Again she shrugged. "We will need to conscript men from Northshore as well. Any man, I should think, who has not fathered a child in a few years.''

Who will then not be available to support children he has fathered, Sliffisunda thought, while keeping silent. The Thraish understood nestlings. Even Talkers understood nestlings. When the parent was lost, the nestlings were lost. Many would die if this woman came to power. The pits would be full. And if that went on for a long time, the Thraish could expand in advance of the day he had planned. The woman was ambitious, but not wise. He could use her, despite her disputatious nature.

"Let us talk," he said, smiling inside himself.

On the day following, Sliffisunda arrived to question Pamra. This was a simple feint or, as the fliers put it, *hadmaba*, a threatening posture designed to bluff rather than injure. Sliffisunda wanted to support Gendra Mitiar; he did not want her to think he did it willingly or for his own purposes. So, let her think he was really interested in this pale, thin woman with the blazing eyes with the child on her lap.

"Tell me of your crusade," he said, expecting nothing more than ranting or evasions.

"You do an evil thing," she said in a level tone, fixing him with her eyes. "All you fliers." The child fixed him with her eyes, strangely.

He hunched his shoulders, staring at her, ignoring her young. "What evil is that?"

"It is for you the workers are raised up," she said. "I did not know that until I came to the Chancery, until my great-great-grandfather Tharius Don told me. I thought it was for the work they did, as we were taught. I thought it was Potipur's will. I had been taught that. It was false."

"It is Potipur's will," Sliffisunda replied, amused. "Potipur has promised the Thraish plenty. The bodies of your dead are the plenty he promised."

"A true god would make no such promise. A true god would not do evil. Therefore, Potipur is not a true god, he is merely your god, a Thraish god. Not a god of man."

"Does man have a god?" Considering the trouble the priests and Towers had been to to suppress all humanish religions, it was amazing that she had come up with this. Despite himself, he was intrigued.

"If the Thraish have a god, then men, also, have a god. My voices tell me that if there is not One, over us all, then there are several, for each race of creatures."

"Or none?" he asked. "Have you thought of that?"

She shook her head at him. "My voices say there is. A god. Of humans and Treeci, for we are like."

Sliffisunda shat, offended, turning his back on her. She did not seem to notice but merely stared at him as though he were some barnyard fowl. He screamed at her, wings wide, and she merely blinked. "Foul Treeci. Offal. Fish eaters."

"The Treeci are wise and benevolent creatures," she said. "As man can be if not brutalized by wickedness. Raising up the workers is a wicked thing to do, Sliffisunda. We know their pain and do nothing. Thereby we condone it. Thereby we are made brutes. Not by the workers themselves, but by the Thraish, who require they be raised. So my voices say."

Gendra, sitting on the other side of the fire, blinked in amazement. She had not heard more than five words from Pamra Don during the entire trip. Now this! What had gotten into the woman?

"Heretic!" Sliffisunda cawed. "Unbeliever in Potipur."

"If Potipur is only a Thraish god, why should I believe in him?" she asked. "If the weehar had a god, would it be the god of the Thraish?"

Theology dictated that the weehar could have no god except the Thraish god, but Sliffisunda had his own doubts about that. He recalled the quasi-racial memories of the fliers' last hunt, as he taught them to nestlings. Certainly the weehar had not seemed to rejoice in Potipur. Perhaps the weehar did not rejoice because they were being punished. But for what? What sins could a weehar commit? The sin of offal eating? The sin of debasement? The sin of doubt in Potipur's care for the Thraish? The sin of failing to breed? The sin of failing to give honor? How could the weehar or thrassil commit any of these? More likely the weehar were only things, needing no god at all. As the humans were things. Sliffisunda shook his head. The woman didn't talk like a thing, which was troubling. Abruptly he rose, stalked to the edge of the encampment, and raised himself into the air. Too troubling. Too much talk.

Behind him, Pamra watched him go, a little wrinkle between her eyes. It was hard, so hard. She could not reach him. She looked around for Neff, for her mother. They would have to help her with this one. She could not feel her way into his heart, not at all. They stood remote, their effulgence dimmed in the light of the day, hard to see. She listened for their voices and was not rewarded. Nothing. Tears crept into her eyes, and she shook them away angrily. If they did not speak to her, it was because they didn't need to. She could not expect them to be with her every minute. Perhaps they had other things to do, other people to guide as well.

Sliffisunda arrived at the Talons in a foul mood. He stalked into his aerie, snatching a mouthful of food as he passed the trough, ripping an arm from the twitching meat and cracking it for the marrow. It had no savor. The human, Ilze, was waiting outside. Sliffisunda could smell him, that sweetish, human stink which only the Tears of Viranel softened and ameliorated into something almost satisfying. Almost. Sliffisunda drooled, thinking of weehar.

A human god? To believe in a human god, that would be a

sin. But if weehar believed in a god at all, what god would it be? Sliffisunda made a noise like a snarl in his throat. Under the Thraish, the weehar had ended. Under the humans, they had multiplied. Which god would the weehar accept? And that could be the sin for which they were punished—except that the punishment had come first.

Ignoring the crouching human on his porch, Sliffisunda launched himself toward the Stones of Disputation. This was not a matter he cared to think about by himself.

Behind him, Ilze pounded his knee with his fist, livid with frustration. Where was Pamra Don? Why hadn't this Talker brought him Pamra Don?

In the camp, Gendra Mitiar watched Pamra Don, her eyes narrowed. She had noticed for the first time that Pamra Don ate almost nothing. The woman seemed built of skin tightly drawn over her bones, like a stilt-lizard, all angles, with eyes like great glowing orbs in her face.

"Doesn't she ever eat?" she asked the Jondarite captain.

"Very little," he admitted. "A little bread in the morning. She seems to like Jarb root, and one of the men sought it for her during the journey."

"You'd better detail him to find more," she said. "The woman may not last a week if she doesn't eat something."

"I can force her if you like," the captain suggested. It was sometimes necessary to force-feed captives, particularly Noor captives, who often tried to starve themselves when their families had been killed before their eyes.

Gendra shook her head. "No. I need her cooperative with the Thraish. If she will eat Jarb root, see she gets it. At least enough of it to keep her alive." She looked up, drawn by a distant cacophony. "What's that?"

"The Talkers on the top of the Talons, Dame Marshal. They do that sometimes, late into the night—sometimes all night long."

"What are they doing?"

"Arguing, so I've been told. Only the high-mucky-muck ones like the one who was here. Sixth Degree ones. They have the highest pillars all to themselves. The less important ones,

SHERI S. TEPPER

they meet lower down. Some nights there will be three or four bunches of them, all going at it. Not always this loud, though. Sliffisunda must have a bone in his craw!'' The captain laughed, unawed.

Gendra's eyes narrowed once more. So. Sliffisunda had talked to Pamra Don, and then some great argument followed among the Thraish. Perhaps Gendra's case was even now being argued. She smiled. Good. Very good.

As she rose from her chair and moved toward the tent, she stumbled, a sudden dizziness flooding over her.

"Jhilt," she gasped, feeling the slave's hands fasten around her arms and shoulders.

"The Dame Marshal has been sitting too long near the fire," the slave soothed, hiding a smile behind her hand. "It makes one dizzy."

"You get dizzy, sitting by the fire?" Gendra said childishly. "You do?"

"Of course. Everyone does." Jhilt half-carried the woman into her tent and eased her onto the bed. "Everyone does." Especially, Jhilt said to herself, when one is some hundreds of years old and is no longer getting any elixir. The woman on the bed looked like a corpse, like something in the pits, gray, furrowed skin gaped over yellow teeth, like a skull. "Everyone does," she soothed, wondering how long it would take. Jhilt had a small supply of Tears in a vial hanging on her chains. She had toyed with the idea of using the Tears before rather than after Gendra's death. She amused herself by thinking of this now, weighing the idea for merit.

"No," she sighed at last. "The captain would know what I had done. If she merely dies, he will not know."

Perhaps she could use the Tears on someone else. That Laugher, perhaps. That would be amusing, too.

The disputation on the stones went on until almost dawn, not merely acrimonious, which most disputations were, but becoming increasingly enraging as the night wore on. Blood was drawn several times before the argument broke up, and only Sliffisunda's quickness in parrying attacks kept him from being among the injured. It was clear the Talkers would not accept the idea of a human god or any weehar god. Only the Thraish had a god, and the god of the Thraish was the god of all. The Thraish were the chosen of Potipur, who set aside all other creatures for the service of the Thraish. So the Talkers believed.

Sliffisunda, bruised and tired, was not so sure. The other Talkers of the Sixth Degree had not heard Pamra Don. He did not like to think what might have happened if they had heard Pamra Don. It might be better if none of them heard her, ever. Better if Sliffisunda had not heard her himself. He settled upon his perch, head resting upon his shoulder. In the afternoon, he would talk with the human, Ilze. In the evening, he would go to the camp of the humans again and make an agreement with Gendra Mitiar. It did not matter what agreement with her was made. The woman stank of death. She would not live long enough to worry him.

"What will you do with Pamra Don?" he asked Ilze.

Ilze's mouth dropped open. He salivated. The stench of him rose into Sliffisunda's nostrils, sickeningly sweet. "Teach her," he said at last, a low, gargling sound. "Teach her she cannot do this to me."

"Where?" Sliffisunda asked. "Where will you do this?"

"Here. In the Talons. Anywhere. It doesn't matter."

"Before those from the Chancery?" Sliffisunda was watching him closely. If, as Sliffisunda thought likely, all those in the crusade had been contaminated by Pamra Don's ideas, then some mere private vengeance against the woman would not suffice. Her followers would have to be convinced that Pamra Don was wrong. "Would you punish her before those from the Chancery and all her followers?"

Ilze shivered. He wanted to say yes, but his soul shrank from it. He had orders not to touch her. If he punished her in public, they would kill him. He knew that. They would kill him at once. Those from the Chancery would do it. Her followers would do it. And no one would care enough to save him from them. "If you would protect me," he whined, hearing the whine and hating it.

"Ah. Well, suppose you don't do it. Suppose we do it, the Thraish. How should it be done?"

Ilze had only thought of whips, of stakes. "Tie her to a

stake,'' he said, then stopped. The Talkers didn't use whips. "Eat her?'' he offered.

Sliffisunda cawed his displeasure, pecking Ilze sharply on one side of his head so the blood flowed. "Take into our bodies the foul flesh of a heretic? Stupid human!''

"Well, do whatever you do, then,'' Ilze sulked, trying to stanch the blood.

"We have a ceremony,'' Sliffisunda said. "A ceremony.''

Night came. Sliffisunda came again. Pamra Don came again, to the fireside.

"Do your followers believe as you do?'' the Talker asked her, already certain of the answer.

"Yes. Most of them. All of them, in time. All mankind, in time.'' It was not the question she had expected, not one of the questions she was ready for, but the Talker asked nothing else. He turned and left her, going to Gendra Mitiar to carry on a lengthy, soft-voiced conversation which Pamra could not hear.

Jhilt could hear it.

"You wish to be Protector of Man?''

Gendra Mitiar nodded. Her voice was very husky tonight, and it tired her to talk.

"What can Thraish do to guarantee this?'' he purred.

"Wait until Lees Obol dies. I will let you know. Then send a messenger. Tell the assembly the elixir will be decreased unless I am elected. In which event it will be increased.''

"And when you are Protector, you will increase the quota of humans? You will eradicate the Noor for this?''

"You have my word.''

"And in return for this agreement, you will give me the person of this woman, this Pamra Don?''

"As you like, Uplifted One. She is nothing to me. What do you want her for?''

"To prove she is a false prophet, Dame Marshal. In ceremony before all her followers at Split River Pass. To show them Potipur will not be mocked.''

Gendra laughed, thinking of Tharius Don. "How may I assist you, Uplifted One?''

Jhilt heard all this, her ear tight to the tent flap.

When Sliffisunda had gone, when Gendra Mitiar was asleep, an uneasy sleep in which her heart faltered and her lungs seemed inclined to stop working, Jhilt walked out to the cage of seeker birds that every Jondarite troop carried with it. The message bone was already in her hands.

"A message for Tharius Don," she said, keeping her voice bored and level. "From the Dame Marshal."

The Jondarite keeper made a cursory examination of the seal. It looked like the Dame Marshal's seal, and who else's would it be? The bird came into his hands willingly, accepted the light burden as trained to do, and launched itself upward to turn toward the north without hesitation, strong wings beating across Potipur's scowling face.

Jhilt shivered, thinking of what was in that message.

"You cold?" leered the soldier, opening his cloak in invitation.

She shook her head. "The Dame Marshal needs me," she said, turning back toward the tent. Though, indeed, if the Dame Marshal needed her at all, it would not be for much longer. Queen Fibji should be told of this conspiracy against the Noor. Jhilt had no seeker birds for the Queen; therefore she must find some Noor signal post that would have them. Gendra would not spend time looking for a slave, not now, not as weak as she was and with so much going on. Jhilt fumbled among her chains for the other key, the one that unlocked her jingling manacles. Moments later she moved off across the steppes, silent as the moons.

22

A yawning servant brought word to Tharius Don in the middle of his sleep time. "The general asks for you at once in the audience hall, Lord Propagator. Most urgently." He waited for some reply, and when Tharius waved him off, he scurried away into the darkness. The midnight bell had only lately struck. Tharius had heard it in his sleep, through the purple dusk that was night in this season.

He wrapped himself in a thick robe with a hood and made his way down the echoing corridors and endless flights of stairs to the audience hall. Muslin curtains hung limp against the closed shutters, like so many wraiths in the torchlight. At the side, where Lees Obol's niche was, the curtains were flung wide, and General Jondrigar stood there, face impassive and his hand upon his knife. Something in his stance recommended caution to Tharius Don, who approached softly, pausing at some distance to ask, "You needed me, General?"

"Dead," Jondrigar replied. "I think. Dead."

"Dead? Who?" Only to understand at once who it was and why this midnight summons. "The Protector?"

The general nodded, standing aside to gesture Tharius forward. In the niche, still overheated by the little porcelain stove which was only now burning itself out, the bed stood with its coverlets thrown back. On the embroidered sheet the body of Lees Obol lay immobile. His eyes were open. One arm was rigidly extended above him, as though petrified, pointing.

"Telling me, go!" Jondrigar said, indicating the hand. "Telling me. As he always did."

"Rigor," Tharius murmured. "All dead men get rigor, General. It doesn't mean—"

"Telling me go," the general repeated, his eyes glowing. "Rigor comes long after. He died like this. The message for me."

Tharius moved to the bed, put his hands gently upon the ancient face, the neck, the arms. Rigid. All. Like rigor, yes. Or blight. His face darkened. So. Plots. Perhaps.

"When was he last seen alive?"

"You were here one time."

"Yes. Last evening. Shavian Bossit and I met in the hall for a few moments. I didn't look in on Lees Obol, though Shavian may have done."

"He did. Through the curtains. Jondarite captain reports this to me." Jondrigar took off his helmet and ran a trembling hand across his mane. "Jondarite captain looked in every hour. Served tea late, as Protector wanted. Then, at midnight bell, he looked in again. This is what he found."

We could have a bloodbath here, Tharius thought. Better defuse that. "We have been surprised he has lived this long, General. We all knew he would die very soon. The elixir does not give eternal life. Only more years, not an eternity."

"No one killed him."

It could have been a question, or a statement. Tharius Don chose to interpret it as both.

"No one killed him. Age killed him. As it will all of us."

"But he left a message for me," the general said again. "He told me to go."

Tharius thought it wiser to say nothing. He had no idea what was in the general's mind and chose to take no chance of upsetting him.

"The Noor Queen. She is coming to Split River Pass," the general said suddenly. "I need to go there."

Tharius thought the general's mind had slipped and said soothingly, "There will be a council meeting within hours. You should be here for that."

The general nodded. "Yes. Then I will go to Split River Pass." He turned and made his way out of the hall, unsteadily, as though under some great pressure. Tharius felt a fleeting

pity. Lees Obol had been all Jondrigar's life. What would he do
now?

He put the question away. There were customs to comply
with. "Send someone to Glamdrul Feynt," he said to the
Jondarite captain who hovered against the wall. "Tell him to
look up what funeral arrangements were made the last time a
Protector died, then come tell me what they were. Send someone else for servants. Wash the body and clothe it properly.
Then get the messengers moving. Let them know at the Bureau
of Towers. Tell them to get the word out to the towns. There
will probably be some period of mourning. Find out who's
running things over there while Gendra's gone, and send them
to me. Oh, and find my deputy, Bormas Tyle, and send him to
me as well."

Tharius chewed a thumbnail. Should a seeker bird be sent to
Gendra Mitiar? Suppose Pamra Don was just now having success with the Talkers? Suppose this message interrupted something vital? He shivered. Better let it alone. Send a message
later, if at all.

He turned, catching a glimpse of a scurrying figure out of the
corner of one eye. Nepor? Here? Surely not. Probably a curious
servant, fearful of being caught away from his assigned duties.
Well, they would all have their curiosity satisfied soon enough.

23

"**D**one," whispered Koma Nepor, pausing at a shadowed doorway.

"Dead? Ah. How did he look?"

"Who can say, Jorn? I didn't look at him. The Jondarite put the tea kettle down on the table by the curtain as he always does. From my hiding place behind the curtain, I put the blight in the kettle. The old man called for tea; tea he was served. An hour later, off goes the captain, here comes the general. Then here comes Tharius Don, much whispering and sending of this one and that one. I didn't stay to listen."

"What happened to the kettle?"

"The servants are in there now, cleaning up. They'll take the kettle and cups away. The blight's only good for an hour or so. All gone now, I should think. That's what took me so long to develop, finding a strain that wouldn't last."

"No evidence to connect you, then."

"No evidence to connect *us*, Jorn. None. Shall we go to our beds now, so's to hear it properly, wakened from sleep?"

They went off down the twisting corridor, two shadows in the shuttered gloom, whispering, heads bent toward one another like Talkers, plotting on the stones.

"When will you give General Jondrigar the letter?"

"Later. There'll be a meeting to discuss the funeral. After that."

Their forms dwindled into shadowed silence.

Shavian Bossit was wakened from sleep to receive the news. He sent a message at once to Bormas Tyle, awaiting his arrival with some impatience.

"Where've you been?" he demanded when the other arrived. "I sent for you over an hour ago."

"So did my superior," the other replied, glaring at him. "Tharius Don. It seems we have lost a Protector. Are we about to gain another?"

"It's sooner than we'd planned."

"Nonetheless welcome."

"True. But we're hardly ready. Gendra's still alive. So is Jondrigar."

"So they're still alive. For a few weeks, perhaps. Support one of them for the post."

"The general? Ha!"

"Well, Gendra, then. In her absence. Elect Gendra as Protector, which will vacate the position of Marshal of the Towers. Feynt will take over there, as we've planned, and that will give you two votes. Meantime, the general will not last long. I will take his position when he dies. Last, Gendra will fade away, and you will have Feynt's vote, my vote, and your own. Enough, Bossit." Bormas Tyle slid his knife in and out of its holster, a whisper of violence in the room. "A few weeks or months more and we will have succeeded."

"I suppose. Still, something's bothering about all this. The servants are whispering about Obol's death."

"Did you expect them not to?" Bormas snorted. "Servants whisper about everything."

"Just the way he died. As though he'd been frozen. One arm pointed out like a signpost."

"Some deaders do that."

"I suppose," Shavian said again. "Very well. We proceed as planned. The council will meet in the morning, an hour before noon. And what about the funeral?"

"I don't know. Tharius has our old charlatan in the files looking up what happened last time. I can't even remember who the Protector was before Lees Obol."

"His name was Jurniver," Shavian said, abstractedly. "Jurniver Quyme. He lived four hundred and sixty-two years. He came to office in his two hundredth year. He made fifteen Progressions. He died long before I was born. Feynt knows all about him. It'll be in the files."

"Old faker."

"Why do you say that?"

"He pretends to be ancient and crippled whenever anyone wants anything. Watch him, though, when he thinks no one's looking. He moves like a hunting stilt-lizard, quick as lightning."

"It's a game he plays for Gendra's benefit."

"It's a game he plays for his own. Keep it in mind, Bossit, when he's Marshal of the Towers. Feynt's no fool."

"Would we be planning together if he were?" Shavian made an impatient gesture. "Get on with it. I'll have to see what happens at the council meeting. If you can find Feynt, tell him we've talked." And he turned away across his room, groping his way to the shutters and throwing them wide. The sweet breezes of summer dawn immediately raised the muslin curtains, flinging them like perfumed veils into the room, where he struck at them impatiently. Outside in the plaza the trees' leaves had unrolled to their fullest extent, glistening in the amber sun, a bronzy green light that covered everything like water, flowing and changing, rippling along the stones and over the walls in a constant tide. "Riverlight," it was called. "Summer Riverlight," created by the wind and the trees.

The fountain played charmingly, the little bells hung in its jet tumbling and jingling. On the nearest meadows the weehar lowed and the thrassil neighed, gentle sounds. With the wind in this direction, one could scarcely hear the axes, far off in the hills.

At the center of the plaza, near the fountain, Tharius Don and Glamdrul Feynt stood in the midst of a crowd of servants and craftsmen, hands pointing, voices raised. Funeral arrangements, Shavian told himself, yawning. Evidently there was to be a catafalque in the ceremonial square prior to entombment. Respected members of the Chancery were not put into pits on their deaths. It was presumed the Holy Sorters would take them directly from their roofless tombs into Potipur's arms. Shavian yawned again. The truth of which would be easy to ascertain, he thought, if anyone wanted to climb over a tomb wall and look. Since he was reasonably certain of what he would find—considering the number of small birds and vermin that congregated around tombs—Shavian was not tempted to do so.

He rang for his servants. There was time for a bath and a massage before the meeting of the council. He ordered perfumes for his bath and others sprinkled upon his clothing. The chamber of meeting would stink of death.

When they met, the body of Lees Obol had already been removed and there was no smell at all. They sat about impatiently, waiting for Jondrigar to arrive. Jorn and Nepor were side by side, pretending no interest in one another, though usually they were collusive as heretics. Shavian watched this, mildly amused. They were up to something. Across the table, in the secondary row of chairs, Bormas Tyle and Glamdrul Feynt bore similar expressions of disinterest. No doubt if Gendra had been present, she would have looked the same. Shavian adjusted his face to one of polite alertness. Why not break the mold, behave somewhat differently, confuse them all?

Tharius Don brooded, but then he always brooded. He had not sent a message to Gendra. He hoped no one else had, though there was no guarantee someone in the Bureau of Towers had not. Or Bormas Tyle, perhaps. Tharius had no illusions about his deputy's sense of loyalty. Bormas Tyle had none, except to himself.

A clatter of feet in the hall, more than one. The doors at the end of the great chamber were flung wide, and General Jondrigar entered at the head of a company of troops. The others stared. Ezasper Jorn bit off an exclamation, throwing a sideways glance at Nepor. What was this?

Shavian, no less surprised than the others, decided to treat it as a normal occurrence. "We have been waiting for you, Jondrigar. Do you wish to sit down?"

"I'll stand," he boomed. "There is little time to do what must be done. I have received the message Lees Obol meant for me. 'Go,' he said to me, and go I must. He wishes me to finish the work he could not finish. He desires I take upon myself the title of Protector of Man."

There was a stunned silence. Into that silence crept the sound of Bormas Tyle's knife, sliding, sliding in its scabbard. Shavian Bossit swallowed, tried to concentrate, torn between laughter and shock. What had he and Bormas Tyle said only that morning? Support either the general or Gendra for the position of Protector. Soon both would be dead. He swallowed his surprise and found his voice.

"I would support you in that, Jondrigar." He turned to find two faces frozen upon his own, Jorn's and Nepor's. Ah, so they had been up to something. "Tharius, you would support Jondrigar's accession to the title, would you not?"

"I would," said Tharius in a strangely husky voice. It was another sign. A sign from heaven. From the God of man, if one cared to say it that way. From Pamra Don. "I would support General Jondrigar. He knows what is needed to protect mankind."

"I have already begun," the general boomed. "When I returned with Pamra Don from the pass, I sent commands to all the mines that the slaves should be released and taken over the mountains to their homeland."

There were gasps from around the table. Shavian bit his tongue. Tharius looked upon the general with loving, glowing eyes.

"Now I must go to the place Queen Fibji is, to beg her forgiveness. And when that is done, I will return to take up this great office, which Lees Obol intended from my birth." He turned away, strode away, the feet of his troops drumming behind him, the chamber echoing with the sound. Behind him was silence.

"No slaves in the mines?" Bormas breathed at last.

Shavian shook his head warningly. "There is metal in the warehouses. Enough for a very long time. We can bear a hiatus."

"Queen Fibji will have evidence of slavery when her people come home."

"Cross that stream when it splashes us."

Ezasper Jorn and Koma Nepor said nothing. They were frozen with shock.

"Let be," said Tharius Don. "It may be we are entering a new age." Jondrigar had not said anything about the fliers, but if he had truly understood Pamra Don—it would not be long before he moved in that direction as well. First the Noor, then the fliers. First those close by, then those more remote. Tharius Don placed his hand over his eyes, covering the weak tears that gemmed the corners. Almost he could see through those hands, so thin they were, so translucent. He should eat. He should. There were things he had to do. His stomach turned at the thought. No. No, he would eat after everything was done.

And everything would soon be done. After which he could die—die in thankfulness that it had not been necessary to invoke the strike, in gratitude that Pamra Don would be safe in the general's care. . . .

As would the world of man.

24

Seeker birds had been bred originally by the Noor. On the vastness of the steppes, messages could be sent, as they were from the signal towers of the Chancery, by heliograph during the day or by reflector lantern at night. Information was exchanged in these ways on a more or less regular and formal basis among Queen Fibji's guards and outliers. For more spontaneous sharing of information or to carry greetings among near-kin, seeker birds were used, flying back and forth between their two masters, sometimes over enormous distances. Possession of a seeker bird was no longer considered de facto proof that the owner was a Noor or Noor sympathizer, though that had once been the case. Many merchants used them now. Medoor Babji had taken half a dozen Fibji seekers with her when she sailed away on the *Gift*. Every troop of Melancholics had two or three home seekers, imprinted to seek some near-kin on the steppes. And, of course, Fibji's spies had seeker birds.

One of these arrived in the cage late in the afternoon, after the audiences for the day were done. Strenge thrust his little finger into the bone message tube and twirled it around, bringing the paper out in a crackling cylinder, frowning as he did so.

"Which one of our people sent that?" the Queen asked, splashing her footbath at him with one toe. The attendant looked reproachfully at the Queen, pumice stone held ready. "That's all right, Jenniver." She smiled. "Give me the towel. You don't need to rub at my horny feet tonight. After half a century walking on them, it's no wonder they're tough as old fish hide."

He put the message he had just received into his sleeve and

took another instead, twirling a finger into the end of it. "This one first, Fibby. It's from Medoor Babji."

"Doorie! Oh, how wonderful. We haven't had word from her in months, months!" The Queen held out her hands, seeing that they trembled a little, to unroll the tight scroll and lay it flat on the little table by her cushions.

"Dear Mother and most honored Queen," she read. "Today the *Gift of Potipur* turns northward. We have found an island chain in center River where men and Treeci live. Many of the men here have seen Southshore with their own eyes. It is there, about a month's sail farther south. There is no question. It is a huge land, empty of men, so these men believe.

"We do not know when or where we will strike land on Northshore, though it will be at least two months, one hundred long days, from now, and probably some distance west of Thou-ne from where we departed. Send a message to me through all the Melancholics of Northshore from Thou-ne at least so far as Vobil-dil-go.

"I have learned that the fliers have found some herdbeasts. They have a plan to raise the herdbeasts on the steppes until there are great herds and then kill all humans. Two fliers were blown to an island in a mighty storm, and I overheard them. I have not told anyone of this but you.

"The Noor must make plans at once to leave for the south. If the Thraish go on with their plans, the plan we have so long depended upon will be only another kind of grave.

"I have found the answer to Grandfather's riddle.

"Your loving and obedient daughter, Medoor Babji.

"P.S. I think I am pregnant."

"Ah," said Strenge, looking perplexed, gulping a little, hardly knowing which part of the message to think of first. "Well, if she only thinks she is pregnant, it happened after she left."

"Rape," snarled the Queen.

"I think not," Strenge said soothingly. "She would not have used those words had it resulted from rape. No. I have had seeker birds from those who were with the troupe in Thou-ne, and they tell me Medoor Babji was fascinated by the boat owner, Thrasne."

"That is not a Noor name!"

"No. And Noor do not own boats. Shh, shh, Fibji. We have children among our near-kin who are not wholly Noor."

The Queen snarled. Strenge petted her and she wept in pain, anger, and frustration.

When she had finished weeping, he said, "And now, Queen of the Noor, you must hear evil news." He took the just received message bone from his sleeve, turning it in his hands for some moments, a sour expression on his face.

"Well?"

"It's from one of our people long enslaved in the Chancery," he replied in a strained, tight voice. "From a sentinel post near the Red Talons. Things are taking a nasty turn, Fibji."

She took the paper and read from it. "Oh, by all the gods. We heard from the scribe that the leader of the crusade was readying for racial persecution. Now some faction in the Chancery plots our extermination in order to settle our lands with paler skins! Have there been any reports of such action against us?"

"We've had no reports, but the Melancholics may not realize what's going on. There's always the chance of more or less random harassment in the cities."

"Get some inquiries out, Strenge. It's unlikely there's been time for the Chancery to act on this, but they may move more swiftly than usual."

"No matter how swiftly or how slowly, Fibby, we must act now, no matter what they do. One message told you a persecution is being built as a fire is laid, with fuel added each place the crusade stops. Another says that now Gendra Mitiar connives at persecution. If her connivance succeeds, our people may find it impossible to gather coin on Northshore. Now comes word from your daughter to say Southshore exists. It is actual, real. It is accessible, too, without such arduous effort as to make it impractical."

"Then why haven't people gone there?"

"Why should they? The journey is very long. There are vast unsettled stretches on Northshore, to say nothing of the steppes. The Towers have long forbidden exploration of the River."

"But she says there are men living there, in mid-River!"

"Who may have been there for countless generations. What I

find more interesting is that she says there are Treeci, but she does not tell us what those are. Another race of creatures, however. That must be what she means!''

"It is unfathomable to me that men would not have settled another land if that land were reachable by any means,'' she grumbled, still preoccupied with Medoor Babji's possible pregnancy and not thinking of exploration or settlement at all.

"And perhaps they did,'' he replied. "And perhaps they are there now. And perhaps they did, and perhaps they all died. And perhaps they did, and some other thing happened. And perhaps, just perhaps, the men who are meant to settle that other land are the Noor.''

She bowed her head, whispered, "You're right, Strenge. As you often are. So. Send word to all the Noor. They are to leave for Southshore by the quickest route, every tribe in its own way. Empty the coffers of the Queen. Hire boats where we can. Take them where we cannot. Arrange provisions. And send word, as Medoor Babji has suggested, to all the Melancholics between Thou-ne and Vobil-dil-go. There must be some plan made for the assembly of our people when we reach Southshore. If we do. . . .'' She took a deep breath, drew herself up.

"We will leave in the morning! We will forget our plans to seek any agreement with the Chancery. It was always a vain hope. Since we are very near to Split River already, we will go down along the river to Northshore. Forced march. We Noor can march in three months or four what would take the Northshoremen a year. She bids us hurry. We will hurry.''

She was silent a time, thinking. With all this threat to her people, still she longed to have Medoor Babji beside her at this time. But pregnant?

"Ah. I am to be a grandmama again. My heir is to have a child. Ah, Strenge, what message shall my heart have for my daughter when she returns?''

Tharius Don slept, deep in the sleep of angels, where no trouble was nor anguish. He flew, as with his own wings, alight with holy fire.

Someone shook him by the shoulder.

He opened his eyes, struggling to penetrate the gloom.

"Your Grace.''

"Ah?"

"A message, sir. It came in this afternoon, but with everything that was going on, it got mislaid. When I came on duty, I knew it should be brought to you at once. It's from the Dame Marshal."

The young officer looked haggard. He offered the message bone with a shaking hand.

"Open it," Tharius ordered, pulling himself up in the bed. Even when the message was unrolled before him, he had trouble focusing on it. It wasn't Gendra's hand. . . .

The thing wasn't from Gendra. The words within were signed by the Noor slave, Jhilt. They spoke briefly of the Noor, and then they spoke of Pamra Don, who was to be given to the Thraish for some kind of ceremonial degradation at Split River Pass. The Thraish had not been convinced or in anywise changed by Pamra Don. They planned this thing in order to discredit her before all her followers.

When he had read the words over for the fourth or fifth time, Tharius Don dried the weak, futile tears that were flowing unbidden down his face, dripping off his chin.

"So," he said, reaching for the bell at his hand. "So is my pride humbled."

"Bring me food," he said to the yawning servant who came in response to the sound. "Something hot and strengthening. Find my musician, Martien, and ask him to come to me here."

When Martien arrived, breathless, he found Tharius Don wrapped in a blanket, eating with single-minded compulsion. His face was drawn into an expression of concentration and pain.

"I am not staying here for the funeral," Tharius said. "I'm going over the pass, leaving almost immediately. Send the alert for the strike, Martien. Have watchmen posted on the heights. Though I pray it will not be needed, I will carry the green banner. When it falls, the word is to go out."

"When the green banner falls, the word is to go out," Martien repeated, himself in shock. He had heard so often of this day; he had thought it would never come to pass.

"I may have been a great fool," said Tharius Don. "A weak, prideful fool. Medman tried to tell me. . . ."

"Oh, well, Mendicants," Martien said, trying to comfort him.

"Yes. Mendicants. They tell us what we don't want to hear, so we don't hear. Oh, another thing, Martien. Send word through my secret channels to Queen Fibji that Mitiar is conspiring with the Thraish to wipe out the Noor. This slavewoman Jhilt may have already told her, but I won't take that chance. Nothing may come of Gendra's plotting, but the Queen must be warned, if she'll believe me. Tell her also that General Jondrigar is on his way to her. To beg her pardon. She may not believe that, either."

"Queen Fibji?"

"She is somewhere near Split River Pass. She's been journeying toward it for some time now. I don't know why. Perhaps she planned another visit to the Chancery." He fell silent, drinking the last of the soup, half-choking on it, a sickness in his stomach at the unaccustomed food. "Half the world is at Split River Pass. The crusade. The general. Fibji. And soon, according to the message I have received, the Thraish."

He stood up, staggering a little. Martien looked at him with concern and offered a supporting arm, which Tharius shrugged away.

"It's all right, Martien. I've been forcibly recalled to myself. Late in life to be taught a lesson like this, but not too late, perhaps. Go now. I trust you to see to everything."

He watched his trusted friend go out, thinking he would not see him again, remembering the flat harp music, the flame-bird, Kessie.

"I am thankful," he told himself resolutely. "Thankful that if I have misjudged, I will have an opportunity not to betray myself, my cause, and those whose lives have been given to it." It was a kind of litany, though he did not think of it in those terms. When the room had steadied around him a little, he went up the endless stairs to make his preparations, wondering what kind of ceremony it was the Thraish planned at Split River Pass and how he could comfort and heal Pamra Don when it was over.

25

Watching Medoor Babji and Eenzie the Clown today. They were washing their hair on the deck, flinging water about, dancing in their small clothes like festival whirlers, making all the men stand there with their mouths open. Some of the men lusting, I'm sure, we've been so long from shore. Medoor Babji has sent all her birds away, and it's as though someone took a heavy burden from her, for she laughs, giddy, like a child, and she comes teasing me during the daytime and inviting me up to the owner-house roof after dark. Sometimes I go, too.

I'm careful not to talk about Pamra Don. I did that once, to Babji's hurt, so I'll not do it again. Still, each time there is happiness with Babji, it makes me ache for Pamra. At first I thought it meant I would rather it *was* Pamra, but that isn't so. If it was Pamra, it would be all tears and pain and sadness instead of this joyousness, and I'm not so silly as to wish that for myself. But I can wish it for Pamra herself, and that's where the hurt is.

Times like this, it would be nice to believe in gods somewhere who took care of things. I could pray, "See to Pamra. Give her joy. Take away whatever the pain is that festers in her."

But there isn't a god to do that. I still love her. I feel unfaithful to her, too, in a strange kind of way, as though it's wrong for me to have pleasure or take joy in life. Good sense tells me that's a wrong kind of feeling. Death lies that way, and I'm no death courter.

So, I'll try to put her and all her pain away, somewhere inside in a protected place. I won't throw it away, or forget it, but I can't go on waving it about like a banner, either, to make Medoor Babji cry.

So, I'll keep it. Quietly. Until I don't have to anymore.

From Thrasne's book

To one coming down Split River Pass toward the cupped, alluvial plain at its foot, the buttes seemed to spread fanwise toward the southern horizon, lines and clusters of level-topped, sheer-sided mountains, all that was left of the great mesa that had lain at the foot of the mountains in time immemorial, now chewed by the river into these obdurate leftovers. Higher up, the pass itself wound along towering canyons and through one enormous valley, more than half-filled by the lake called Mountain's Eye, fed at this season by a thousand hurrying streams carrying melted snow from the heights, itself the source of Split River's flowing both north and south. The south-flowing stream was the larger one, in this season capable of violent excess, sometimes tumbling great boulders into its own path, detouring itself east or west at the foot of the pass to flow in any of a hundred ancient channels among the buttes. This year it had ramified into a braid of smaller streams on either side of the vastly swollen main river, and Tharius Don looked down from the pass to see the buttes glittering among tinsel ribbons of water in the late sun.

Tents were thickly scattered among the buttes, an agglomeration and tumult of peoples. Tharius put his glass to his eye and scanned the multitude. To the south, at some distance down the main stream, were the tents of the Noor, a large party of them with more arriving. Near the Noor, the banners of the Jondarite select guard and the tent of the general. Nearest the pass, the crusaders, thickly sown, like fruit fallen beneath a tree. To the east, not far, a party of Jarb Mendicants, their distinctive round tents identifiable even at this distance, surrounded themselves in a haze of smoke. Tharius put the glass away and went on down the pass, toward a Jondarite guardpost.

Near Red Talons there had been two days of argument, stretched out partly by Gendra Mitiar and partly by Sliffisunda, who wanted to be sure there were plenty of witnesses present at

Split River Pass. When his scouts returned to say that a vast multitude of crusaders and Noor and even Mendicants were gathered there, Sliffisunda delayed no longer.

"I will take the woman now," he said.

"You'll take me, too," said Gendra grimly, drawing on her last reserves of strength. "I must return to the Chancery the fastest way." Jhilt's defection had made her think of treachery, and treachery had made her think of the elixir. Though the bottle did not look in any wise different, its effects were not what she had counted on. She had to get back to the Chancery and a new supply, bartered off old Feynt.

"Take me, too, Sliffisunda."

He had consented, not caring greatly, rather more amused by the request than not. He would take her and the Laugher, Ilze. He wanted to watch Ilze during the ceremony with Pamra Don, see what he did. Abnormal human behavior was very interesting to Sliffisunda, and there would not be many more years of humans in which to study it.

"Very well," he said in a calm voice that any flier would have recognized as dangerous, "I will take all three of you. The others may follow after." He did not like the Jondarites with their crossbows this close to the Talons and was glad to hear Gendra order them to return to the Chancery.

Three of the coarse flier-woven baskets were brought. Pamra Don would not give up the child, which Sliffisunda thought odd, but it added little to the load. There was no hurry. Fliers had gone on ahead to prepare, and Sliffisunda himself had ordered what was to follow. There would be an announcement first, to get the attention of the mob. Then the ceremony with the nest. Then the woman from the Chancery would order the mob to disperse. It was all agreed.

Pamra heard only that they were returning to the Chancery. She rejoiced in this. It did no good to talk to these fliers. Neff comforted her by telling her she had not been sent to the fliers, but to man, which she understood. "We're going back now," she said to Lila, jouncing the child on her knee.

"Back where?" Lila asked. "Do you know where, Pamra Don?"

It was the first time the child had called her by name, and

Pamra looked into her face, wondering at this adult, understanding tone. "Why, to the Chancery," she said. "We will see Great-Great-Grandfather again."

The child shook her head, reaching up to pat Pamra's face. "Pamra Don," she said. "You don't listen."

"Where are the Thraish?" Tharius asked the Jondarite officer who was stationed at the guardpost.

"The fliers are mostly on those two buttes over there, Lord Propagator," the man answered, pointing them out. The rocky elevations he indicated were so near the pass that the river washed their feet. They were about forty or fifty feet high, very sheer-walled, their bases carved inward into low, smooth-walled caves by the water's flow. Tharius put the glass to his eye and stared at their slightly sloping tops. There were fliers there, certainly, quite a mob of them on both butte tops, but there were fliers on several of the farther buttes as well, coming and going, all of them staying well away from the edges.

"Did you plan to shoot at them?" he asked the Jondarite, noting the crossbow case on the man's back.

The Jondarite shook his head. "Not unless ordered to, sir, and even then not so long as they stay in the middle of the butte that way. It's too far from here, and we can't get them from below unless they come to the edge. They're too smart for that."

Tharius shook his head, wondering why they always thought of weapons first and talking later. "Do you have any seeker birds for the general?"

The Jondarite saluted and ran off to get one from the cage. Tharius laid paper on his knee and wrote out the message. "To the Protector of Man. The Thraish plan some ceremony to discredit Pamra Don because she defends the Protector of Man. They seem to be gathering on the buttes at the entrance to the pass. Tharius." They sent the bird off, watching it winging down the river toward the Jondarite tents.

"I've sent three messages by that bird already today," the Jondarite said. "That bird knows right where he is."

Tharius reached into his pocket for bread. He had been eating constantly since he left the Chancery, trying to convince himself he had strength enough to do whatever would need doing. "Can you get on top of that thing?" He indicated the nearest butte. If the ceremony was to occur on that height, it might be necessary for them to get close in order to talk with Sliffisunda.

"With grappling ladders, sure. Trouble is, we start to climb it, they'll just move to another one. We don't have enough men here to put a guard on all of them. The general's already sent a message for all troops at Highstone Lees to join him here."

All the troops? Tharius stared at the man in amazement. There had never been a time when all the Jondarites had left Highstone Lees. "What are the fliers up to?"

"I don't know. They've been coming and going all day. Carrying trash. Look like a bunch of birds building a nest."

A nest, Tharius thought. For nestlings. Juveniles. One could be discredited in the eyes of a multitude by being reduced to the status of a juvenile. Would the mob understand that? Or would Sliffisunda explain it to them? He was too shrewd to let them misunderstand it, that was certain.

"Have any of them come in carrying people?"

The Jondarite shook his head. "Not that I've seen."

Tharius sighed. If Pamra Don was not yet here, then he was in time. There could still be negotiations. He gave quick instructions to the Jondarite. "You can see better from here than I'll be able to from below. The minute you see any fliers carrying people—or any people approaching across the valley from the direction of the Red Talons—send me word. I'll leave a man here with half a dozen of my birds."

He took another bite of the bread and started on down the pass, Martien close behind him. Martien was holding the green banner. Somewhere high above them among the encircling peaks there were signal posts and watchers, their eyes on that banner. Since Pamra Don had failed, he would have to send the signal for the strike soon. Better for everyone if he had sent it a year ago. "Weak," he castigated himself. "You're weak, Tharius Don."

"What are you going to do?" Martien asked.

"I don't know. Try to get to whoever's in charge. Sliffisunda, maybe. Gendra, maybe. Or that Laugher, Ilze. The message I got said he was involved."

"How did the general get so far down the river? He couldn't have left more than a few hours before you."

"He's in better shape than I am, Martien. I have to face it. I've been a fool. Starving myself. It felt right, you know. Light. As though I were taking off weights, enabling myself to fly. I saw everything so clearly. The light was limpid. Nothing was complicated. I'd half convinced myself God was talking to me through Pamra Don. All the time it was only pride pretending to be something else. And Pamra Don the same. Familial stupidity, maybe. Well, I sent her into this. Now I have to get her out."

Far down the valley, Queen Fibji heard the reports of her own scouts. They had not expected this great mob of people. They had not expected to find the originator of the anti-Noor doctrine here, either, but Peasimy Flot was said to be present as well.

Though mobs were always dangerous in the Queen's opinion, and Strenge agreed with her, this one on this occasion was doubly, trebly dangerous. No matter what the general had said. She was not sure she believed him. If she believed him, she was not sure he could do what he promised. Too late, she told herself. His pleas for forgiveness had come too late.

"I think we'd better move south, away from this, don't you?" she said to Strenge, breaking into his musing.

"I think it would be wise," he agreed soberly. "I'll call Noor-count and march." He was out of the tent before she could say anything more, and she had to summon her own people with a trembling hand on the bells. "Pack it up," she said. "We're moving within the hour."

She did not want to think about the mob. General Jondrigar had just left her, and she did not wish to think of what they had said to one another, either. She distracted herself by helping with the packing, scandalizing her people thereby.

From the air, the steppe looked like a carpet of ash and dun and grayed green. Pamra Don stared down at it, fascinated despite herself. If she could convince some of the fliers to carry her like this, her crusade could grow that much faster. Less time would be spent in travel. Though perhaps it was not necessary for the crusade to grow any more than it had. She had not spoken to Lees Obol yet, and when she did, perhaps he would believe her all at once as the general had done. Neff flew beside her, turning his shining face toward hers in the high, chill air. "Don't you think so?" she cried. "Neff?"

He didn't answer but merely sailed there, driven on the wind, just out of her reach.

Tharius and his men continued their descent, the plain coming up to meet them as they twisted back and forth along the downward road. When they arrived at the bottom, a breathless runner confronted them with the general's message. "Wait for him here, Lord Propagator. He follows close behind me."

It was an hour before the general arrived at the head of his battalions, during which time the fliers went on clustering at the butte tops and nothing changed.

"Did you see Queen Fibji?" Tharius asked, wondering at the expression on the man's face. It was full of pain.

"I saw her," heavy, without intonation. For a time Tharius thought he would not explain, but then he went on, "She heard me. She said if the God of man forgave me, ever, then so would she and her people. I do not know if the God of man has forgiven me or ever will, Tharius Don."

"I think—I think he probably has," Tharius said, astonished. Whether the God of man had forgiven Jondrigar or not; whether there was any such deity, they could not afford the time to worry about it now. "What is Queen Fibji doing here?"

"It was the shortest route to Northshore from where they were, because of the good roads along Split River. The Queen said they would be leaving very soon. South. While there is time."

"Time?"

"She says the crusaders plan to kill the Noor because the Noor are black. She says the crusaders have betrayed Pamra Don. A devil has come to lead them. So says Queen Fibji. She called upon me, the Protector of Man, to put an end to him."

Oh, clever Queen, Tharius thought half-hysterically. Turning her enemies or former enemies against one another. "What is this devil's name?"

"Peasimy Flot. He calls himself Peasimy Prime. He teaches no breeding, no children, no Noor. He cries, 'Light comes,' and brings only darkness and death. So says Queen Fibji."

"Where is he?"

The general gestured toward the west. "There. She showed me where. His people and wagons have recently arrived. If you will look with your glass, you can see him between those two buttes, high in his wagon, a crown on his head. I have looked at him. When we have talked, I will go kill him."

Tharius laid a hand upon his shoulder. "First we must take care of Pamra Don." He pointed out the buttes, showed the general the message he had received. "Two days ago, Jondrigar. Almost three. They would be here by now, wouldn't you think?"

"If they flew. Perhaps they didn't. Perhaps they sent her back as she came to them, traveling over the steppe with Gendra Mitiar."

Tharius stared at the high buttes. They couldn't have picked a more visible place to do whatever they planned. Accessible only from the air, only by fliers, yet sloped enough to be unconcealed to all except those at the foot of the butte. Even as he stared, the seeker bird arrived.

"Fliers carrying baskets, slow, coming this way."

From the air, the butte tops looked like tables above the colorful carpet of the valleys. Nearest the pass were two where many fliers clustered, and it was to one of these that Gendra and Ilze were carried and tumbled out with no ceremony. Ilze was on his feet at once, shaking his fist and screaming, but Gendra lay where she had rolled, unable to move. Some link within her was broken, she thought dully. Some vital connection. At last she gathered her remaining strength and struggled to her feet. At the very center of the space they stood upon, Sliffisunda crouched among a few weathered boulders, invisible to anyone looking from below, staring across Gendra's shoulder. She turned. Across from her, level with her eyes, was another butte, perhaps a hundred yards away. Fliers clustered on it like flies on puncon jam, getting in each other's way.

They are building a nest, she thought to herself. The stupid fliers are building a nest. She looked down. Thousands of faces stared back at her, white ovals, mouths open. A ripple moved from the base of the butte outward as people turned, staring, faces and faces. A murmur came, like a murmur of waves. She had not expected this many, not this many.

A new emotion came to her, all at once. Dismay. There should not have been this many crusaders. And there should have been only a few Jondarites, but there were Jondarites everywhere. With their bows. Why were there so many Jondarites?

Beside her Ilze stood, still waving his fists at the crouching Talker, screaming at him. "You owe her to me, Sliffisunda. You owe me!"

A flier came screaming low over the crowd below. Gendra could not understand what it said, but the crowd seemed to understand, for the murmur deepened, became a roar.

Tharius crumpled the message and raised his glass. The fliers had reached one of the buttes near the pass and dumped the basket on it. Someone stood up, shaking his fist. "Ilze," Tharius breathed. "The Laugher. They've brought him. There's another one." This time the tumbled figure did not stand up at once; when it did, Tharius could hardly recognize it. Gendra Mitiar? It looked dead, a staggering corpse. An errant wind brought Ilze's shouts to their ears, though they could not see whom he was shouting at.

"You owe her to me, Sliffisunda. She's mine!"

"Where are the Jondarites who were with Gendra?" the general asked. "What has happened to them?"

"I don't know," Tharius answered. "Gendra and Ilze seem to have come willingly. They haven't been hurt."

He tried to think. He had to get a message to Sliffisunda somehow, get him to talk. But where was Sliffisunda? Was he even here? His frantic thought was interrupted by a harsh cawing as a flier came over them from the east, flying low, screaming its message so that all could hear: "Pamra Don is a heretic. Pamra Don denies Potipur. See how the Thraish deal with heretics!" Elsewhere upon the plain other fliers soared, all screaming the same message.

The flier turned and came over once more, still screaming.

The general spoke to his aide. Before Tharius could intervene, men reached for their crossbows and quarrels flew. The flier choked, sideslipped, tumbled from the sky in a crumpled heap. Elsewhere on the plain, other crossbowmen began to shoot and other fliers fell. From the butte came a cry of rage. The Talkers had not expected this. Fliers and Talkers rose from it in a cloud, straight up, offering no further targets.

Oh, gods, Tharius thought. Now they won't listen to any offer of talk.

The roar became a howl. Gendra sank to her knees. The stupid fliers shouldn't have done it. Shouldn't have threatened Pamra Don. It was all going wrong, all wrong. "Sliffisunda," she croaked, trying to warn him. He ignored her, his eyes glowing. "Don't," she croaked. "You'd better take the woman down to them and let her alone."

He turned his back on her, shat, walked closer to the edge of the butte, eyes still fixed on the other tabletop.

When they began to descend, Pamra leaned over the basket side, seeing everything from above, a great, scattered carpet of followers, her followers. She took a deep breath and the rapture came, glowing. All her followers, waiting for her.

"Pamra Don," said Lila again.

She scarcely heard the child. Above her, wings tilted toward one of the flat-topped mountains. It had a huge nest built on it, a flier nest.

Before she could think about that, they had taken her out of the basket and tied her to something in the nest. What did they think she was? A nestling? The fliers were screaming in rage. They wanted her to look like a nestling, that was it. Wings lifted in a cloud, leaving only one or two of the fliers behind her. She could not see them. She could not see the nearby followers, either, only the distant ones, a wave of faces, turning toward her, thousands of faces.

She smelled smoke. Smelling smoke always made her think of flame-birds. In her arms, Lila grew very still. Still and hard.

Tharius had no more time to think of talking with the Thraish. A laboring pair of fliers appeared high above the butte and dropped onto it, burdened by the load they carried. "Tell your men not to shoot," Tharius cried. "That's Pamra Don."

Too late. The bowmen were already shooting, but it had no effect. The edges of the butte effectively blocked the bolts, which rattled harmlessly on the rocks. Tharius focused his glass upon the butte top. There was a huge pile of twigs and branches there, an untidy cupped mass, as all Thraish nests were. His stomach heaved, and he vomited violently, Martien holding his shoulders. "Stop them," he croaked. "We've got to stop them!" Suddenly he knew what they were about to do.

There was no time. There was scarcely time to feel horror. The distant figure was tied upright in the nest and it was set alight, all in a moment. A moment. They could scarcely see her through the smoke. "She's carrying the baby," Tharius cried, as horrified at this as at the distant puff of smoke. Flames rose up, almost invisible in the sunlight. Word spread among the crusaders, and they turned toward the butte, seeing the fliers circling above it, the flames, the struggling form there disclosed, then hidden by blowing smoke. A cry rose up, a great shout. One of the bowmen made a lucky shot, and a Talker tumbled from the sky. The fliers rose, screaming, then darted downward, claws extended, only to fall victim to the cloud of bolts. Some fell into the plain still alive and were beaten to death by crusaders as the shout rose, louder and louder.

Ilze watched, his eyes bulging, his body twitching. "Oh, yes," he said. "Oh, yes."

"Don't," Gendra begged. "We've made a mistake, Uplifted One. It won't happen as you expected it to. Put out the fire. . . ."

The first flames touched Pamra Don. Neff, she thought. She tried to look over her shoulder to see his face, but she couldn't. He was there, she felt his blazing glory. Before her on the rimrock were her mother and Delia, but Neff was behind her. He was hurting her. "Neff," she cried. The flames were all around her, and she cried his name again, the word rising up in an agonized howl to fill a silence that had fallen over all that multitude, rising and rising from a throat that could not stop it nor end it nor consider what it was doing, on and on and on into a silence that seemed to resound with it still when it had ended.

"Get grappling ladders onto that butte," the general shouted, not seeing that Jondarites had already done so and were scaling the sheer wall, being attacked by furious fliers, thrown down, replaced by others, with the smoke still blowing. The first man reached the top, was pitched off by buffeting wings, was replaced by two more who flailed with their hatchets at the fliers guarding the fire. Other men poured up the ladders after them. The wind stilled for a moment, falling into an enormous, awful silence. Into this silence the scream insinuated itself as though dropping from the heights of the sky itself to fill all the world. It had all agony in it, all pain, all loneliness. Pamra's voice. One endless scream. Then again the silence.

And after the silence a roar of fury which moved across the multitudes like a mighty wave, from the base of the butte to the farthest edges of the encampment. Fliers had landed here and there to strut and crow before crowds of unarmed crusaders. They were clubbed to the earth, clubbed into the earth, pounded into bloody soil and scraps of feathers.

"You should not have done it," Gendra muttered, falling to the stone. She had no more strength. Nothing mattered now. She knew what would happen next. It was inevitable. From beside her, Sliffisunda watched, amazed and wild-eyed. This was not the way it should have gone. The humans should have cowered before this. On the Stones of Disputation it had been decided, they would be frightened, they would be abased, obedient. But they were not. They screamed. They howled. Sliffisunda felt a strange, unfamiliar emotion. Terror.

"Hostages," he screamed to three fliers near him in the sky. "Take these two humans. We may need hostages."

Obedient, as frightened as Sliffisunda himself, they dropped straight down and took off again, Ilze struggling in their claws, Gendra Mitiar hanging limp, unconscious. They tilted, spun, flew toward the Red Talons. Behind them, bolts filled the air and other, less wary fliers fell from the sky.

*   *   *

Tharius Don found himself running, not remembering when he had started running, only that he was. The general pounded along beside him, both of them headed for the butte that was about a quarter mile away, close to the main river. Without the glass, they could not see its top. They panted their way to its bottom, leaned against the stone, puffing. A Jondarite came down the ladder.

"The woman?" the general asked. "Pamra Don?"

"I think she's dead, General."

"You think?"

"Something there. Strange. The men won't go near it."

They were climbing the ladder then, swaying. Tharius had never liked heights. He didn't think he could climb this ladder, but he was being pulled over the rimrock before he could determine whether it was possible or not. A smoking pyre was before him, a great heap of glowing wood. In the center what remained of Pamra Don, black, contorted, its teeth showing between charred lips, held upright by a partially burned stake.

And in its arms a sphere of softly moving light which pulsed. And pulsed. And breathed.

And broke.

Something came out of it. Winged. Or perhaps finned. Or both. Whatever it was spoke to Tharius Don. "Poor Tharius. She was the last of your line." Then it was gone, falling or flying from the edge of the rock to the river below, entering it with scarcely a splash, moving in it as though born to it, south, southward, away toward the River that encircled the world.

"Lila?" breathed Tharius Don. "Lila?"

The general did not seem to have seen. He leaned from the rimrock to shout in a stentorian voice, "The fliers have burned Pamra Don."

From far off came a treble shout. "The Mother of Truth has been killed. War against the fliers. Night comes, night comes, night comes!"

Tharius looked across the plain to the place Martien waited. He made a chopping gesture, made it again, and again and again. Four times. The far green speck that was his banner dropped and then rose, four times. So. Let it begin. Let it all begin. Let it all come to a bloody end. Let the damn Thraish die as they deserved. He began to weep.

Below he could see Jondarites fighting against a party of crusaders. "Why?" he demanded of the general.

"Someone has said it was Jondarites who killed Pamra Don," he growled. "Perhaps the devil with the crown has set his people against the Jondarites. I go to lead my armies. See, he flees!"

The cart that Peasimy Flot had traveled in was moving away, pulled by a dozen running men. Voices were calling out, wanting to know who it was who had killed Pamra Don. "Jondarites," said some, attacking the nearest ones and falling in their blood. "Fliers," said others, marching off toward the Red Talons, clubs and bows in their hands. And still others said, "Chancery. Those of the Chancery."

"The Noor," cried some, looking around for dark faces. "The blackfaces." Tharius stared out over the valley. The Noor were moving rapidly south, visible now only as a trail of dust upon the horizon, too far away to become victims of this general holocaust. Below him a thousand battles were being waged, generalized slaughter was going on, and Jondrigar moved ponderously down the ladder to get his troops around him.

Tharius sat down where he was, staring at the blackened corpse of Pamra Don. The pyre still smoked.

The Jarb Mendicants left their encampment and began to move onto the battlefield, their pipes smoking, the haze around them thickening. Slowly, slowly, as the Mendicants covered the field, the fighting stopped. Shouting stopped. Cries of fury stopped. Sobbing and cries of pain and grief came after. Beside Tharius Don the ladder quivered, and Chiles Medman climbed onto the stone to regard him with calm, awful eyes.

"She was mad," Tharius said, his eyes red-lined with weeping. "Mad, and I did not see it."

"Was she?" asked Chiles Medman, glancing at the blackened corpse, shuddering, turning his eyes away.

"Of course! Look at the slaughter down there. All madness. Madness."

"Oh, that is probably true, Tharius Don."

"Let it end."

"I do not think it will end, no. Peering through the smoke, I
see what is to be." He stood at Tharius's side, taking the
oracular stance: hands held out, facing the weeping multitude,
head thrown back, the pipe between his teeth so the smoke rose
before his eyes. He called in a trumpet voice, "Millions will die
in her name. The steppes will be soaked in blood. I see a future
in which women are herded into one set of cities, men into
another. I see endless processions, mindlessly stamping puddles
of light. I see age, coming inexorably, with no youth to soften
it, no children to bless it. I see Peasimy Prime immolating
himself at last when death draws near, in order to assure for
himself the immortality promised by Pamra Don."

"Millions?" Tharius faltered. "What would be left?"

"I see a dozen, a hundred interventions, heresies, rebellions,
all of which might succeed, any of which might fail. Still, the
Jarb Houses will try, and try. And in the end die or flee, as all
else dies or flees. Then there will be remnants, scratching in the
ashes, ready to begin again." He lowered his hands, took the
pipe from his mouth, put his hand on Tharius's shoulder as
though in comfort.

"Madness!"

"Not to Peasimy Flot," he said calmly. "Not to the fanatics
who follow him. They do not see this world at all, but only their
hope of the next. He has crossbowmen, did you know that?
Men he has hired. They have instructions to shoot any Jarb
Mendicant who comes anywhere near. He has named us the
ultimate heretics. Us, and the Noor, and the Jondarites, for he
has heard that General Jondrigar has been named the Protector
of Man. Peasimy says no, the general is not Protector. He,
Peasimy, is the Protector."

"No hope." Tharius clutched at himself, as though he had
been stabbed.

Chiles Medman laughed bitterly. "Oh, there is always hope.
Even now the Noor are marching toward the Rivershore. Every
boat able to float will soon be headed south with Noor aboard. I
do not know why, but they are a saner race than most. There is
a riddle there. With the great numbers they have lost to slavery
and war, one would think quite otherwise, and yet because of
some chance they seem inclined, particularly in recent genera-

tions, toward peace and good sense. Medoor Babji has begged a
boon of her mother, the Queen, so the smoke tells me. Because
of the love she bears for a certain Northshoreman, the Noor
have said they will take certain—peaceful—others, as well.
That proud, persecuted people will take others as well. It is
remarkable."

"Ah."

"So I suggest you go with them, Tharius Don. There is a
future for you, too. It is not long, but I see it in the smoke."

"Kessie," he murmured.

"Kessie as well. She is in Thou-ne, where you sent her,
where all of this might be said to have begun. Send word for her
to meet you in Vobil-dil-go."

"Your sources of information are better than mine, Medman.
But this did not begin in Thou-ne. It began in Baris, long and
long ago."

"Well, if you must talk of ultimate beginnings, it began long
before that."

"Why? Why? Medman, I read the books in the palace, again
and again. They are old books. If they tell the truth, our history
is full of this. We humans have done this again and again. In
the face of truth we choose madness! Over and over. We choose
madmen as leaders, clever players who will tell us pretty lies.
We repudiate those who promise us honesty and cleave to those
who promise us myths. Never the truth, always the Candy Tree.
Like flame-birds, we do not feel the flames even while they
burn us, as we hatch our like to make the same mistakes in their
time. And I, I who sought to do everything in my power to
achieve life and peace, I have fallen into the trap. Why? Why?"

"Ask the strangeys, Tharius Don. Perhaps they know. I
don't." Chiles Medman stretched wearily, his nostrils flaring at
the stench of the fires. Among the dead and dying moved the
Mendicants, hazing the valley with smoke. On the far green
horizon, Peasimy Flot's cart gleamed in the sun, its bright
banners fluttering as the men drawing it ran at top speed away
from the battle. "Do not let that one get hold of you," said
Chiles in a conversational tone. "Power has come to him, and
he will drive it as a child drives a hobby. He has it between his
legs, and he will make it take him where he will."

"The general will catch him," Tharius said wearily. "He cannot run forever."

"So reason says, and yet that is not what I see," said Medman, putting his pipe away as he started down the slope. "Vobil-dil-go, Tharius. Now. Do not return behind the Teeth. There is nothing there for you."

And indeed, there was little enough left behind the Teeth for anyone. The Jondarites had flowed from Highstone Lees like water; after them the servants, for who would stay if there were no Jondarites to enforce discipline? Split River Pass ran like a river with soldiers and slaves and servants and all, out and away. Tharius Don was gone; Gendra Mitiar gone; the general gone; Lees Obol dead, and none caring that he lay all alone on the catafalque in the ceremonial square.

Shavian Bossit wandered through the empty rooms, wondering where everyone had gone, down the long, echoing corridors to the winter quarters, through those to the deeper caverns of the files. "Feynt!" he called, hearing his own voice shattering the silences. "Feynt!"

There was no answer. Glamdrul Feynt and Bormas Tyle were together in a deep, hidden room of the place, unaware of their abandonment, plotting. In another room, distant from the first, Ezasper Jorn and Koma Nepor were doing likewise. They knew nothing of the slaughter beyond the pass, nothing of the strike that had begun, nothing of the war that had started while they whispered, all unwitting, in the dark cellars of the Chancery.

"Jorn!" cried Shavian Bossit. "Nepor!"

There was no answer, and he struggled up the endless stairs to a high terrace, where he stepped into the light once more. In the ceremonial square a herd of weehar milled about the unguarded catafalque. Around them lay the scattered bodies of dead herders, and over the bawling animals fliers struck and struck again.

"Stop that!" he howled, unthinking that there were no Jondarites to enforce his commands. "Stop that!"

He scarcely felt the claws that seized him from behind and lifted him into the high, chill air. Sliffisunda had told the

SHERI S. TEPPER

raiding party to bring bull calves, but also, if they had an opportunity, to bring hostages.

In the deepest corridors below the Chancery, those on whom Koma Nepor had tested his improved strain of the blight began to stir. Bodies began to twitch, to move, to stand up and look curiously about themselves. The incubation period was over. Now they moved, seeking others to touch, to infect, to make as themselves. In all of the Chancery, there were only four live persons remaining. All else had been taken, or had fled.

26

When Tharius Don stood upon the height where Pamra Don had been burned, it was the fifth day of the week. He raised and dropped his arm as a signal four times. Four days later, on the ninth day, that which had been long planned would take place. With that gesture, the signal so long awaited had been sent.

From a ledge high upon the Teeth of the North the birds went out near dusk, a flurry of them, like windblown flakes of white, twirling for the moment on their own wingtips with a murmur of air in feathers, a light rustling as of satin, a sound so innocent, so quiet, that no apprehension could attach to it. They were only birds, silver in the light of late afternoon, a little cloud of wings breaking into dots of fleeing light which beat away and away, some along the precipices east and west, others southward, still others in long diagonals away from the wall of mountains.

After the first flurry came a second and a third, glittering spirals, fleeing jots of amber and rose as the sun dropped still lower, and finally a fourth cloud of wings, blood red in the last of the light, darkening to ominous purple as they fled into the waiting dark.

There were thousands of birds, gathered over the years for this purpose alone. Each bird sought a separate person in a separate place. Each bird carried the same message. "On the ninth day, let the strike begin."

Below the ledge from which the birds went out was another on which a signal tower stood, and from here went winking lights like spears cast into the dusk, to be answered by other gleamings in the distance east and west, and then by others farther still, twinkling stars in the dark void of earth's night.

There were many thousands of towers transmitting the lights, ranks and files of them marking the edges of areas and zones, of townships and rivers, manned by newly volunteered zealots for the cause or by rebel Awakeners or by Rivermen, and it was to these the word came.

"On the ninth day, let the strike begin."

In far-off places, villages remote from the River, and to the townships themselves, the birds came bearing the same words "On the ninth day, let the strike begin."

To the nearer places first, to the farther places only after days had passed, still the word ran like fever in the veins of Northshore, corrupting the blood of the world into a fatal hemorrhage.

In Zephyr, the husband of her who had been Blint-wife went to his bird cote at dawn. It was the morning of the ninth day. He read the message almost with disbelief. So long, so long planned, So long in the coming. And so suddenly was it *now*. This coming night. He went down the stairs, the message in his hands. "Murga?"

She was bustling about in the kitchen, making a cheerful clack with her tongue as she fed stewed fruit and grain to the grandchildren. "Murga."

She appeared at the door, wiping her hands. "Raffen? What is it? Are you ill?"

He realized his voice had betrayed him, edged with half excitement, half fear; like a knife, it had cut into her contentment. "The word has come."

She shivered. She had had to know, as all the Rivermen knew, and yet she had kept it closed away in the back of her mind somewhere, along with other unwanted and dangerous lumber. "When?"

"Tonight."

"So soon!"

"Once the word came, it had to be soon. Immediate. We could not expect to keep it quiet long after the word was given. Too many birds. Too many messages."

"So." She wiped her hands again, as though by wiping them she might wipe away the need for acting, for responding. "What am I to do?"

"You are to stay here, in the house. I'll need the children as

messengers for a time, then they must come in and stay close. I
will spread the word now. We will spy out the pits during the
day to see how many men will be needed.''

"The River?''

"Yes. The barge is ready. The stone sacks are ready. We
have men to man the lines.''

"I worry,'' she said, tears in the corners of her eyes. "I
worry the barge may break loose. You may end up west of here.
You could not return to me. How would I find you?''

He laughed, a quick, unamused bark of laughter. "Silly
woman. Such a silly Murga. After tonight, dear one, it will not
matter east or west. When we have done with the Servants of
Abricor, do you not think we will have done with their gods?
And then do you not think we may walk where we choose? East
or west?''

That night he came with others to the pits, well after dark, to
pile the bony remnants and twitching corpses into barrows,
careful not to touch them with naked skin lest there be some
infection from the Tears of Viranel. The barrows creaked down
through the town and were emptied into the barge, and there the
heavy sacks of stone were tied to the bodies while the barge
made its laborious way out into the River, sweeps creaking and
men cursing at the unaccustomed labor. The line that connected
them to shore reeled out, span after span, and at last Raffen
gave the word they had waited for. The bodies went overboard,
into the massive currents of the ever-moving River, and the
Rivermen turned to the winch to take up the line and bring the
barge back to the place it had left.

When morning came, there was nothing different, nothing
remarkable, nothing to show that the world had changed. Except that the worker pits were empty.

In Xoxxy-Do, where there were no piers and great rocks
encumbered the Riverside, a great pit had been prepared, dug
by Rivermen over the decades, deeper and deeper with each
succeeding year, the stones taken from it piled above it on
teetering platforms of poised logs, the earth piled behind the
stones. "A quarry,'' they had called it, taking from it small
quantities of carefully crafted blocks, chosen, so it was said, for

their veining and color. There the Rivermen came to the quarry late, bringing with them the harvest of the worker pits of towns both east and west, their wagon wheels creaking in the dark and lanterns gleaming. It was early morning when the last of the bodies was laid in the great stone hollow, almost day, with the green line of false dawn sketched flatly on the eastern plains. Then the engineers moved certain logs that braced certain others in place, and the mountain of piled rubble fell, the accumulation of years fallen into the place from which it had been taken.

If the Rivermen were to try to dig it up, it would take a generation. The Servants of Abricor could not unearth the bodies in a thousand years.

In the towns of Azil and Thrun and Cheeping Wells, the Rivermen carried the corpses to the ends of the long piers, weighted them well, and tossed them out into the River's deep currents.

In Crisomon a great pyre had been built, and in that township every man, woman, and child danced around the pyre as the bodies of the workers were burned to ashes. In Crisomon, conversion to the cause had been total and unanimous.

Elsewhere that was not so. In some townships the Awakeners were vigilant or wakeful and came out of the Towers to defend the pits. In a few places the Awakeners prevailed, but in most the Rivermen won and the corpses of Awakeners were merely added to other corpses which had to be disposed of before dawn.

Dawn.

Worker pits empty when the sun rose. In B'for, just east of Thou-ne, an Awakener returned in some haste to the Tower to speak with the Superior, who was in company with the lady Kesseret, said to be Superior of a Tower farther east who had come to B'for on urgent business and was receiving Lord Deign's hospitality before going on.

The Awakener was panting so much it was hard to discern the message that the pit was empty.

The Superior was silent, but the lady Kesseret seemed to understand what had been said.

"Then you will not need to go to the fields today," she said calmly. There were great wrinkles around her eyes and lips, and her voice was thready. "Rejoice."

"But, but," the young Awakener stuttered, "but, what shall I do?"

"Go to the chapel and pray," she suggested.

"What should I pray for?"

"Enlightenment. Patience. Resignation."

Were these not what she herself had prayed for? She searched Deign's face for signs of shock. None. Both of them had been ready for this. Now it had happened, and she must plan to leave B'for to travel westward to Thou-ne. In a few days or weeks, if they were permitted to live that long. She would not fail to be in that place where Tharius Don would come for her or send her word.

In a few towns the word had not arrived in time, or there had been no Rivermen to receive it. In a few towns there had been no strike, no disturbance at all. The Servants of Abricor fed as usual in the bone pits, looking up with surprise to see their fellows from neighboring townships circling high above, dropping down to sit with them in long, dusty lines upon the pit edges, talking of this thing.

"No workers in our town," the fliers said. "No workers."

"Sometimes there are no workers," they told one another. "Sometimes it happens."

"Not often," they agreed. "Not so many places all at once."

It was almost noon of the day after the strike before they sent some among them off to tell the Talkers at the Talons.

"How long?" the Rivermen asked one another. "How long will it take before they do something?"

"Pile the fish upon the wharves and wait," they said to each other. "Each day, fresh fish, there for the eating."

It took only another day before Servants descended upon the towns, snatching at children or smaller adults. In Baris one among them distracted a group of townsmen while others made off with a living, pleading victim. In some towns, the Rivermen were ready for this; ready with crossbows and stone-tipped bolts, ready with nooses and obsidian clubs. In other towns the victims screamed into unheeding air, were flown away to be dosed with Tears and left in some pit or other until ready for eating.

The Servants had never considered human anger. In the wake of these seizings, anger rose like a veil of smoke around the towns, palpable as wind. Even they who had not been Rivermen, who had revered the Awakeners, even they could feel nothing but anger as they saw their children hoisted aloft, blood dripping from sharp talons as the screaming prey were carried away. Towns in which the first victims were easily taken proved to be impregnable on the second try. Doors and windows were closed. Farmers were not working in their fields. Children were not playing in the streets. Where groups moved, armed men moved with them.

On the wharves the fishermen, guarded by bowmen, drew in their nets and piled the bounty of the River upon the wharves.

On the third day after the strike, Servants attacked some of the towns, tearing at shutters with their talons and beaks, screaming rage at the inhabitants, making short flights to the Riverside to attack the fishermen and to drop tiny blobs of stinking shit upon the fish piled there. The bowmen were practiced by now and used their bolts to advantage. The fliers, in their rage, scarcely noticed how their numbers were being reduced.

In Zephyr, Murga and Raffen sat in their kitchen, listening to a fury of wings outside, like the sound of a great, windy storm. The children cowered beside them, both frightened and excited by this frenzy. "When will it be over?" they asked, not sure whether they wanted the excitement to end.

"Soon," said Raffen. "They will weaken soon." He sighed. Thus far, not a single one of the fliers had taken any of the fish from the shore. Though many of the Rivermen were not unhappy about this, Raffen believed in the purity of the original cause. He had not wanted the flier folk to die. "They will weaken soon," he repeated, hoping they would grow weak enough to succumb at last to reality and eat what was offered them.

In most Towers, Superiors ordered their Awakeners to stay within. Even those most dedicated to the worship of Potipur, and to the virtual immortality that worship might have gained them, learned that discretion was needed. Blinking lights told them of Awakeners in neighboring towns beaten to death by mobs of outraged citizens. Seeker birds arrived to tell them of Awakeners burned in their Towers because they had seemed to favor the Servants of Abricor. These messages had been planned by Tharius Don and long arranged for, designed to be sent a day after the strike to prevent the Awakeners from interfering with what was going on.

And in the Talons was a fury such as Northshore had not seen in a thousand years. Upon the Stones of Disputation the Talkers sat in their tattered feathers, screaming at one another of fault and blame and guilt and shame, while below them in the aeries the last of the Talkers' meat struggled mindlessly in the troughs. Sliffisunda brooded alone in his own place, considering the likelihood of survival, his mind sharpened by the knowledge that there had indeed been a heresy afoot.

"Promise of Potipur," the surviving fliers cried, dropping from the sky like knives of black fire upon the Stones of Disputation while the Talkers scurried for cover. "Promise of Potipur!" From his concealed room, Sliffisunda heard them, heard the shrieks of pain and rage as those like himself were slaughtered by the angry flocks, his mind working relentlessly as he determined to go on living whether any other of the Thraish lived or not. He would wait until dark. He would fly into the north, to the Chancery, to that place he had flown once before, against his own will, where the herds of thrassil and weehar still grazed on the grasses of Potipur's Promise. Enough to feed himself, he thought. For years. The hot, lovely blood of thrassil. In the north.

He forgot that others of the Thraish had already been sent to hunt among the herds beyond the Teeth.

On the great moors of the Noor, Peasimy Flot learned of the conflagration to the south. Some among his entourage could read the flicking lights. There was even one who was sought out by a seeker bird. The days brought increasing information, until even Peasimy could not but be aware of what was happening.

"Light comes?" he asked, almost whimpering in his hatred for whoever had done this without him. "Light comes?" He had sworn vengeance upon those who had burned Pamra Don, and now those who had burned Pamra Don were dead or dying without any action by Peasimy Flot. Without his hand in their guts, his knife in their throats. He had fled—though, he told himself, he had done so only to consolidate his strength—but still they died. How dared they?

"Who did it?" he asked at last, while they conferred and tried to come up with an answer. "Who killed them?"

"Someone in the Chancery," they said. "It had to be someone in the Chancery."

"Heretics," he hissed. "All those in the Chancery. We go to war!" For it had been near the Chancery that Pamra Don had died. And near the Chancery that the great assembly had seen him flee away. And from the Chancery that some troop of soldiers had been seeking him ever since. He would make sure there were no witnesses to that defection left to speak of it.

"War," he said again, telling his close advisers to make that message manifest among the multitude.

During the night some among the followers faded away to the south, but enough others were still there when the sun rose, polishing their axes and making ready new bolts for their bows, to make a great army.

Not far to the east, General Jondrigar pursued Peasimy Flot, eager to chastise him for his insults to the Noor.

After about a week, and in only a few towns, a flier or two descended upon the wharves to gorge themselves on the fish piled there. They did not return for another meal. Scarcely had they time to arise from their feasting before the talons of other, more traditional Thraish hurled them from the sky. Then there was screaming and feasting of flier upon flier, with much buffeting of wings and thrusting of beaks. For the most part the Rivermen were faithful to the instructions of Tharius Don, taking no action against the fliers unless they themselves were attacked—they or other humans in the towns. In some, however, it was an excuse for general slaughter, and more of the fliers died.

"When?" asked the children. "We don't hear anything anymore."

"Now, I think," said Raffen the Riverman. "Let us go out."

The streets were littered with bits of broken shutter, with blown feathers, with the wind-tossed refuse that accumulates in every town unless swept away daily by those whose business it is to keep the streets. People wandered here and there, peering around them as though to see whether there might not be just one Awakener among them, just one group of workers. There were none. The Tower stood in its park. No one had looked inside it yet, but it gave the appearance of a place that was tenantless. Empty. Like a shell when the nut has been eaten away.

A bustling man came to Raffen for advice. There were dead in the town to be disposed of, and Raffen went away with him to instruct the townsfolk how this should be done in the future.

Murga and the children went on wandering the streets. On the highest point of the town, the Temple still stood, its high dome gleaming white with paint. From inside came the sound of hammers.

"What are they doing?" Murga asked a passerby.

"Taking the moon faces off the wall," came the answer. "They are setting up an image of the Light Bearer instead."

Murga took the children by the hands and led them to the Temple to see what was going on. The Temple floor was littered with shattered stone before the wall where the masons' hammers were at work, but the image that stood at the top of the stairs was one Blint-wife had known well. She was carved in ivory stone, her arms curved around a child. It was a copy of the statue in Thou-ne.

"Thrasne's woman!" Murga whispered to herself. "That's Thrasne's woman!"

The serene face gleamed down at her, unmoved, unmoving, just as it had always seemed aboard the *Gift*.

"Well, at least she's got her baby," said Murga, unawed by this elevation to divinity. "At least that."

27

The *Gift* had returned to Northshore, thanks to the skill of the sailors, three towns east of Thou-ne. Those who had sailed in her gathered at the rail, watching the familiar shoreline grow closer, each of them aware that something was wrong, was missing, without knowing precisely what until Medoor Babji said, "There aren't any fliers!"

It was true. There were no wings aloft except for the little birds. There were no great, tattered shapes floating above the Talons.

There were great heaps of fresh-caught fish on the piers, which no one seemed to be eating or selling. Within an hour of their arrival, they had been told why and how, and Thrasne had gone to the Temple to see the wall where the moon faces had been. A stone carver was there, working on a large figure. When Thrasne asked what it was to be, he said it was to be the Light Bearer. A woman, with a child in her arms. It did not look at all like Suspirra, but then the carver was not very talented. Or so Thrasne thought, wondering what Pamra would think of this image. He said something of this to the carver, twitting him only a little, saying the image was not really like unto her.

"Well, as to that"—the man spat rock dust at him—"likely she will be carved in a hundred fashions or more. What was left of her after they burned her, so I'm told, didn't leave much for us to model from."

Thrasne had him by the throat before the poor man knew what he had set off, and it was only when two people came up from the Temple floor, pulling at him and screaming in his ear, that he let the carver go. They told him then what they knew, which was not much and already overlaid with myths.

"She rose," one woman whispered. "Like the flame-bird, burning, into the very heavens, singing like an angel."

Thrasne stumbled out of the place.

There was a hurt place inside him, one he could cover with his outspread hand, a hot burning as though he were being consumed from within. He burned as Pamra Don had burned. The fiery spot widened, spread, reached the limits of his body, and then erupted through his skin in a fleeing cloud of spiritual flame, vaguely man-shaped, the heat of it an emotional blast which fled away as a hot wind flees. He could feel it as a presence departing, an actuality with motivations of its own, now vanishing from his understanding. In that momentary excruciation he felt he had emitted an angel which now expanded to fill all the universe, becoming more tenuous with every breath until all connection with Thrasne was teased away into nothing.

He flexed his hand across the place the angel had left, somewhere near his stomach or heart, an interior place that had nothing to do with thought but only with the tumbling of liquors and the rumbling of guts, the living heart-belly of his being. Where the fire had burned was a vacancy. A hole. He poked a finger at himself, half expecting it to penetrate into that emptiness, but he encountered only solid muscle and the hard bones of his ribs. Whatever the emptiness might be, it was not physical, and there was no pain associated with it. The angel had taken the pain with it when it departed.

"Pamra Don," he said, testing himself for a response. There was none. Perhaps a twinge of bittersweet sadness, like dawn mist blown across one's face, carrying the scent of wet herbs, evocative of nothing but itself. "Pamra Don?"

And then again he tried, "Suspirra?"

To find her gone as well.

So, what was it that had fled? A ghost? A fiery spirit? A succubus who had lived beneath his heart?

Or was it some soul-child of his own, self-created, dreamed, hoped-for, stillborn in this world but released into some wider universe?

Whatever it might have been, it would not be. "I can do nothing," he said to himself in wonder. "There is nothing I can do for Pamra Don."

Except perhaps, his hands said of themselves, twitching for his knife or a chisel as he remembered what the carver was making in the Temple. Except perhaps. Whatever she was, whatever she had become, Thrasne could show her as she had been.

"I knew her, after all," he said to himself wonderingly. "I knew her."

28

The days of the strike had fallen into memory. In Vobil-dil-go, order had been restored. The heights of the Talons on the eastern skyline were empty of wings. The Tower was empty of Awakeners. Only Haranjus Pandel had occupied a room there when he had come with the lady Kesseret and the widow Flot from Thou-ne. He came down to the town occasionally to greet this one and that one, well accepted by all. To the north, it was said, great armies moved, but at the Riverside there was a precarious calm, like that at the eye of a storm before the great winds come again.

On a stone above the River, Queen Fibji drew her feet beneath her and sat thus, cross-legged, looking across all that mighty water to the place she hoped to arrive with her people in a little time. Below her the Noor and some Northshoremen toiled among the boats, carrying endless bales and barrels into the holds. She approved this, searching among the busy forms for the tall bulky one her daughter had just mentioned. Thrasne. Boatman. Not a Noor and, to hear Medoor Babji tell it, in love with someone else to boot. And yet, her daughter's choice.

"How long before we leave?" she asked for the tenth time.

"Three hours," answered Medoor Babji. "Perhaps four."

"And how many boats?"

"A dozen have gone that we know of. Fifteen are readying to go. There will be more. There are Noor in every town, buying boats, hiring boats. There will be hundreds, thousands."

"If we get away before they kill us all."

"We will. The battles are all on the steppes, behind us where the Jondarites are fighting the crusaders. The towns are not involved."

"Not yet!"

"Oh, I agree, great Queen. They will be. But they are not, yet."

"How will we find one another, when we get there?"

"Those who leave from towns west of Vobil-dil-go are to march east when they arrive at Southshore. Those who leave from towns east of Vobil-dil-go are to march west. When we arrive on Southshore, we will build a great tower upon the shore. We will light beacons on the top of it at night. We will leave messages in cairns upon the beaches. We will send runners. We will find one another, great Queen."

"And the islands of the River . . ."

"Are full of friendly folk, human and Treeci. And the strangeys of the depths are not to be feared."

"And Southshore waits."

What they said to one another was a litany. A ritual. They had repeated it a hundred times. Perhaps the Queen would say it a hundred times more on the boat, convincing herself.

"Does that man know you're pregnant?"

Medoor Babji looked at her swollen belly and laughed. "It would be very hard for him not to know."

"What does he say about that?"

"Thrasne says very little about anything. I have told him it is his. He got a strangely bemused expression on his face. It seems to me he smiles a great deal more recently, though he still goes into those odd abstractions and stares at the water. I know then that he is thinking of Pamra Don."

The Queen had resolved not to remonstrate, and now she shut her teeth firmly upon her tongue. Her whole self writhed at this self-imposed silence, and she sought a subject that was not—or would not seem to be—related. She would talk about . . . about something global.

"Medoor Babji, since you are my heir, let me share my mind with you as my father once shared his mind with me. Since I received your message, I have spent much time in thought. Perhaps my thoughts will interest you.

"When I was very young, I often wondered what I was for. The boys, most of them, seemed to know. They were to be warriors. The girls were to bear children. But my father told me

I was to be Queen, and we did not have a queen then, so I could not see what one was. Whatever it might be, I was quite sure it was something wonderful and eternal. Then, when I was about seven or eight—with some it happens earlier, I suppose; there may be some with whom it never happens—the understanding came all at once, in one hot burst, that Queen or no, I would not always be, that someday I would die and stop being. I screamed and wept. I thought I knew something no one else knew, but my father comforted me. He told me it was the first accomplishment of mankind, to know our own mortality, a thing the beasts and fishes never know.

"So, it seemed my father knew all about it. At that age, grown people seem to know everything about everything—you accused me of that once, I remember.

"Well, when it was time to sleep, back then when I was a child, I would lie on my blankets and go drifting into a certain world. I remember little of it now, except that there was music everywhere, and fountains of pearl, and beasts one could ride, and funny little furry things that talked. . . .

"So, one day I said to my father that I wished he would get me a—what was it I called them? a foozil or some such—get me a foozil. And he asked me what a foozil was, and I explained that it was one of the furry, talking animals, and he told me I had made it all up. Imaginary, he said.

"Well. I had not known that the world I drifted in before sleep was only my own. I had thought it was a world everyone knew of. I thought we shared it, other people and I. It was the first time I knew that we all have separate worlds, Medoor Babji. No one else knew of my foozil. No one else had seen my fountains of pearl, or my wondrous beasts. How sad for them, I thought. Until I realized that they, each of them, had a world of his own.

"And I was shut out of them, daughter! Oh, the tragedy and wonder of that! The wonder of knowing that my own universe, much of it unexplored, bright or dim, shadowed or sunlit, full of every possible expression of dream and imagination—that the universe I have inside me was *not shared*. But more tragic, to know that all around me were a hundred thousand others, also dim or bright, full of dream, none of which I could ever see or know. The tragedy of knowing I would never know! Do you understand what I mean, Medoor Babji?''

Medoor nodded, thinking perhaps she did, perhaps she did not. Her mother did not wait for a response.

''I was a child. I didn't realize how limited our lives really are. I decided to learn all about the worlds of others. I asked them to tell me stories of their worlds, and they gave me words, daughter. Do you know how limited words are? People try to describe their worlds to you, but their words are like a map drawn with a burned stick beside a campfire. At best they let you in a little; at worst they hide the way entirely. I found that people go through life giving each other these little maps and little passwords. We explore one another, and gradually the maps accumulate, the passwords become more numerous. The more we are alike, the more we share, the more we understand. So, we Noor can see further inside one another than most. We can share each other's worlds better than most. But we can never really see it all. . . .

''So, you have a world inside you, child of my heart, which I can see a little. And the one you love, this Thrasne, he has a world as well, and it is utterly strange to me, to all the Noor. You ask me to love him for your sake. And I have not even a little map drawn with a burned stick to find my way to that.'' She smiled at Medoor Babji, shaking her head ruefully, receiving an equally rueful smile in return.

''So, I must do what we all do. I will take it on faith. His world is real because you tell me so. I cannot perceive it. I can only assume it. I will love him for your sake, Doorie.''

Medoor Babji took her hand and held it tightly. There were tears on the Queen's cheeks as she went on.

''Perhaps you will ask him to show me what he can of his world. Perhaps he will give me a map. From his map, I will travel in his strange world of water and boats if I can.''

''Oh, great Queen . . .''

''Call me 'Mother,' child. There may be no Queen of the Noor where we are going. There may be no throne for you to ascend.''

''I think he is afraid of you, Queen Fibji.''

''Well, so, and I am afraid of him as well. We must do what

we can about that. I will give him passwords to walk in my world, and he must give me passwords to walk in his, so we can pass each other by without disruption. There are many passwords, child. 'Be careful,' or 'Forgive me,' or 'I love you,' or 'Take care of my child.' ''

"What do I do if he still loves Pamra the Prophetess? Or believes he does? Or remembers doing so?"

"You have told me he is an artist, and she was beautiful. I never saw her, but I have seen the image of her in the Temple here. He may always love that image of her. But it will not matter. Pretend it is God he loves, or his art. It is much the same thing."

"And you will give me your blessing?"

"You have had my blessing since I conceived you, Dorrie. It is not something one can take back. But if you want it renewed, so be it. Have your Thrasne, child. To whatever extent you can. Take whatever password he gives you, and be grateful."

The Queen brushed at her trousers and threw back the long tassels of her hair. "It is time we were done with this serious talk. All day has been full of weeps and moans. I cried this morning, thinking of all those who would not come with us to this River. How many there were who would not follow me! How many there were who stayed, to revenge themselves upon those who had persecuted us. How many there were who chose that, rather than this. . . ."

"The River is frightening," Medoor admitted. "I was frightened by it."

"They were not frightened of the River," Queen Fibji contradicted. "They were frightened of going where there would not be any enemies to fight. These were the young men with battle in their blood. They thumped their spears on the ground and leapt high in a battle dance and sent their spokesmen to me to explain. They spoke of honor. Of glory. I tried to tell them what I have told you, but it meant nothing to them. I told them of my father. I told them the riddle he had given me as a child. 'Of what good are dead warriors?' I asked them. It did no good. They stayed behind. They did not see my world, child. They would not see my world. . . ."

She gazed out over the water, not seeing Medoor Babji's eyes fixed on her, wide and terrible.

And she, Medoor, within herself but without speaking, said to her mother, "Mother. I found the answer to your father's riddle. I sent a message to tell you. . . ."

She imagined that the Queen was silent for a moment, thinking. "Of course you did. And you told me you were pregnant. And that Southshore awaited. And those things drove the other from my mind. So. You have the answer. Will you tell it me?"

"It is the answer to your riddle of long and long ago. The riddle your father set you. 'Of what good are dead warriors?' I found the answer to that."

"Where did you find it?"

"I learned it from the Treeci, by chance."

"So? Come, child. Why this hesitation? Tell me!"

Medoor imagined herself delaying, knowing she was right, and yet the answer was a hard and hurtful one. "Warriors are those who desire battle, Mother."

"Yes?" The Queen would be puzzled.

"Warriors are those who desire battle more than peace. Those who seek battle despite peace. Those who thump their spears on the ground and talk of honor. Those who leap high in the battle dance and dream of glory. . . .

"The good of dead warriors, Mother, is that they are dead."

The Queen would stand staring at her for a long time. After that time, tears would begin to run down her cheeks. Medoor saw them clearly. If she told her mother the answer to the riddle, her mother would cry once more and there had been enough tears today. She would not tell her mother the answer. Not today. Perhaps not ever. It was a stony answer, a hard answer.

When all the warriors were dead, when they made no more children like themselves, then others might live in peace. She would not tell the answer, but she would keep it in her heart.

"Let us go down to the River," said the Queen.

They walked together down toward the *Gift*, the ship that was to take them to Southshore.

There were some others who would sail aboard the *Gift* as well: Haranjus Pandel, the widow Flot, and two very old and feeble people, Tharius Don and the lady Kesseret. Tharius had sent word for her to meet him in Vobil-dil-go, and here he had begged passage for them both from Thrasne.

"I have not seen a flier in weeks," the lady said, her voice quavering. "I think the last was a month ago."

"They are probably all dead," answered Tharius, his voice emotionless. He had done grieving for the Thraish. His grief over Pamra Don had been all the grief he had left. "I was wrong, that's all. A few survived for a time, eating stilt-lizards and the lesser birds, until there were no more. Except for a few, they wouldn't eat fish, even to save their lives."

"Medoor Babji told me a strange thing," the lady said. "She said that at the time of the hunger, long and long ago, all the Thraish who could eat fish had done so. They left Northshore then, in fear of their lives. Only those who couldn't do it had remained here on Northshore, and there were very few of them. And all those who lived here on Northshore were descendents of those few who could not. It wasn't your fault, Tharius. It was bred in them. They couldn't. That's all."

"It's no one's fault," he said.

"Medoor Babji told me something else. She says that when the dead are put in the River, they are touched by blight and then taken by the strangeys to the islands. They go on living there, Tharius. They grow slower and slower, rooting themselves like trees, time all quiet around them. I want to go there."

"Why? Why?"

"Because there has never been time for me. Only for the cause. It would be nice to have time for me."

He buried his face in her hair and said nothing. He would grow roots beside her if she liked. He didn't know whether to believe Medoor Babji's tale or not.

"It's a pity Pamra Don could not have been put in the River. What did you do with her body, Tharius?"

"Buried it," he said. "Wrapped it in a robe and buried it beneath a thorn tree. There was nothing but bones. And a kind of child-shaped shell that Lila hatched out of. I think it was Lila."

"Lila?"

He told her of Lila. He had heard more about Lila from Thrasne, though he wasn't sure how much of that he believed, either. "I don't know what it was that went into the River," he said. "The strangeys called her their child. She was something strange."

"They're taking up the plank," she said. "The oars are beginning to sweep."

He looked out across the railing. The River slid between the *Gift* and the shore, and they began to move out onto the waters. All the deck was crowded with Noor amid a sprinkling of other folk. "Half a year," he said. "To Southshore."

"It is unlikely we will see it," she said, contented. "I don't care."

Behind them on the bank, a few standabouts stood watching their slow progress. Most paid little attention. Too much else was happening. There were no workers anymore. The Towers were empty. There were no fliers, not anywhere. All of them had starved to death, it was said, though a good many had been killed when they'd attacked humans, trying to dose them with Tears or carry them off to the Talons. If one wanted excitement, one might think about joining the war going on, back on the steppes. Two Protectors of Man, one true, one false, fighting each other, and who knew which was which? There was even talk that one side wanted to kill off all the Noor. People were taking sides, joining up with one or the other, getting irate about one side or the other in taverns. Some were Peasimites, some Jondarites, and the gods knew where it would all end.

The gods knew; not that anyone meant the old gods. Potipur was finished. His image was scratched right off the Temple walls, and so were Viranel and Abricor. The Mother of Truth stood there now, shining, and people came from far away to make measurements of her so they could carve copies for their own Temples. The man who had carved her had actually known her, so it was said, before she was the Light Bringer. He had written it, right there on the image, for all the doubters to see.

Still, other carvers carved her differently. Sometimes they carved her with a child in her arms, sometimes with a flame-bird chick, for it was told how a flame-bird had hatched in her arms when she was put in the fire. Her soul, some said, which flew straight to the God of man. Something else, others said, which had not looked like a flame-bird at all. She had been burned by Jondarites, some said. By Peasimites, said others. By the fliers, said others yet. But who knew the truth? Priests used to answer questions like that, but they were gone, along with the Awakeners. Who knew where? They unbraided their hair, laid down their staffs, wiped the paint from their faces, and disappeared. Just like anyone else, now.

The gates were gone now. People went east if they felt like it, though some felt very uncomfortable about it. And sure as sure, some oldsters couldn't stand the changes and had to carry their dead west for the Holy Sorters, even though everyone knew there weren't any such things. The Rivermen kept watch, though. There weren't any bodies left lying around to attract fliers, even though no one had seen any fliers for weeks. Sooner or later, everyone ended up in the River.

Or across it. For there was word of a new land there, a far land, a land where the Noor were going—and smart of 'em, too, if the Peasimites were coming. Now and then someone might stop a moment and look in that direction, saying the word over as though it had some magical meaning.

Southshore.

• 30 •

They were somewhere near the Island of the Dead when the two old people died. First Tharius Don, all at once, with one deep, heaving breath; then Kessie, calling his name once and then not breathing again, as though there were no reason to breathe once the other was gone. Thrasne found Medoor Babji crying over them, the tears lying on her cheeks like jewels, and he kissed them away, comforting her.

"Aiee, Medoor Babji, but those were old, old folk. Tharius Don told me he'd lived hundreds of years. More than you and me put together ever will."

"I know," she wept. "It's just they loved each other, Thrasne."

She would not be comforted, but she did stop crying. The late evening mist hid the waters, and he couldn't see whether the island was really near or not, though he smelled it, or another one like it, and had been doing so all day. There was a peculiar odor about the Island of the Dead, a tree fragrance unlike any other, and he could detect it now, faintly borne on the light wind. The two old people lay on the deck, side by side, and the Noor Queen came out of the owner-house to say some words over them in a high, singsong voice before Obors-rom slid their bodies into the River.

They sank down, out of sight, quickly, as though eager to depart. Medoor Babji clung to Thrasne almost fearfully, and he held her close beside him, bringing her into his bed that night, big belly and all, feeling the babe kicking inside her with a kind of quiet joy and fear all at once. There had still been no words, no real words, between them. They had not talked of Pamra

Don or of Thrasne's feelings. He did not know how she felt about him, really, or how a queen's daughter would be allowed to feel. He was afraid to ask. And yet she lay there beside him, deeply asleep, and he took it to mean something.

In the night he dreamed of Lila.

She had become a creature wholly strange, not human at all and yet, one could have said, not totally unlike. There was something one thought of as a head, with organs of sight and smell and perhaps taste and hearing, this part already fringed at the edges. There were parts that could have been arms and legs on their way to being something else, not flippers or fins, precisely, and yet fulfilling those functions as well as other, unimaginable ones. Her voice, when she spoke, was Lila's voice, a child's chuckling voice using words that set up unfamiliar chains of association in his mind as he heard her demanding to know why Medoor Babji was grieving.

"Medoor Babji was crying because they died, and they loved one another," he explained to her.

"My people tell me humans are maddened by death," she said. "It comes too quickly, severing love. People need time to become accustomed to it. Either they dwell on it all the time, worrying their lives away to make monuments to themselves, or they refuse to think of it at all, like Queen Fibji's young warriors. It becomes an obsession with men, one way or the other, so they forget to live. Like you, Thrasne."

"I don't understand," Thrasne said in his dream. "What has that to do with me?"

"Your mother died, Thrasne, and you could not bear that she was gone. So you created her again, as Suspirra, a carving, which was safe because it could not die. And then you found the drowned woman, and she was safe, too, because she was already dead. Then, when she fell into dust—I know; I was there—when she fell into dust you chose Pamra to continue to be Suspirra. You told yourself you wanted her to love, to bear your children. In truth you only wanted her never to change. You wanted her to be Suspirra.

"It is easier to honor the dead than it is to love the living."

"That's crazy," he said in his dream, but weakly.

"Oh, but men are crazy," Lila said in her bubbling voice.

"Only crazy people would have had things like Awakeners and workers. Only crazy people would dream of an eternal life in Potipur's arms." She laughed. "A baby, held in arms, rocked to and fro, unchanging. Ah, ah, that is not eternal life, Thrasne. That is eternal death. Only a crazy man would have loved Pamra. . . ."

"But I did love her," he argued, angry even in his dream, knowing he did not quite believe it.

"Only because she was Suspirra. What was she otherwise? A narrow, ignorant woman. Maddened by death into rejecting life. Holding fast to a childish naiveté which protected her from seeing reality. A believer in impossible futures. A simple, totally selfish woman who saw no one's need but her own, who invented a doctrine to meet that need and voices to validate it, who walked a way upon the world convincing others her myth was better than their myths, letting others suffer and die in the service of her madness, starving herself into spasms of self-generated rapture, not seeing, not hearing, only to be burned at last by that which she would not hear or see."

"She wanted to free the slaves. She wanted to stop the workers. She was a saint," he muttered.

"There are those who say so now. There are those who will say so," Lila whispered. "What is a saint? Delia was a saint."

"You're saying she never could have loved me!" he cried, angry at this in the dream, though he knew it was true.

"I'm saying you never should have loved her," Lila said, her voice somehow changed into something remote and terrible. "For she was like the blight, a terrible thing that kills. . . ."

"And preserves," whispered Thrasne in his dream.

"And preserves," whispered Lila as the dream whirled about him, giving way to the sounds of the River, the soft, eternal sluff of water.

He woke then, the dream at first clear, then fading from his mind. Medoor Babji lay heavily beside him, her cheek flushed and warm where it had rested against his own. He rose without waking her and went out of the owner-house onto the deck. In the dawn light the Island of the Dead loomed to the south, mist and tree behind mist and tree and yet again, mist and tree to the limit of sight, with the blessed ones—for so he now called them in his mind—the blessed ones moving slowly in the mists, like swimmers. There on the water the strangeys danced, calling to one another in their terrible voices, and among them their young sported themselves, standing winged upon the waves.

One of these came very close to the ship and looked up at Thrasne with eyes that seemed somehow familiar.

"Thrasne," it said to him in a bubbling voice. "Kesseret is here, Thrasne. And Tharius Don. They have been given the time we created for them. They live. You live, too, Thrasne. And come to us." It sank beneath the flowing surface, its eyes still fixed on Thrasne's face.

There was a hand on his shoulder.

"Come," said Medoor Babji, her dry and watchful eyes on the waves where the strangeys danced. "Let us go on to Southshore, Thrasne. This is not the place for us."

He heard the rattle of the anchor tackle, the call of the sailors as the sails were raised. On the shore of the island, one of the blessed raised its hand to wave. Tharius Don? Too soon for Tharius Don. Someone else. Bending across the rail, Thrasne let a few tears come and fall and wash away the last of whatever thing there had been tight inside himself.

And then he stood to take Medoor Babji's hand and nod acceptance. "To Southshore."

• 31 •

As they sailed on into the south, Thrasne rigged a chair over the bow and laboriously chiseled away two of the three words that had been carved into the prow of the ship. The *Gift of Potipur* became simply the *Gift*. The winged figure that had leaned into the wavelets of the River for decades was replaced with another carving, one that Medoor Babji called, only to herself, "Suspirra in ecstasy," taking comfort in the fact that Thrasne had carved it, for it was not a face or figure any living man would lust for. It was Pamra's face, but a face beatified, glorious, and inhuman, the face of a departing spirit. Before her in her wooden hands she held the gift, a strangely shaped being that might have had either wings or flippers and was carved as though eternally poised to drop into the waters below. Tharius Don, before his death, had told Thrasne about Lila as he had seen her, Lila transformed, the child of the strangeys.

On a calm and starry night when there were no moons, the child was born. When it had been cleaned and wrapped and laid in a blanket, Thrasne stood by the basket and the baby grasped his hand, curling infant fingers around one of his own in a gesture as old as time and demanding as life itself. "Mine," said Thrasne wonderingly. "This is mine."

"Ours," said Medoor Babji firmly. "He belongs to us, and to the Noor."

"And to the *Gift,*" said Thrasne stubbornly. "And to Southshore."

"That, too. I pray we find good fortune there, for our ancestors alone know what is happening behind us." She reached for

Thrasne's other hand. The birth had been more than she had
expected; more in the way of pain, of effort, and of fulfillment
when it was done. It was time to say. Time for words. "And
what of the baby's mother, Thrasne? Do you claim her, too, or
only the child?"

"Oh, yes," he said, suddenly surprised that it should need
saying. "Oh, yes! She, too, is mine if she will be."

"And Suspirra?"

He shrugged, rather more elaborately than the question
warranted at this stage, but he needed to be sure that both
of them understood what he meant. "At the prow of the *Gift*,
Doorie. Where dreams are put. That was a different thing from
this."

She was content, and Queen Fibji, hearing this exchange
from outside the door, sighed a great sigh of relief.

They had come to the baby's tribal day, that day on which he
was to be given a name, when the hail came from the steering
deck. They thought it might be only another island and sent
someone scurrying up the mast to spy out the cloudy land. He
came back down to say there was no end to the land he could
see, not south nor east nor west, but ahead of them were white
beaches and a great, towering smoke. They gave up any thought
of ceremony then, preferring to crowd the rails for the earliest
glimpse of the new land.

By the time dusk came they had anchored in a shallow
bay rimmed with pale dunes. On the beach were three boats
that Thrasne recognized, and scattered across the dunes were
the tents of many earlier arrivals. High above them to the
west was a towering scaffold bearing a clay firefox, and in
this a great beacon burned, smoke roiling above it as from a
chimney.

Some of those aboard the *Gift* splashed into the water and
swam ashore while others plied to and fro on hastily rigged
rafts. The *Cheevle* bore Queen Fibji, Medoor Babji, Thrasne,
and the child, with Strenge plying the rudder as they ran the
little boat up on the sand. The Noor crowded around, not too
closely, making obeisance, pointing at the child, who regarded
them with wide, wondering looks from his not altogether Noorish
eyes.

"Let me see this land," the Queen called, waving them aside as she staggered toward the tops of the dunes to peer inland, seeing there a vast prairie of grass and scattered copses in the light of the moons.

Thrasne came up behind her, one arm around Babji's shoulders, the baby in the other. From behind them, far down the beach, came a hail, and they turned to see another ship against the darkening sky, and beyond that one still another.

"The Noor are gathering. On Southshore," said the Queen. "We have made landfall. All my hopes, Doorie. All my hopes. I feel—oh, I feel I might die now, knowing the best thing I could have done is done."

"Do not talk of dying," said Thrasne, shaking her by one shoulder, much to her astonishment, for the Noor did not presume to touch their Queen. "There is much planting to do if all this mob is to be fed, and who will see to that if not you?" He sounded, she thought, really angry at her. "And this one is a month old today and still has no name. Who will name him if you go dying?"

"Ah, babe, babe." She laughed, half crying as she turned to take the child. "Your father speaks the truth. You have no name." She held the baby high so he might peer away, as she did, toward the wide plains before her and the nearest line of hills. She wondered what mysteries would lie behind them, for it was sure that something wonderful awaited, just beyond the horizon. Then she turned to look into Medoor Babji's eyes, full of trust and pain, wonder and joy intermixed, then to Thrasne's craggy face, which held the same mixture of feelings. So they stood for some time, regarding each other without speaking.

"I name this child Temin M'noor," she said at last, passing him into Thrasne's keeping as she moved away from them down the hill. "Temin M'noor," she called again, her voice like that of a shore bird, hunting.

"What does it mean?" Thrasne asked, thinking he had heard the words somewhere before.

Medoor Babji was smiling at him, holding out her arms for the child, her eyes swimming with tears.

"Temin, which is to say *a key,* and M'noor, that which is *spoken. . . .*"

He did not understand, and she explained it to him.

"We have given him to one another between our worlds, Thrasne.

"His name is Password."

SIGNIFICANT INDIVIDUAL PEOPLE

Arbsen: One of the Treeci of Isle Point, Saleff's sister, Taneff's mother.

Binna: One of the Treeci on Strinder's Isle.

Blint: Owner of the Riverboat the *Gift of Potipur.*

Bormas Tyle: Chancery official, Deputy Enforcer to Tharius Don, conspirator with Shavian Bossit.

Burg: A human resident of Isle Point.

Chiles Medman: Governor General of the Jarb Mendicants. A frequent visitor at Chancery.

Delia: Nanny to Pamra Don, called Saint Delia by the townsfolk of Baris.

Drowned Woman, the: The drowned wife of Fulder Don, taken from the River in a blighted state and kept by Thrasne. Her given name was Imajh.

Eenzie the Clown: Member of a group of Melancholics to which Medoor Babji belongs.

Esspill: A flier, blown by storm to an island far in the River.

Ezasper Jorn: Ambassador to the Thraish; member of the Council of Seven in the Chancery. Conspirator with Koma Nepor.

Fibji: Queen of the Noor.

Fulder Don: A man of the artist caste in the town of Baris. Father of Pamra Don.

Gendra Mitiar: Dame Marshal of the Towers, member of the Council of Seven in the Chancery. Conspirator with Ezasper Jorn.

Glamdrul Feynt: Master of the files in the Bureau of Towers, Chancery. Conspirator with Shavian Bossit.

Haranjus Pandel: Superior of the Tower in Thou-ne.

Ilze: Senior Awakener in the Tower of Baris, mentor to Pamra Don. Becomes a Laugher.

Jhilt: Noor slave of Gendra Mitiar.

Jondrigar: General Jondrigar, member of the Council of Seven in the Chancery; leader of the armies of the Protector.

Joy: Surviving resident of Strinder's Isle.

Kesseret: "Kessie," "the lady Kesseret," Superior of the Tower in Baris.

Koma Nepor: Director of Research, member of the Council of Seven in the Chancery.

Lees Obol: Protector of Man, member of the Council of Seven in the Chancery.

Lila: The slow-baby. Born from the drowned woman.

Martien: Musician, close friend and follower of Tharius Don.

Medoor Babji: Daughter of Queen Fibji; chosen heir of the throne of the Noor.

Murga: Wife of owner Blint. Called Blint-wife.

Neff: A young male Treeci living on Strinder's Isle.

Obers-rom: Thrasne's trusted assistant, first owner's man after Thrasne takes over the *Gift of Potipur*.

Pamra Don: Awakener in the Tower of Baris, who leaves the Tower to begin the great crusade.

Peasimy Flot: Resident of Thou-ne, childlike adult son of the widow Flot. Follower of Pamra Don. Also called Peasimy Prime.

Prender: Half sister to Pamra Don.

Raffen: A Riverman in the town of Zephyr. Second husband to Murga, Blint-wife.

Saleef: A Treeci talker, resident of Isle Point, brother of Arbsen and son of Sterf.

Shavian Bossit: Maintainer of the Household; member of the Council of Seven in the Chancery.

Shishus: A semimythical typical flier of the past, used as an eidolon for young Talkers.

Sliffisunda: A Talker of the Sixth (highest) Degree among the Thraish.

Slooshasill: A Thraish talker of the Fourth Degree, blown by storm to an island in the River.

Sterf: A Treeci resident of Isle Point, mother of Saleff and Arbsen.

Stodder: Resident of Strinder's Isle.

Strenge: Favorite consort of Queen Fibji.

Suspirra: The idealized woman of Thrasne's dreams. A carved image of that woman.

Taj Noteen: Leader of a group of Melancholics to which Medoor Babji belongs.

Taneff: Young male Treeci, resident of Isle Point, son of Arbsen.

Tharius Don: Propagator of the Faith; member of the Council of Seven in the Chancery. Ancestor of Pamra Don. Leader of the cause.

Thoulia: Semimythical "Sorter," the Talker who first discovered the efficacy of the Tears of Viranel.

Thrasne: Third assistant owner's man aboard the Riverboat the *Gift of Potipur*. An orphan, adopted by the owner, Blint. Later, owner of the *Gift*.

Threnot: Servant to Kesseret.

Werf: One of the Treeci on Strinder's Isle.

GROUPS, PLACES, AND THINGS

Abricor: Male, second god in the Thraish trinity. Also the second-largest moon.

Awakeners, the: Religious order living in the Towers who oversee disposal of the dead.

Baris: Township. Homeplace of Pamra Don, Tharius Don, and the lady Kesseret.

Blight, the: A fungus living in the World River that seems to turn living flesh to wood.

Boatmen: Those who make their living on the boats that travel westward on the World River. Merchants. Not to be confused with Rivermen, q.v.

Chancery, the: The administrative center of Northshore, including the officers, buildings, and bureaucracy, located at Highstone Lees, behind the Teeth of the North.

Direction of Life, the: Movement to the west, as the sun, tides, and moons move. Movement to the east is considered antilife and forbidden.

Flame-bird: A species of Northshore bird that sets its nest afire in order to hatch its eggs.

Fliers, the: Ordinary—nontalker—members of the Thraish.

Gift of Potipur: Riverboat belonging first to Blint, then to Thrasne.

Glizzee; Glizzee spice: A euphoric substance of pleasant flavor, provided by strangeys, sold in the markets as a food additive.

Highstone Lees: The name given to the Protector's palace, as well as the Chancery offices and residence grounds in the lands behind the Teeth.

Holy Sorters: Those human or superhuman creatures who sort the dead into categories of worthy or unworthy.

Isle of the Dead: Any one of many islands to which the Strangeys bring blighted humans.

Isle Point: An island of mixed Treeci, human population in mid River.

Jakes Island: An island of mixed Treeci, human population in mid River.

Jarb Houses: Places of residence set up by the order of Mendicants for the treatment and housing of madmen.

Jarb Mendicants: Madmen enabled to see the truth by smoking Jarb root; visionaries; oracles.

Jarb Root: A food root often eaten by the Noor whose toasted peel contains an anti-illusory drug.

Jondarites: The military personnel under the command of General Jondrigar.

Laughers: Pursuivants and inquisitors sent from the Chancery to find heretics in Northshore.

Light Bringer, the: The name given to Pamra Don by the crusaders, particularly by Peasimy Flot. Also, "Mother of Light."

Melancholics: Wandering pseudoreligious bands of the Noor who collect coin for the Queen of the Noor in the cities of Northshore.

Noor, the: The black people of the northern moors, from whom the Melancholics come.

Northshore: That area of land immediately to the north of the World River which is occupied with separated townships.

Pamet: A fiber crop in which armlong pods open to reveal sheaves of white strands used in making cloth.

Potipur: Chief god in the Thraish trinity. Also the largest moon.

Priests of Potipur: Awakeners assigned to Temple duty, distinguished by blue-painted faces and mirror-decked garb.

Progression: The circumnavigation of the planet done once every eighteen years by the Protector of Man. Ship of the Progression: The gilded and highly ornamented ship on which this journey is made.

Puncon: A spicy fruit, most often used in jam and confections. The bloom of the puncon tree.

Rivermen: A heretical group who put their dead in the River.

Servants of Abricor: Another name for the fliers who frequent the bone pits. The Thraish.

Shorefish: Derogatory term used by the Noor to describe the non-Noor inhabitants of Northshore. Term also used by the Talkers to describe all humans. The implication is of a thing which can be easily caught or eaten.

Song-Fish: A shallow-water fish that grows to great size and which sings in the evenings and early mornings, the pitch and tempo dependent upon the size of the fish (smaller fish having higher, more frequent tonal eruptions).

Sorting Out: Theologically, that process by which the dead are sorted into categories of worthy and unworthy.

Southshore: The land to the south of the World River, considered almost mythical.

Split River; Split River Pass: A river originating in a mountain lake in
the Teeth of the North, running both north and south from that
point. The pass cut by that river. The shortest route from the
Chancery to Northshore, ending in the town of Vobil-dil-go.

Stilt-lizard: A lizard with very long rear legs that stalks the shallow
waters of the River or swamps, snapping up small fish or aquatic
bugs.

Strangeys, the: Creatures of vast size and unknown habits living in
the World River.

Strinder's Isle: An island not far from Northshore that is occupied by
a tribe of Treeci and a few surviving members of the Strinder
family.

Talkers, the: Infrequently hatched members of the Thraish who have
the talent of articulate speech over and above that found in
ordinary Thraish.

Tears of Viranel: A fungus that reanimates recently dead bodies or
takes over live ones, changing the composition of the flesh.

Teeth of the North: The mountain range separating Chancery lands
from the moors of the Noor and Northshore.

Thou-ne: Township. Birthplace of Peasimy Flot. Site of the origin of
the crusade.

Thraish, the: Race of large, carnivorous fliers in the world north of
the World River. A flier can lift a small person easily. Two or
more of them can carry a large adult human. While light-boned,
their talons and beaks are formidable weapons.

Towers, the: One in each township, residences of the Awakeners.

Towns, the: Areas along Northshore, each approximately thirty
miles wide, largely agricultural, usually centered on a village or
urban area, extending northward into unsettled or Noor country.
Typical towns are Thou-ne, Baris, Cheeping Wells, Xoxxy-Do,
and so forth. There are 2,400 towns on Northshore.

Treeci: A race of ground-dwelling Thraish whose wings have
atrophied because of their diet. Their wings, however, are still
large and their wing-fingers are capable of adroit manipulation.

Viranel: Third, female, deity in the Thraish trinity. Also the third
moon.

Vobil-dil-go: Township. Some distance west of Thou-ne. Historically
called the site of the embarkation of the Noor.

Xoxxy-Do: Township. Birthplace of Thrasne.

CPSIA information can be obtained at www.ICGtesting.com
Printed in the USA
LVOW10s0111220713

343905LV00012B/115/P